THE SHEPHERD BOOK ONE

SHE WHO WATCHES

ANTHONY PRYOR

A PERMUTED PRESS BOOK

ISBN: 978-1-68261-087-9
ISBN (eBook): 978-1-68261-088-6

SHE WHO WATCHES
The Shepherd Book 1
© 2016 by Anthony Pryor

Cover art by Christian Bentulan

**PERMUTED
PRESS**

Permuted Press, LLC
275 Madison Avenue, 6th Floor
New York, NY 10016
http://permutedpress.com

ACKNOWLEDGEMENTS

The Shepherd trilogy has been in development for far longer than I want to admit, and many folks have been of invaluable assistance over the years. Thanks are due to all of them—first and foremost, the members of my awesome critique group, all fine writers in their own right—Shawna Reppert, Danielle Myers Gemballa, Rebecca Stefoff, Garth Upshaw, and my BFF Dale Ivan Smith, who has been my most persistent and insightful reader for many years. Thanks also to my beloved Beth Peters, my other BFF Rhiannon Louve (another one of those fine writers), and my friend Jennifer Cantrell for their valuable input. Thanks especially to the folks at Permuted Press for bringing The Shepherd to the world and to my agent Kimberley Cameron, who has been tireless in her guidance and support. Also, a shout out to my amazing daughter Devon whose faith, intelligence, and determination have been an inspiration to me, and to the weird people of Portland Oregon—please forgive me for taking some slight liberties with the locales and geography of our hometown. And finally, an affectionate RIP to the Portland Gas and Coke Building, a dark gem of local architecture that served as the creepy model for the Petroco Building in this story, and which was finally demolished in November of 2015.

PART ONE

EYE ON THE UNKNOWN

“**A**re you the Shepherd?”

Wide and red-rimmed eyes stared at me from a grizzled, filthy face framed by a tangled mat of black hair. The man looked up from where he sat on the sidewalk, sheltered from the rain by the department-store awning.

I knew most of the homeless who panhandled for change near the Pioneer Building—I even gave them money sometimes. But I'd never seen this man before. The hungry look in his eyes made me nervous.

I tried to avoid his gaze. “No, I'm not. Sorry.”

He looked disappointed. Then his eyes darted up and down the street.

“You seen the Shepherd? We gotta find the Shepherd.” He licked his lips. “Spare any change?”

It was a gray day in Portland. I'd been up late the night before and wasn't feeling terribly charitable, especially toward a scary-looking panhandler I'd never seen before. In my pocket, my fingers touched a handful of bus change, jingling there beside my keys.

"No." I tore my eyes from the man and concentrated on looking ahead. "Sorry."

"He's comin' back. Haven't you heard?"

I walked away as quickly as I could.

"God bless." The man's voice faded into the cacophony of morning traffic. "He's comin' back, and hell's comin' with him."

I pushed through the brass and glass front doors of the Pioneer Building. By the time the elevator reached the sixth floor, I had put the incident almost completely out of my mind.

The *Ranger's* office was quiet, filled with a few other employees, all about as inspired and energetic as I was. I poured myself a cup of bitter coffee and slouched into my office, turning on my computer and wondering whether anyone would notice if I just stayed home in bed.

"Good morning, sunshine." An unkempt figure appeared in my doorway. He was thin and rangy with a long face and a scrap of beard, and he had no right to be so enthusiastic. His t-shirt said *Will Game for Food*.

I rolled my eyes. "Well, if it isn't Loren Hodges, my own personal herald of doom. What have you got for me, sport?"

He grinned madly and dumped a pile of envelopes and printouts on my desk. "Terri's going to the printer after lunch and needs layout done by noon."

"Of course she does." I looked dubiously at the pile. "This is going to be a weird day. Some transient outside just asked me if I was a Shepherd."

"Maybe he's lost his sheep."

"If he did, it's because he scared them off. He was creepy looking."

"Maybe he thought you were Jesus."

"Oh, yeah. That's it. People get us confused all the time." I shuffled through the papers. "Anything good in there or just the usual crap?"

He pulled a manila envelope from the stack like a magician producing a white dove. "It's your lucky day, Alex. The mysterious Damien Smith has submitted a new *Eye on the Unknown* column. All you have to do is copy and paste."

"Thank God for small favors." I looked at another document. "On the other end of the spectrum, this is a review of the Megatherium show at Slabtown that appears to have been written in crayon. I can't run it through the scanner, and I have only four..." I glanced at the clock. "Oh, crap—three hours to turn this into something readable."

Loren looked back over his shoulder as he walked back toward his desk. "Cry me a river. At least you don't have to figure out how to get those escort services to pay for their ads."

"Take it out in trade." I put the music article on my copy stand. "I get to deal with illiterate rock critics."

The Portland Ranger wasn't exactly a Pulitzer Prize winning publication. It was a rag, given away free at bars and nightclubs, surviving on ad revenue, full of badly-written articles, crappy photos, and editorials that were borderline polemics. We made do with a staff that fluctuated between three and eight. Respectable journalists wouldn't come within ten miles, but at this point in my life I was grateful for any paycheck, whatever the source.

And besides, my name was on the masthead, right below Teresa "Terri" Rosenblum, Publisher. *Alexander St. John, Editor in Chief* sounded a hell of a lot grander and more important than it really was.

I didn't pay too much attention to the rock critic's grammar and spelling, but typed it up as best I could before moving onto Terri's editorial. It was a follow-up on a series of articles that I'd written, and harshly took state authorities to task for failing to catch the I-84 Killer. I gave it a quick read-through, fixed a couple of misplaced commas, and called it good.

The other articles were thankfully in electronic format or printed out so that I could scan them. I gave them my usual editorial once-over and figured that our readers wouldn't care that they read like grade school book reports. I saved the best for last.

As usual, Damien Smith's *Eye on the Unknown* was an easy edit. He'd sent us a clean printout with electronic copy on a flash drive. As Loren had said, all I had to do was drop it unaltered into the issue's InDesign layout. When I read the article, it wasn't to check for errors, it was because I enjoyed reading it.

This week Damien considered identical aberrant behavior that took place in widely-separated locations, suggesting a number of explanations—ancestral memories, madness that spread telepathically or even remote possession by the same paranormal entity.

Many Crimes, One Mind. I typed the title manually, mostly so I could feel that I'd done something constructive other than copy text, then settled in for a pleasant read.

It was vintage Damien Smith. I'd never met him; Loren told me that he was a friend of Terri's, a recluse who rarely left his house. He insisted that Terri always bring him his payments in cash. His manuscripts never bore an address or phone number, and the only bio that the paper ever ran read, "Damien Smith is a local freelance writer specializing in the occult."

Eye on the Unknown had been a fixture at the *Ranger* for years. It came out irregularly, whenever Damien Smith wanted

4

it to. Topics varied. One week, the article would deal with reincarnation and past-life regression, a month later came a piece on spontaneous human combustion or the nature of mysterious undersea noises.

They were models of impartiality, with equal consideration given to all sides of each argument. It was this very logical approach, and the bizarre conclusions to which each story led the reader that gave them their power.

Of course, despite being entertained I knew it was all nonsense. Like watching *X-Files* or *The Exorcist* it was a good way to while away an hour or two, but I knew the truth—there was nothing out there that couldn't be explained by simple science, rational thought, and logical interpretation. Nevertheless, Damien's column provided me a few minutes of pleasant irrationality every few weeks, giving me a glimpse into a more dangerous, frightening and, frankly, more interesting universe. He entertained me. And I appreciated it.

Ghouls, werewolves, alternate dimensions, ghosts, ancient gods, vampires, demons, sorcery, the walking dead... However silly the tale in the warm light of day, when Damien wrote, the shackles of logic fell away, the world narrowed, growing dark and mysterious, and the impossible seemed—mad and unlikely though it was—possible.

After I closed the file and the issue went to press, however, the real world reasserted itself and my sensible mind returned, fueled by skepticism and cynical disdain for my fellow man.

I read happily, letting the mysterious Mr. Smith's words draw me into an exotic world of strange phenomena. Unfortunately my happy diversion from daily drudgery lasted only until the middle of the article.

It was as if a cold hand had just touched the back of my neck, and I stared uncomprehending at the screen.

Certain crimes, far removed from each other both geographically and temporally, include bizarre similarities that are difficult to dismiss as mere coincidence. Beginning in 1947, for example, a series of brutal assaults occurred in a number of widely separated locations—among them Poland, China, Australia and Brazil. In each of these attacks the perpetrator claimed to be looking for someone named "Shepherd" and later claimed to have no memory of the actual crime. The name "Shepherd" was uttered in the criminal's native language or—even more remarkably—in a language that the assailant did not normally speak. At least five murders and four sexual assaults were associated with this mini-crime wave, which ended in 1953 as abruptly and mysteriously as it had begun.

What are we to make of these crimes? Certainly the sheer number of incidents—at least twelve in widely separated locations—lends credence to the suggestion of common motive. It has been said that one incident is an accident, two is a coincidence, but three is a movement. And if what we can call the "Shepherd Crimes" is a movement, who then could be the one responsible?

Red-rimmed eyes stared at me from memory. *You seen the Shepherd? We gotta find the Shepherd.*

"What's wrong, Alex?" Loren's shaggy-haired face appeared in my doorway, making me jump. He had one earpiece of a pair of headphones in his ear and I heard distorted dubstep "wub-wubs" blaring from the other as it dangled against his chest. "You find a typo or something?"

I suppressed the impulse to throw a paperweight at him. "Nothing. Just a really good column. Now scram or I'm going to make you go write meat substitute reviews."

"Yum." Loren reattached the second earpiece and went back to his business.

My heart was racing uncomfortably. Slowly it settled down as I finished off the issue and copied it onto a flash card.

Still distracted, I was trying to choke down the last of my horrific coffee when Terri showed up. She was a short spitfire of a woman, and just the rumors about her private life were enough to curl my hair. As usual, she had a cigarette dangling from her lips and she zeroed in on me like a heat-seeking missile.

"Got it done, Alex?" she took a long drag and crushed her cig out on the *Slabtown Review*. Smoking in offices was illegal in Portland, but she didn't care. "I've gotta drop it off before one, so I sure as hell hope the answer is yes."

I handed her the little flash card. "Right here, all neat and tidy. I presume this means I can take the afternoon off?" I didn't relish going downstairs to face the strange street person again, but right now I wasn't in the mood for work.

"Heh." She made a sound mid-way between a snort and a laugh. "Yeah, sure. Go crazy. I'll even pay you for it, college boy." She looked around my office at the posters and clippings I'd tacked to the wall—copies of my old articles, photos of me fishing and target shooting with my family in Wisconsin, political cartoons, Dilbert strips, advertisers' business cards. In one corner was a small photo of a younger me grinning, clad in a plastron, a foil in my hand, my mask resting atop my head. I'd been on the fencing team in college, but that was all over now.

Notably absent was a diploma or any kind of reward or recognition for my journalism.

"I guess the *Ranger* isn't the kind of place you wanted to end up working when you were in college, was it?"

"It pays the bills," I said. "I'm not sure whether I want to go mainstream anyway. The news is just too depressing these days."

"Anything in particular?"

"Not really. Just a general disdain for humanity. Maybe I prefer proofreading articles about strip clubs to working someplace where I'll end up as morally bankrupt as the rest of the world."

"That's the spirit, champ. I'll put your name in for the next Humanitarian of the Year Award." She pulled the cellophane off a fresh pack of smokes and tapped one out. "Anyway, if you're off this afternoon maybe you can do me a favor."

"Name it. Just don't get ash on my keyboard."

"Perish the thought. Like I said, I need to drop these files off at the printer by one and I've got an ob-gyn appointment at two."

"That's a little too much information, Terri."

"Sorry; my ex-husband said I had no tact."

I smirked. "Which one?"

"All of them. Anyway, I need to pay Damien for his column today." She rummaged in her purse and pulled out an envelope. "Any chance I can get you to drop it off for me? Assuming you don't have a hot date or something."

I hesitated for a moment. The notion of talking to Damien Smith had never occurred to me before. But now, with the words of his column still echoing in my head, joining the street person in strange dissonance, I suddenly felt as if I needed to. It was as if another voice was speaking to me, compelling me to leave, to meet Smith and ask him...

Ask him what?

I didn't know, but the compulsion remained.

"Sure," I said. "I need an address."

Terri turned the rock review over and scrawled an address on it, then handed it to me along with the envelope. "He lives out in Woodstock. You really are a life saver, you know that?"

"Don't get any ideas, now. I don't save lives for just anybody."

"It's because you love me, isn't it?" Terri stepped backward out of the office and blew me a kiss. "See you next week, boychik."

I looked at the address and the envelope, then out the window. My office had a lovely view of the adjoining building's wall. For the first time, I wondered what was happening on the other side.

* * *

The street person was still there when I left the building, and now he had an equally dirty, equally disturbing friend—an emaciated older man with a waxen complexion, hooked nose, and a fringe of white hair. My first thought was that he looked like Uncle Creepy from the old EC horror comics.

"I'm Pine Street Bob," the first man said. "What's your name?"

"Alex," I said, still walking.

"Hi, Alex. He says we gotta find the Shepherd."

Uncle Creepy only stared in rheumy-eyed silence, his thin lips twisted into something that looked vaguely like a not-at-all-friendly smile. Something dark seemed to flit across his face, like the shadow of a flapping moth.

I quickened my pace and walked toward the transit mall.

Pine Street Bob's words continued to echo and churn in my head as I rode the train from downtown then waited for my bus at the Lloyd Center Station.

The air smelled of diesel fumes. It was getting cold and rain was beginning to fall. My feet were already wet and cold and all I had to keep warm was a cheap windbreaker. I made a mental note to hit up Goodwill for something heavier. Nearby a busker sang and played guitar, his open case on the brick pavement beside him. I pulled all the change from my pocket and dropped it into the case. The man nodded and rewarded me with a smile.

I felt better, but as I rode the bus to Woodstock I felt a chill that was deeper than the cold, rain-soaked day around me.

He's comin' back, and hell's comin' with him.

I wasn't sure what to expect when I got to Damien's house—a disintegrating hovel, a lean-to made of old egg cartons and soup cans, a gothic castle complete with howling wolves and fluttering bats? God only knew. As I stepped off the bus into the fresh, rain-scented air, I was curious to find out.

Woodstock is a working-class neighborhood with ornate old houses in a dozen different styles, narrow streets, and ancient overhanging trees. Its colors contrasted with the leaden sky above—green trees fading to yellow with oncoming fall, and the varied hues of the brightly-painted homes.

Damien's house lived up to none of my expectations. The only word I could think of to describe it was "shabby." Dirty concrete steps led up to the yard, flanked by an unruly maple with its leaves just starting to turn and a decrepit hemlock, each competing with the other to completely overhang the path first. The yard was full of weeds, overgrown as if it hadn't seen a mower in weeks. The walkway to the front porch was like a tunnel through patchy shadows beneath the trees' looming branches.

The house had once been green but now it was gray, flaking paint over weathered wood. It was an old Queen Anne, the better part of a century old, boasting two stories, an attic, and a basement with small ground-level windows. A diminutive balcony perched on the second floor and there was a large, much more recent garage out back, shaded by yet another tree, this one an ancient willow.

The steps protested as I walked up to the porch. I pressed the bell and listened as its muffled tones echoed from inside, then rapped on the door with mixed emotions. As I had speculated about the house, so I speculated about its owner, my imagination generating anything from a mad-eyed, razor-thin savage to a suave elder in a fine silk suit. Once more, the ordinary-looking man who came to the door fit none of my imaginings.

He was in his middle- to late forties, in good shape save for a slight thickening around the waist. He was dressed in jeans and a white t-shirt. His brown hair was sparse and shot with gray, and he hadn't shaved in a day or two. His eyes were riveting—brown so dark they were almost black, deep-set and intense.

"Yes?" He sounded annoyed. Maybe I'd interrupted him.

He looked at me skeptically as I tried to introduce myself. "Hi. I'm Alex St. John. I work at the *Ranger*. Terri was busy and asked me to drop your money off for her."

He extended a hand. "Thanks."

Automatically, I handed him the envelope. He accepted without evident emotion, stepped back inside, and began to close the door.

"Uh, Damien," I said. "One more thing?"

He paused. "Yeah?"

"I would..." I faltered. "I'd like to talk to you. I've edited your column for months now, and I'd like to tell you how much I enjoyed it."

"Thanks. I appreciate it." He started to the close the door again.

"No, wait!"

Damien stopped short in surprise."What?" There was growing irritation in his voice.

"I'm sorry. I was just wondering whether I could talk to you about your column. I'd like to learn more."

He frowned. "You'd like to learn more?"

I nodded. "Yeah. I read today's article and—"

"You don't want to learn more. Believe me." This time he finally managed to get the door closed, firmly and loudly. From inside, I heard a muffled singsong "Thank you" and then he was gone.

I stood on the porch for almost a full minute, staring stupidly at the closed door, wondering how much of a fool I'd just made of myself. I briefly considered the notion of ringing again, but given how little I knew about the house's owner, it was entirely possible that the next time he came to the door he'd have a shotgun in his hand. I drew a deep breath, shrugged, and walked down the weathered porch steps, back toward the bus stop. Rain began to sprinkle down, darkening the pavement.

Behind me the door opened and I heard a voice.

"Hey, wait!"

I turned. Damien was there with only his chest and head outside, as if reluctant to expose himself.

"You wrote the I-84 Killer articles, didn't you?"

"Yeah, I did." I walked back up the steps, extending my hand.

He looked me up and down with a dubious expression, like a man inspecting an overpriced used car. He didn't take my hand and I lowered it.

"Alex Sinjun. Spelled Saint John. You use the English pronunciation. That's why I didn't recognize you. Those articles..." His expression changed and he looked almost amused. "They had a certain native talent."

My initial reaction was to raise my middle finger and leave with my last few tatters of dignity still intact, but I restrained myself.

"Thanks, I guess."

He nodded, seemingly unaware of how rude he sounded, then looked down at my sodden shoes. "I assume you came all the way on the bus?"

I nodded.

He smiled humorlessly. "Oh well, I won't make you stand out in the rain waiting for another one. Come on in. Do you drink coffee or tea?"

* * *

The inside of the house mirrored the yard—crowded, dark and unkempt. Books, magazines and boxes were piled everywhere. It smelled musty, as if it had been sealed for years, away from the eyes of prying outsiders. An old light fixture overhead provided wan yellowish light that barely cut through the tree-shaded gloom.

I sat uncomfortably in a faded wingback chair between two piles of old books, afraid to move lest I knock something over. Damien drank tea from a large coffee cup, which he placed on an ironwood coffee table with a polished slate top, crowded with more books and papers. He spooned sugar from a white china bowl and stirred it in, not speaking.

I contemplated my coffee and realized that I didn't have any idea what to say. Damien's weirdness and my own doubts combined to make me feel profoundly uneasy. All the same, the compulsion that had caused me to help Terri was still there, pressing me, and I went with it.

"I've really enjoyed your column," I said. It was a weak opening gambit, but it was all I had. "It's the best-written thing we publish at that damned fishwrapper."

"Yes, it is, isn't it?" Damien sat casually on a battered leather couch that looked as if he'd found it on a curb somewhere. He sipped his tea delicately. "That says more about your other writers than it does about me, unfortunately. I think Terri just publishes it as a favor to me. We're old friends."

"She told me."

"It's easy to stand out when you're an island of quality in an ocean of garbage. You're another exception. As I said, your I-84 Killer series was decent. Not great mind you, but decent. With some work you might even be a good writer."

"Thanks. That's what my professors at U of O said." I was clearly dealing with a raving egotist. I tried not to feel insulted and finally tasted my coffee. It was very good. "I got some decent feedback from the dozen or so people who actually read the series."

Damien gave a short sniff of laughter. "You actually have a dozen readers? Fortunate. I have no idea if anyone reads my column at all."

"I read it. Of course, it's my job." I paused, and the silence stretched out between us as rain drummed softly on the roof.

Damien leaned back, regarding me with a neutral gaze. "So what brought you here, Alex Sinjun? You seem a cut above those other Neanderthals who work at the *Ranger*. I can't imagine you came all this way just to tell me what a brilliant writer I am. Not that I mind, of course."

I set my coffee down on the table, a little too hard.

"I don't..." I faltered, trying to formulate something that made sense, something that gave a name to the compulsion that I felt. I knew what I wanted to ask about—Pine Street Bob and the Shepherd—but I couldn't say so, as if simply mentioning my fears would give them greater validity.

Damien looked at me indulgently. "It's okay. Be honest. So few people are these days."

I forged ahead, hoping that I didn't sound stupid. "Do you really believe all of that stuff you write about?"

I regretted it almost immediately. I had discarded my desire not to sound stupid almost the instant that I'd expressed it.

Damien looked as exasperated as a science fiction writer who had just been asked for the thousandth time where he got his ideas.

"That's a rather imprecise question, especially for a journalist," he said. "A more interesting question is whether *you* believe it."

That threw me for a loop. "What?"

"Seriously, Alex. I have a reason for asking. Do you believe what I write?"

I sighed. "You're one of those people who answers questions with questions, aren't you? You and my dad would get along great."

"I doubt that, Alex. I'm not exactly a people person. The question stands. Do you believe what I write?"

I swallowed my growing annoyance. "I guess. When I'm reading it, anyway. You write well enough that I can believe. Or at least you make me want to."

Damien's face lit up in triumph. "Good. That's exactly the response I want to generate. I don't especially care what you think when you're done with the article, but if you believe it when you're reading then I've done my job."

"I see. And what job is that?"

"To make you want to believe."

We were going in circles. "Okay, Damien. *Quid pro quo*. Do you believe what you write?"

Damien leaned forward and refilled his cup. He regarded me thoughtfully for a moment. "Look, Alex. What do you know about the nature of reality?"

Now there was a question you don't hear every day. In spite of myself, I began to eye escape routes in case he turned violent.

"As much as anyone else," I said. "Water is wet, ice is cold, up is up, and down is down. We're part of a material universe that obeys the laws of physics."

"Of course we are. Everything is scientific, rational, and predictable, right?"

"For the most part, I guess."

"What if that isn't the way reality works?" His eyes were suddenly intense, almost crazed, and my discomfort at being under his gaze increased. His hand trembled slightly as he lifted his cup. "Or rather, what if that's only part of the way reality works? What if reality is actually chaotic and incomprehensible? What if we can only understand the portion of it that we occupy? What if rational thought is nothing but a defense mechanism?"

I frowned. "I'm sorry?"

If Damien noticed my irritation he didn't show any sign. His voice abruptly grew steady and he spoke like a professor addressing a bored class of undergraduates. "What if our universe is just one of many different realities, all coexistent and coterminous—in other words, all occupying the same physical space? It's not a new concept. Some physicists theorize that this universe coexists with others like one slice in a loaf of bread, or a single bubble in a bubble bath."

I didn't reply. I'd read about alternate realities in science fiction novels since I was eight years old. How it related to my question was another matter entirely.

"You're not following me, are you?" Damien asked.

"I'm following you, Damien, but I'm not entirely sure where you're going."

He stood up abruptly and gestured at my coffee cup. "I'm going to make more tea. Want a warm up?"

I heard the rattle of dishes from the narrow cluttered kitchen, and a moment later he was back with a fresh cup. I accepted it and took a sip, still trying to fit my head around what he'd said.

"As you say, we live in a very rigid reality." Damien carried on as if there had been no interruption. "It's hard, if not impossible, to alter. Maybe you can influence the behavior of a gluon or a quark, but nothing more. Maybe you can alter reality near singularities, but have you ever actually seen a singularity?"

"Uh, no. No, I can't say that I have."

"I write about times and places where reality changes, where it's bent and things happen that the laws of science and logic tell us shouldn't happen. UFOs, sea monsters, psychic phenomena, spontaneous combustion, angels, demons. Irrational things. I want to know how such things can happen if we live in a reality that's rigid and obeys specific laws."

"Maybe because reality isn't really bending? Because people are gullible and believe what they want to?" I felt slightly less annoyed. I wasn't sure what he was getting at, but at least he was being entertaining instead of merely arrogant.

He favored me with a slightly indulgent smile, as if I'd just scored a point, but he was still in the lead. "Oh, of course—human error or exaggeration is responsible for a lot of it. Probably even most of it. Let's face it, Alex. Most people are stupid, only barely functional. But if ninety nine point nine nine percent of all supernatural phenomena are hoaxes or human error, what about that other zero point one percent?"

In the kitchen the kettle began to whistle. Damien stood up again. "Hang on a second."

Once more he vanished and once more returned, this time with a steaming teapot. He dropped in a tea ball and let it steep.

"I think those physicists are right. I think there really are alternate realities, coterminous with our own. And the stuff that makes up these universes... It's different from ours. And sometimes, for lack of a better term, Alex, it leaks through into this reality."

I tried not to look too skeptical.

Damien continued. "The Celts knew about it. You know what a thin place is? It's a place where the barriers between our world and the others are weak, where you see and hear strange things—ghosts, will o' wisps, banshees, spirits. They were right. A thin place is where this reality and another coexist and bleed into each other like two soap bubbles stuck together."

"And what happens there?"

He poured himself tea and proceeded to load it with sugar. "Weird things like the Celts talked about. And more. Fortean things like UFOs, psychic phenomena, rains of frogs. It all leaks through. Like through a door. That's what they are—doors. Not very good ones, either. Screen doors, or doors with really bad weather stripping, that let in the cold and rain in winter."

"Very interesting," I said. "And would you like some tea with your sugar?"

He ignored me and continued. "The rational mind is an amazing thing, Alex. It built the pyramids and it wrote *The Lord of the Rings*. But it's also a defense mechanism that kicks in when those barriers grow thin, when things get too chaotic, too incomprehensible. Maybe what some people see as supernatural phenomena are really chaotic, alien entities. Our minds can't comprehend them so all we see is little green men or sea monsters. Maybe without the filter of rational thought the reality of the universe would drive us insane, so we make laws, we study science, we build cars and computers, keeping our world stable and the wolf away from the door."

I felt as if I were watching Damien peel away the layers of his psyche, each a little stranger than the last. I wondered what I'd find when he reached the center and whether I'd want to see it.

Damien blew on his tea and took a sip. "I'm chronicling the collapse of this reality and its replacement with something else. Something new."

Although by now I was almost entirely convinced that Damien was delusional, something in his tone made me keep listening.

"Reality is infinite and infinitely complex, Alex. When we look at the universe, we're like the blind men with the elephant. When we confront things we don't understand—*can't* understand—the rational thought we use to defend ourselves grows less certain, the barriers grow weaker, and other realities intrude. We start to believe, and our belief is the roadway down which truly alien things travel."

Okay, I thought. *That's it. Have a nice day. Thanks for the coffee. See you around.*

But I didn't move. I remained sitting, letting Damien's words percolate in my head.

Part of me said that it was all nonsense and that Damien was completely unhinged. But I still felt an inexplicable pressure in my mind, a strange need to say just one more thing.

I tried to keep my voice steady. "Damien, this morning a homeless man asked me if I was the Shepherd."

That caught Damien up short. The cup froze halfway to his lips and he looked at me, his expression unreadable.

"What?"

"He asked if I was the Shepherd. Then I went up to my office and read your column. *Many Crimes, One Mind.*"

Damien set his cup down and placed one hand over the lower half of his face, stroking his cheek contemplatively while his eyes flashed from certainty to confusion, then back again, as if his mind were racing and he could barely follow.

He lowered his hand. "Interesting."

I waited a few moments. "Is that all? 'Interesting'?"

He gave me a thin smile. "Well, isn't that what it is? Interesting?"

"I thought it was kind of creepy myself."

"Yes, that too." Damien took a deep breath. Outside the rain had slacked off, but the shadows of late afternoon were falling. "Tell me about this homeless man."

I described what had happened that morning, about Pine Street Bob and his strange friends. Damien listened, staring at the floor, nodding occasionally until I was finished.

He rubbed his chin. "Interesting."

"There's that word again."

"'He's coming back?' That's what he said?"

"Yeah. 'And hell's coming with him.' That isn't something that normally comes up in conversation. What did it mean? Could it have anything to do with what you wrote about?"

"Damnation." Damien sat in contemplation for a while. "I can't give you any answers right now, Alex. As I said, the universe is incomprehensible, and sometimes coincidences happen."

I felt disappointed. "I got the impression you didn't believe in coincidences, Damien."

"Oh, I believe in coincidence. I just don't believe they happen as often as some people think."

I looked around the room. The coffee gods were demanding tribute. "Can I use your bathroom?"

He chuckled. "I'd be offended if you didn't, Alex. It's right down the hall there."

The bathrooms in a lot of old Portland houses seem as if they were added as an afterthought, and Damien's was no exception. It was little more than a closet with toilet, sink, and shower shoehorned in. When I'd done my business, I washed my hands and then, on impulse, opened Damien's medicine cabinet.

Yes, I was snooping. I always hated it when people did it to me, but I still felt annoyed by Damien's superior attitude and didn't feel terribly guilty.

There was the usual stuff—aspirin, vitamins, disposable razors, shaving cream, toothbrushes, dental floss as well as a diabetic testing kit. There were also three pill bottles. One by one I picked them up and looked at the labels.

Zyprexa. Metformin. Ramelteon.

I had no idea what they were. They certainly looked potent, but all drugs have impressive-sounding names. I committed them to memory, then hurriedly put the bottles back and closed the cabinet, wiping my fingerprints from the glass.

Back in the living room, Damien was busy rifling through a manila folder full of computer printouts, photos, and newspaper clippings.

He looked up as I walked in. "Shepherd crimes. Pine Street Bob. Hell's coming with him, huh? You've got me interested in spite of myself, Alex. I'll look into this matter further."

He glanced at a clock on the wall nearby. "Your bus is coming in about ten minutes. You should get going." He put down the folder and stood, extending his hand. "Thanks for coming by, Alex. I've really enjoyed it."

The suddenness of his dismissal stunned me. I shook his hand numbly then hurried out, pulling on my jacket. Behind me the house was dark, shrouded by its guardian trees. The bright colors of the neighborhood faded into twilight gray as I rode the bus back to my apartment.

I looked up the medications as soon as I got home. Metformin was for diabetes and Ramelteon was a prescription sleep aid. Just as I was beginning to relax and reconsider my misgivings about Damien I found an entry for Zyprexa.

It was an atypical antipsychotic, also known as olanzapine, and was used to treat schizophrenia and severe bipolarism.

I usually locked and deadbolted my apartment door, but tonight I fastened the security chain as well. I didn't expect anything to come bursting through in the middle of the night, but after today I wasn't going to take any chances. I tried to tell myself that it was all foolishness, that Pine Street Bob was just a harmless street person, and that the only difference between him and Damien was that Damien lived in a house. It didn't do much good. I took two melatonins and tried to sleep.

When slumber finally came, my dreams were dark and confusing. I walked alone through a devastated landscape. The sky overhead was a boiling mix of purple and indigo, glowing faintly like neon. All around me was the detritus of civilization— broken and abandoned houses, overgrown yards, the rusting hulks of cars, discarded appliances, fallen utility poles. I walked down a rutted street, my gaze fixed straight ahead, knowing that if I looked either left or right I would find some rotted, toothy horror staring at me through a broken window, or from under a diseased-looking bush.

Ahead lay a freeway overpass, but the freeway had long fallen into ruin. Wrecked cars were strewn about like Matchbox toys smashed by an angry child, and the space under the freeway yawned darkly, a fetid stench issuing from it like an open sewer.

I kept walking. As I approached the tunnel I saw a rumpled figure crouching in the shadows, regarding me with red, sunken eyes. Was it Pine Street Bob, I wondered—even dirtier and more menacing than before after weeks of starvation and disease?

The creature's mouth opened and he spoke in a scratchy, hissing voice.

"Shepherd..."

More whispers emerged from the rank darkness behind him and I saw shadowy motion there. More bodies emerged, as if the darkness itself was birthing them. They were like Bob, only worse—stick-thin bodies covered in welts and scratches, black with filth, their faces like so many skeletons, all staring at me with mad, hungry eyes.

"Shepherd," they whispered. "Shepherd."

As one the horde began to creep toward me, still whispering. I turned to run, but my feet felt as if they were trapped in muck, and I moved at snail's pace. A cry for help died in my throat as dirty fingers and jagged claws touched my face...

I awoke to a darkened room, my cry of terror still ringing in my ears.

As I lay, panting and telling myself that it was only a dream, I found myself wondering whether the neighbors had heard me.

A week passed. Another issue went to press, I heard nothing from Damien and never saw Pine Street Bob or his friends. The other homeless who normally populated the area were gone too, but I assumed they'd simply moved on to greener pastures.

As the week sputtered to its end I was starting to feel normal again, sitting in my office, working on one of the few projects that meant anything to me.

The Search Goes On.

I looked at the words, all by themselves on my screen. Outside my closed door, the office was quiet, as was usual for the Friday after we went to press. Loren was busy editing random copy for future use when we had extra space for it, doing layout and assembling ads for strip bars, swingers' clubs, medical marijuana clinics, and cheap bankruptcy lawyers. In her office Terri chain-smoked, blowing pungent gray clouds out the window and pretending no one noticed.

I'd written six articles about the I-84 Killer; this one was the last installment. It should have been easy.

But today it wasn't. Even if I hadn't seen him, Pine Street Bob was still there in spirit, lurking in the shadows. Sometimes in my imagination Damien Smith was there too. They were things of chaos—unpredictable, unknown—and my rational mind could find no defense against them.

Just like the I-84 Killer.

I rubbed my eyes, and focused on the page.

The I-84 Killer has terrorized the region for over five years, I typed, *blazing a trail of death that extends from Salt Lake City to the Pacific coast. He has brutally murdered at least six men and eight women. Only three victims are known to have survived his attacks, and they have proved unable to provide any useful evidence. As of this date, the police are no closer to catching him than they were half a decade ago.*

I stopped and read what I'd written. I was no Damien Smith of course, but it would do.

The killer is unusual in that he combines violent sex crimes against women with non-sexual serial murder of men. With that exception, his victims are treated similarly—bound, tortured for long periods, their flesh cut with random, possibly ritualistic symbols. Men are eventually stabbed repeatedly and their bodies mutilated, while women are left to bleed to death. One female survivor, pregnant by her attacker, chose to terminate her pregnancy.

I looked away from the screen. After months of working on the story, its details were familiar to me, but it was still difficult to write, conjuring up images of mindless savagery that combined uneasily with memories of my own past. I'd dreamed about the killer many times now, often waking up in the middle of the night convinced that he was in my bedroom with me, knife poised in the darkness. Sometimes—even more alarmingly—I dreamed that I was the killer.

The articles were Terri's idea. She was a sex abuse survivor. She didn't talk about it much, but she still bore scars—internal and external—of an abusive relationship many years earlier. Something about the I-84 case struck a chord with her and she wanted to do something. Though the *Ranger's* ranking on the scale of journalistic excellence could barely be measured, she used it as her own bully pulpit, writing articles and editorials demanding that the authorities do something, anything, to apprehend the killer.

Back in May, she had suggested that I write the series, and had given me unlimited editorial freedom to do so. It was the kind of assignment I'd dreamed of in college, but now it seemed little more than a routine aspect of my unglamorous job.

I did the best I could because Terri had asked me, and I both respected and cared about her. About once a month I wrote an article chronicling the saga of the I-84 Killer, his victims, his *modus operandi*, the police response, their lack of progress, and conflicting theories on the crimes. The articles generated some reader mail, and even a couple of messages from law enforcement, complaining about my lack of objectivity. Beyond that, they did little for me besides make me even more cynical about my fellow human beings and their capacity for violence.

The killer has slain at least fourteen victims, and even those fortunate enough to survive his attentions will bear both physical and emotional scars for the rest of their lives. The mutilated body of his most recent victim, Francine Harris, was found only two months ago. Authorities in four states, as well as representatives of the FBI, insist that the case is ongoing, and that they are following several promising leads. But as the body count grows and atrocity piles upon atrocity, one cannot help but wonder how many more innocents will suffer at the hands of a monster before the authorities finally catch up with him.

I clicked "save," drew a deep breath, held it for a moment, then released it slowly. There. Assignment completed.

The only problem was that it didn't feel like the end of the story. Not by a long shot.

A soft tone from my computer told me that I had an urgent flagged email. I opened my inbox and read.

Alex: I don't have your cell number so I'm emailing; I need to speak with you immediately. Please come over ASAP – Damien

"God damn it," I muttered. I'd almost decided that Damien and Pine Street Bob were two sides of the same crazy coin, and now Damien wanted to talk to me again.

I stood up. No. I was done with that lunatic. It was Friday night. I was going to go home, make myself a pizza, and watch Netflix until I fell asleep.

Terri was in her office nursing another cigarette, a full ashtray on the desk in front of her.

I rapped softly on her open door. "I just finished the I-84 story. Is everything under control?"

She nodded and took another drag. "You can take off if you need to. Loren said he'd stay and keep me company."

"You sure?"

She nodded again and waved a hand. "Take off, sweetie. You've done your time. I'll call if anything comes up."

With what I hoped was calm determination I rode the elevator down and strode out through the front doors of the Pioneer Building.

As soon as I stepped outside, I stopped short, my heart in my throat.

Pine Street Bob was outside the building, sitting on the sidewalk, hand extended, eyeing each person intently as they walked past. Beside him sat Uncle Creepy, looking at me with big watery eyes.

When Bob saw me, he froze for a moment, his eyes locked on my face.

"You seen the Shepherd?" His voice was grim, almost menacing.

I felt a sting of fear, but I couldn't look away. "No, I haven't."

Uncle Creepy's gaze joined Bob's. He held up a dirty hand and waved.

"Hi, Alex," he said, his voice barely audible over the snorting roar of a passing bus.

My nerve broke and I practically ran down the street, Pine Street Bob's voice fading behind me.

"Spare some change, sir? God bless."

* * *

It was dusk by the time I got to Damien's place, and it had grown still more forbidding. The two big trees formed an arched gateway, with only the faint suggestions of a walkway and porch beyond them. As I set my foot on the cracked concrete steps, the notion occurred to me that I was stepping across the threshold into one of Damien's other realities and that I might not return in one piece.

I chided myself as I reached for the doorbell. There was a rational explanation for what was happening—for Pine Street Bob, the Shepherd, Uncle Creepy, everything. I'd just panicked and jumped on the Woodstock bus, and now I was here.

But, I thought to myself, if there was a rational explanation, why was I seeking out a madman to find it?

The bell rang hollowly, and the curtains on the door window moved, revealing Damien's wan face. He looked different now—haggard, his hair out of place, his eyes staring and worried. I waved and mouthed, "Hi."

"Come on in," he said, opening the door. "God, Alex, I have to apologize for my behavior last week. I was a complete dick to you, wasn't I?"

"Well, I wouldn't call you a— "

"Of course you wouldn't, because you're too polite. So allow me to do the honors. I was an ass and I'm surprised you even bothered to read my email."

He ushered me into the living room—even more cluttered now, with yellowed clippings and computer printouts strewn everywhere, alongside the unruly piles of books and magazines in several different languages. The overhead light seemed even dimmer.

"I'll get you coffee." Damien shuffled into the kitchen as I sat down in the wingback. He moved slowly, without energy. It was as if he'd grown as dark and untidy as his house. In the kitchen I heard the crash of a dropped coffee cup and a muffled curse.

He returned a moment later with two cups in one hand and a sugar bowl in the other, making room for them amid the clutter on the coffee table.

"Listen, Alex, I know we got off on the wrong foot. But you got me thinking. About, you know… patterns and…" He paused. "God damn it, I'm stupid sometimes."

I stared, trying to reconcile the humble, self-effacing creature who sat on the couch, nervously blowing on his steaming tea with the arrogant man I'd met a week ago. I wondered idly if this was the real Damien, who kept his evil twin chained in the basement.

His expression changed to one of deadly seriousness as he set down his cup and gripped the edge of the coffee table.

"I don't want to alarm you, Alex, but I've found something important. Very important. And it kind of scares me."

I forced down a swallow of coffee. This time it was awful, but I didn't pay much attention. "What is it?"

He gestured at the computer printouts that covered the coffee table. "The Shepherd crimes, Alex. I took another look at them after you left like I said I would. I found more...more similarities. I don't know why I didn't see them before. Maybe I was overly impressed with my own abilities and rushed the column. I do that all the time when I'm on an upswing."

He paused, as if gathering his thoughts with difficulty. "But when I looked over the stories... Given the era in which the crimes occurred, the papers were fairly circumspect, but I was able to pull out some details... These men... The ones who said they were looking for the Shepherd. They were all drifters with histories of mental illness. Some of them killed men. Some of them raped women. Some of the women died, others survived. Sound familiar?"

It was dark outside, and now it felt as if we were in a tiny island of yellow light, surrounded by an abyss of shadow. I felt a chill as the skin on the back of my neck prickled, and didn't reply.

"How about this, Alex? The perpetrators ritually tortured their victims, carving their bodies with strange symbols."

"Jesus." The chill spread to my shoulders and down my back. I felt a sudden urge to look into the shadows beyond the living room to see if something was lurking there, watching me. "You mean like the I-84 Killer?"

"Exactly."

I looked down at the printouts. Most of them looked like copies of old newspaper articles, pulled from on-line archives. They were all old—1948, 1951, 1953... and in a variety of languages—Spanish, French, German, Russian, Japanese.

I picked up an article from an Irish newspaper with a 1949 dateline. The headline read *Suspect Arrested in String of Assaults*. The article was discreet, but what it implied was unmistakable—Michael Nolan, a drifter and petty criminal, had been arrested for sexually assaulting and mutilating two women with a knife. His face, muddy and indistinct from crude digital scanning, stared at me from the middle of the page.

I'd seen his eyes before, staring at me on the streets of Portland. But they'd been part of a different face.

He's comin' back. And hell's comin' with him.

I forced myself to look away. Nonsense. The article was over six decades old. Michael Nolan was dead and buried.

"You're saying that the Shepherd crimes were the same as the I-84 killings?"

Damien drew a deep breath and fell back onto the couch. "I don't know, Alex. We can't know that, not really. They had certain similarities, yes. But we can only use coincidence as an explanation for so long before we have to look elsewhere, don't we?"

Skepticism and science struggled to maintain control of my mind in the face of growing irrationality.

I put the printout down and covered it with another, so I wouldn't have to think about the eyes, or acknowledge the truth I'd seen there. "Damien, this all sounds... well..."

"Crazy?" Damien leaned forward. "You think I don't know that? Look, I know you think I've got a screw loose somewhere. You may even be right. I don't blame you at all after you looked in my medicine cabinet."

I felt a surge of shame and the sudden realization of how truly creepy my behavior had been. How had he known?

"Damien, I'm so sorry. I didn't mean to..."

He waved his hand in a careless gesture. "It's okay, it's okay. I wouldn't have noticed, but you put the bottles back on the wrong shelf. Blame my mania. I snoop in other people's bathrooms too. It's a good way to learn more about them. It scares me that these Shepherd crimes were committed by mentally ill men, Alex. It scares the living hell out of me."

"Are you... " I couldn't think of the right word to say. Crazy? Delusional? Mentally ill? Given that I'd been the one caught snooping in Damien's medicine cabinet, I didn't feel as if I had the right to judge.

Damien sighed. "I'm pretty severely bipolar, Alex. What they used to call manic-depressive. I've been that way all my life. My sainted father never believed it. He just told me to pull myself up by my bootstraps and act like a man. He was a corporate lawyer type. A real Reagan republican hardass. When I was sixteen I told him to go fuck himself and walked out. I tried to live with it, but it finally got to me. A few years later I opened my wrists up and would have bled to death if Terri hadn't found me." He held up his wrist, and I saw faint white lines of scar tissue.

My mouth hung open at Damien's sudden rush of revelation. Now I understood why Terri was so protective of him, and what a jerk I'd been for prying. "My God, Damien, I'm sorry. I didn't know."

"There's no way you could have. Anyway, after that I got my act together, got on meds, started writing. My folks died in a plane crash back in '99. I hadn't spoken to them in years, but I cried for three days straight after it happened. Then I found out that they hadn't bothered to change their will and I'd inherited everything. I bought this this house, set myself up with a little investment portfolio, and presto...I'm a full-time freelance writer specializing in the occult."

I felt ashamed and somehow chastened by Damien's confession. "Damien, I don't know what to say."

He shook his head. "Don't bother. I know how I come across. When I'm manic I'm a great writer, an awesome editor, and a certifiable genius—at least in my own humble opinion. When I'm down, I think I'm the most talentless and horrible person on earth. It's weird living your life alternating between the top of Everest and the bottom of the Marianas Trench. The meds help a little. At least they keep me from killing myself. And when I'm up, I'm an asshole."

He leaned back like a rag doll, entirely absent the energy that had driven him the last time we'd spoken. "I'm also energetic, driven, careless. But the bottom line, Alex, is that I'm not delusional. I'm not making any of this stuff up." He held up another printout, this on in some Scandinavian language. "And when I find an article about a kid in Norway going berserk at a club and trying to slash people with a broken bottle while screaming that they're all *hyrde,* it's a fact, not a product of my mental illness."

"*Hyrde?* Sorry, Damien, but I don't speak Norwegian."

Damien's eyes narrowed. "I think you know what it means, Alex."

I swallowed. "Shepherd?"

"Bingo. And look at the date. It happened only six weeks ago."

I cast my eyes across the coffee table and to the cluttered living room and dining space beyond. It looked as if a snowstorm of printouts had hit.

"Are you saying that they're still..." I bit off my next words. We both knew what they were, but I couldn't bring myself to say them, to acknowledge the madness that was staring at us like the monsters in my childhood closet.

Damien smiled. It was a grim, humorless smile, but a smile nonetheless.

"Come upstairs," he said. "There's something you need to see."

* * *

Damien's small and surprisingly tidy bedroom was upstairs facing the back of the house, but he'd knocked the wall out between the other two bedrooms, creating a large space that was a computer geek's wet dream.

"After the house and my car, this is where most of my inheritance ended up," he said, indicating a tall black structure that lurked in the corner, humming ominously amid more piles of books and papers. "It's a 64 blade Linux server enclosure. Multi-terabyte RAID-6 array for storage, high-performance workstation, incoming fiber optic line, generator for backup, the whole nine yards."

I was impressed. "How much did all this cost?"

Damien shrugged. "You don't want to know. And the power consumption makes the cops think I'm growing weed or something. But I need it, given the sheer amount of data that I have to deal with. I wrote a series of scripts that search the net for key words and phrases, looking for patterns and similarities. Then it sends me a report and I look at the references that seem most relevant. Those I store and use in my articles." He tapped the big enclosure gently. "I've got texts and images of thousands of rare occult books, out of print periodicals, obscure articles, publications, comics, pulp magazines, blogs, journals, everything. This could be the most extensive collection of occult materials in the world, right here in the corner of my office. I've got hundreds more printed books downstairs in my library."

He gestured toward an office chair. "Sit, please."

The workstation had a monstrous twenty-seven inch screen, and when Damien sat beside me and gave his mouse a few clicks, a world map appeared, with fifteen or so colored pin icons scattered across several continents.

"I can filter my searches any way I want," he said. "These are the results of my original search when I was just looking for violent crimes in which the word 'Shepherd' appears."

I remained silent, watching as Damien did more arcane things with pop-up menus and search criteria.

"After we talked, I took a closer look at those crimes and saw that they all involved knives or stabbing weapons, along with the ritualistic cutting of symbols into the victims' flesh."

Damien described the crimes with almost clinical detachment, but I'd been living with the victims' ordeals for the past six months. I shivered.

The mouse pointer darted across the screen. "There were other similarities. Some babbled gibberish while they killed or raped their victims. Some butchered their dead victims and engaged in cannibalism. I missed all of that, of course. I can be really blind when I'm manic. So focused on one idea that I don't see what's staring me in the face." He pulled down a menu and tapped another button. "I added all of those criteria to my search and look what happened."

Dozens more dots appeared, each with a date beside it.

"Over a hundred now," he said. "And in each case, the killer used a stabbing or slashing weapon, cut symbols on the victim's body, babbled in an incoherent fashion, or used a language that he didn't normally speak. Not all of them mention the Shepherd, but in most other aspects they're identical. Most of them aren't assaults, either. They're murder. Lots more than I originally thought. The perpetrators that were caught were all either imprisoned, executed, or committed to mental institutions. Many of these crimes remain unsolved to this day."

I leaned forward to look at the screen, reading the dates. "Jesus, Damien. They didn't end in the '50s."

More dots appeared with later and later dates. Damien clicked again, and the dots changed to different colors according to the decade in which they occurred.

"They happen in waves," Damien said. "The blue ones happened in the late '40s, yellow in the mid-'60s, green in the '80s..." Red dots appeared in western North America, along the route of the I-84 Killer's spree. "And now it's happening again."

There was a sick feeling in the pit of my stomach. "These crimes are all identical to the I-84 Killer? Over a hundred murders over sixty-plus years?"

"I count a hundred and twenty-two. Maybe more, but the records get scarcer the farther back you go."

"All over the world."

"All with three or more similarities." Damien stopped, as if reluctant to continue. He rubbed his cheeks with one hand. "Some are spot-on identical. The Shepherd pattern was only one aspect of a larger crime wave. All around the world, men have been killing and raping with the same M.O. Just like the I-84 Killer. I didn't see the pattern, Alex. I should have. If it hadn't been for you, I'd have missed it entirely."

"I don't like where this is going, Damien."

"Neither do I. In most cases there's no record of the supposed gibberish that the killers babbled. In one case, I was able to find a transcript of one of the interrogations from 1988. It was in Nice, France, and the guy who did it was a Spanish transient named Ramon Soto." He picked up a stack of papers that sat beside one of his printers. "I printed it out and highlighted the important parts." He handed it to me.

I looked at it. "Damien?"

"Hmm?"

"I don't speak French either."

He took it back. "Sorry. I keep forgetting…"

"Forgetting that not everyone is as gifted as you are?"

"Take it as a compliment, Alex." He opened the transcript to a series of highlighted paragraphs. "Most of it really is nonsense. The transcriptionist did her best, tried to type some of it phonetically in case he was actually speaking another language. *Itcheloot. Agunaba. Bagnakunachee.* But here he actually starts to talk in Spanish. He never says anything about a Shepherd, but he does say some interesting things. The interrogator asks him in Spanish why he killed the man and Soto says, '*él me ordeno*'— 'he ordered me to.' The policeman asks who *he* is, and Soto says '*el bestia dentro cabeza me,* '—'the beast in my head.'"

I looked away, as if not seeing the printed words would help me to feel less helpless, less confused. "The beast in my head? What the hell does that mean?"

"We'll never know. After that Soto refused to respond and they finally ended the interview. He died in custody a week later, cause unknown."

"You're scaring me, Damien." I felt as if dark, mad eyes were staring at the back of my head, across scores of years and thousands of miles.

"Yeah, well I'm pretty scared myself. I don't have an explanation for any of this, and even if I did I don't think I'd like it. All that cosmic uncertainty I talked about is suddenly right in front of us."

I looked outside. A pair of doors with large glass windows led out onto the upstairs porch. Night was spreading across the neighborhood. The streetlights were almost invisible through the thick trees in the front yard. I wanted to deny it, to find some logical reason to reject everything Damien had told me, but I couldn't.

"If this is all true, what the hell is going on?" I asked. "Has some bizarre cult been committing rapes and murders for the past sixty years?"

"It's one possible explanation, Alex. But only one of many."

"You said it yourself—three incidents is a movement." I waved my hand at the screen. "You just found over a hundred."

"I think there was at least a small amount of hyperbole in that statement. Besides I wrote it when I was manic and thought I was right about everything. There's really no way of knowing for certain why this is all happening. Or whether it's happening at all." He hung his head. "Damnation. Sometimes I wonder whether it's just my own mind screwing with me."

Damien was silent for a moment, then perked up.

"Oh, yes. I found something else interesting." He rummaged through the stack of papers and handed me another printout. This one looked like a high school yearbook photo.

"A little present for you, Alex. Meet Robert Leslie, aka Pine Street Bob. Born 1961, graduated 1979, Holy Grace Young Men's Academy, Seattle, Washington."

I frowned at the picture. "Pine Street Bob? How did you get this?"

He shrugged. "I can find just about anything about just about anyone. It just depends on how hard I want to look and what laws I want to break. Finding out about Bob was easy."

"Are you sure this is him?" I held the printout up, trying to connect the smiling, fresh-faced youth in the picture with the burnt-out street person who had been haunting my imagination. Had the delusional Pine Street Bob really started out life as a Catholic schoolboy?

"Reasonably. You can never be certain with transients—no fixed address, no socials. Many don't even use their real names. But I'm relatively sure—young Robert here seems to have devolved into your friend Pine Street Bob."

Damien read from another printout. "Young, intelligent, deeply religious. His yearbook bio says that his goal was to join the priesthood, but he never did. He ended up with a history of emotional problems, a string of jobs, increasing mental disturbances, reports of violent behavior. He moved all over the Pacific Northwest—Seattle, Olympia, Anacortes, Post Falls, Boise, Eugene, finally Portland. He's been here for a few years, and he has quite a dossier. Disorderly conduct arrests in '11 and '13, later assault charges dropped because the victim was another homeless man and they couldn't find him. The report says that Bob kept screaming that the guy was the Shepherd and cut him up pretty badly with a broken bottle."

I felt my neck hairs raise again.

Damien continued. "They arrested him by that abandoned cement plant out in the industrial area near Blue Lake. You remember—the one that had a fire last fall?"

"Yes, I remember." It had been a bit of a scandal—an abandoned site that the owner had let go completely to seed. When someone saw smoke and called in the fire department, they'd discovered a fairly extensive homeless community there. The sheriff had fined the owner, kicked the homeless people out, and promptly forgotten about the place.

Damien took the photo back from me and contemplated the innocent, smiling face. "Something happened to our little Bobby. Something took this kid and made him into what you saw outside your building."

"Schizophrenia, maybe? It can happen to anyone." I was still looking for a rational explanation, for some way to make it all make sense.

"No arguments here." Damien stroked his chin thoughtfully. "But no. It's got to be more than that. Certainly he's disturbed. His history was pretty clear. But why the Shepherd? Why is he following in the footsteps of all those other men? Disturbed, loners, petty criminals who start demanding to know about the Shepherd and eventually kill and rape because of it?"

"He read about the Shepherd crimes somewhere and decided to add them to his delusions? Maybe he read your articles, Damien." I was busy searching for some other explanation, something that would make sense of it all.

"Not unless he can travel in time. He had a history of violence well before my article was written. Besides, he asked you about the Shepherd before the article was even published. No, there's some other influence at work. God knows, maybe he's part of our hypothetical serial murder cult. He certainly fits the profile."

"Damien, are you suggesting that Pine Street Bob is the I-84 Killer?"

There it was, plain and ugly as an open wound.

"No, I'm not suggesting anything. I'm just observing, looking at patterns. And noting that Robert Leslie fits them."

He was starting to sound like Manic Damien again, but it didn't bother me. Manic Damien was who I wanted to talk to right now.

"He's got friends too, Damien. That first day I saw him with another homeless guy who looked like Uncle Creepy. He was there again today. He waved at me. Said 'Hi, Alex.' They both looked at me like..." I shivered. "Like they wanted something from me. God damn it, Damien, do you think they could be..."

Again, I let my voice trail off, unwilling to finish a thought that was too awful to contemplate.

I suppressed a shiver. The fact that Damien kept his whole house underlit didn't help matters. "What do you think we should do? Call the cops?"

"And tell them what? That we think Pine Street Bob and his buddies might be part of a murder cult that's been raping and killing people for a half century? That he's going to be a murderer at some unspecified future date?"

"Shit."

"Exactly. You see the position we're in, Alex. It's where I've been for years, seeing patterns and thinking things that no one in their right mind would believe."

Damien held up Robert Leslie's photo. His eyes stared out of the picture—younger, healthier, brighter. But they were the same eyes that I'd seen in the picture of the Irish rapist, and the same ones I'd seen staring out of Pine Street Bob's face.

"Gaze into the abyss, Alex," Damien said. "It's already gazing into you."

* * *

Damien led me outside to the garage. Inside, safe from the rain, dark and bulky in the gloom, was a relic of another century.

"Is this what I think it is?" I asked.

Damien grinned, some of his former manic energy returning. "This is a 1968 Chevy Camaro SS with a non-stock 454 cubic-inch, 425 horsepower V8, AFR210 eliminator competition heads, custom ground cams, Isky Red Zone lifters, mandrel-bent exhausts with MagnaFlow mufflers, Cloyes billet roller timing chain—"

"Damien."

He stopped, looking at me blankly. "Huh?"

"I have no idea what you're talking about."

He grinned. "Sorry."

It was a magnificent beast of a car—sleek and muscular, its aggressive lines speaking of barely-restrained power. Its shiny black body was painstakingly polished, chrome bumper and fender strips gleaming as if it had just rolled off a Detroit assembly line.

"How did you get it?"

"It was my dad's. His pride and joy, from a forgotten age before he sold his soul to corporate America. He bought it stock, added the new engine, leather interior, custom wheels, all out of his own pocket. He named it Yngwie for Yngwie Malmsteen. His favorite guitarist, I guess. I inherited it along with everything else when he died." Damien faltered for a moment, and I perceived the faintest trace of unidentifiable emotion in his tone. "Maybe keeping it helps me remember the part of him that still loved me."

I didn't reply immediately and finally decided to change the subject. "You take it out much?"

"I try not to. It's a work of art, after all."

"Works of art are for people to look at," I said. "Besides, how do you get around? The bus, like me?"

He shrugged. "I don't. I ride a bike. I walk in the neighborhood. I have food and computer parts delivered. Mostly I stay at home and write, or I come out here and tinker. I've got enough auto equipment to open a business."

"This is the most beautiful car I've ever seen." The disparity between the thin, slightly unbalanced hermit and this shiny black automotive monster was remarkable.

"Thanks. It still runs like a Swiss watch but parts are getting harder to find. Maybe I'll just start machining my own."

"You know, after today I believe you would, Damien."

He beamed. I guess he didn't get too many compliments.

"Come on inside. I'll make you dinner. It's the least I can do after scaring the hell out of you. You're not Vegan or anything, are you?"

"Hell no."

We talked until nearly ten o'clock when Damien drove me home in Yngwie. It was raining, and I realized what a concession this was for him, given his concern for his automotive masterpiece. The engine purred like a happy tiger, and the heater pumped out hot air like a furnace. Outside the dark streets scrolled by, slick with rain and full of secrets, well-lit bars full of happy patrons, houses snug against the autumn chill.

That night I lay in bed, plans and ideas half-formed in my mind then vanished, along with memories of my days at University of Oregon and my loss of innocence and faith. I'd wanted to be a journalist once, not a hack working for a giveaway street rag. As I drifted into a haunted sleep, it occurred to me that part of me still did.

IV

"So he lives all alone in this house and never comes out?" Loren nursed his pale ale, regarding me with a mixture of curiosity, skepticism and fascination. His t-shirt said *Reverse the polarity of the neutron flow!*

"Not much." I downed the last bitter swallow from my pint of Terminator stout and wiped foam off my lips. "He drove me home in that battleship of his, but I guess that was pretty unusual for him."

Loren considered this. He'd wondered about Damien Smith too, and now at last he had some answers.

Outside it was a characteristically gray Portland Saturday. We were seated in the loft at the Barley Mill—private, warm, and slightly cramped, surrounded by surreal murals, perched above the hubbub of the main floor where people played billiards, drank microbrews, and admired the tavern's collection of Grateful Dead memorabilia.

Loren frowned into his drink. "He thinks that this Pine Street Bob guy might be the I-84 Killer?"

"Well, he doesn't want to say one way or the other, but it's obvious that's what he's thinking. And maybe because I'm

45

hanging out with the guy, I'm starting to think like him too. And it's got me worried, since this nutcase attacks people he thinks are the Shepherd, whatever the hell that means."

Loren reached for a French fry. We'd ordered a large and he'd eaten most of them. He was an eating machine, but for some reason continued to stay thin as a rail.

"What about that Uncle Creepy guy? You think he's involved too?"

"I don't know. I don't know anything, not really. For all I know they're just a couple of scary street people who like to stare at me." I faltered, shaking my head. "But something keeps telling me that they're not. That there's something really dangerous about them. Don't ask me how. Maybe it's Damien's influence or something. But I just... can't write them off as just another couple of transients."

Loren watched the game below. A woman carefully lined up her shot, then sent the cueball spinning flawlessly into the corner pocket without hitting anything else, earning a round of applause from her friends. "Have you told the cops about this? If you think you've got a maniac stalking you, it might be a good idea."

I sighed. "Damien and I discussed it. The police don't have the resources to keep track of every unstable homeless guy in Portland. They'll take my report, tell me that they'll look into it then roll their eyes at each other after I leave."

"So if you don't want to go to the cops, what are you gonna do? Leave town?"

"Of course not. But right now I've got no idea what else to do. I'm even spooked about going home."

Loren rested his chin on his fist. "Want to stay at my place? My roommate won't mind."

"I wouldn't say no, especially since it's possible that a homicidal maniac and his friends are stalking me. I know it sounds paranoid, but I can't get it out of my head."

"Well maybe you shouldn't hide. Maybe you should act like a journalist."

"How so?"

"It sounds like Mister Pine Street was crashing at that old cement plant in Blue Lake. Maybe we should drive over there and check it out."

My eyes widened. "You're not serious. Are you?"

"I'm serious. I know you don't want to admit it, but you've always wanted to be a real reporter, not a guy at a desk retyping other people's crap. And I need to do something this weekend besides playing *Modern Warfare* and wishing I had a girlfriend. What do you think?"

"When do you want to go?"

"How about right now?"

I felt a knot in my stomach ease a bit. Strangely enough the notion of throwing ourselves directly into the lion's mouth seemed better than just cringing behind a locked door and never learning the truth. "Okay. But if I get killed I swear I'll haunt your ass for all eternity."

"Deal. You think we should go armed?"

"Hell, yeah. God knows how many other weird friends Pine Street Bob has. I'll buy a can of bear mace. You got anything?"

Loren leaned back, interlacing his fingers across his chest and beaming.

"Yeah. I'll bring Beowulf."

"Beowulf?"

* * *

Beowulf turned out to be a large black dog with soft, floppy ears, intelligent brown eyes, and a heavy muzzle. He sat patiently in the back of Loren's Taurus as he guided us into the wilds of eastern Multnomah County. I guessed that he had some black lab, Staffordshire terrier, and maybe even mastiff in his background—in short he was as much of a mutt as any other American. He'd greeted me with enthusiasm, his stumpy tail wagging as if to tell me that any friend of Loren's was a friend of his too. There was something about him that made me feel safer.

High clouds had given way to grim foggy overcast. Winter seemed to have come early this year. The trees were jagged and skeletal, and a few tattered scraps of orange and yellow continued to cling against the stiff cold breeze. Fallen leaves accumulated in gutters and drains, and when it rained the streets overflowed with dirty water.

We drove along Marine Drive with the muddy expanse of the Columbia River on our left, fringed by stands of shaggy evergreens and clusters of freight terminals, silos and warehouses. On our right was the Portland Airport. A light commuter plane raced along the runway beside us and rose into the low clouds, vanishing quickly.

Loren sat at the wheel of his battered Taurus, glancing down at the Google map printout I'd given him. "Jesus, Alex. We're heading into the ass end of nowhere."

I laughed. "Where the hell is your journalistic spirit? This was all your idea, remember?"

"I see you've recovered your enthusiasm for reporting. Next stop, Pulitzer Prize."

Rain began to fall. We drove on, splitting off from the Columbia and driving past rain-dimpled sloughs filled with dirty brown water, corrugated warehouses and heavy equipment yards where backhoes, cranes, skip loaders, and steamrollers sat and rusted, past junkyards surrounded by chain link and barbed wire, overgrown with blackberries and overhung by ancient willows and oaks. The clouds descended lower, curling foggy tendrils around trees and fences.

On days like this, Damien's theories seemed more plausible. Somewhere out there in the mist I could imagine beasts from nightmares emerging through open doorways. These were the days when my faith in science and reason seemed weakest, when the barriers grew thin and even the darkest fantasies seemed possible.

Loren sighed and shook his head. "I don't know about you, but I'm keeping my eye out for a guy with a chainsaw and a hockey mask."

I grunted but didn't say anything, listening as windshield wipers flipped methodically back and forth in time with the music. It seemed as if we were the only ones on the road.

The compulsion was still there, though—the one that had made me go to Damien's house and accept Terri's assignment against my better judgment. It was something I hadn't felt since college, back when I truly wanted to be a crusading reporter and tell everyone the truth.

Harsh reality and my own failings had crushed that particular dream, but part of me knew it had survived, wounded but alive. And part of me wished it hadn't.

And there was something else too. Something I couldn't tell Loren.

I wanted things to be ordinary. I wanted Pine Street Bob to be a random crazy, and I wanted the whole Shepherd thing to be a stupid coincidence. I wanted the world to be rational, scientific, measurable. The idea that Pine Street Bob was the latest in a long series of criminals, influenced and controlled by forces that I couldn't explain didn't fit into my logical universe.

The truth was that I had come this far and was willing to risk both myself and Loren because I wanted to prove Damien Smith wrong. And if he was right...

If he was right, I didn't want to know it. Facing Damien's reality meant facing my own, and that wasn't something I was prepared to do.

With that realization I almost told Loren to turn the car around and head home, but as I started to form the words, Loren spoke.

"There it is."

An aging metal frame surrounding a cyclone preheater rose above a stand of trees like a rusty obelisk, alongside a cluster of silos that bore the fading logo *Western Pride Cement.* An unpaved road led toward the river. It was marked *No Trespassing*, but Loren drove down it without hesitation, our tires crunching in the gravel, bumping through ruts and potholes. The main road quickly vanished behind us.

I swallowed my doubts as Loren pulled to a halt at a padlocked gate topped with patchy razor wire.

"End of the line, everybody out." Loren stepped into the cold air and Beowulf scrambled after him. I grabbed my camera out of the back and joined them. Loren was bundled up in a down coat, and Beowulf looked so eager that he didn't seem to care about the weather at all. Rain drifted down like a chilly blanket. Beyond the fence rose a towering complex of concrete and rusty metal—preheater, silos, a tangle of broken-down conveyor belts, and cylindrical mills that led to an ancient precalcinator kiln. Some walls were streaked with black from last year's fire. Grass and weeds grew across the grounds, pushing up through cracks, spreading over the faint yellow stripes of the old parking lot.

Loren gestured at another *No Trespassing* sign and a human-sized hole in the fence behind some brush a few feet away. "Looks like someone's already been here. You still up for this, Woodward?"

"I am if you are, Bernstein." I didn't feel very enthusiastic. "Let's get this over with before the sheriff shows up."

We crawled through the breach and made our way down slippery gravel toward the plant, Beowulf trotting along without hesitation as if it were a trip to the dog park.

The preheater rose above us like a rusting skyscraper as we walked across the parking lot. I heard cawing and saw a flock of crows circling its upper scaffold.

As I stopped to snap a couple of pictures the wind picked up, brushing at us with a rising rush of sound.

Alex.

The word seemed to emerge from the wind's low moan like an intimate whisper. I felt a deeper chill than the cold air, then lowered the camera and glared at Loren.

"Okay, cut that shit out. I'm freaked enough already."

He looked puzzled. "What shit?"

I sighed. "Nothing. I thought I..." I paused, then gestured toward the main building where a door yawned, half open. "Come on, let's get out of the rain."

Loren looked at the plant dubiously. "Shit. The cops kicked like fifteen people out of this place last year. Who the hell would want to live in a place like this?"

"Someone with no other options."

I leaned on the door, pushing it fully open against piled debris and stepped through. Inside was a dimly-lit tangle of metal and broken concrete. It stank like a porta-potty left unattended for a couple of weeks. Beowulf whined uneasily.

I wrinkled my nose. "It sure as hell smells like someone was living here. When you've got no place else to go, this kind of thing probably looks pretty good."

Loren pulled an LED flashlight from his pocket. The beam was almost swallowed up by the gloom.

The place resembled a war zone, full of trash and twisted rusty metal. Two corridors led off, one toward the kiln, the other toward a larger, open room with dim light shining down from above.

"Where do we go from here?" I asked.

"Search me. Follow the smell?" Loren pointed the flashlight toward the big room. "How about that way?"

"Looks as good as anything else." I slung my camera around my neck. "If you've got a spare light, I'll even take point."

He handed it over and pulled a second from his other pocket. "Lead the way, Rambo."

I slipped the light's lanyard over my wrist. I didn't feel much like Rambo as I approached the doorway. Beyond it I only saw more trash.

"I'm not sure anyone's been here for years."

"I respectfully disagree." Loren shone his light at an empty cigarette packet under my right foot. The floor near the doorway was littered with flattened butts and discarded bottles.

"Could be kids," I said.

"Yeah, maybe. When I was sixteen I used to drink beer behind an abandoned house. It made me sick as a dog, but at least I was drinking beer."

"That kind of logic only works when you're sixteen." I prodded a bottle with my foot. The label said *Mogen-David 20/20*.

I laughed. "Mad Dog? Yeah, it's probably kids. They have no taste in liquor."

"Or Pine Street Bob and his transient friends." Loren looked down with distaste. Steam curled from his nostrils. "There's needles over here, Alex. Careful where you step."

The room was big—it looked as if it had once been warehouse space. Faint sunlight shone through dirty skylights. The floor was littered with debris and burst cement bags, their contents long since coagulated and solidified. At the far end, dim in the distance, a rickety rusted staircase led up.

Chunks of concrete sprouting rebar lay everywhere like dead plants. We picked our way around them. Beowulf moved slowly, as if he was stalking prey. He seemed even less at ease now that we were inside. Occasionally, he shot Loren a worried glance.

I grimaced. The smell was getting intense. It stank of garbage, stale urine, old cigarettes, and worse. It seemed almost solid, like an invisible fog reaching down my throat and choking me.

Loren held his hand over his face. "What the hell smells so bad? Something's weird here."

He was right. There was trash everywhere, but nothing that could account for the overwhelming strength of the stench. Beowulf seemed unaffected, but I reminded myself that he was a dog and bad smells were among their favorite things.

Above us, rain drummed against the skylights. For a moment I thought I heard a babble of voices amid the noise—voices softly whispering in a dozen languages at once. I closed my eyes and drew a long breath. The sound became rain again.

I flashed the light across a wall where several piles of blankets and dirty pillows were set up like camp beds. Above them the concrete wall had been tagged. Paint, charcoal, dirt, and probably even more unpleasant things were smeared across the cold stone.

After studying the wall for a few moments I saw that the scrawls made some kind of sense. There were frightening images—winged monsters, giant insects, fanged mouths and glaring bulbous eyes, something like a child would draw when remembering a nightmare. There was writing, but at first I couldn't read the letters.

ουγατοχη

"Is that Cyrillic? Greek, maybe?"

Loren stepped toward the wall. "Shine the light here." He stood for a moment, lips moving silently. "Yeah, it looks like Greek. What's it say? *Ovyatoxin?* Maybe it means they're selling Oxycontin or something."

I ignored him. I'd slept through Classical Studies 101, so I struggled to remember my Greek alphabet. As I frowned at the letters, I heard a rustle and the sound of something falling outside. Beowulf barked, I jumped and flashed the light but saw only the gray silhouette of the doorway.

Loren released a shuddering breath. "Damn, Alex. I'm getting kinda spooked right now."

"Yeah, me too." I looked back as the wall, straining to pick out the crudely-daubed characters. "Stay cool. Beowulf is here."

Beowulf looked up at mention of his name, then looked stoic and sat down beside Loren.

I frowned, studying the daubed letters, repeating them out loud. "Omicron... upsilon... nu... alpha... tau... omicron... chi... eta... ?" I began to sound it out. "Oh... No, no... Oo... It's a dipthong... n... ah... t... oh... kee? *Oonatokee?*"

Loren frowned. "*Oonatokee?* That sounds like just random shit someone smeared up there."

"I think it sounds vaguely Indian. What are they doing spelling it in Greek? While I'm at it, what the hell are homeless people doing writing in Greek at all?"

The cold suddenly grew deeper, as if it had formed claws and grabbed my insides.

"What the hell's that one say?" Loren gestured at another word, this one in entirely different letters.

"Those don't even look real, Alex. Now tell me that isn't just random crap some lunatic scrawled on a wall."

I uncapped my camera and aimed it at the wall. My neglected classical studies and anthro classes still nagged at me. "They look familiar. Maybe I can look it up once we get out of here."

As I took pictures, individual flashes illuminating the room like lighting, I saw that there was graffiti all over the walls, some of it ordinary, some of it in the ancient letters. I saw Hebrew, Russian, Arabic, and others I couldn't identify.

"Alex," Loren's voice echoed, "You'd better look at this."

I lowered the camera. He was crouching beside one of the piles of grimy blankets and old bedrolls. On the floor, I saw a collection of dirty plastic cards, crumpled bills, jewelry, keys, and other knick-knacks.

I squatted down and Beowulf sat beside me. He looked very serious. "What is all this?"

"Stolen stuff I bet." Loren picked up one of the cards, holding it by its edges. It was a Visa, its gold surface covered in grime. "The cops searched the place last year, so this must all have been left here since then. Trophies, maybe?" He put the card back and continued to rifle carefully through the pile. "Crap. Look at this."

It was a Washington driver's license, as dirty as all the other cards, but a pair of gentle female eyes gazed from the picture, and below it the name read, *Francine Harris*.

Icy hands ran down my spine. I recognized the name. I'd been typing it at my workstation for months.

"Oh, Jesus." I stood up quickly, stepping backwards as if the card was radioactive.

Loren looked at me in alarm and Beowulf whined nervously. "What's wrong?"

"She's one of the I-84 victims," I said, my voice sounding faint and distant even inside my head. "The most recent one. Murdered. Just a couple of months ago."

Beowulf stood up quickly, legs splayed, as if he knew something was up.

I was suddenly alert, my eyes darting to the dark corners of the room, searching for motion. There was a hollow sickness in my stomach. "Call the cops, Loren."

"Yeah." Loren pulled out his phone and looked at the screen. "No signal. We'd better get out of here."

I checked my phone. It was similarly useless. I turned toward the gray doorway. "Come on. We can try outside."

"Alex, wait!"

Loren had stopped and was shining his flashlight around the room.

"Did you hear that?"

"Hear what?" I felt a rush of annoyance. "God damn it, Loren, we've got to get— "

"No, wait!" He shone his light toward the rusty staircase. "Listen!"

Though my instincts urged me to leave, call the police, and take my medicine for trespassing, I forced myself to stop and listen.

Beside me, Beowulf's ears pricked up. I strained to hear.

Alex.

I shook my head. The voice wasn't there. I was just freaked out, nervous, scared. There was no one whispering to me.

Then, from the direction of the stairs, barely audible over the steady tattoo of rain, I heard a voice—faint and tortured, but clearly human. There were no words, only a muffled moan.

Loren and I exchanged a fearful, wordless glance.

There was someone up there.

V

The stairs creaked and groaned as we ascended. I gripped the rail for support with one hand and held Loren's flashlight in the other. The can of mace was a reassuring weight at my belt. Beowulf followed, crouching low, his eyes fixed on the yawning opening at the top of the stairs. Occasionally I heard a low, husky growl.

The voice hadn't come again, but by now, with the stairs protesting at each step, we'd made enough of a racket that stealth was out of the question.

The smell was getting worse, wafting from the opening above like the foul breath of a giant. Common sense demanded that we behave rationally—run outside until our phones had reception and call the police. But my head was filled with thoughts of what had happened to the I-84 Killer's victims. If there really was someone in danger up there, I wasn't going to go scampering off in terror and leave them to die.

Despite the alarming noises, we reached the top of the steps without triggering a collapse. The space beyond the small landing looked like a walkway between two buildings, with

58

grimed-over windows on either side. The stench felt like a solid wall here, a barrier that we had to push through.

With effort, I stepped into the room, shining the light. Loren and Beowulf followed.

"Hello? Anyone..."

The words died in my throat as the circle of blue-white light illuminated what was inside.

It was an abattoir. The graffiti was thicker here. The corrugated metal walls were smeared in paint, dirt, blood, and filth, explaining some of the smell but not all. The floor was awash in junk—rusted metal, splintered pieces of furniture, broken concrete, stained and burnt paper. Amid the tangle, I saw chunks of rotting food, alongside the bloated corpses of small animals—

rats, possums, birds, even a cat. On the wall, a few paces inside the entrance, was a pile of junk—a rusty bicycle, an old car door, a bald tire. A pyramid of dirty wooden slats and other undefinable garbage formed what looked almost like a shrine. On the wall above it was a crude graffiti image that looked like a mass of multicolored clouds full of angry eyes and jagged-toothed mouths.

Loren made a disgusted sound. "This is really fucked up, Alex."

Almost without thinking, I raised the camera to my eye and took more pictures, lighting up the room with instants of blue-white brilliance.

Then the voice was back—a strangled moan from the far end of the room where a second staircase led down.

"Alex! It's over there..." Loren started to move and Beowulf uttered a single bark.

I was already scrambling through the rubble, racing toward the place—I shone the flashlight and at first I didn't see anything save another pile of stained cloth, blankets, and soiled paper. Then I saw it move.

At first she looked like just another piece of garbage, tossed carelessly against the stair railing. Then I picked out the body of a woman—naked, crusted in filth, her dark brown skin crisscrossed with knife wounds, her hair torn out in chunks. She was bound to the railing with rusty wire, torn pieces of cloth, plastic packing straps, and dirty duct tape.

But she was still alive. Her head lolled back weakly when I shined my light on her. Her cheeks were slashed, making her mouth look almost comically huge; her face was stained with blood and rusty dirt. Her eyes were untouched, and I had a good idea why.

So she could see everything they did to her, I thought, nausea and fear swimming in my stomach, gagging me.

Her eyes opened. I shifted the light so it wouldn't blind her, and when she caught sight of me hope flickered on her ravaged face. Hope, and something else...

Recognition?

"You," she whispered in a weak, cracked voice through ruined lips. "It's you..."

"Oh, God!" Was it Loren's voice or mine? I couldn't tell. "Oh my God! Oh, Jesus..."

I moved without thought, leaping through the maze of junk toward her, Loren and Beowulf a step behind. I'd almost reached her when my foot struck something solid and meaty. My ankle went sideways and I felt a bone-deep crack as I fell, pain lancing up my leg.

I landed on my shoulder, smashing painfully into a chunk of concrete. I lost my grip on the flashlight and it swung off the lanyard, clattering to the floor beside me, its beam shining backwards, illuminating the object that had tripped me.

I choked back an acidic wave of bile. It was a headless, limbless human corpse. It must have been days old—its greenish flesh was bloated and carved with weird symbols. It looked as if it had once been male, but when I looked down toward the junction of its thighs...

"Oh, God." Bile rose again and I forced it down, looking away in disgust. I lay atop a severed arm, also covered with the same carved symbols, and rent by semicircular bite marks, as if someone had chewed on it like a huge turkey drumstick.

I struggled to my knees, trying not to look at the mutilated mass of flesh beside me. My ankle throbbed. Was it broken? Jesus, I didn't know.

Loren hadn't seen any of it—he was crouching beside the woman now, muttering frantically, trying to untie her bonds. Beowulf stood beside him, his face was set in a feral glare, growling softly.

"You're gonna be okay," Loren whispered. He pulled a multitool from his belt and began slicing at the tape and cloth that held her. "You're gonna be okay. We'll get you out of here, and we'll call the cops. You're gonna be okay."

I got up on one knee, then tried to rise to my feet. Pain stabbed through my injured ankle, and I gasped, falling back to my knees.

"Loren..."

"Jesus, Alex. Oh, Jesus." He didn't hear me. He was trying to cut the heavy rusted wire that held the woman's wrists to the railing, but his tool didn't have wire cutters. He tried to use the pliers to untwist the metal. The woman convulsed in pain when he turned it the wrong way.

"Oh Shit. I'm sorry. Are you okay? I mean..."

A feeble whisper escaped from her ruined lips.

"Help me. Please. Please... *Nomeus.*"

The word sounded strangely familiar, and I was struggling to identify it when Beowulf's growl rose to a ragged, angry snarl. Behind me I heard the groan of metal and a shuffling footfall.

"Loren..."

He didn't look up but continued untwisting rusty wire. "God damn, Alex... Help me, man. Help me..."

"Loren, there's someone on the stairs."

Loren stopped, falling silent and staring toward the doorway with frightened eyes. A soft footfall echoed from the shadows as a figure appeared, silhouetted in the rectangle of dim light.

My hand went to my belt, but my canister of mace wasn't there. It must have come loose when I fell. Fighting down panic, I scanned the floor, shining the light this way and that, searching.

Beowulf stiffened, spreading his feet, his head low, his growl dropping to a bass rumble. Loren fumbled with the multitool, clumsily trying to pull out the knife blade.

I found myself hoping that it was a cop and that all he'd do was arrest us for trespassing. The figure that emerged was about as far from a policeman as you could get.

"Hi, Alex."

Pine Street Bob was even dirtier and more starved-looking than I remembered him. His face was almost black, and his clothes looked as if they hadn't been washed in a decade.

He moved slowly and deliberately toward us. In his hand he held a jagged, rusty piece of sharpened metal, one end wrapped in grimy surgical tape to form a crude grip.

Loren stood in front of the woman, the multitool in one hand, knife blade out.

"Hey, asshole! Back off!" His voice was laced with fear masked as courage. "Get out of here or I'll mess you up!"

Bob continued to shuffle forward, chuckling softly.

"Itchiloot..." He sounded like a man with a mouth full of sand. *"Onatochee."*

"No..." The woman's voice was a terrified whisper. "No, please. No more."

I couldn't look away. Bob moved toward us, step by step. My hands moved mechanically, without thought, searching for the canister by touch.

"I'm warning you!" Loren's voice trembled. Behind him the woman moaned in terror. "Get the fuck out or you're a dead man!"

Bob's eyes were mad and almost joyful. He grinned, revealing a mouth full of jagged yellow teeth and black stumps.

"Gatchink... wo'igunaba..." The words seemed to rumble up from his chest as if something was speaking from deep inside him. *"Iltsim'unachee."*

"Oh, shit..." Loren's voice finally broke. "Alex, what..."

Bob suddenly flung his arm forward, winging a chunk of concrete at Loren. It struck his head and he fell with a cry. Instantly, Bob transformed from a shuffling transient to a sprinting predator, knife poised. Loren lay helpless on the floor.

Uttering a savage snarl, Beowulf exploded into motion, launching himself at Bob. They met in a maelstrom of black fur, teeth, and filthy flesh. Beowulf bit unerringly on Bob's right arm, teeth crunching down. Bob howled in pain and the crude knife fell from his grasp. Then Beowulf lashed out with his front paws, overbearing the already off-balance transient, and they both tumbled to the floor.

Bob recovered quickly, his fingers encircling Beowulf's throat, while Beowulf continued to strain and snap and snarl. It was a deadly stalemate, and as I pulled onto one knee, still searching fruitlessly for the mace canister, I realized that I wouldn't be able to help.

I tried to stand, ignoring the screaming pain in my ankle. It felt thick and frozen, and refused to move. Loren still lay, not moving. "Loren, wake up!"

The woman cried out again as a wet, muffled chuckle sounded from behind me.

I turned, fear stabbing me in the pit of my stomach. A second man emerged from the stairs near the bound woman. I didn't recognize him—he was almost the complete opposite of Pine Street Bob, clad in baggy khaki shorts, expensive athletic shoes, and a t-shirt with a beer logo. His face was clean and his hair was kempt and well-trimmed, but his eyes were as wild and demented as Bob's. Slowly he stepped toward me.

"*T'igunaba'unatchee*. We are his claws. *T'igunaba'ichiatku*. Onatochee's claws." His voice was hollow and scratchy, and he held a brown-stained butcher knife.

The woman gave vent to a full-throated scream. The man threw himself forward and slammed into me like a linebacker. A bottle shattered painfully between my shoulders as I fell, glass stabbing my flesh. The knife was coming down—old and dirty, but sharp enough to easily tear through my eye or mouth or neck.

My mind was a mosaic of horrified fears as I thought of the headless, limbless corpse that lay a few feet away.

No. He wouldn't do that to me.

With a surge of strength, I rolled on top of him, pinning his wrist to the floor. He was strong—stronger than I thought possible, and as he pushed back the knife began to rise.

"*Onatochee,*" he whispered, his breath foul and rotten in my nostrils. "Feel his claws. Feel his teeth."

I reached out with my left hand, searching for a piece of rock, metal, glass—anything to defend myself with, and touched the smooth cool surface of the bear mace canister. I fumbled for a moment, then brought it up, pulling the trigger, sending a stream of liquid directly into the man's wild red eyes.

The stinging sensation hit me too—I could tolerate it—but my attacker received a full dose. He screamed, squirmed out of my grasp, and stumbled away from me. His knife fell as he raced blindly toward the staircase, clawing at his face.

Anger of a sort that I hadn't felt in years pumped through me—anger at what they'd done to the woman, what he'd done to me and what he'd done to others. And there was anger at others too—long-suppressed rage emerged in a red, roaring torrent. Rage at one who had betrayed me, at one who had stolen something precious... Rage that I thought I had forgotten...

Inside my head, the voice spoke again—the voice I'd been listening to ever since coming here, the one that had whispered my name. Now it spoke again with words that weren't really words, just impulses, memories, flashes of wrath that I had tried to forget long ago.

Vengeance. Vengeance for what he did to her. *Memory.* Memory of what I'd done to him. What it had felt like. The mad, bitter joy of it...

I got back on my feet, savagely forcing myself to ignore the pain in my ankle even as it threatened to collapse under me. I ran unsteadily but unerringly toward the man as he stood at the top of the stairs, shrieking and trying to rub the mace from his eyes.

I struck him as hard as he'd struck me. He tumbled over the railing and onto the stairs, a tangle of limbs crashing down on the metal steps. His shrieks cut off suddenly as he vanished in a boneless heap into the shadows below.

Adrenaline still pumped through me. My ankle screamed and protested, but I turned, limping toward Loren, the mace in hand. My leg lagged as if it were a second or two behind, pain biting me with each step.

Beowulf stood atop Pine Street Bob, worrying his throat while Bob feebly flailed at his flanks with blood-covered hands.

Loren was on his knees, blood-stained but alive. "Enough, boy." His voice was cracked and raw. "C'mere!"

Beowulf looked back at Loren, his expression almost proud and happy, then bounded toward his master.

Pine Street Bob's face was a mask of blood and dirt. He began to crawl away, but I limped over and shot him with a long dose of mace, eliciting a satisfying shriek.

Vengeance, you bastard. Vengeance for her…

For her…?

As quickly as it had come, the burning rage drained away, and I felt a wave of nausea.

"I don't think he's going anywhere," I said, and finally sat down heavily, the mace pointed at Bob as he writhed. "The other one's at the bottom of the stairs. I think he's dead."

…And I'd killed him. The sickness in my gut redoubled, and I felt a growing compulsion to throw up.

I'd felt it before. I remembered, even though I didn't want to.

Loren looked down at Bob, then toward the bound victim. "You sure you don't want to finish this fuck off?"

The voice was still inside me, screaming for me to avenge all those victims, surrender to the bloodlust that I'd kept hidden. But it was faint now, overwhelmed by shame and sickness. All I wanted was escape back to the comfort of a safe, rational world.

"No. Go help her. We'll call the cops."

Loren nodded. "Okay."

Beowulf stayed with me, glaring at Pine Street Bob. He lay still now, breathing heavily and moaning.

"It's all over, you bastard," I said softly. "Time to pay the piper."

Bob continued to moan, and among the random sounds I heard the strange words.

"Gatchink... Itchiloot... Onatochee."

He rolled onto his side and I started back, aiming the canister at him.

His face was a welter of cuts and scratches, and one eye was swollen shut, but he grinned at me.

"Onatochee," he whispered, blood and saliva drooling from cracked lips. *"Onatochee."*

* * *

"You said the second suspect attacked you?" Detective Maitland asked. He was a chisel-featured black man with a touch of gray at his temples and a reassuring professional manner.

I nodded, wincing as a paramedic wrapped my ankle with an ace bandage. "Yeah. He came at me with a knife. I hit him with my bear mace and pushed him down the stairs. Is he alive?"

Maitland shook his head. "Broke his neck on the way down. We're investigating, but it looks like self-defense to me. I can get you in touch with a counselor if you need to talk to someone about this."

I suppressed a shudder. The nausea had faded, but I still felt sick and weak. He'd gone over the railing and down the stairs like a load of wet laundry. I'd never seen him before, and he'd been dressed normally, but he was Pine Street Bob's accomplice. I thought about Uncle Creepy. How many others were there, and what would they do now that their fellow killer was in prison? My numbed brain was in no condition to speculate.

The weed-covered parking lot was crowded with deputies, detectives, and paramedics. Lights from a dozen vehicles flashed like blue and red Christmas trees. Groaning and babbling to himself, Pine Street Bob had been cuffed and hustled away as soon as the police arrived. Upstairs the rest of the medical team was seeing to the victim.

The paramedic finished binding up my injured ankle. It felt as big as a grapefruit.

"It's a bad sprain," she said. "Another inch or so and you'd have broken it. You're lucky."

Beowulf rested nearby, staring with concern at his master. Loren sat in the open door of an ambulance nearby, getting his cuts and bruises patched up. He was pale and shaken-looking, and there was a big bandage on his forehead, but when I looked toward him he returned a weak grin.

"Great way to spend a Sunday, huh?"

I managed a feeble nod.

There was commotion at the entrance to the cement plant and a crowd of medical personnel emerged, guiding a gurney where the woman lay, swathed in bandages, a drip bottle in her arm. Ignoring angry protests from my ankle, I stood and limped alongside the gurney as it rolled toward a waiting ambulance.

"Is she going to be okay?" I asked, but the paramedics ignored me. I struggled to follow.

When she heard my voice, the woman's eyes flickered open.

"Alex?" she whispered despite a paramedic's attempts to keep her quiet.

I felt my eyes go wide. "How do you know my name?"

"I saw you." Feeble words emerged from her cracked lips. "You and the other man. And the dog. You were wearing a long black coat, you had a sword in your hand. She told me you'd come."

"Who?" My voice rose. "Who said I'd come?"

"Tsagagalal." The strange word emerged without apparent effort, alien syllables that nevertheless rang in my ears with warm familiarity. "She said... Tell him... Tell *Nomeus*... Tell the Shepherd..."

The paramedics lifted the gurney and stowed the wheels. It slid into the ambulance bay and, as the paramedics slammed the doors, the woman's voice issued forth one last time.

"Tell him that Onatochee is coming."

PART TWO

WORSHIP ME

D amien's house was even more cluttered than it had been during my last visit, but the man himself was clean and neatly dressed with not a hair out of place. He was manic again, and I wasn't sure whether that was a good thing or not.

"Tsagagalal," he said, scribbling on a steno pad. "How is that spelled?"

"Damned if I know, Damien. I'd never even heard it before." I moved a stack of papers so that I could set my coffee mug down amid the chaos.

He continued scribbling. "Onatochee? That's what she said?"

"Yeah. And so did Pine Street Bob and Maurice McMahon."

"McMahon?"

"The guy I pushed down the stairs." I couldn't bring myself to admit that I'd actually killed someone. I pounded the arm of the wingback. "He was a carpenter. A goddamned carpenter. No one suspected him of anything, not 'til the cops found a huge stash of kiddie porn on his computer. Real sick stuff too."

"I don't want to know about it. I'm more interested in this Onatochee angle." Damien nodded toward printouts of the photos I'd taken. "It's scrawled all over the walls of that cement plant too, isn't it?"

"Uh-huh. Or something very close to it. In Greek. Greek, Damien. A language none of those assholes had any business knowing."

"Oh, it's way better than that." Damien put down his pad, then drained his mug. "There's graffiti in that building from a dozen different ancient languages—Demotic script, Hebrew, Arabic, Pelasgian, and some I don't even recognize. And they all say the same thing, with minor spelling variations. Onatochee." He paused, shuffling through the pile until he found the printout he was looking for. "With one exception."

He held up the image. I remembered it. The graffiti that had looked like random scrawls that we hadn't been able to read.

"This is Linear B, Alex. Mycenaean Greek. It's the only instance I can find of a different word."

"What's it say?"

"It says *Nomeus*. In Mycenaean dialect it means Shepherd."

It took a long moment for Damien's words to make sense. Then realization of what he had said crashed down on me.

"My God, Damien. She said that too. She looked straight at me and said it just as they were closing the ambulance doors. *Nomeus*. 'Tell *Nomeus*.'"

"Tell the Shepherd. Alex, she was speaking in an ancient Greek dialect, and called you the Shepherd."

"Me? What the hell, Damien? Pine Street Bob, McMahon—they keep babbling about something called Onatochee and they're looking for the Shepherd? They scrawl words on walls in alphabets that no one's used in thousands of years? A woman talks to me in ancient Greek? What the hell is going on? And what about Bob's friend Uncle Creepy? I know he's mixed up in this too, for fuck's sake."

"Well, it's certainly a mystery, isn't it? Your friends in the media have dubbed it the 'I-84 Murder Cult' and it's already hit the national news channels."

"Yeah, I know. If it bleeds, it leads. Loren and I are staying out of the spotlight. I told that detective about Uncle Creepy, and they're looking for him. They said it's probably best that I keep a low profile."

"Hmm." Damien looked amused. "You'd think the local stations would eat it up—two intrepid reporters and their faithful dog crack a baffling serial murder case and heroically rescue its next victim from the killers' clutches. It's tailor-made for a summer blockbuster." He paused. "Sorry, Alex. I don't mean to be flippant. Where's Loren? Is he dealing with this all okay?"

"Not bad. His head needed some stitches, and he had some cuts and bruises, but he'll be okay. He took Beowulf and is visiting his folks in Kennewick for a few days." I sighed. "I wish I was with him."

"How about the woman? How's she doing? What's her name? Mia something?"

"Mia Jordan. She's still in ICU, but they say she'll live. She's got to be messed up, though. Tied up, tortured, raped for days. Her boyfriend murdered and butchered in front of her while she was forced to watch. That's not something she's ever going to get over. And they cut her up too, just like the others. Carved shit all over her body. She's going to have scars for the rest of her life."

"Damnation." Despite Damien's protective cloak of mania, it was obvious that my words disturbed him. "Who could do such a thing?"

"Crazy ass sons of bitches, that's who."

"Yeah. Crazy..." Damien's voice trailed off and his eyes wandered across the coffee table, cluttered with books and papers. "Just two more crazy men doing horrible things, like they've been doing for the past century or so."

I didn't say anything. My mind was still searching for a rational explanation of what I'd seen. But reverberations of a hundred other crimes still echoed like the ravings of a lunatic across a canyon of decades.

"I wonder," Damien said quietly, "if any of the other Shepherd killers ever talked about Onatochee."

* * *

An hour later Damien looked up from his monitor. "Got it."

I looked over his shoulder at the image on the screen— the scanned image of an old book, *A Preliminary Report on the Languages and Mythology of the Upper Chinook Cultures,* published in 1910.

Damien read out loud. *According to the legends of the Multnomah band, Onatochee was a* chiatku*—a demon or evil spirit—whose very presence corrupted men's souls, compelling them to commit rape, murder and other atrocities. Tribal storytellers claimed that he was worshipped by a band of outsiders called the Chilut, who came to Multnomah territory from far away, possibly the Oregon or Washington coastal region. According to legend, the Chilut were weak-willed, evil men easily swayed by Onatochee's promises of power and vengeance.*

The Chilut band included a warrior cult called 'T'igunaba'unatchee' (Onatochee's Claws) or 'T'igunaba'ichiatku' (Claws of the Demon), fanatics who engaged in self-mutilation in an effort to look more like their demonic god. Onatochee's Claws were said to engage in particularly egregious acts, such as cannibalism, sadistic torture, and rape. Women were treated particularly cruelly, subjected to gang rape and mutilation. Those women who were impregnated during the cult's savage attacks gave birth to Onatochee's offspring— half-human, half-monster.

"Oh, hell," I muttered. "That's what McMahon said when he attacked me. *T'igunaba'unachee*. Claws of Onatochee. Claws of the Demon."

"Damnation." Damien studied the screen for a moment, then continued.

The Multnomahs, members of a relatively peaceful band who made their living by fishing and gathering foodstuffs, at last allied with several other tribes under the leadership of a famous monster-hunter called Klale-Mamuk to destroy the Chilut, but always feared the influence of Onatochee. If a man of the area committed an especially despicable or violent act, he was said to be one of Onatochee's followers and dubbed with the derogatory title 'i'Chilut' or 'Man of the Chilut.'"

"*Ichiloot*," I said softly. "They said that too." I looked away from the screen, rubbing my eyes as if to wipe away the words' reality. "Oh God, Damien. Oh my fucking God."

Damien didn't seem terribly swayed by my outburst, but was instead busily copying the information to permanent storage.

"Fascinating. Amazing. You realize that we now have solid evidence of a demon-worshipping cult that goes back continuously for literally centuries? What do you think happened, Alex? Were the Chilut part of a larger Onatochee-worshipping cult, or did the cult spread from remnants that escaped when the Multnomahs destroyed the Chilut?"

"Damien, I..."

"At this point I'm willing to wager that it was the former, given the multiple languages of that graffiti you saw. But when did the Onatochee Cult originate? And what's the connection to the Shepherd? Could it be related to this Klale-Mamuk character?" He began typing frantically. "I think that Carl Lind from Idaho State wrote the definitive book on Chinook myth. I can send for it through interlibrary loan, but I don't..."

"Jesus Christ, Damien, will you please just shut up for a minute?"

He stopped abruptly, looking like a five year old caught shoplifting candy.

"Damien, I don't care how old this damned murder cult is, or where it came from. All I know is that the cops haven't found Uncle Creepy, they have no idea who he is, and I have no idea how many other friends Pine Street Bob had out there."

Fear crept into Damien's expression. For him, this had been nothing more than an intellectual exercise, a sick proof for his strange theories. Now, at last, as the enormity of what was really happening began to sink in, Damien's enthusiasm drained away like dirty bathwater.

His eyes widened. "Alex, I just thought of another possibility."

"What?"

"That maybe this cult is still around because Onatochee is real."

I didn't answer. I wanted to roll my eyes and make a snarky comment, but I couldn't. I still remembered what Mia Jordan had said to me as they took her away.

Tell the Shepherd... Tell Nomeus... *Tell him that Onatochee is coming.*

* * *

Under the circumstances I didn't especially want to go home, and when Damien offered me dinner I took him up on it. He didn't get many chances to use his dining room, and it turned out that he made pretty decent spaghetti.

"I have groceries delivered most of the time," he said, handing me the pot of marinara sauce. "I don't buy that sauce in jars, though—it's usually full of sugar and preservatives. I prefer to make my own. I also use low-carb pasta. Tastes just as good, I think."

I spooned the sauce on my pasta and tasted it.

"Damn. You ever consider changing professions? You'd make a decent chef."

Damien rolled his eyes. "Yeah, right. I make spaghetti, salads, and scrambled eggs. That'll take you far in the restaurant industry."

He poured me some red wine and we ate in silence for a while. I tried not to think about Pine Street Bob, Uncle Creepy or the Chilut Indians and their demon-god.

"I need to ask you something, Alex." Damien held his wine glass in front of him, staring at the dark red liquid inside. "I know it's personal, and you don't have to tell me anything if you don't want to."

I set down my fork. "Go on." I had an inkling what was coming.

"I took the liberty of doing a little research about you. I didn't pry. Not too much, anyway. I know you were a journalism student at U of O, and that you made the dean's list four times. You wrote a series of articles on campus drug abuse for the *Daily Emerald*, and you got nominated for a couple of awards. You were active, too—wrestling, swimming, varsity fencing team. You even played bass guitar in a band. You had quite a career ahead of you."

I listened in stony silence as point by point Damien brought up things that I wanted to forget.

"You were working on a thesis on the future of digital media. You were a semester short of your master's. Then you quit. You turned your back on a promising career and went to work for Terri, editing a no-name street paper that no one cares about, doing a job that any trained ape could do."

"I don't want to talk about it, Damien." I stared down at the table, feeling anger begin to bubble. Damien's lack of tact was only a minor symptom of his mania, but it was easily the most annoying.

"Alex, I'm sorry for prying, but it's important to me."

Steam was building up. After the past couple of days it wouldn't take much to push me over the edge. "Damien, please. I told you—"

True to form, Damien couldn't let it rest. "Alex, why did you—"

I slammed my hand down, making the tableware jump. My wine sloshed alarmingly but the glass didn't fall.

"Because it doesn't make any difference!" The pressure inside me finally overflowed and burst out, but I didn't care. It was all boiling through me—the fear, the anger, the frustration, the unexpected horror of revived memories. Damien had opened the closet door, and now what had been hidden inside was free.

I glared at him, seeing confusion and possibly a dawning recognition of the lost reservoir of emotion he had tapped. "The whole fucking world keeps circling the goddamned drain and you know what? No one cares. No one even reads anymore! You waste your time talking, and no one *listens!*"

"Alex—"

It was too late. Damien had finally dragged my memories into the light, and I was angry with him for it. "No one listens! Humanity is bankrupt. You try to help, try to tell them... You can't. No one cares. They don't listen."

She didn't listen.

"Alex, I'm sorry." There was a trace of the depressive Damien there, the one who had been so apologetic and ashamed.

"I spent five years of my life pursuing a career and then discovered that I didn't believe in it anymore. You talk and write and edit and work and when you're done, nothing is different." Tears stung my eyes. "Nothing. It's a waste of time trying to save humanity, when the fact is that humanity doesn't want to be saved. That's why I'm wasting my time doing a job that any trained ape can do. That's why I don't care anymore."

There it was, after three years of hiding. No one had ever asked me about it—not Terri, not Loren, not anyone. But here at last was someone who truly wanted to know who I was and why. Slowly I felt my anger drain away, replaced by weariness and the irrational desire to finally unburden myself.

"Damien, I've never talked to anyone about this. Maybe it explains something about me. I don't know." I swallowed and blinked away tears. "You read my articles in *The Daily Emerald*. You know what I wrote about. Drug abuse on campus, cocaine and heroin, pills and booze. Even meth. Colleges don't like it when you talk about that. I got in trouble for it. I had to go talk to the dean. But the editor and my journalism professor intervened on my behalf and they let me write what I wanted to write."

"Why did you want to write about drug abuse so badly?"

"My girlfriend. Cheryl. Cheryl White. We met freshman year. We were friends for a long time. Finally she told me she was in love with me. I'd been in love with her of course, but I hadn't done anything about it. I wanted..."

I swallowed the rest of my wine in a single gulp. "She was a junkie, Damien. She kept it secret. They're good at that. Once we were together though, well, it was impossible. I caught her stealing money. I confronted her. She confessed to it all. Showed me her stash, her baggies, her needles, her spoon. She even had a rig hidden at my place in the bathroom. I hadn't found it. Shit."

Damien nodded. "I knew a lot of junkies back in the day, Alex. My drug of choice was coke, but I know how much smack can mess you up."

"She swore she'd get clean, and I believed her. We went to rehab together. I drove her to her appointments. She was getting better. I loved her, but I was so pissed off at the situation... I wrote those articles to show her how widespread it was, how dangerous, how many people were involved. She told me how much it had meant to her, how she'd learned her lesson, how much she loved me..."

"She didn't quit, did she?" Damien knew more than I'd realized.

I shook my head. "She was hooking up with her dealer all along. Some fuck named Alan Coleman. She was even giving him..." I stopped again and wiped away tears. "Giving him *favors* in exchange for smack. God damn him. You can guess the rest. She OD'd. I heard she was in the hospital, but by the time I got there she was gone. That bastard as good as murdered her. I went to the cops, told them everything. They'd been after the guy for a long time. They found Cheryl's stash, got information that Alan had sold it to her. Charged him with manslaughter."

"What happened to him?"

I snorted. "He copped a plea. He'd done it before. Ratted out his suppliers and a bunch of his customers. Got a suspended sentence."

"He got away with it?"

"I guess that depends on what you mean by *got away with it*. He split town, but he'd gotten himself a reputation as a rat. He was hiding out here in Portland, dealing to make money. I..." I stopped again, almost afraid to continue, to admit to what I'd done. "I did some research. I found out where he was. Then I..."

I faltered. How much of the truth could I admit to Damien? And how much could I admit to myself?

"I located one of the suppliers Coleman had burned," I said at last. "It wasn't too hard."

"You told them where he was?"

"Yeah. They found him. Made him sorry he'd ever been born."

A look of horror crossed Damien's face. "They killed him?"

"Oh, no. He lived, if you want to call it that. He's a paraplegic now, living with his mother. They... They fractured his skull so he couldn't even say who did it. Hell, maybe he did know and was too scared to say. Anyway, the police never arrested anybody, and they never suspected I was involved." I looked down at my plate, half full of spaghetti and sauce. I wasn't hungry anymore. "But I did it. Me. He killed her and I... Well, I sure fixed everything, didn't I? I sure made myself feel better. I sure got even for everything that happened, didn't I?" I let my head sag. "To hell with revenge. It's a lie. It's not worth it."

"Winston Churchill said nothing is more costly or more sterile than vengeance." Damien's voice was soft, lacking the tone of pontification that he normally affected.

"He was right. That's why I quit school. That's why I didn't want to be a journalist anymore, why I figured people didn't care. Because of one woman who told she loved me. Everything I did, everything I tried, everything I wrote, every drop of blood I shed. It was all for nothing. It made me..."

I faltered again. "It made me hate. It made me hate Alan, it made me hate myself. It made me believe humanity is worthless. She's gone and nothing can bring her back. I don't care that that son of a bitch can't walk anymore. It didn't change a damned thing, no more than my articles or the praise of all my professors."

There it was, the story I'd never told anyone. I was telling it to a man I'd only met a few weeks ago, and I had no idea why.

Damien looked stricken, the careless arrogance of his mania gone. "I'm sorry, Alex. I didn't mean to... I mean I don't know what to..."

I felt suddenly weak and vulnerable. "Don't apologize. It's my fault for hiding it all this time. And it wasn't you, anyway, it was..."

I paused. My scalp was crawling again.

Damien frowned. "What, Alex?"

"At the plant." I looked away, my gaze wandering to the ceiling as I remembered. "When I was fighting McMahon. I stood up on a sprained ankle, and I knocked the bastard down the stairs."

Damien looked confused. "What does that have to do with...?"

"I felt it, Damien. I felt the same anger I'd felt years ago. It was as if someone was talking to me, whispering in my ear, telling me to let go, to give in. To take out all my anger on Maurice McMahon."

Damien blinked, comprehension dawning. "Onatochee? Promises of power and vengeance?"

I leaned forward, my face in my hands. No. It wasn't possible. That the killers were part of an old cult that had inexplicably survived for centuries—that was at least plausible. That there really was a demon-god who could influence the actions of weak and mortal humans...

No. My mind simply refused to accept it.

"God, Damien." I glanced across the table for reassurance, only to see that Damien looked as disturbed as I was. "What's happening to us?"

* * *

After dinner, we watched TV in Damien's living room. He had a big plasma screen hidden behind the doors of an antique wardrobe that he'd converted into a media center.

The program was called *Paranormal Investigations Unlimited*, one of those myriad "Ghost Hunter" reality shows. This one featured a team of misfits who ran around buildings, filming themselves with night vision cameras and not finding anything. The gimmick was that in between not finding anything the show included interviews with supernatural "experts" who explained what the team was looking for, giving history lessons and spouting metaphysical mumbo-jumbo.

Given what we'd been talking about all afternoon, the notion of a bunch of reality show bumblers stumbling through a deserted house was kind of comforting and quaint. When we got to the expert, however, we both sat up and took notice.

He was a suavely handsome, red-haired man in a simple green sweater and spotless gray slacks, who spoke mildly and convincingly with a pleasant Irish brogue. The text at the bottom of the screen identified him as *Michael O'Regan—author and supernatural investigator.*

"Hey, I know him," Damien said. "I have some of his books."

O'Regan gazed into the camera with comfortable confidence. "Ghosts are one thing. Demons are quite another. I'm of the opinion—as are a number of occult experts—that demons are actually entities from alternate realities, creatures that coexist with us on a different plane. There are many such planes, but from time to time the barriers between our reality and theirs grow weak or thin, allowing demons and similar entities access. Humans can even weaken the barriers themselves through arcane ritual, acts of violence or even simply by believing that they exist."

"Do you think the team is dealing with a demon, Mister O'Regan?" the off-camera interviewer asked.

"I can't say. So far I haven't seen any manifestations that couldn't be explained by purely mundane phenomena. If this were a real demon, they'd know it."

"Have you dealt directly with demonic entities?"

There was the briefest and most subtle of pauses before O'Regan continued.

"Yes, yes I have. And believe me, it isn't the kind of thing one undertakes lightly."

"So if the team is actually dealing with a demon—"

"I would recommend that they get out immediately and consider an entirely new line of work."

The show cut to commercial, leaving Damien and me staring at each other.

"Maybe he reads your column," I said.

Damien nodded. "He's good. He knows his stuff. I don't know what he's doing on a stupid program like this."

"They offered him a lot of money?"

"Yeah, that's always a possibility, isn't it?"

We watched the rest of the show. Unsurprisingly, the *Paranormal Investigations Unlimited* team found no evidence of demons or ghosts, but shot a lot of night vision footage and got opinions from a couple of other supernatural experts. Damien changed the channel before we could get to the next reality show, this one about throwing pumpkins from catapults.

"I think they're telling me I need to go home," I said.

"Sounds good." Damien pulled on a coat. "Want a ride?"

Damien took Yngwie out into the elements again and drove me home. I had mostly stashed my fears away by the time I got there, but I checked under the bed and in the closet nevertheless, finding nothing but boxes of miscellaneous junk, a pair of steel-toed engineer's boots that I hadn't worn in a couple of years, clothes, and my dad's old Stingray bass gathering dust in the corner.

I stared down at the instrument, then back at the clothes. There in the shadows hung a black leather duster. It had hung there untouched for three years now, and I couldn't bring myself to either wear it or give it away.

Then in a single chilling rush I remembered what Mia Jordan had said as I limped beside her gurney.

I dreamed you were coming. You were wearing a long black coat, you had a sword in your hand. She told me you were coming.

Cheryl had given me the coat for my birthday, and I hadn't worn it since the day she'd died.

I didn't go to bed but stayed awake with all the lights burning, hunched over my computer keyboard.

Searching.

* * *

Damien wasn't the only one who could do online research. Around 1:00 a.m. I found what I was looking for on a small folklore site. I felt my body trembling slightly as I read the words on the screen.

Long ago, before people were real people, a woman chief lived up in the rocks above the village of Nixluidix, where she could look down on her people and see that they were well.

One day, Coyote visited the woman. "Are you a good and wise chief?" he asked. "Do you see to the welfare of your people, or are you cruel and spiteful?"

"I watch over my people," the chief replied. "I teach them to hunt and fight and how to protect themselves from enemies and evil spirits."

"Very well," replied Coyote. "Soon the world will change, and people will become real people. Then women may no longer be chiefs. But you, who care for and protect your people, will remain here, watching over them for all time. You will be called Tsagaglalal—She Who Watches."

And to this day Tsagaglalal stands watch over her people, her great eyes seeing all that occurs.

* * *

I went to bed after that, but lay awake for a long time, thoughts churning, fears growing and receding. I tried to relax, staring upward as if daring something to leap out of the darkness and onto my face. When nothing came, I felt my breaths grow longer and deeper.

I could see the dim outline of my bedroom curtains, the door, the dresser. They all seemed suffused with a faint silver-blue luminescence like moonlight on a clear summer night.

Night fears subsided, monsters fled. My eyes slowly closed. Was I seeing the real room through slitted eyelids, or was I dreaming of a duplicate room, ethereal and silver-blue?

Blue sparks danced lazily through the shadows. It was as if they belonged in my room, as if they had always been there, like unseen guardian angels. They moved together in graceful harmony, forming strange symbols and letters, then swirling into an even more intricate pattern—a spinning mandala, a whorl of thin lines, a triskelion, a spiral...

Memory stirred, as if I had seen this sign many times, over many years, in dreams, in visions, in my imagination. It meant something, but I could not comprehend it any more than I could read the alien letters that surrounded it.

There was a sound—a deep groan like metal being pounded with hammers and pressed into alien shapes against its will...

...And I felt myself pulled back to consciousness by the sound of the clock-radio and the opening chords of *Back in Black*. It was six o'clock and the rain beat a desultory tattoo against my window.

D amien rifled through yet another handful of printouts. "I think the coincidences are starting to pile up. We've got serial killers spouting off the name of Indian demons, and their victim saying that she had a vision of you and heard from a Chinook goddess. I'm beginning to believe there really is a supernatural element to all of this."

"Not so fast, Agent Mulder." I yawned and rubbed my eyes. The coffee wasn't perking me up as much as I'd have liked. "You sure you aren't indulging in just a *little* bit of magical thinking?"

I was tired—after about four hours of restless sleep I'd dragged myself to work and tried to write a new I-84 Killer article that included all the new information about Pine Street Bob and his cult. I'd made almost no progress, though Terri had been solicitous. Loren and I were her new star reporters, and she told me we could both expect a little something extra in our next paychecks.

Loren was still in the Tri-cities, though I knew that more than three days away from his X-Box would have him climbing the walls. I expected him back at any moment.

I'd made my way back to Damien's after work despite my weariness and desperate desire to get some real sleep. The information I'd found about She Who Watches was compelling, but my mind felt locked up and defensive, refusing to think it was anything more than evidence of a mundane conspiracy.

"I can buy that there's a murder cult," I continued. "I can buy that it's got a bunch of crazies killing people in the name of some kind of evil spirit. But if you're suggesting that some kind of Native American evil spirit called Onatochee is real and that he's truly influencing people's actions, I think you're as crazy as Pine Street Bob."

I was trying to be funny, but I immediately regretted my words—Damien might not think jokes about mental illness were especially amusing.

Fortunately, he didn't take offense. "You may be quite correct there. I'm seeing ghosts and goblins where I should be seeing facts. Maybe we should collaborate on my next article— you can provide the unyielding skeptic's perspective."

He was a little less intense today—I guessed that his mania was fading and that he had begun the transformation back into his depressive self. The irony of the situation was that while Depressive Damien was much more likable and easier to get along with, he wasn't anywhere near as skilled a writer or researcher as Manic Damien.

He went on, typing as he spoke. "I'm afraid most of the conspiracy nuts out there probably think the Gordian Knot is how a guy named Gordon ties his tie. I promise I won't jump to any conclusions about Onatochee yet. However, I'm not going to discount the possibility that he's real, either."

I took it in stride. I'd said my piece and he'd responded in typical fashion. I was getting used to Damien's world view, even though I didn't necessarily agree with it.

"Okay," I said. "I accept that. Maybe the difference between us is that there are some possibilities that are so far-fetched I refuse to consider them. Sure it's possible that Pine Street Bob and Maurice McMahon were members of an ancient murder cult. Possible but unlikely. On the other hand, as much as I admire and respect you Damien…"

To my surprise Damien's eyes brightened slightly at that. "Thank you, Alex."

"I mean it, Damien." It occurred to me that he didn't get compliments very often—probably never. "But as I was saying as much as I admire you, I think that the possibility of a real, live demon being responsible for this isn't just unlikely, it's impossible. And if I have to choose between unlikely and impossible, I'm going to vote for unlikely."

"Fair enough. I can't necessarily fault your logic. Well, I could but you'd just argue with me."

I chuckled. "You got that right."

Damien opened his email client. "I'm getting in contact with Michael O'Regan. Remember the guy from that silly reality show last night? I want to see if he can provide us with any insights into what's going on here in Portland."

I eyed him suspiciously. "So you want input from a guy who makes his living working on bad reality shows? You sure he's a reliable source?"

Damien nodded, still typing. "He's been writing books on demonology and magic for years. His blog says that he's in LA wrapping up work on the next season of the ghost show. Apparently it's being retooled with a new cast."

I frowned. "Retooled? Why? Bad ratings?"

He opened a web page that showed a news article with the headline *PIU's a Yawner— Showrunners Hope New Cast Boosts Buzz.*

"According to *Variety,*" Damien said, "one of the cast members saw his reflection in a mirror and thought it was a ghost. It scared him so much he ran right through a sliding glass door and over a porch railing, destroying four thousand dollars worth of video equipment and a fifty dollar EMF meter. They're changing the show's name to *Ghost Stalkers* and hiring an ex-NBA player and a couple of SI swimsuit models as their new team."

I facepalmed. "There goes what's left of my faith in humanity."

"Don't worry. If they keep Michael O'Regan employed, he'll be able to continue writing books. And maybe even help us." Damien rotated his chair and looked at me. "What do you say, Alex? Want to collaborate? I know I'm an insensitive asshole half the time and a useless non-entity the other half, but in between I need someone around to keep me centered. We've already uncovered some amazing things about the I-84 case. Who knows what else we'll find?"

I looked out the balcony windows at the sky, deepening from indigo to black as the sun vanished below the horizon.

"So you want me to be a cynical, ironic skeptic and help you do research into ancient demons and monsters? You sure you don't want someone a little more open-minded?"

That got a smile. "No, Alex. I like you just the way you are—a cynical, ironic skeptic."

I shrugged. "What the hell? I've already almost gotten myself killed, so what are the odds that it'll happen again?"

Damien looked at me appraisingly. "Gambler's fallacy, Alex. The odds of it happening again are exactly the same as of it happening in the first place. People just don't understand probability."

"God damn, Damien. If I work with you, am I going to have to put up with that kind of crap all the time?"

Damien affected a thoughtful look and gazed down at his keyboard. "Not all the time. Sometimes you may find yourself talking me down from a ledge."

I sighed again. "Okay, Damien. You've got yourself a collaborator. Bring it on."

Damien crossed his arms and looked strangely content. "Thanks, Alex. For some reason I feel pretty good right now."

Oddly enough, so did I.

I accepted another ride from Damien, and he chattered the whole way back to my apartment, though later I didn't remember what he'd said. I was tired. I didn't care about ancient demons or goddesses or serial murder cults. Right now I just wanted to sleep.

* * *

I stood in a clearing in the midst of a dark forest. I was wearing the black leather coat that Cheryl had bought me, and I was on my knees.

Before me I saw a stone outcropping. Barely visible on the weathered surface was the carving of a strange, owl-eyed figure. As I knelt, I felt a faint breeze that quickly grew to a strong wind. All around me the trees twisted as if in torment, and the stone began to fluoresce, glowing silver-blue.

I wasn't afraid when I saw her. It was as if she'd always been there, floating just beyond my perception, a presence that was at once close and distant. Only now did I remember how she'd come to me when I was a child, scaring away monsters and giving me courage.

Now, in my lucid dreaming state I saw her at last, a voluptuous, naked woman floating in the air above the outcropping, her hair surrounding her like silvery gossamer. A pair of graceful swan-like wings rose from her back, and blue lights traced intricate patterns across her skin.

"Tsagaglalal," I whispered, transfixed.

She gazed on me with soft eyes that shone with the same silver-blue, and held out her hand. Drawn on her palm in flickering blue sparks like fireflies was a crude spiral pattern. As I watched, it grew more complex, becoming the shape I'd seen in my waking dream the night before, spinning like a galaxy, crawling with tiny characters that I couldn't read, radiating a sensation that I could not describe.

Now the firefly lights that darted and danced across her skin swirled in the air, sketching an elongated shape like a neon-glowing sword, suspended in the space between us. She spoke, but her words sounded like someone speaking underwater.

I reached out and my fingers almost touched the pulsing, iridescent sword-shape.

Then I heard the sound again, the groan of tortured metal, but this time it was more vivid, deeper, as if it issued from the throat of a living being, and other sounds echoed—screams of the dying, cries of infants, the tormented howls of animals...

She looked away, past me, into the storm-tossed forest. The sword-shape vanished into a swarm of agitated points of light. A look of alarm crossed her face...

...And I was awake again.

I sat on the edge of the bed for a long time, images from my dream strobing through my head like a slideshow. The images continued to cycle through a hurried breakfast, a cup of microwaved instant coffee, the long bus ride downtown and my sleepwalker's journey to the Pioneer Building. They only began to fade when I sat down at my desk to consider what horrors the *Ranger* would visit upon Portland this week.

For two weeks things regained a semblance of normalcy. Pine Street Bob, aka Robert Leslie, sat quietly during his arraignment, muttering and drooling on himself while his court-appointed lawyers announced, unsurprisingly, that they planned to present an insanity defense. Bob himself then bolstered their claims by attacking the bailiff, screaming Onatochee's name until he was repeatedly maced and tased, then carried off in shackles.

Mia Jordan recovered—at least as much as anyone could. After her release from the hospital, she dropped out of sight. Rumor had it that she'd gone to live with her parents in San Diego, and also that her doctors had quietly terminated a pregnancy. I made a few attempts to confirm the rumors, but the wall of patient confidentiality was thick and in the end I didn't really try all that hard. She had been through enough, and she deserved her privacy.

The mutilated body had been that of Mia's boyfriend, Byron Sears, and parts of him—most notably his head—remained missing. The media horror show continued for a while until the sharks moved on to other fish, relegating the I-84 killings to the "Also in the News" portion of their broadcasts.

As I'd expected, Loren was his old self when he returned from Kennewick. True, he was a nerd and he considered an evening of playing *Grand Theft Auto* to be the height of culture, but he was also possessed of a strong will and a ferociously resilient constitution. We got together a few times, drinking microbrew beers in taverns, playing video games that he invariably won by a wide margin, and taking Beowulf for walks. We didn't talk much about Pine Street Bob or Maurice McMahon, but the bond that had been forged between us was still there, unspoken but strong.

Uncle Creepy never turned up. I almost succeeded in convincing myself that my fears were overblown—he wasn't even part of Pine Street Bob's cult, or he'd blown town in the face of police pressure. I finished my follow-up article on Bob and the murder cult, but I didn't include anything about Onatochee or the connection to ancient Chinook mythology— suggestions about Native American demons seemed more appropriate to Damien's column, and besides I was having a hard time believing it myself.

My less skeptical side came out when I worked with Damien. Together, we delved deeper into supernatural connections to the I-84 murders. Pretty soon it was obvious we had more than just a series of articles—it was well on the way to being an entire book.

Damien fixed coffee and sandwiches, I cooked burgers and chicken. Occasionally, we tooled around in Yngwie, taking expeditions to the library or to bookstores, gathering either blank stares or delighted grins from onlookers as we roared noisily past. His growing willingness to take his precious classic out into the cruel elements seemed to me a sign that his mental health was improving.

As days went by, I began to grow accustomed his eccentricities—his obsession with detail, his wild-eyed rants, his sudden mood swings and personality changes. In the end it all seemed, if not normal, at least appropriate for the brilliant, lonely man that Damien was, and to the life he'd chosen to lead.

Perhaps what I'd seen had changed my way of thinking— perhaps now his talk of gods and demons and transdimensional gateways didn't seem quite so bizarre. Friends are good at changing one's mind, and despite his peculiarities and the constant pain of his struggle with illness, Damien Smith had certainly become a friend.

Loren threw a Halloween party, and we spent the night handing out candy, playing *Halo,* and drinking microbrews with his roommate, some people from the *Ranger* office and a score of other friends of friends. Damien chose not to attend, but we had fun without him.

As if sensing the lightening of my mood, the weather improved and the first half of November was sunny and unseasonably warm. The city's beauty emerged from the gray, basking in the last bright light of autumn. Crews cleaned up drifts of dead leaves, coats gave way to sweaters, hats and gloves were left at home.

Riding the bus wasn't so bad now with the window open, fresh scents of cool air and earth rushing across my face, and the sights of a city that reveled in its eccentricity dancing before my eyes—an Asian man selling Bento from a food cart, a dreadlocked white man juggling, a businessman in a dark suit stopping to watch a boy on a skateboard, a gang of street musicians playing acoustic versions of heavy metal songs to the delight of passersby. Portland seemed more than just a city—at times like this it was a great amorphous entity made up of a half-million elements, each of them unique.

Other aspects of life weren't quite so perfect. Portland's economy was in the tank, necessitating cuts in fire and police services. Violence increased in the homeless communities of Old Town and North Portland. Bored with the I-84 story, the media had started to call the rash of killings "The Homeless Wars."

It was a sunny Saturday in early November when I arrived at Damien's house amid a red-orange riot of fall foliage, and my long journey finally began.

* * *

Damien was sitting in the wingback when I entered. He'd made me a key so I didn't have to ring the damned bell every time I came over. I knew this was another huge concession on his part, and I was grateful.

He looked up from the book he was reading, a wide and slightly demented grin on his face. He'd been oddly erratic for the past few days, as if his two personalities had been stuck in a blender. I told myself that it was probably because he'd been working so hard on the new project and that it was good for him to keep busy.

"He's coming to Portland." There was a note of triumph in his voice.

I frowned, throwing down my backpack and settling on the couch. I was a bit put off—usually Damien let me sit in the wingback.

"I see. Exactly who is *he*? Or do I have to guess?"

Damien rolled his eyes. "No you don't have to guess. Remember Michael O'Regan? The occult expert?"

"From the reality show?"

I must have sounded dubious. "Damn it, Alex. I told you he's done other stuff." Damien waved his hand over the coffee table. It was cluttered with books.

"I told you I had several of his books. Check this out." He selected a volume from the table, a hardcover with an acetate library cover. "*Demons and Banishments*. It describes a ceremony he used to send a demon back through the rifts. That's what he calls my leaky screen doors. I cross-checked, did some more research last night. Damn, Alex, the man was onto something. He describes the banishment in detail here in this book."

"Damien, are you..." I faltered. "Are you still suggesting that Onatochee is real? I thought we'd been over that."

"As I have told you repeatedly, it's one possibility among many, Alex. And Michael O'Regan may have the means of testing it to see if it's correct."

"How, Damien? By dancing naked around a fire and waving dead chickens or something?"

Damien ignored me. "O'Regan seems to know what he's talking about. He's considered one of the most knowledgeable occultists in the western world. He wrote a biography of John Dee and papers on Enochian magick. He's memorized the Lesser Key of Solomon, lived with Haitian houngans—the whole bit. Of course he also claims he's summoned and exorcised real demons too, so it might all be hype. But what I've read so far suggests otherwise."

"Has he lived at the North Pole, helping Santa make toys too?"

"No, of course not. He's not some occultist wingnut, Alex—he acknowledges that the whole Onatochee thing could have a mundane explanation, but he's interested in learning more. He could be a complete charlatan, or he could be a valuable resource. I think I'd like to find out. We've been corresponding for a couple of weeks now."

In the kitchen the teakettle began to shriek, and Damien leapt up to go deal with it. His voice echoed off the tiles. "I sent him all the information we've gotten about Onatochee, and the Shepherd murders, Pine Street Bob, She Who Watches. All that stuff. What I've told him seems to dovetail with a project that he's working on, and he just got into town a couple of days ago. We're meeting for lunch today."

I closed my eyes. Normally I admired Damien's even-handed approach and his careful consideration of differing points of view. But giving credence to the beliefs of someone like Michael O'Regan seemed to be taking things a little too far.

"I want you to come too, Alex." Damien returned with his teapot and cups. Over the past few weeks it had become a familiar ritual, but I didn't feel terribly comforted by it now. "Look, Alex, I know you're skeptical. That's one of the reasons I want to work with you. You don't have to buy into any of the supernatural stuff. I'd probably be disappointed in you if you did. But I think it's important to look at all the angles, not just the ones that make sense to you. Besides, you're my collaborator. If you're not there, I'll miss out on your keen, razor-sharp observations."

I sighed and forced a thin smile. He was making sense, damn his eyes. "Okay, sure. It might be fun to talk to a real live TV personality. When are we meeting him?"

Loren checked his watch.

"Oops. In an hour. Must have lost track of the time. Better drink up."

* * *

Dressed in a spotless white sweater, a gleam in his eye and a jaunty brogue in his speech, Michael O'Regan proved to be every bit the rugged, handsome gray-touched redhead we'd seen on TV.

"I'm familiar with your work," he told Damien as the three of us sat in a dark corner of Huber's Restaurant. "It's very..." He paused, searching for words. "...informative."

Michael and I drank microbrew beers, while Damien sipped at his ever-present cup of tea with a quick, nervous manner. He was out of his element, far away from the comforting womb of his home, but meeting O'Regan was a significant enough event to draw him out.

"Thanks," Damien said. "I've seen you mentioned quite a bit in occult publications, even if you don't have a lot of mainstream recognition."

O'Regan nodded sagely. "I'd as soon not have even that much notoriety, but when you move in such small circles, you're bound to attract attention."

"You mean from cable TV producers?" I felt suspicious.

He smiled and seemed to take no offense. "Yes, I'm afraid so. Unfortunately I'm not a wealthy man, as I'm sure you appreciate, Alex. Most of my resources go into research, and when a show like *Paranormal Investigations...*"

He paused and chuckled. "Excuse me... *Ghost Stalkers* is looking for an expert and willing to pay, I tend to forget some of my professional scruples. I must admit it's given my book sales something of a boost. And, oh yes—my blog seems to be getting a lot more hits these days."

"So working with the swimsuit models is just a fringe benefit?" I was a little put off by Michael's self-proclaimed status as an expert, but I let it go. "What other circles do you move in, Michael?"

Michael took my jibe with good humor. "All sorts. People like you and Damien—the curious, the enlightened, the mystical." He fixed me with a knowing stare. "Even skeptics like yourself."

"Touché."

He took a sip from his frothing glass. "Exquisite. I'd always heard your beer was excellent but I haven't had the chance to prove it until now."

"I don't think you came all the way to Portland for the *hefeweizen.*"

O'Regan considered me for a moment, savoring his drink. "You know I've been active in my... pursuits... for many years."

Beside me, Damien nodded eagerly. He wasn't immune to O'Regan's charms.

O'Regan continued. "It started in school. I read voraciously. Everything by John Dee, Edward Kelley, Aleister Crowley, Nicholas Flamel, Anton Lavey. And not just non-fiction—I devoured the works of Poe, Machen, Lovecraft, Barker, Louve, Glancey and others. It wasn't enough, though. I felt as if these authors had just scratched the surface, as if they'd been granted a brief glimpse at the mystical or the infernal, and wrote of it as if it were nothing more than fantasy."

"Exactly," Damien said, unexpectedly abrupt. He seemed to be getting more excited by the moment. "Like the blind men and the elephant."

"That's the situation we're in, isn't it—seeing only a portion of a larger picture? In any event, I began to visit the places I'd read of, talk to some of the actual authors, and learn more about the truth behind the stories. By the time I wrote my first book, my head was a virtual library, containing every aspect of supernatural research and fiction imaginable."

Once again I felt a faint stirring of annoyance at his casual egotism.

"In your books, you claim you've actually summoned real demons," I said. "I don't mean to be rude, but given that skeptical nature you mentioned—"

"You have a hard time believing in ghoulies and ghosties and demons," he finished for me. "I can't say that I blame you. You've lived your entire life in the physical world. You've never seen any real, solid evidence of the supernatural, and those who claim to have it are all proved to be frauds and charlatans."

I hesitated a moment, then nodded. He certainly didn't seem offended.

"Frauds and charlatans," I said. "Yes. With all due respect, Michael, the people on your reality show certainly fit the bill."

He sighed. "Don't they? I regret to admit that I agree with you. You're looking at a man who has largely sacrificed his credibility in exchange for a paycheck and wider exposure. It's a painful admission."

I was almost impressed by his candor, but my doubts still nagged at me.

"Tell me about these demons, Michael," I continued. "What was your first experience?"

I noted a brief, almost undetectable pause before Michael spoke, much like the one I'd seen during his interview.

When he spoke, there was a faint catch in his voice as if he were physically willing the words to emerge. "It was nearly twenty years ago, in a stone circle near Boleskine—Aleister Crowley's house at Loch Ness. I was there with my friends Bryce, Donald…" He paused and spoke quietly. "And Moira. We were young and foolish, and I had a book. A very old book of spells and summonings."

I bit my tongue, holding back the urge to walk out of the restaurant and let Michael stew in his own ego. But enough had happened in the past weeks to keep my rational mind quiet for the moment. He paused for a long time, then something behind his eyes seemed to shift almost imperceptibly, like a lock finally clicking into place.

"We used a spell in the book to call something out of the rifts. It was something called Abatu. It didn't manifest physically, but it got into our heads, almost drove us mad." He raised his hair off his forehead, revealing a white scar. "Under its influence Donald hit me in the head with a rock, then leaped on Moira and tried to rape her. Bryce tried to stop him and they fought. Donald fractured Bryce's skull, but then he slipped and fell, breaking his neck. Barely conscious, I managed to recite a dismissal spell." He shook his head slowly. "We were never the same after that, none of us. The authorities investigated and concluded that Donald's death was accidental. Bryce was in a coma for nearly a year. When he finally recovered, he remembered nothing of his ordeal, and he'll be in a wheelchair for the rest of his life. And Moira... Dearest Moira..." He paused again, staring into his glass. "She took her own life."

"My God," I said. "I'm sorry."

O'Regan seemed genuinely saddened by the memory. At the same time, the cynical part of my brain wondered whether he wasn't exaggerating, or telling us a sad story to elicit sympathy, and make the whole overwrought tale seem more plausible. I suppressed such thoughts—Michael's story was tragic enough without my questioning his version of events.

Nothing he'd said proved that demons were real—his friend Donald may simply have snapped and gotten violent. I didn't argue the point however. It didn't seem very polite to start interrogating Michael about such a personal tragedy.

"As for me," Michael concluded, "well, I ended up obsessed with demons and the occult."

"I'd have thought you'd want to get as far away from the occult as possible."

Despite my doubts, Michael's evident sincerity and sadness left me feeling numb. Thoughts of my own past were almost unavoidable.

"That's what you'd think, isn't it? The fact, Mister Saint John, our contact with Abatu affected us all. I believe that I'm cursed to pursue demons and try to destroy them, until I'm destroyed myself. After all that happened to us I felt nothing but a burning desire for more knowledge and through it, vengeance."

There was that word again. Vengeance. It echoed uncomfortably in my mind.

I felt a sudden desire to change the subject. I tried to move the conversation back to something a little less controversial. "You talk about demons... that's Christian mythology. You don't seem especially Christian."

"I'm not. Demons are not unique to the Christian mythos. Look around you. Almost every culture has them—Buddhist, Muslim, Hebrew, Hindu, Native American, African. The Sumerians revered Mimma-Lemnu, called the sum of all that is evil. Babylonian culture practically revolved around demons like Pazuzu, Lamashtu, and others. They are malevolent extra-dimensional entities of enormous strength, psychic power, intelligence and cunning. I find it interesting that though most humans worship different gods, we all fear the same demons. I wrote a book on the subject in fact. *Eyes in the Darkness—A Compendium of Demons and Evil Spirits*. I think you can still find it on Amazon."

Michael had clearly played the self-promotion game before. He had already admitted that his TV work was as much for publicity as for a paycheck.

"You can summon demons?" I asked.

"I can. To my own deep regret, I have. Through the rifts."

"You mean through Damien's screen doors?"

O'Regan frowned. "Screen doors? I normally call them interdimensional rifts. It's an interesting analogy. Yes, I suppose it works."

"You've seen them? Physically?"

For an instant he looked uncomfortable. "That's exceedingly rare. Usually demons make themselves known through other senses—alien thoughts, malign influences, whispered voices barely heard. A demon that could fully manifest itself physically would be a powerful—and dangerous—creature indeed."

"I see." It seemed like a cop-out, but once more I let it slide.

"In many cases, what we call demons may not even be conscious entities at all—simply manifestations of their own alternate reality, reflected in this universe through our own limited perceptions. They bring pieces of their reality with them—small bubbles of chaos existing in our material world. As mere humans, we can't tolerate their presence for long. Brief exposure twists the mind. Longer exposure twists the body and the soul as humans absorb elements of the demon's alternate reality."

"Are they really evil then? Or are they just bad for our health?"

He looked at me with a stern and almost angry gaze. "Demons—or rather, *entities*—like Onatochee and Abatu may not be actively malevolent or evil as we would know it—a better word might be *inimical*—they are simply incompatible with our existence in this world. Our desperate attempts to comprehend them, to make them fit into our conception of reality drives us mad, makes us do violent, evil things. No, Alex—I wouldn't necessarily call Onatochee evil but he is very, very bad. And very, very dangerous."

"Do you have any thoughts on our research?" Damien asked. "Or on the possibility that Onatochee might actually be one of these extradimensional entities or phenomena?" I noticed that he avoided using the word *demon*. Maybe terms like "entities" made the entire thing seem less crazy, less frightening.

O'Regan replied thoughtfully. "Your research looks solid, Damien, but I appreciate Mister St. Johns' skepticism. I prefer the ordinary solution to the extraordinary myself, but the connection to the Onatochee entity is intriguing, and it parallels my own investigations." He drained his glass and set it down. "I'd like to see more of your work, Damien. If it's as extensive as you say I think you would be an excellent resource for my future researches."

Damien nodded. "You can come over today if you like."

"I would. It will give us a chance to compare notes and investigate our options."

"And if you think there really is a supernatural cause for all of this? What then?"

"Let's take this one issue at a time, Damien. We haven't even confirmed that it exists yet. Alex... Excuse me, can I call you Alex?"

I nodded.

"Alex, is it your suggestion that the I-84 murders are the work of mundane serial killers who might think they worship Onatochee, but are simply garden-variety sociopaths?"

"In as many words, yes. I'd even consider that they're part of some kind of cult that's been around for decades or centuries, but there's no demon involved. They're just crazy."

"And the female victim? Mia Jordan? She said she had a vision of you, and spoke of the goddess Tsagaglalal, who may represent some kind of counterbalance to this Onatochee entity. How would she know such a thing?"

I shrugged. "She was pretty messed up when we found her. My guess is that she just repeated something that she heard Pine Street Bob and his friend babbling about, in among all the nonsense about Onatochee and the Chilut."

"And their graffiti? The name Onatochee scrawled in obscure ancient alphabets? And what about that Spanish killer that Damien found—what was his name? Ramon Soto? He apparently said many of the same things as your current suspects."

"Pine Street Bob wasn't stupid, just mentally ill. I'm sure he was exposed to ancient languages when he was studying for the priesthood. As for Soto, who knows? Maybe he really was babbling gibberish and it just happened to resemble words from the Chinook language."

"In other words, coincidence?"

I felt suddenly very self-conscious. For years I'd criticized others for using tortured logic and ignoring facts when they promoted conspiracy theories and mysticism. Was I doing the same thing now—searching for any explanation that fit my world-view, however obscure and unlikely?

Doggedly, I clung to my argument. "Yeah, coincidence. No matter how weird it sounds, in my mind it's a hell of a lot more likely than the work of demons and evil spirits."

O'Regan smiled. "Alex, there's an old Irish proverb that says the believer is happy, but the doubter is wise. You make a decent argument. If it turns out that you're right, I'll be happy to buy you a few rounds of this wonderful Portland beer."

"Thanks. I appreciate it." I was surprised that he didn't also offer me an autographed copy of his latest book.

"However, right now I want to dig a little deeper into the matter. I'd like to start as soon as possible. Is that acceptable, Damien?"

Damien nodded. His antisocial tendencies seemed completely overwhelmed by Michael's charismatic, oversized personality. Even I had to admit that, despite his flashes of egotism, the man had charm to spare.

"Good." Michael produced a pen and scrawled an address on a napkin. "Damien and I will be doing our research tonight. You can meet us here tomorrow night at eight. You can decide then whether you want to help. I'd also like you to meet my friends."

"I'll see you then, Alex," Damien said.

I accepted the napkin, then watched, vaguely jealous in a way I couldn't entirely understand as Damien and Michael bid me good night and departed, leaving me with my coffee and a half-eaten turkey sandwich.

I sighed. Michael O'Regan had been friendly, polite, and respectful. He'd even picked up my tab. Why then did the man annoy me so intensely?

I had no idea.

* * *

It took a couple hours of searching on my own before I found a small article from the *Glasgow Daily Record*, dated November 1, 1993 describing a tragic accident near Inverness that had taken the life of a young American backpacker named Donald Grace and left one of his fellow hikers, Bryce MacGowan, in a coma. Two other hikers, a man and a woman were mentioned but not named. The local constabulary lamented the tragedy and warned that the Scottish Highlands could still be a dangerous place, especially for inexperienced travelers.

The piece was short, and said nothing about a fight or any injuries to the other two hikers. While Michael and his friend

Moira weren't in the article, it seemed to confirm the story he'd told.

Still, as I printed out the story and filed it in my desk, I felt troubled, though I didn't know why.

IV

It was clear and cold the following evening when we drove Yngwie to a small but neat downtown apartment, and were ushered in by a thin, chestnut-haired woman.

"Hi," she said. She seemed as nervous and flighty as a small dark bird. "I'm Kay. This is my husband Ronald." She indicated a tall, friendly-looking man with short dark-blonde hair and round wire-rimmed glasses.

He nodded. "Hello. Nice to meet you. And for God's sake call me Ron." He paused. "Is that your Camaro out front?"

Damien smiled graciously. "Yes, it is."

Ron grinned. "Kew-el! I always wanted one of those."

"It's an expensive hobby, believe me."

Michael's other friends were a mixed lot. Vince, an overweight man with a fringe of red beard, had brought his own eight pack of Zap, the Cola with Attitude. He specialized in history and research.

"Glad to have you here." He held out a can. "Wanna Zap?"

I shook my head. "I'm wired enough. Thanks anyway."

Vince shrugged and settled down on the couch.

Kay indicated a handsome man with a long face, lustrous chestnut ponytail and goatee who lounged on the other end of the couch. He wore a tight t-shirt and I could see that his arms were thin but wiry and muscular.

"This is Eric. He's the artist of the group."

"Hi." He spoke with little enthusiasm and returned to the dog-eared paperback he'd been reading. I was getting ready to feel slighted, when Kay introduced the last member.

"And returning from the kitchen is Patricia." I tried not to stare as a pale-skinned woman in a frilly black outfit entered. Long, shining black hair framed an oval face with a large, expressive mouth. A collection of necklaces, bearing an assortment of ankhs, Thor's hammers, pentacles, crosses, hexagrams, goddess figurines, and other symbols I didn't recognize hung around her neck, glittering as she moved.

"Actually, it's Trish." I accepted her proffered hand. "Call me Pat at your peril, and if you ever call me Patty I'll have to kill you."

I grinned. "I feel the same way about Xander."

I was just about to make another stab at conversation when Michael O'Regan appeared from the bathroom.

His arrival signaled an end to conversation, and our companions fell into respectful silence, settling themselves on the couch, on chairs, or—in my case—the floor.

O'Regan wore a dark purple collarless shirt and black slacks, making him look uncomfortably like a priest. He carried a folder full of papers.

"I'm glad you could all make it," he said. "I think everyone knows everyone by now."

Not as much as I'd like, I mused to myself, surreptitiously appraising Trish, who also sat on the floor, back against the couch, gazing at Michael with wide, adoring violet eyes. Beneath

112

her frilly outfit her body was a lush landscape of soft curves and ivory skin.

I'd been virtually celibate since college, and despite my best efforts to concentrate on Michael, I found my thoughts drifting toward speculation about what sort of underwear Trish was wearing and what she'd look like without it. At that point, Trish's gaze shifted, and her eyes met mine for a moment. I forcibly broke my reverie and turned my attention back to Michael.

"About three years ago I began to see a pattern to many crimes that were committed in varied locations around the world. Lone madmen driven to attack couples, savagely murdering the man and raping the woman." Kay and Ron exchanged a worried look. "It seems that I wasn't the only investigator on the case—my new friend Damien Smith and his associate Alex St. John were researching a series of local murders, the I-84 killings, and discovered the same pattern. Tell them what you found, Damien."

Awkwardly at first, but with growing confidence and an increasingly relaxed manner, Damien recounted our research and discoveries about the old killings and their connection to the I-84 case. When he finally got to our discoveries about Onatochee, he turned to me.

"Alex investigated one of the suspects, the one who called himself Pine Street Bob. I'll let him tell you what happened."

It caught me by surprise and I considered refusing, but then I met Trish's gaze again.

"I, well... I found out that Pine Street Bob sometimes crashed in an old cement plant out near the river," I began and launched into my own story. I didn't name Loren, only calling him "another reporter" but I told them what had happened at the plant—seeing the graffiti, finding Mia Jordan alive, stumbling over Byron Sears' corpse, fighting Pine Street Bob and Maurice McMahon. I left out the part about hearing whispered voices and the compulsion to kill McMahon, however. By the time I finished, Michael's friends were all staring at me in fascination.

Vince whistled. "Holy crap. These were actual worshippers? Do you think they were possessed by this demon—Onatochee?"

"I think that's quite a stretch," I replied. "I think it's a lot more likely that they were just garden variety sociopathic rapist-murderers."

"Onatochee's claws?" Michael O'Regan's voice was urgent. "You're sure that's what they said?"

"Well, that's what it sounded like to me. We correlated the words to an Upper Chinook dialect, but neither of us are linguists, so we could be completely wrong on that as well."

Eric rolled his eyes. I swallowed my growing dislike and tried to ignore him.

Damien said, "The legend says that he preys on the weak-willed, like the Chilut. Like mentally ill homeless people, or pedophiles like Maurice McMahon."

Vince nodded sagely. "So you think that this entity might be recruiting followers again?"

"It's a possibility, yes."

"And what's the connection to this Shepherd aspect? Any clue as to why all those guys say they're looking for him? And any idea about the connection to the Chinook goddess? A competing cult, maybe?"

"No idea. Not yet, anyway. We've found no mention of Tsagaglalal in any of the material we've studied, and the Shepherd business just seems to be another manifestation of the cult's activities."

I leaned my head on my fist. Michael's friends seemed determined to stampede toward a supernatural explanation for the crimes, disregarding all the other, more likely options. I sighed but held my piece, my gaze wandering back toward Trish.

When I finally tore my attention from inspecting the curve of Trish's neck and the way the light shone on her black hair, Damien was reading from an open book.

"This is another study of the local Indian tribes, published in 1897. The Multnomahs had all but disappeared by that time, and the government sent a team out to survey the area, including regions that had been inhabited by Indians."

"What happened to the Multnomahs?" Ron asked, polishing his glasses then replacing them. "Smallpox?"

"No one knows. All they know is that in 1830 they were thriving and less than three decades later they were gone. This survey lists several settlement areas—more semi-permanent campsites than actual villages. The biggest was on northern Sauvie Island and was called Cathlepotle. There were several other Chinook bands and tribes in the region besides the Multnomahs—the Cathlamet, the Clackamas, Watlala, Clowwewalla, and others. The survey also mentions some outside tribes that migrated to the region, such as..." He pointed to a word in the middle of the page. "The Chilut."

Vince grunted. "Our cannibalistic demon-worshippers."

"The same," said Michael. "The Chilut's main camp was called Chittequawla. It was located along the Willamette River, about five miles south of where it joins the Columbia. The authors investigated the place and although the Chilut were long gone by that time, they did find evidence of settlement. They even provide coordinates. Painfully accurate, those old surveyors." He withdrew the printout of a satellite map from his folder and held it up.

"This is the industrial area in North Portland, near the Saint Johns Bridge. This building corresponds to the coordinates of the Chilut settlement." The printout showed an ugly expanse of gray structures and oil tanks on winding gravel roads. In the middle of the district was an incongruous edifice, a sprawling industrial gothic building made of dark stone, its red-brown slate roof choked with moss and weeds. It was surrounded by a chain-link fence and piles of pipes, old crates, rusted trucks, and other junk.

"I know that place," Ron said. "You can see it from the highway."

"It's an old office building for what was once called Petroco—the Oregon Petroleum Company," Damien said. "It's been abandoned for years. The company refuses to tear it down or clean it up, so it just sits there and rots."

Eric looked impressed. "You mean that building is where the Chilut village was?"

Michael nodded. "Precisely, according to the survey that Damien found. I believe that this Petroco Building was built on one of Onatochee's places of power—one of several in the region that we've manage to locate." He cast his warm gaze toward me. "Now I want you to know that I believe it to be entirely possible that these killings and the horrors that went with them are the work of sick, twisted madmen as Alex suggests. But as a student of the occult, I must maintain an open mind. If—and please keep in mind that I am saying *if*—if this creature—for convenience's sake, let's call it a demon even if that's a terribly inadequate and specific term—truly exists and is truly influencing the actions of unstable personalities, I think it is beholden upon us to find the truth, and find some way of ridding the world of this evil."

He surveyed the rest of the room. Even I had to admit that the man oozed charisma, and my first instinct was to enthusiastically agree with him. I wondered why. Maybe it was the accent. Maybe it was because what he said actually made sense.

I spoke in the well of silence that followed. "Okay, I know I'm the newcomer here. And I've made it pretty clear that I'm the skeptic, too. I've said this to Damien many times, and I'll say it to you. I think that it's possible that this is all the work of a cult—a very old and secretive cult. But I also think the likelihood that such a cult can exist is small. No, tiny. Infinitesimal. But even then, that's still more likely than being the work of a demon, because demons aren't real. They don't exist. They're an impossibility."

Eric snorted. "Skeptic." He said it like an insult.

"Eric!" Trish spoke sharply. Her voice was soft but assertive. "Behave yourself! He's here because he's Michael's guest!"

Eric looked mad for a moment, then contrite, and fell silent.

Damien and Michael had heard my spiel before, and they took it well. Michael nodded and looked thoughtful, while Damien smiled slightly, almost indulgently. The others responded with silent gazes that ranged from Kay's dubious and sympathetic expression to Eric's look of outright hostility.

I wasn't finished.

"That said..." I paused, trying to find the exact words I wanted. "That said, what if after all the logic and reason we can apply to the problem, after we've explored every avenue and every other explanation, what if the impossible is the only alternative we have left? What do we do then?"

It took a few more seconds for my words to finally sink in. Damien's smile widened slightly.

O'Regan put a hand on Damien's shoulder. "As you say, Alex, what indeed? Thanks to Damien's hard work, I have far more information now that I had before. I'm not going to rush headlong into things and assume that this demon is real. I intend to investigate further, and as best I can ascertain, either confirm or deny Onatochee's existence. If he is real, I intend to make a summoning circle in a place of power—probably the Petroco Building—call it up and perform a banishment ritual that will permanently return it to the nether regions from whence it came. And if that's the case, I'll need help from everyone in this room."

There was another long moment of silence.

I rubbed my forehead. "I'm not a hundred percent sure that's the best way to proceed, Michael. If this really is a cult, there may be more of those bastards out there. And if they really do believe in this Onatochee thing, then they'll take a dim view of our meddling and stomping around in their territory. I've seen what they can do, more clearly than anyone else here. Doing your ritual at the Petroco Building could put everyone in this room in serious danger. Besides, you yourself say that exposure to extradimensional entities can twist the mind and the body." I didn't believe it myself, but I wanted to make an argument that Michael and his friends would pay attention to.

Kay spoke up. "He has a point. Michael, you've been my..." For a moment she faltered then exchanged the briefest of glances with Michael before looking away. "You've been our friend for years. This is the first time you've ever asked us to actually participate, and it makes me nervous."

Ron put his arm around her shoulder. "We knew this time would come eventually, Kay. We can't know someone like Michael and not be involved at some point."

Kay's expression was unreadable. She seemed determined to avoid meeting Michael's gaze again. I wondered if there was something more than friendship between them. "Well I think it's either foolish or dangerous, and either alternative isn't terribly encouraging."

"Of course it's dangerous, Kay." Trish sounded almost excited. "Crossing the street is dangerous. Just living is dangerous these days. I'm willing to risk it."

"So am I." Eric ran a hand across his shiny dark hair. He looked over at Trish, then at me. His manner was still angry, as if he was trying to prove something, though it wasn't clear exactly what. "I'm not scared. Michael knows what he's doing."

"Not just Michael," added Vince. "We all know what we're doing. We wouldn't be here if we didn't. Right?"

Michael nodded. "I trust every one of you to do what's needed. I want us all to go out to the Petroco Building tomorrow, and confirm that it is indeed a place of power. If we go as a group, it's very unlikely that any surviving cultists will try anything. And together I think we can generate enough positive psychic energy to hold off any ill effects arising from exposure, especially if we keep it relatively brief."

He looked at me. "I'd like your help, Alex. I understand how you feel and how irrational all this must seem to you. All I ask is that you be there and lend us your support. The more of us there are, the better our chances of success. I've dealt with this sort of situation enough to be confident that none of us will face any serious danger."

I felt a sudden chill of fear at the prospect, as if my intellectual concession to Damien and Michael had sent me down a long, treacherous slope. "Michael, I really don't—"

"Damnation, Alex." Damien's voice was almost pleading. "What's the harm? We'll all be there, and if we're lucky we can get the proof we need, one way or the other. I need to know, Alex. Please."

They were all staring at me now, expectantly. Michael, Vince, and Damien were all for me joining up. Eric didn't seem to care—he'd taken an instant dislike to me and the feeling was mutual. Ron and Kay both looked doubtful. If I backed out, I had no doubt they would too.

I fixed Michael with the most cynical gaze I could manage. "So if I come, should I bring my EMF meter and a camera crew?"

He looked up, smiling. "Oh, that. This will be very different from television, Alex. I promise there won't be any night vision cameras. Are you with us?"

My gaze finally came to rest on Trish. Her riveting eyes brimmed with excitement and anticipation. I realized that I didn't want to disappoint her. Our moment of contact, and my flash of lust for the woman were enough to send me over the edge.

"All right. I'm in. I'll come with you."

* * *

I had always heard about violet eyes, but I had never actually seen them before. Of course in reality they weren't truly violet, but a very deep, almost lambent-blue. I found them slightly unsettling, especially when they were staring at me with rapt interest over a steaming cup of coffee-like substance on a small table at Java Planet.

"Where were you born?" Trish asked, in a voice that made everything sound exciting and somehow sexual. "I want to know all about you."

I laughed, briefly. "I never thought of myself as that intriguing."

I started to reel off my biography, but she interrupted. "I don't want a chronology of your life, Alex. I want to know about you. Who are you? What do you believe in? Why do you think you're here? You're a man of science, but you're confronted by the irrational and you see everything changing. I feel privileged, Alex. It's exciting to be around someone when his eyes finally open to the possibilities of the world around him."

I frowned. "So why the intense fascination?"

Her eyes narrowed, exotic and suggestive. "I like to know as much as possible about the men I go to bed with."

Well, she certainly put matters in perspective. Stunned by her forthrightness, I stumblingly tried to explain who I was and what I believed in. I skipped over my experiences with Cheryl and her drug habit, falling back on my old argument about not wanting to talk to people who didn't listen.

She laughed at that. "Misanthrope."

"You're not the first to call me that." I shrugged. "Maybe you're right. I haven't seen much to encourage me these past few years."

She touched my arm reassuringly. "It's not too late to go back if you want to. Maybe Michael and I can help prove people are trustworthy."

Now that all the cards were on the table, I felt less self-conscious about looking her over, and noted with approval the faint outline of a lacy edge to her bra, also black. Through the semi-opaque fabric of her blouse, her breasts seemed ready to escape given the slightest chance. There was so much to her— the desire to lose myself in her wilderness of soft curves was almost overwhelming.

"So you've pretty much told me we're going to end up in bed together," I said.

"Unless you turn out to be a complete asshole, but that doesn't seem likely."

"I hope not." The server refreshed my coffee, and I waited until she was gone. "Now it's my turn. I like to know about my friends and lovers, too. I take my time—I like to wait at least two hours before getting naked. Tell me about yourself. Don't spare any details."

"Mm." She rolled her eyes briefly. "This should be interesting."

I can't say that I got as clear a picture of Trish as she had of me. She had dabbled in the occult for many years, starting out with the kind of bizarre, fringy gothic paganism that attracted many disaffected young people.

"I did the usual stuff. Dressed in black, wore pasty make up, pretended to be a vampire. Had sex with girls because it was chic. Never got any tats or piercings, though."

"Bucking the trends?"

"I just like to keep my skin intact."

"Good call. It's very nice skin."

"Why thank you."

When the black lipstick crowd proved inadequate and, in Trish's opinion, largely phony, she moved on to more dedicated groups such as Wicca, Asatru, and neo-Celtics, without success.

"I finally ended up getting into Satanism, but they were all poseurs. They only call themselves that to piss off the Christians. In reality they're more like Ayn Rand fans with fake devil horns. Nothing worked for me."

Her voice was low and laced with passionate intensity. "Not until I met Michael. Those others—all they wanted to do was bask in the light, stare at the stars, and sing songs about how wonderful it all was. Me, I want to be part of it, not just an observer. I want to become one with the things we can't see, Alex. Michael has given me a chance to do that."

"Michael? What does he give you that no one else does?"

"He gives me a chance to get closer to all this than I've ever been. We were lovers for a few years, you know." She tossed off this tidbit casually. "He shows me the most direct route to where I want to go. The others... Well, Vince is smart but hasn't any common sense. Eric—we've been to bed a few times, but it's never worked out—he's good enough with drawing pentacles and making inscriptions but doesn't have any real skill with true magic. He really has it bad for me, but I've been kind of avoiding him lately."

"That explains the look he gave me back at the apartment. I guess he noticed me ogling you."

"Probably. He's reliable, but he can be a prick sometimes. Kay and Ron—God, I don't know why they're here. She's a nurse and he's some kind of personnel manager or something. I think they met Michael in college. I think he used to sleep with Kay, too, though God only knows whether Ron knew about it or not. Under that reserved Irish exterior he's really a randy old goat."

I sighed. My intuition about them had been right. Michael was yet another guru who couldn't resist the charms of his female devotees.

"Michael's the only one who really counts," she continued. "With him I experience things that I've only imagined before. We've done amazing things together."

I frowned. "What sort of things?"

She snickered. "I know what you're thinking, you jealous boy. Yes, we've done those things too, but we've explored other areas. Now, if Damien's theories about Onatochee are correct, I'll really have something to see."

"Damien's theories?" I frowned. "I think you may be reading too much into what he's saying. I've worked with him—he's only speculating about Onatochee right now. He hasn't made any final decisions. At least I hope he hasn't."

"Oh, he will. Soon. And so will you."

She seemed strangely excited, stimulated by her own declarations. Why, I wondered? The excitement of the unknown? Or perhaps more to the point, the forbidden?

"Well, you'll find out tomorrow. It's likely to be strenuous. We'll need our rest."

She cut me short with a cold, icily sensual stare. "Not so fast, Mister. You've still got work to do. Shall we get the check?"

I nodded, and flagged down the server.

T rish's place was dark and shadowy, but warm. When we arrived, she bade me sit, then lit candles, illuminating the apartment with dozens of yellow-glowing tapers.

She lit two cones of incense. "Wait right there. I'll be back."

Her apartment was a lot like mine. Both were tiny and cramped, the best we could afford on our respective salaries (she was a bookstore clerk, I learned). However, where my apartment was a trashed-out lair used primarily for sleeping and lazing about watching TV, Trish had transformed her minimal space into a showcase of occult objects and images. Candles stood on almost every open surface, posters and pictures of various significant topics filled the walls—the Venus of Willendorf and a Green Man here, Herne the Hunter and Osiris there, a Doors poster and a chakra chart elsewhere. Books filled the shelves, most of pagan or mystical subject matter, though there was a smattering of classic science fiction and fantasy as well. She had an old Macintosh, and I didn't see a TV.

Trish reappeared, gliding into the room like a ghost. She wore a long peignoir of black lace, and underneath I could see the tantalizing outlines of her substantial breasts. She had retained her numerous necklaces, and they rested comfortably in her cleavage, glittering faintly in the candlelight. Below the curve of her belly, I could see that she wore black lace panties, the rest of her vanishing into shadow.

"Well?" she asked. "Like it?"

I nodded.

"Only one rule, Alex," she said. "After that it's whatever you want, however you want it. The charms stay. Don't remove them. They're my wards and are very important to me."

After three years of celibacy I'd have agreed even if she'd asked me to stand on one foot and sing the Star Spangled Banner. I stepped close and wrapped my arms around her, bending her back, my lips seeking hers.

"Oh." She gasped in surprise. "Actions speak louder than words, don't they?"

"Enough talk." I covered her face and neck with small kisses. I was feeling impulses and desires that had lain dormant for years. "I wanted you the minute I saw you."

She gasped again and stiffened, then met my kisses with her own, and we stood there for long minutes, lips and tongues exploring. When she dropped to her knees and loosened my belt and fly, I grabbed her head and set the pace, then shed the remainder of my clothes and carried her bodily to her bed.

There was something about her manner that seemed to demand I take control. It wasn't my usual mode for sex. I'd always been equitable, even conventional, in bed, giving women what they wanted, and how they wanted it, before getting around to my own pleasure. But then again, I hadn't really been in bed with that many women.

Now, fired up by the near-forgotten passion she awoke in me, I surprised myself, toying with her in a manner I'd never dreamed of before. It was as if my three year dry spell didn't exist.

Despite her requests, which soon became insistent pleas, I gently held her wrists with one hand, toying with her breasts, stroking and rubbing through the fabric of her black panties. When she tried to take them off herself, I pushed her hands away and kissed her deeply. I held her only lightly—she could have broken away easily, but she didn't resist. I released her hands and she began to stroke herself.

At last, I allowed her to undress completely, and I applied my fingers to the warm center between her thighs, rubbing and petting all around it until her groans grew in intensity and urgency.

"Please," she said. "Oh, please. Please. Don't tease me."

God help me, it drove me on. The more she begged, the less inclined I was to give her what she wanted. I gave her only a few strokes with my tongue, then looked up to see her face twisted with desire, staring in what I could only describe as supplication. In the depths of my mind, I was troubled that she submitted so readily to someone she barely knew, but I wasn't about to stop and be rational.

At that moment, something seemed to snap. A look of anger and unvented frustration contorted Trish's features, and she rose up, grabbing me by the shoulders, forcing me down on my back with unexpected strength.

"Fuck you." She leaped astride me, nails raking my neck and chest. She grabbed a condom from the nightstand, upsetting her clock and reading lamp. Ripping the package open with her teeth she slid the condom over my erect organ, then drove down onto it with an intensity I was afraid would hurt her. "I want it now, you son of a bitch... Give it to me..."

And she rose and fell on me, breasts bobbing, belly and chest heaving, teeth bared, neck straining, grating out angry exhortations as she did so.

"Fuck me, you bastard. Fuck me. Do it..."

So it went for several minutes. Torn a half dozen ways between excitement, astonishment, shame, passion, puzzlement, and a strange, logical detachment, I had little to do besides ride out the storm until she came with gut-wrenching intensity. Moving off me, she removed the condom and once more applied her lips. I unleashed my own pent-up orgasm, to her apparent delight.

"Oh, yes..." She sighed, fumbling for a towel beside the bed, and cleaning up our mutual mess. "You do that all... so well..."

After a few moments, I was seized by some sort of post-coital depression, and the full realization of how I'd behaved washed over me.

"I'm sorry I was so... Was I being a jerk just now? It just..."

She stared at me strangely. "What do you mean, Alex? It's what I wanted."

"You liked it?"

"Of course I did. You were nice. We'll talk about it later." She gazed down at me with an affectionate expression, though behind it I could detect something like sadness or unfulfilled longing. She sighed. "You'll do, Alex. You'll do quite nicely. Now, you have to go."

It took me a second to comprehend what she'd said. "What do you mean?"

"You're lovely, Alex. I'd love to do it again. Soon. But I sleep alone, Alex. I'm sorry. It's the way I am. I have to know a man for weeks before I'm comfortable sleeping with him."

It was no weirder than anything else she'd said or done, so with only a few cursory complaints, I allowed her to talk me into dressing, slinging my backpack, and leaving her apartment, for the long, cold bus ride back to my place.

She kissed me deeply before I left. "Until we meet again," she whispered, then closed the door behind me.

There wasn't anything wrong with what we'd done. She'd let me be in control, then she'd turned the tables and taken it herself. I sighed. I'd liked it, too, though I didn't fully understand why.

I was so tired and drained I hardly had time to think about it. The bus home was a blur, although some of her words continued to resonate, especially her desire to experience and be part of things, and her apparent fondness for the forbidden and the strange.

And, I thought with mixed feelings, her willingness to give up control to a man she barely knew. I shook my head. It didn't matter.

She was, I decided as I unlocked my apartment, staggered to my bed, undressed and collapsed, one spooky chick.

Tomorrow. Tomorrow I would see her again. And then we'd have some answers.

* * *

Morning wasn't promising. After two weeks of nice weather, November gray closed in again, shrouding everything in cold, misty fog.

I sat in silence as Damien drove and didn't even bother turning on the radio. We were both dressed for exploration, in jeans, heavy boots, sturdy shirts, and hooded coats. I held my digital camera lightly against my chest, and at my belt was a new can of bear mace. Even though this was supposed to be just a reconnaissance, I wasn't about to go unarmed.

The Northwest Industrial District was a colorless, joyless wilderness of train yards, offices, warehouses, oil tanks, and pumping stations sandwiched between the lush forested slopes of Forest Park and the brownish-green expanse of the Willamette River—the usual depressing facilities that help every city run, but never appear on tourist brochures.

Damien broke our silence. "I did more research into the Petroco building." He shifted with practiced ease. "They processed coal and turned it into natural gas. Back in the 1930s, people would actually come to the plant to inhale the *healing vapors* it produced."

I made a face. "Ugh. Are you serious?"

"Yeah. I guess they figured if something smelled bad it had to be good for you. Anyway the building housed the company's main offices. Would you believe that there was a rumor it was haunted?"

"No kidding." Beyond the warehouses and docks, a tug pushed a barge along the river, white foam trailing behind.

"People heard noises, lights went on and off, doors opened and closed. There was a basement where they had huge gas meters and a furnace—a maintenance man was found murdered there, stabbed. They never found out who did it and after that the maintenance staff refused to go down there alone."

I snorted. "Sounds like a job for the Ghost Stalkers." I suspected that Michael O'Regan was going to be in his element at Petroco—exploring an abandoned building and not finding anything. I didn't say as much to Damien, however. He seemed to have gotten on board the O'Regan train just like everyone else.

He continued. "A night watchman reported seeing goblins in the shadows, but they decided he was drunk. In 1938 a company vice president fell from the clock tower and was killed.

No one knew what he was doing up there. It went on and on. They finally closed the place in 1957 and never gave a reason. It's been locked up ever since."

"Great. So we'll be trespassing, then."

"You've committed that particular offense before, Alex. By this time it should be part of your journalistic nature."

I grunted. I wasn't really in the mood for humor.

Only the thought that I'd soon be seeing Trish had given me the resolve to get into the car when Damien showed up at my door. I still had mixed feelings about Michael and his friends, but when I thought of her I felt the stirring of emotions that I hadn't felt since Cheryl's passing.

The Saint Johns Bridge rose ahead of us. The irony of its name wasn't lost on me, though unlike me the locals pronounced it like it was spelled. It was a classic suspension model, with soaring green towers and graceful curved cables. The near end rose toward the sky, tall and proud, but the tops of the towers vanished into the fog, dim and indistinct, merging with the featureless gray above.

"There it is." Damien pointed to a maze of structures under the near span. In the middle was the dark edifice I'd seen on the satellite photo, an artifact from another century in the midst of modern oil tanks and facilities. "You ready for this?"

"No. But let's go anyway."

VI

The closest place to park was off the highway a half-mile from the building, against a concrete jersey barrier in the shelter of a rail embankment. It was cold and wet and I didn't feel like sitting silent in a car while we waited for the others to arrive. My mood grew sour, as unsettled as the sky above.

As fog slithered down from the hills and surrounded us, I passed the next half-hour wandering around Yngwie, kicking rocks, and watching cold water gush from an irrigation pipe that ran under the embankment. Damien stayed in the car, probably worrying about what the rain was doing to Yngwie's finish.

I felt a gulf growing between us, one brought on by the arrival of Michael O'Regan and his crew. I thought I had tried to be reasonable, giving O'Regan and his tales of demons and magic a fair hearing. I'd tried to think like Damien, avoiding letting my treasured rationality blind me to the obvious, but I still felt drowned out by a chorus of unreason, by people who wanted demons and evil spirits to be real, refusing to see how insane it all sounded. I was fearful that I'd lose Damien to them.

I studied the rush of cold water across dark rock. Was it possible that I was wrong? Was I just too terrified to accept a truth that was staring me in the face?

Not for the first time, I wished I could go back to living a boring and pointless but safe existence, in blissful ignorance of Pine Street Bob, Michael O'Regan, and his demons.

I was in a fine state when the others finally arrived, a half hour late. All six were crammed into Eric's battered blue van, and none of them looked terribly happy. Perhaps they were having second thoughts now that Michael had dragged them outside their comfort zones. At least in my present mood, that's what I hoped.

Ron looked glum until he caught sight of Yngwie and took the opportunity to give the vehicle a closer inspection.

"This is awesome," he exclaimed. "Can we get a ride sometime?"

Kay smiled indulgently. "Old cars. His secret passion."

Damien brightened slightly at that. "Sure. Ask nicely and I might let you drive."

Trish lit up when she saw me, flashing me a warm smile. Her hair was braided, and she wore a down coat over a utilitarian sweatshirt and jeans.

Eric must have noticed for he regarded me with ill-concealed contempt as he opened the van's back doors and pulled out a heavy duffel bag.

Vince moved slowly—he didn't look like a morning person—and hefted a blue backpack. I suspected that it contained, among other things, a six-pack or two of Zap Cola.

Michael was last, his bearing as regal and confident as ever, dressed in a wool jacket and sturdy hiking pants. He reached into the van and pulled out a titanium walking stick with a compass in the head.

"Hi Michael," I said. "I don't think you'll be needing the compass." I pointed down the railroad tracks toward where the Petroco Building rose, a dark shadow in the mist. "It's easy to find."

He grinned. "It never hurts to be prepared, Alex. So is everyone ready?"

Unenthusiastic nods and mumbled affirmations followed, and we set off beside the embankment, hiking past more tank farms and razor-topped cyclone fencing with Michael in the lead.

I trudged behind Trish, admiring the way her hips moved and feeling regretful that she'd chosen to wear baggy jeans. She cast a couple of backward knowing glances at me, her eyes a stormy complement to the unsettled sky.

We reached the fence and crouched behind it. A gravel lot packed with junk lay between us and the building.

The place was even more intimidating up close. Its stone walls were almost black with soot, streaked here and there with water and rust. An ancient fire escape climbed up the wall nearest to us. Shaggy green grew around the foundation, across the slate roof and from corroded gutters. Some of the plywood had fallen from the windows, revealing fragments of broken glass. The empty clock tower stared down at us like the eye sockets of an old skull.

Eric pulled out an entrenching tool from his duffel bag and began to dig gravel from under the fence.

"You sure you can actually get into this place, Eric?" Ron cleaned his glasses and looked nervously toward the front doors, which were secured with heavy chains and padlocks.

"I'm reasonably confident." Eric's voice had lost none of its superciliousness. He dug tirelessly for several minutes, hollowing out a space under the fence and pushed the bag through. "Now follow me."

My pants caught on the fence but I made it. The others came too and for a moment we stood, regarding the building and its barricade of junk. Two old transformers stood nearby, wreathed in the cold mist, and a pile of plastic pipes pointed the way toward the central edifice. The air smelled of rain, wet dirt, and rust.

"Come on, then. We've work to do." Michael strode confidently toward the building with the aid of his walking stick.

Damien looked worried now, but he trudged after Michael, his feet crunching in gravel and squelching in mud. Behind me I could hear Vince huffing and puffing as he struggled to keep up.

We threaded our way through the rusting labyrinth. It was like a battlefield strewn with broken, decaying machines. The ground was treacherous, littered with broken glass and nail-covered pieces of wood, but at length we made it to the rough stone wall several feet below a window covered with weathered, separating plywood.

Eric pointed toward a big wooden cable spool. "Ron, help me with this."

Damien and I pitched in too, though Eric pretended not to notice, while Vince stood nearby, catching his breath and knocking back a Zap. We rolled the spool under the window and Eric clambered onto it armed with a crowbar. After a few moments, the lower sheet of plywood was gone and Eric knocked the last few jagged shards of glass from the frame. I gave the man credit—in addition to artist, he was also the athlete of the group.

He placed his hands on the stone sill. "Someone else want to go first or shall I?"

Damien boosted Michael up, then me. Ignoring Eric, I climbed through the window, tumbled inside onto dirty concrete, then took Trish's hand and helped her through.

"Thanks," she said, giving me another warm smile.

I could get used to this, I thought.

Grunting and swearing under his breath, Eric had to practically stuff Vince through the window, then pushed his bag inside and followed.

We were in a large office area that had once been painted pale green. Now the plaster walls were disintegrating, revealing wooden slats beneath. Naked wires hung from the ceiling where fixtures had been torn out, the floor was littered with rubble, glass and fragments of broken furniture. A few ancient desks and chairs stood, covered in dust and broken plaster. A few still had rusted desk lamps. Outside was a hallway lost in gloom.

"Come on. No sense in delaying." Michael pointed to my camera. "Alex, get some pictures and we'll move on."

There wasn't a whole lot to photograph, but I took a few anyway, including a view out the window at the junk piled around the building, and a lone oil tank in the distance.

"Does it seem overly cold in here?" Damien slapped his hands together

"Yeah, it sure as hell does." My breath steamed. "You'd think it would be at least a little warmer indoors."

The hallway was clear, but almost totally dark. Eric pulled several Maglights from his bag and handed them out. Damien took one and Michael took another. Wanting to keep both hands free for the camera I pocketed mine.

There were several more rooms on the main floor, all in similar condition. Bathrooms with their fixtures removed. Walls streaked with water and rust. Closets full of moldering plaster and rusty metal. A small office with a desk covered in mud-caked ledger books. I took more pictures, but the entire expedition was starting to feel like a waste of time.

At the end of the hall a staircase led up. Eric flashed the light up the stairs, and I heard a sudden rattle and scuffling noise. Kay uttered a soft shriek.

"Raccoons? Possums?" Ron said. "Rats, maybe?"

"Who wants to go find out?" Vince asked. He was breathing slower now, but his face was sheened with sweat despite the cold.

The stench still curled in my nostrils, but that was the least of my concerns right now. I swallowed. My throat was dry. I suddenly wished that Loren and Beowulf were with us.

"Come on," I said. "Let's get this over with."

I was beginning to feel irritated with myself for jumping at shadows, but I remembered what had happened at the cement plant. Sometimes there were good reasons to be afraid of the dark.

I made as much noise as possible as I climbed the stairs in the light of Damien and Michael's torches. If anything lurked on the second floor it already knew we were here; I wanted it to know that I didn't care.

The stairs were broad and turned 180 degrees to emerge on the second floor. When we reached the top, the smell hit us—the same nauseating stench as the concrete plant, but combined with the odors of dampness, decay, and mold. I tried to hold my breath but choked and spat. Michael was having the same trouble, trying to breathe only through his mouth.

Vince made a face. "God damn," he gasped. "What died in here?"

"Maybe we should have brought gas masks," Ron said. He held Kay close, his arm around her shoulder. She looked nauseated and ready to bolt. I saw her glance over at Michael, who gave her a brief smile and a reassuring nod. She forced a smile in reply.

"Damnation." Damien's voice echoed in the huge room.

I forgot all about the smell as soon as I saw our surroundings.

We stood at the head of a long, wide high-ceilinged hallway that extended the length of the building. Grime-covered glass globes hung from the ceiling. At the opposite end was a pair of tall windows, gray light streaming through gaps in the plywood outside. On either side, doorways held sagging wooden doors or stood empty and dark.

"Oh my God," Kay whispered.

We could only see isolated pieces of the hallway, surrounded by gloom. But my mind arranged them together into a disturbing picture.

I'd seen it all before. The walls were covered in scrawled letters. Some were familiar, some strange, spelling out words I couldn't comprehend. Someone had cleared debris from the floor and sketched elaborate geometric patterns, with more of the crude letters. Piles of charcoal and burnt wood were carefully spaced out to create a circle, ten feet across.

"This is like nothing I've ever seen before," Michael muttered, crouching down to look at the symbols and patterns on the floor. "No ritual, no magical tradition. Nothing."

"Alex! Look." Damien shone his light at a wall.

There, smeared in mud or dirt or worse, was the image of a menacing figure covered with eyes and toothy mouths. The light darted upward and there, crudely scrawled across the pitted plaster...

ουγατοχη

"Onatochee," Michael whispered. "Alex, is that the same thing you saw at the cement plant?"

"Yeah."

"Onatochee." Damien's voice was faint and for the first time, he actually sounded frightened.

Damien moved the light. On the wall beside the Greek letters were the Linear B characters that Damien had translated, the word that Mia Jordan had whispered to me. *Nomeus.* Shepherd. Except these were defaced, covered with smears of dirt and charcoal, the plaster pitted and gouged until the letters were almost unrecognizable.

"What the hell does it mean?" Damien whispered.

The cult had set up shop in the spot that Michael had said was a place of power, the site of the old battle where the Multnomahs defeated the Chilut. There was a cold knot of fear in my stomach as my brain numbly tried to find some explanation—any explanation—for what we were seeing.

I heard a rattle from one of the nearby rooms and something fell to the floor. Everyone jumped at that. Damien shined his light into the room, revealing nothing but more junk.

"I'm not liking this, Michael," Ron said. Beside him Kay shuddered.

"Neither am I," Michael admitted. "There's a presence here. I can feel it." He started clearing a space on the floor. "Sit tight, everyone. I need those ritual items, Vincent. Alex, can you get some more pictures, please?"

I forced my screaming ape brain back into its cage. Later. Later I'd try to figure out what I really believed. For now I had to stay calm.

I pointed my camera at the graffiti, the cleared space on the floor, and the fearsome image on the wall. Gazing through the viewfinder, watching the flash light up the room, I felt as if I was entirely alone, suspended in this strange chamber, far from civilization and reason, sucked through a doorway and drifting in one of Damien's alternate realities. Fear plucked at me like a cold hand on my shoulder, my breath coming faster, my body almost anticipating the touch of something foul and alien.

Hidden among my dark thoughts were dim memories, rapidly growing stronger—of Cheryl's eyes, her hair and hands, the softness of her body, the touch of her lips. She'd promised me, told me with desperate sincerity that she would never hurt me again, never steal, never touch the foul chemicals that had wasted her body and soul. Maybe she'd known she was lying and had been ashamed. Maybe she didn't care. Maybe she meant it when she said it...

Something dark, like a fast-crawling shadow, seemed to pass between the viewfinder and the wall and I looked away from the camera. No, there was nothing there—only the trash and filth and graffiti.

"Do you feel that?" Vince's eyes were wild, darting every which way. "Like someone's staring right at the back of my head no matter which way I look."

Cold gooseflesh ran along my arms and up my spine. I felt it too—cold and slimy, writhing in my mind like a handful of worms...

God damn it. This was just like that fucking reality show that paid for Michael's groceries—a bunch of naive amateurs scaring each other in the dark.

"You're just freaking yourself out." I said it as much to reassure myself as Vince. "Stand your ground. Breathe slowly."

Vince shut his eyes tightly for a second, and when he opened them they were steadier.

Michael gestured impatiently. He held a piece of chalk in one hand. "Eric? Help me with the circle, please."

"Okay." Eric sounded weak and out of breath. He knelt on the dirty floor beside Michael and began drawing with the chalk.

I returned to the viewfinder, shooting the words on the walls.

The sense of dread was still there, despite my attempts to ignore it. I wanted to keep looking through the viewfinder, and not lower the camera for fear that Michael and the others would be gone, or worse yet, that they'd been replaced by some multi-eyed horror like the thing on the wall...

Something else prodded me, something from where my memories of Cheryl still lived. These thoughts had nothing to do with matters at hand, but they rose up inside me anyway. I remembered my anger at her and the dealer, Alan. I remembered the satisfaction I'd felt when I heard he'd been arrested. Then he'd gotten off with a slap on the wrist and my anger had returned, redoubled, driving me to find out where he was, and my savage joy when he'd been beaten and crippled...

Alex...

Icy fingers touched my arms and neck. Was it the same voice that had whispered to me before, urging me to unleash my pent-up anger on Maurice McMahon, to surrender to the hatred that I felt for a thoughtless, uncaring humanity? Or was it just my own mind playing tricks on me, freaked out by the strange place and the terrifying stories I'd heard?

With effort, I stopped taking pictures and lowered the camera. To my relief everyone was still there. Michael and Eric crouched on the floor, inscribing a complex circular pattern with chalk. Trish watched them with an excited and fascinated expression. Vince stood nervously, gulping another Zap. Kay and Ron stood holding hands a bit back from the others, but as Ron looked at Kay, she was focused on Michael. Damien was beside me, eyes darting around the room with increasing nervousness.

It's nothing, I told myself. You're freaking yourself out. Nothing is talking to you. Nothing talked to you at the cement plant. This is all stupid witch doctor crap that won't do shit.

Thoughts of Cheryl and Alan continued to churn and bubble, despite my best efforts to suppress them. Yes, there had been a sense of vindication—triumph, even—at what had happened to the bastard, at least initially. Regret, sadness, self-loathing, and with it loathing of the entire human species—those had all come later. But what if I'd never felt those things? What if that horrid elation had continued? Wouldn't I have wanted it again? Wasn't it just simple human weakness that made me feel regret?

"There," Michael said, standing and brushing himself off. "This should be sufficient for basic communication with any entities that are here. It can't physically summon anything so we won't be in any danger if it's broken."

Eric took one last look at his handiwork, then stood up beside Michael. The chalk pattern on the floor didn't look familiar. It consisted of two nested circles with an intricate pattern of lines and angles inside the inner one. In the band between the two circles was a string of characters that looked vaguely Hebrew. There was a lit blue candle in a holder at each of the four compass points.

Michael drew a deep breath. "Quiet, please," he said. "I'm going to begin the invocation."

He gazed down at the pattern on the floor and clenched his hands into fists, crossing them over his chest.

"Chochmah! Binah! Nezah! Malchut!" he said. "In the name of the archangels Uriel, Rafael, Gavriel, Mikhael, Nuriel I call forth what is hidden! By seventy-two names I adjure you, you all the retinues of evil spirits in the world—Be'ail Lachush and all your retinue; Kapkafuni the Queen of Demons and all your retinue; and Agrat bat Malkat and all your retinue, and Zmamit and all your retinue. I adjure you and call you forth, and bid you speak!"

The last echoes of Michael's voice faded into silence, and then there was no sound save the drip of water from outside. Seconds passed by and we stood without speaking.

After a minute or so, I began to wonder how long I should wait before calling bullshit.

Then it was back, speaking in my head in an angry but seductive whisper. It didn't speak in words, but in sensations—emotions, memories, primal thoughts that emanated from the deepest recesses of my mind where the simplest and most terrifying of impulses lay.

Rage. Vengeance. Exultation. Delight in suffering. Revelry. Joy.

With a rush of loathing, I remembered now. I had reveled in it. I had felt such utter, guiltless elation at Alan Coleman's downfall. Part of me still knew, beyond all doubt, that he richly deserved what had happened to him.

The thing that had awakened the memories now urged me to embrace them, to accept the thrill that I'd felt. Images of blood, murder, rape, and slaughter flashed in my mind like a sickening slideshow. And the whisper grew louder, now at last forming words, or something like them.

They'll fear you. You'll take what you want, free of conscience, free of guilt, free of the burden of self... Accept me... Join me... Love me...

Worship me...

On the nearby wall, the darkness around the picture of the multi-eyed thing seemed to gather and deepen. In the shadow it shifted and flickered, changing shape...

I felt the soft touch of fingers against my face and I jumped, heart racing.

Trish stood there, her eyes burning with the same strange passions I'd seen last night.

"Alex." It was a whisper but it reverberated inside me. "Alex, I want..."

A massive blow struck me from behind, and I fell in shock and confusion, red and yellow stars dancing in my head. I rolled and tried to rise, but then Eric fell on me, screaming, fists flailing. His face was flushed and spittle flew from his lips.

"You fucking bastard! I'll fucking kill you, you son of a bitch!"

His knees pinned me down and he beat at me wildly. His blows were driven by rage and not reason, but he was strong and struck me heavily, jarring my head first one way, then the other.

There was no subtlety to it, only mindless fury. I managed to pull one of my arms free. I reached for the mace canister at my belt but it was jammed tight against my body by Eric's leg. He hit me again. Sparks flashed, my head rang. I threw my arm up to shield my face, struggling to push him off.

I hated him. I hated the man who wanted to take my woman from me. He had attacked me because he knew I was better— stronger, smarter, a better lover. Eric hated everything that he couldn't be.

He would kill me if I didn't kill him first.

My own rage flared up, hot and bloody red in savage counterpart to Eric's. I struck out, driving my fist into Eric's face, feeling the harsh impact of bone on bone, but not caring. His lip was split open, blood ran from his nose, but I still didn't care. Through a fog of anger, I saw another face that was not Eric's.

Alan. His name was Alan, and I hated him.

Then, as suddenly as he'd come at me, Eric's weight was gone and I struggled to my feet, fumbling for my mace. Killing rage flared white-hot.

Then as swiftly as my anger had come, it fled, vanishing like fog in sunlight. I let my arms hang limply by my side.

What the hell had happened to me? For an instant I had forgotten who and what I was, caught up in a red, bloody rage that swept away my identity and my consciousness.

I didn't want to kill anyone. I wasn't a murderer or a bloodthirsty animal. I was human.

I was Alex.

Michael and Damien held the struggling Eric down on the ground. His shrieks began to subside, transforming into groans and finally sobs.

"God damn you." There were tears on his face, now mixed with blood from his split lip. "God damn you."

The strange urges that I'd felt, and the dark whispering in my head was gone. Exhaustion was setting in, along with bruises and a pounding headache.

The others seemed similarly affected. Vince sat, hugging himself and weeping softly. Kay and Ron embraced and whispered to each other. Trish's face was flushed as she looked from me to Eric and back again. Her eyes were wide and her breath was quickened, almost as if she were torn between confusion and excitement at what had just happened.

I looked down at the floor. One of the candles was upset and the chalk pattern was disrupted, as if someone had smeared it or dragged a foot across.

Eric had stopped fighting. "It's okay. It's okay. You can let me go." His voice was weak, tired, and almost broken. "You can let me go."

Michael and Damien stepped back. Eric remained sitting on the floor, his head in his hands.

I looked down. There was chalk on Damien's shoe.

"What the hell just happened, Michael?" I demanded.

"Something tried to contact us," Michael said. "You felt it, didn't you?"

I nodded. What had happened was too raw and fresh in my mind for me to try to rationalize or lie. My usual defense mechanisms were simply too exhausted to work.

"Something inside. It saw my memories, felt my anger. It... It was as if it was telling me that I..." I faltered. "I don't... It was like something was speaking to me from inside my mind, but it didn't use words."

"*El bestia dentro cabeza me,*" Damien said softly. "The beast in my head."

"Did it talk to you?"

Damien rubbed his eyes. "I don't know if *talk* is the right word. It was as if it sent me pictures, sensations, made... Promises, I guess. That I could act anyway I wanted. Stop taking my meds, stop trying to fight the bipolarism, just let the sickness guide me. Live free, unfettered, do what I pleased. Give up the pain of being human. I know it sounds crazy, but it all made a strange sort of sense. It seemed to be emanating from that chalk pattern on the floor. It took pretty much everything I had for me to knock the candle over and erase the circle with my foot."

Trish knelt beside Eric and spoke to him quietly. After a moment, he turned and embraced her, burying his face in her shoulder. She looked up at me and I saw she was crying too.

"Alex. Alex, I'm sorry."

I nodded. "It's okay. Really. We have to get out of here, Michael. Now."

Michael looked shaken and almost fearful. I wondered what had gone through his head.

His voice was unsteady, shorn of all its normal confidence. "Whatever we're dealing with, it's far more powerful than I suspected. You're right. We need to get out of this place and figure out what to do."

Slowly and painfully we rose and slogged down the stairs. I didn't look forward to clambering out the window, or the long trudge back to the cars.

We walked in stunned silence. Michael went first, followed by me and Damien. Behind us, Trish helped Eric as he shuffled along, head downcast. Ron and Kay came last, arms round each other's shoulders. He looked at her with concern, but she didn't meet his gaze, instead flickering glances at our surroundings, as if she was afraid that something lay in wait. The rain came down in a steady drizzle, but I didn't notice.

Rational thoughts had fled. Desperately I tried to bring them back, but I knew the truth then. I knew what had happened.

The impossible had become possible. We had just met Onatochee.

VII

Trish's nails dug painfully into my back as she bucked and writhed against me, coming to her third or fourth orgasm. My hair was tangled in her charms and wards but staring into the feverish depths of her violet eyes, I didn't care. Her breasts were pillowed against my chest, her legs twined around me.

She had sex with the raw enthusiasm of a lost soul in the desert who had suddenly found an oasis. For a brief moment I wondered whether I was different, or whether this was how she had sex with everyone—with Eric, with her former lovers, with her Wiccan or Asatru or Satanist boy- and girlfriends...

No, my sex-drugged subconscious screamed, it's you. Only you.

With a sudden surge of strength, Trish pushed back, rolling on top of me, long black hair joining the snarl of chains and talismans in a sweaty mass. She pinned me, rising up and plunging down, crying out with each stroke. There was a tone of both desire and need in her voice as she called out to me, demanding me to finish it.

When I finally came, I almost blacked out, feeling something deep inside breaking loose, a rush of sensation and emotion, like a broken dam flooding the green lands below it.

It must have gone on for quite some time, for it was several minutes later, as we lay in a naked, sweaty tangle, that I finally heard her speak.

"You really have been saving it up, haven't you?"

I was breathing heavily and barely managed to nod. "Be advised we'll have to do this a lot more before I've caught up."

She grinned. "Are you sure you're only twenty six? You go like a teenager."

I shrugged and remembered a line from a Woody Allen movie. "When I'm by myself, I practice."

"Silly." She kissed my nose. "Very silly man."

We lay that way for quite some time as the darkness deepened around us, not bothering to turn on a light or do anything other than soak in the warmth and comfort of each other's company.

It wasn't how I'd expected to end the day. After the debacle at the Petroco Building, we'd all gone our separate ways. Damien had dropped me at home and I'd stumbled into the shower then thrown myself on the couch, intent on sleeping the rest of the day. Trish had texted me around five o'clock informing me that she was on her way over and asking for my address.

After a long while, she finally broke the silence. "Why did you come with us to that place today? Really?"

I wasn't in the mood for a discussion. I also didn't want to admit my real reasons.

"Because Damien's my friend, and I wanted to watch out for him. We don't know Michael or his friends very well, and I thought... Well... I thought they might..."

"That we might be up to something sinister? That maybe we were going to lure him to the Petroco Building and sacrifice him to Baal or something?"

I snorted. "No. I just wanted to make sure he was okay." I hoped she would let it go at that. The last thing I wanted right now was an argument.

She persisted gently, stroking my chest. "Was that the only reason, Alex?"

I stared at the ceiling.

"No. No it wasn't."

"Well what was your other reason?"

I rolled on top of her, nuzzling her breast as I replied, my voice muffled by warm flesh.

"Because I wanted you. Because you're beautiful. Because you're the most beautiful woman I've ever met." I teased at her nipple with my tongue. "Because, I'm starting to want you even more right now."

"Flattery will get you everywhere." Her fingers teased at my thighs. "What did it say to you, Alex? What did it offer?"

Her questions took me aback for an instant. "You mean that damned voice in my head? Why are you asking now?"

"Because I want to know. And I didn't say you could stop."

My rational mind was wary, but my libido was slowly coming back. I returned to my business, keeping my eyes locked with hers as I did. Her gaze smoldered with curiosity and lust. My excitement rose, and I didn't especially care what she wanted to know.

"The same as Damien," I told her. Memories of the morning were coming back, whether I wanted them to or not. "It didn't really speak. It felt like memories and sensations that my mind put into words. I wanted to surrender to my anger and my hatred of humanity. Give in to violence and revenge without worrying about consequences. It was almost appealing for an instant. At least until your ex-boyfriend sucker punched me."

"Maybe it told him that he could have me again if he attacked you."

"Now there's a happy thought."

"Mmm." She sighed. "Lower, please."

I kissed my way down her stomach, toward her thighs.

"What did it say to you?" I asked between nibbles.

"It said... You're right. It just spoke in feelings, primitive thoughts—that I could have the knowledge and understanding that I've been looking for you. And that I could have you, and Eric, and Michael, and anyone else I wanted. That I could make you or anyone else want me more than anything else."

I kissed my way up one pale thigh. "Not possible. I already want you more than anything else."

"Oh, yes... Right there, Alex... Right there... I saw it. I felt it. I could have the power. Become part of it. See the real nature of the universe, see the truth." Her black hair spread across the pillow as she stared up with dreamy eyes, giving herself over to my touches. "Give myself to the truth. Surrender to it."

"Surrender?"

"Yesss... Like this. Like this. Oh, please don't stop..."

There were no more discussions of philosophy or our experiences at the Petroco Building. When we were done I expected her to gather up her clothes, kiss me, and slip away. Instead, she whispered in my ear.

"Is it okay if I spend the night?"

* * *

When classic rock awoke me the next morning it felt as if I hadn't slept at all. My face and arms were sore from my fight with Eric, my legs protested, my knees made noises I'd never heard before. I stumbled into the shower, and when Trish slipped in beside me I didn't have the wherewithal to do anything more than wash her back.

"Poor baby," she said, suds running down her hands as she rubbed shampoo into her hair. "I wore you out, huh?"

"Yeah," I mumbled. "You and Michael and Eric."

"All three of us? Hm," she said. "Sounds sexy."

I made a face.

"Sorry. I'll try to be more gentle next time. I can't promise anything, though."

The shower and breakfast resurrected me somewhat and I gratefully accepted a ride downtown in Trish's decade-old VW bug. Outside the Pioneer building I kissed her through the open driver's window. She grabbed my collar, holding me close and keeping the kiss going until horns began to honk. She threw me a last smoldering deep-blue gaze and then she was gone.

It was Monday, so the office was busy—so busy that I was able to slip unnoticed into my office. Unfortunately Loren had gotten there ahead of me.

He flashed a grin. "So who is she?"

He'd been more reserved since his fight with Pine Street Bob, and today he wore a plain gray t-shirt with no clever slogans. Still, the old Loren was irrepressible and seemed determined to come out again.

"Who is who?" I asked, throwing myself down in my chair and hoping that I could lock the door and catch a nap.

"Bite me, Casanova. The brunette in the VW. I saw you guys tonsil-jousting. What's her name and does she have a sister?"

I sighed, feeling my shoulders droop. "Patricia. Patricia Martin. Trish for short. Don't ever call her Patty."

There was a glint of Loren's impishness in his eyes. "Is she why you're looking like a zombie this morning?"

I grinned. "What's wrong, Loren? Jealous?"

"I think envious would be a better word. How'd you meet her?"

I looked away. Despite my growing affection for Trish I still felt like the outsider in Michael's group. After what had happened yesterday, I suspected that only O'Regan's force of personality would keep them together. And I felt as if Damien was falling under his spell as well. Where was it all going? A sense of sad realization came over me.

More than anything else, right now I needed a friend.

"Loren," I said, "close the door. We need to talk."

* * *

I did my best to bring Loren up to date. The past few days had been a whirlwind of events and I'd barely had time to slow down and comprehend them myself. By the time I finished telling him what had happened—avoiding as many details about Trish as I could—Loren looked stunned.

"So this Irish dude goes around the world exorcising demons and writing books about it?"

I nodded. "Sort of. He makes most of his money appearing on reality shows. It sounds completely crazy, doesn't it?"

"Yeah, well everything about this sounds crazy. You actually felt something at that old building? Telling you to go start something? That you could kill this Eric asshole and nothing would happen?" There was real concern in Loren's voice, and he leaned forward in his chair, staring at me intensely.

I closed my eyes, trying to make sense of it. I felt exhausted, both physically and mentally and simply didn't have the energy for my usual skeptical denial song-and-dance. "Eric's not an asshole. But that's not what I was thinking when it happened. I felt it. I felt it at the cement plant, too. Loren, it's scaring the hell out of me. I want to think it's just my imagination—just me being freaked out by Pine Street Bob and Michael O'Regan and all those articles I wrote, but that's getting harder and harder to do."

"You're thinking this shit is real?"

"God, Loren—I don't know. If I start really, really thinking that this Onatochee thing exists, then... God... Am I crazy? Am I losing my grip on reality?"

"You're not crazy, Alex. Well, you're kind of weird and annoying, but you're not crazy."

"Gee, thanks."

Loren's tone grew somber. "Look, Alex—you've been trying to be the sensible one ever since this all started. Remember it was my idea to go to that cement plant. I thought it sounded cool."

"Yeah, well I agreed to it. And you almost got killed for your trouble."

"So what?" Loren's brows furrowed. "You know, Alex, I never really gave a whole lot of thought about what I wanted out of my life. My folks, well, they're really supportive, no matter what. They say they don't care what I do as long as I'm happy."

"They sound cool."

"Yeah, they're great, really. But sometimes I wish they'd pushed just a little harder, made me do something more serious than party my way through college and take a crappy job in Hipsterville just to feed my video game habit." He sighed. "I thought that was what I wanted. Just slacking and relaxing, playing games, doing my job so I could blow my check every weekend."

His expression grew harder, more determined. Strangely, it reminded me of Beowulf. "Alex, I've been reading fantasy and SF since I was six. I watch cop shows and action movies. And then I just basically sit and do nothing."

I forced a smile. "Hey, it's good work if you can get it."

He shook his head. "No, Alex. I want more. You helped me see that. I watch those cop shows and I want to be the guy who breaks down the door and takes down the serial killer just in time to save the girl."

He paused. There was real emotion in his voice. "Hell, you gave me the chance to do that. We saved the girl. We caught the killer. We did it. Us. We got to be heroes, and maybe they didn't show our pictures on the news, but I don't care. I know what I can be now."

"Loren, I don't want you to end up hurt or dead. I feel like you're my responsibility."

Loren stood up and leaned over my desk. "You know what, Alex? I don't give a fuck. If I go down, it's gonna be for something important. Not for sitting on the couch slacking and playing games all day. I want my life to mean something." He blinked quickly, and his old expression returned. "So can I meet these assholes or what?"

* * *

Despite the day's good beginning, it turned out to be a real nightmare, punctuated by a computer crash and several hours of lost work. I shuffled along like a zombie, trying not to get too cranky, buying the office a couple of pizzas out of my own pocket to keep morale up, and finally sleepwalked to the elevator and onto the bus.

Outside the streets moved by in a sodium-lit blur. I resolved to contact Damien and Michael about Loren tomorrow—right now I was too tired to do more than shove something in the microwave and watch TV.

At nine o'clock the world outside was pitch-black and quiet. I was in the midst of my 547th viewing of *Iron Man II* on cable when I realized that I'd slept through Scarlett Johansson's first scene. It was obvious that I wasn't going to make it to the end. Grimly I turned the TV off and dragged myself into the bathroom to brush my teeth.

The bedroom was warm, dark, and welcoming. Pants, shirt, socks dropped off in my wake and I crawled under the comforter, determined to go to sleep thinking about Trish. I wanted to feel the same dreamy lethargy I'd experienced that night when I'd seen the fireflies, but instead sleep fell on me like a brick—sudden, dark, and very heavy.

I didn't dream, at least not immediately. It was an incalculable time later that something nagged at me—a light, distant and silvery like the moon behind a stand of trees, glowing and indistinct.

The bathroom light. I hadn't turned it off. Through the heavy blanket of darkness the light shone insistently, urging me to open my eyes, to crawl out of bed and extinguish it.

Then I heard a sound.

It was like a short, soft hiss. After a moment I heard it again. It came from nearby.

Somehow I managed to stay still, lying with my head on one arm, urging myself to wakefulness.

It was as if my eyelids had been glued shut. I forced one open, then the other. Disoriented at first, I made out the shapes of my room, blurred and indistinct in the light from the hall, shining faintly through the semi-closed door.

I heard the sound again—something softly pressing down on the carpet. Still not moving, I rolled my eyes, looking toward the sound.

The closet door was slowly sliding open.

A hand appeared on the door, gently pushing from inside. It was thin and pale with dirty broken nails like claws.

I was paralyzed—eight years old, huddled under the covers, staring at the closet door, afraid to close my eyes for fear of what I'd see when I opened them.

There was one difference. When I was a little boy my closet door had never, never actually opened, and never revealed the monsters that lurked inside. This time it was different.

Almost two feet of darkness now yawned open. The thing that emerged from the shadows was more skull than head—emaciated, mostly hairless with a hooked nose and eyes like dark pits in sunken sockets. In the gloom below it, I saw a pale, nearly naked body covered in scars and dark sores. I'd only seen him twice before, but there was no question who he was.

Uncle Creepy.

The realization broke my paralysis. In a heartbeat, I threw aside the covers and bounded off the bed, racing for the hallway. There was no thought of fighting—I'd seen what this creature's friends had done to other men and women, and now all I wanted to do was get away.

"Heeey! *Heeeeeey!*" It was an incoherent scream. My panicked lizard-brain desperately hoped that it was enough to alert the neighbors. If the walls were thin enough for me to hear them having sex, they should damn well be thin enough for them to hear me being murdered.

A wordless gurgle exploded from Uncle Creepy's throat. He launched himself out of the closet, intercepting me halfway to the door and hitting me like a runaway truck.

There was unbelievable strength in his wasted body. He bore me backwards and we crashed painfully into my nightstand. My water glass went flying and the clock-radio shattered into jagged pieces.

His face was only inches from mine, grinning like a rotting jack-o-lantern. He gnashed his remaining teeth, and inside his mouth I saw something writhing and squirming, something pale that wasn't a tongue.

"*Ichiloot. Wo'igunaba.*" His voice resonated, echoing through my head, as if it was speaking directly to my brain. "Be one. *Ichiloot.* Join with him..."

The nauseating otherness that had invaded my consciousness at Petroco was back—stronger now, more insistent, eating away at my mind like a nest of carnivorous insects, crawling and biting, digesting my consciousness, nibbling at my very self.

I could be like him. I could shed the burdens of my humanity and surrender to my basest, most animalistic urges. If I let those cold, slimy fingers dig into my brain and my soul they would strip me of my nagging conscious, tear away the troublesome fears that had festered in my heart all these years. If I gave in, I could be one of Onatochee's Claws, and bring the gift of action without consequence to the world. They would fear me and I would have power.

And the only price was something I hated already.

Myself.

Darkness rose, almost covering me, and for a moment I was in that desolate broken world from my dreams, empty and devoid of light or hope. Yet through a sea of inky gloom a single word echoed, ringing like a distant trumpet across a desolate plain of ruin.

Nomeus.

Uncle Creepy's grip grew weaker for an instant, and his frightening gaze turned into a mask of confusion.

The horrid tendrils of foreign intelligence drew back in pain as if burnt, slithering from the crevices of my psyche, fleeing back into the worm-eaten depths of Uncle Creepy's soul.

His expression hardened and his glare deepened into black hatred.

"Shepherd," he hissed, drool dripping from his thin lips. *"SHEPHERD!"*

It was the feral scream of a wild animal, and I saw that now in one hand he held a knife, its blade almost pristine, gleaming in the reflected light from the bathroom.

Instinct was in command now—if I'd thought about it I'd never have been able to grab his wrist in one hand and his neck in the other. I pushed back against his knife-hand, but he countered with more impossible strength, straining and pressing down.

His yellow teeth bared in a macabre grimace. The fell stink of his breath washed over me as he snapped and snarled, trying to bite my wrist. There was a mad inhumanity to him, a strange combination of morbidity and vitality, as if he were charged with an unearthly energy that redoubled his strength while wasting his body.

As panic and adrenaline raced through my limbs, it didn't occur to me to scream something coherent like "Help! I'm being attacked! Call the police!" Instead I kept yelling, swearing, screaming, making any kind of noise that would say that I was in trouble.

He struck at me with his free hand and the side of my face went numb. I felt the strength in my arm begin to waver, and the knife point crept closer.

Through clenched teeth, Uncle Creepy growled fierce, horribly familiar words.

"Ichiloot. Feel his claws..."

But as he gained advantage over me, Uncle Creepy's body shifted enough so that I was able to move my leg, twisting it underneath him, then kicking out with all my strength.

It wasn't enough to get him off me, but his grip loosened and with another surge of effort I tore myself loose, kicking his head so that it rebounded off the wall. Self-preservation was still in control and I dodged backwards as he slashed at me, running desperately for the door.

I plunged into darkness as yielding softness stopped me and I fell.

Jesus.

In my panic I'd run straight into the closet.

I turned around, trying to rise. I was tangled in clothing, shoes, boxes of junk. In the faint shadow of the bathroom light, Uncle Creepy rose and advanced, knife in hand.

"Onatochee. Ichiloot."

I fumbled for anything I could use as a weapon, blindly grabbing at sneakers, a cardboard box full of old CDs and computer games...

My hand fell on something—something solid and woody, and closed around it.

He was only a few feet away. He'd be on me in an instant.

"Feel his claws..."

With both hands, I seized the neck of my father's electric bass guitar, launching myself out of the closet, swinging the heavy body edge-on at Uncle Creepy's skull.

It struck him with bone-crushing impact, knocking him to the floor with an animal howl of pain and shock.

Self-preservation still drove my actions, but it was joined by a healthy dose of murderous anger. Now that my enemy was down, I wasn't going to just abandon the fight and flee like the victims in so many bad horror movies.

I raised the bass up again and brought it down on Uncle Creepy as he struggled to rise. He fell, limbs twitching.

Again. Blood splattered across the wall and the carpet, but I didn't care.

Kill him. Revel in it.

Again. Again. Again.

Remember the joy. Remember the savage exultation... Kill...

But as I raised the bloody instrument for another brutal blow, I felt a sudden cessation of my rage, just as I'd felt at Petroco after Eric attacked me. Murderous anger drained away into a river of silver-blue calm.

I held the bass over my head for a final blow, but as strength left my limbs I stumbled, letting it fall to the floor.

Nomeus.

I slumped against the wall, staring wide-eyed at what I'd done.

Uncle Creepy's head was caved in like a broken eggshell. His eyes were lifeless, staring up from hollow sockets. Something seemed to wriggle and squirm in the shadows, as if his skull had contained a nest of thread-thin worms. I blinked and the motion vanished, draining away with his lifeblood.

I was still slumped beside the corpse when the manager burst through the door, letting a phalanx of police into my apartment.

* * *

"There's no sign of forced entry," Detective Maitland said as I sat on my cheap futon couch, trying to force down a cup of coffee despite roiling nausea. "It looks as if he'd been in your closet for hours, waiting for you to go to bed."

I grunted. "How the hell did he get in, then?"

"We don't know. We're talking to your manager about improving security. I saw your bedroom window was unlatched. Is it possible you left it that way?"

"Hell, I don't know." I rubbed my eyes. In addition to everything else, I had a headache coming on. "I might have left it open last summer and never bothered to latch it closed."

"Well if he did that, he must have removed the screen and then put it back after he was inside." Maitland glanced over at the gurney where Uncle Creepy's remains lay, covered in a green sheet. "He didn't look like he was all that thoughtful a guy."

"He was thoughtful enough to get even for his friends at the cement plant," I said. "Do you have any idea who he is? I mean was?"

Maitland shook his head. "None whatsoever. We'll find out now, thanks to you. I'm sorry you had to go through all of this. Right now we're pretty sure he's the last of the I-84 cult."

My shoulders slumped. I wanted to believe him, but right now I wasn't so sure.

"Detective Maitland." I spoke quietly. "I think you'd better check out the old Petroco Building out on Highway 30. I think that they were camping out there, too. And I think there might be more than just three of them."

Maitland's eyes narrowed. "Petroco? What were you doing in that place?"

I stared at the floor as I spoke. "I was working on a story about the cult. I heard a rumor Pine Street Bob hung out at Petroco, so I went there." I shrugged. "There's cult graffiti all over the place. More weird stuff like at the cement plant."

I returned my gaze to Maitland. He looked at me appraisingly.

"You went there? When?"

"Yesterday morning." My words sounded as glum and helpless as I felt.

"Alone?"

"Yeah," I said. "I just wanted to get more information for my story."

"Who told you he was there, anyway?"

I shook my head. I suspected that Damien hadn't obtained all of his information about Robert Leslie legitimately. "Sorry, detective. Confidential. No one connected with the cult. I'll take full responsibility, but I'm not going to rat out my sources."

I also wasn't about to get Damien and Michael and the others in trouble. I certainly wasn't about to tell Maitland that I'd gone to Petroco with a bunch of strangers so we could talk to evil spirits.

Maitland gave me a stern look. "That was really stupid, you know that?"

"Yeah, I know."

"You could have gotten yourself killed, and we wouldn't have found you for weeks."

"I've been telling myself that ever since I got back. I was going to report it. I just wanted to get my story done first."

Maitland looked at me like a grade school teacher deciding how to punish a student.

"Okay," he said. "I'll let it slide this time. We'll go check out the Petroco Building and see if we can find anything. And we'll keep an eye out for more of Bob Leslie's friends, okay?"

I nodded. "Okay."

"And thanks for the information."

"Great." I slumped back. "You're welcome. Just..." I paused. "Just keep my name out of the news, okay? I don't want to talk to anyone about this."

"I hear you." Maitland stood, extending his hand. "If you happen to remember anything else, you have my number."

My arm felt limp and boneless as cooked pasta as I shook his hand. "No problem."

The gurney and its gruesome inhabitant vanished out the door, toward the waiting meat wagon.

"Do you have a place to stay? Friends? Family?"

I nodded. "Yeah. I've got a friend coming over."

As if on cue, Loren and Beowulf appeared in the doorway. Beowulf was nervous and excited by all the people, and no doubt the smells of blood and violence so Loren held him tight on a leash.

At the sight of them something shifted inside me—a tension in my chest finally let go and I felt a tidal wave of emotions that I couldn't clearly identify. When I saw that Loren was wearing a Sunnydale High Razorbacks sweatshirt, I almost wept.

"Loren, I..." I faltered, then without hesitation I threw my arms around him, feeling tears begin to flow. "God."

Though he was a bit surprised for an instant, Loren did his best to deal with it.

"Jesus, Alex. It's over. You're gonna be okay."

More than anything else I wanted the wall I'd built between me and the rest of the world to be gone. For the first time in years I wanted contact, I wanted people.

The police were real, they were human, and they at least gave the appearance of caring. But Loren, and even Beowulf, who seemed to catch on to my mood and looked at me with deep concern, were more than just humans. They were something I needed more than anything. They were real friends.

* * *

I was calmer now that Loren was there and the cops were busy packing up. I desperately wanted to call Trish and tell her what had happened, but something kept me from doing it. Maybe I was afraid I'd break down when I called, and I wasn't ready to be that vulnerable around her. Maybe it was something else.

Loren looked at the bass lying on the bed. One end was covered in congealing blood. Maitland had offered to have it cleaned but I told him I'd take care of it. It would need a hell of a lot more than a simple cleaning to work right and at this point I didn't want to let it out of my sight.

"Wow, man—an Ernie Ball Stingray?"

I looked at him wearily. "Yeah. Vintage 1972. It was my dad's. When he was in his twenties, he wanted to be a prog-rocker. Big Yes fan."

I'd played it with a band myself at U of O. Then, like everything else from those days, I'd put it in a closet and forgotten about it.

"That's so cool. Good thing it's a neck-through or you'd have broken it when you hit the guy."

I managed to force out an appreciative chuckle. "Yeah, that was my first thought when I grabbed it."

"I've got a nice fake Strat myself. We should jam some time."

I sat down on the edge of the bed. "You know what, Loren? You have got to be the most resilient person I've ever met."

"Wow, man. Thanks." He grinned. I reminded myself of what he'd done at the Western Pride site.

He drove me back to his apartment, and for the next twelve hours I slept on his couch. Beowulf thought I needed company and lay almost on top of me, but I didn't mind.

To my relief, I didn't dream.

VIII

Damien and Michael reacted in very different ways when I told them about my encounter with Uncle Creepy. While Damien listened in wide-eyed, mounting horror, Michael's expression remained frozen in a concerned, but not overly emotional grimace. If his tales of past horrors and demonic confrontation were true, then this was probably par for the course.

"Jesus, Alex." Damien looked me up and down, scanning me for signs of the fight beyond my bandaged head and knuckles. "I... I'm so sorry."

I nodded. "Thanks."

Michael's comments were predictably reserved. "You're very lucky, Alex. I'm glad you're still alive and well enough to tell us about it."

We sat in Damien's living room with our various favored beverages. It seemed awfully early in the morning for Michael to be drinking beer, but I let it slide. I hadn't told them that I'd thrown up most of my breakfast on the way over from Loren's apartment. The bus driver had been royally pissed.

My stomach was still queasy, but I swallowed a mouthful of coffee nevertheless. It tasted bad. Damien was on a downswing.

"Have the police told you anything?" Michael asked. "Have they at least figured out who this bastard was?"

"Nothing yet," I replied. The attack had been all over the morning news, but once more I'd managed to stay relatively anonymous, identified only as an a victim "whose name has been withheld."

"Maitland said he'd contact me once they had information," I continued. "So far Uncle Creepy's a blank—no name, no identity, no family. Nothing."

"Just Onatochee and the other cultists," Michael muttered. "They were his identity, his family."

I put down my coffee and cleared my throat. With a willful effort I kept the tremor out of my voice. "I told Maitland about the Petroco Building."

A look of alarm flashed across my companions' faces, but I raised a hand. "Don't worry—I didn't mention you. I said I did it all by my lonesome. He said they're going to go check the place out and see if there's evidence anyone else is involved in the cult."

"Of course there are others," Michael said grimly. "As long as the entity is allowed to influence weak minds, he'll have followers."

I looked away, steeling myself for what I was about to say.

I chose my words carefully. "Look, I acknowledge that all of the hypotheses you—we— have come up with seem to be proving true. There really is a cult, they kill people in the name of some kind of ancient horror, and they have a lair right where you suggested it would be. I'd be a fool if I ignored evidence that's staring me in the face."

Michael nodded. "I have a suspicion that your next word is going to be *but*."

"Yeah. It is. But after having one of those cultists show up in my bedroom with a knife, I don't think I have to tell you that I'm scared to death."

"That's not only understandable, it's sensible," Michael agreed. "I've been in the same situation myself, many times." He seemed more blasé than concerned.

I forged on. "Maybe we really felt the influence of a demon on Sunday. Maybe we all just got completely freaked out and lost it. That doesn't matter to me. What matters is that there really is a bunch of sociopathic weirdoes out there and one of them tried to kill me. If, as you say, there are more of them—and I have no reason to doubt that—then they're likely to try and kill me too." I paused, looking as steadily as I could manage into Michael's eyes, then Damien's. "And they'll be after you and everyone else who was at Petroco."

It was what I'd feared, and what I'd warned them about, but I resisted the urge to say "I told you so." Michael's stoic countenance didn't waver, but Damien looked suddenly alarmed, his eyes darting left and right as if looking for cultists in the shadows of his living room.

"My God, Alex," he said. "You're right."

I felt a moment of relief. I'd actually gotten through to him. "I think we need to lie low for a while. We can keep writing, keep researching, but we should keep in touch, not go anywhere alone, and for God's sake stay out of spooky buildings for a while."

Damien nodded so hard that I was afraid he'd slip a disc. His words were almost frantic. "Yes. Yes, that's definitely a good idea, Alex. We'll just work here, do our electronic research as usual. I've got a security system but I never used it. I'll have it turned back on. Yes. I think that's a very good idea."

Thank God. "We'll need to tell the others, too."

Kay and Ron could keep an eye on each other, but I didn't know whether Vince and Eric had anyone. They'd all need to know. Eric wasn't my favorite person at that moment, but I wasn't angry enough to commit him to the cult's tender mercies.

As for Trish, I'd called her at the book store and asked her to meet up with me after work. She'd be safe today, surrounded by customers and coworkers, and I didn't want to alarm her. I'd give her the whole story later.

Michael observed our exchange quietly, his fingers steepled in front of his face.

"I agree that we need to be cautious," he said. "Safety is our prime concern right now. We'll keep a low profile, at least until we perform the banishment."

I stopped dead, as if Michael had just thrown cold water in my face.

"Banishment?" The word sounded alien on my tongue, as if I'd never spoken it before. "You're still planning on that? After everything that's happened?"

Michael spoke with his usual air or erudite confidence. "Even more so now, Alex. We know from the legend that Onatochee can control the actions of weak-minded people. No matter how many cultists are killed or arrested, there will always be more.

We also now know that the Petroco Building is a place of power where he can be summoned."

My mouth was dry and the nausea was back. Damien's awful coffee swam unpleasantly in my gut.

"So you're planning to go back to Petroco and give Onatochee the finger again?"

I felt uncomfortable, as if saying Onatochee's name gave him power, kindling in my mind the tiny spark of belief that said he was real. I hadn't told them about the compulsion that I'd felt when Uncle Creepy attacked—the horrifying possibility that he'd been trying to recruit me, to make me into one of Onatochee's Claws, and to kill me if I refused. Nor had I said anything about the word that Uncle Creepy had shrieked after I'd resisted.

Shepherd.

Why wasn't I telling them? Maybe it was because I simply didn't want to believe any of it myself. Or perhaps I didn't really trust either of them with the information.

Michael nodded. Now his manner was patriarchal, almost authoritarian. "I intend to follow through with my original plan—return to Petroco on *Hecate Trivia,* the Feast of the Crossroads, there to summon the entity and perform a ritual that will return him to his place of origin."

It took several moments for me to find my voice.

"Are you serious? Michael, I don't know what to..." Words failed again. "I... I think that's a very bad idea. The police are there now, and God only knows... Michael, we'd be trespassing again. We might be walking into the middle of a crowd of cultists. For God's sake, we might be violating a crime scene. Just think about what you're saying."

"I assure you that I have, Alex." The authoritarian voice was stronger, but it was wrapped in Michael's comforting, fatherly tone. "*Hecate Trivia* isn't for another week. I'm sure the police will be finished with their work by then. They're probably doing us a service in any event—it's unlikely the cultists will return if the police know about their lair. In any event, we can take precautions—bring mace, tasers, other defensive weapons, just as you did at the cement plant. That should keep us all safe. If we succeed, then it will be well worth the risk."

His voice was so calm, so reassuring that I felt trapped in a cage of words. It was clear to me that Michael intended to go ahead with his risky scheme whether I agreed or not.

"Michael, I'd have thought that you of all people would see how insanely dangerous this all sounds," I said. "Even assuming that Onatochee is real—and by God I'm not ready to do that yet—we don't even understand what it really *is*. Something like this happened to you before. Remember your story about Scotland? Remember Bryce, and David? Remember Moira, Michael? Remember going in with your eyes closed, not understanding what you were truly facing?"

He looked away and spoke in a quiet monotone. "That was different, Alex."

"Different? Different how, Michael?"

I felt bad for dredging up tragedies from his past, but I pressed on anyway. He was talking madness, and I had to convince him.

"For one, there are more of us," he replied. He raised his head, fixing me with a misty-eyed gaze. "For another, we have more experience. We know what to expect. And we'll be better prepared."

I turned a beseeching look on Damien.

"You can't be considering this, can you?" I asked.

Confusion flickered in Damien's eyes as he looked desperately, first at me then at Michael.

"Alex, I don't..."

Michael cut him off. "Damien, we need you. We need your assistance, and we need you at the ritual. I'm in total agreement with Alex regarding security and caution—Onatochee's followers will be everywhere. It's imperative that we stick together and never give them the chance to attack us as they attacked Alex. But this ritual—"

I felt anger smoldering alongside fear. "What is this ritual going to accomplish, Michael? How is it going to change anything? I suspect these cultists won't be terribly thrilled if you do end up banishing their god. Or even if they think you did. We'll be in even greater danger than before."

"No." Michael's denial brooked no argument. "I'm completely certain of that. Once their connection to their demonic god is cut off they'll be lost, bereft. The cult will collapse into chaos and the world will be forever free of a monstrous evil."

I threw up my hands in frustration. "Do you know that, Michael? You only even learned about the cult a few days ago. How can you be an expert in what they will or won't do?"

"I've seen it before, Alex. I've quite a bit of experience in these matters. I assure you, it's typical behavior for a cult of this nature. Most of them are so deeply disturbed that they'll barely be able to remember their association with Onatochee. They certainly won't be able to engage in any more coordinated behavior."

I fell silent. It was like arguing with a brick wall. There was a hint of unreason in Michael, an irrationality and stubbornness that I hadn't seen before. Something burned behind his eyes that I didn't fully understand. There were pieces missing from his puzzle, and until I found them I'd never be able to reason with him.

"Damien," I said, "please don't do this. I've seen what these bastards can do to people. You're my friend, Damien. I can't let you do this."

Damien's gaze wavered, then grew steady. "Alex, I know you're worried about me. And about the others, too. But Michael's right—we can take precautions. We can check the place out and make sure it's safe before we do anything. And if Michael is right—if—then we'll have done what no one else could have done. We'll have gotten rid of this monster. And we'll have proof. Proof that the universe works the way we say it does."

Unspoken, but clear as crystal, were the words, *and proof that I'm not crazy.*

The place where my head had hit the wall throbbed and my hand ached. I couldn't hide my nausea.

"You're willing to risk your life for that kind of proof, Damien?" My voice felt small and weak compared to Michael's rich baritone.

Damien nodded after the briefest of hesitations. "Yes. Yes, I'm willing. I understand if you don't want to. But I need to. I need to know, Alex."

He spoke with a new recklessness, as strange to me as Michael's declarations.

I slumped forward, my head in my hands. My choice was bleak but inevitable. I couldn't leave Damien to face what I'd faced.

"Okay," I said. "I'll help."

"God, Alex." Damien sounded almost sorrowful, as if he realized that he'd put me into a corner. "God, thank you. I'm sorry if I..."

"Thank you, Alex." Michael's rich, reassuring tone had returned. "I know it was difficult—

I've had to make many such decisions myself. But I think you'll find it was the right one."

I raised my head. The room swam and I felt terribly tired.

"If I do this, we need to take precautions just as you suggested, Michael." I paused. "We'll need to get weapons—anything else we can come up with to defend ourselves. And I was going to talk to you about including Loren Hodges, too. He's told me that he wants to help and I want him there with us if anything goes wrong."

Damien frowned. "How much does he know, Alex?"

"Everything," I said. "I told him everything. All about the cult, all about Onatochee. Everything."

"What?" Damien's face fell.

I felt too weary to be polite. "Don't give me that look, Damien. You brought in Michael without asking me, now I'm doing the same thing."

Damien looked down, chastened. I felt as if I'd just kicked a puppy.

Michael was far more enthusiastic. "Loren sounds like an excellent addition to the group, Alex. I was going to suggest him myself if you hadn't."

Yeah, right. I didn't want to talk anymore.

"Okay, I think we're done now." My tongue felt thick, my words slow and leaden. "And I need to get to work at least for a few hours."

I wasn't going to tell Terri about Uncle Creepy, but rely on her usual indulgence when I came staggering in two hours late looking like death warmed over. In her heart I suspected that Terri was just as much of a slacker as me and Loren, and I was grateful.

Damien stood with an eager expression. "Need a ride?"

I shook my head. "No, I'll be okay. I'll take the bus."

He looked hurt at that and I felt bad again.

I rode the bus downtown with the window open, letting cold, fresh air wash over my face, watching storms of yellow leaves swirl and dance in the wind.

Most of the nausea was gone by the time I got to the Pioneer Building. Terri only gave me a disapproving stare and assumed that I was hung over. I let it pass.

* * *

Trish's eyes went wide with fear and shock as I told her what had happened.

"Oh my God, Alex. I saw the story on the news but I had no idea it was you. Why didn't you call me when it happened?"

"I didn't want to freak you out in the middle of the night," I said. It was at least partially true. "I'm okay, really. It's going to be okay."

At the thought of last night and my memory of Uncle Creepy emerging from my closet I felt a renewed sense of fear. My apartment was going to be a mess for days, and I still desperately wanted to be close to another human being. Loren was a good friend, but he couldn't provide what Trish did.

"Oh thank God. Thank God." She repeated the words again and again, shaking her head slowly as she sat at her little dining table, nursing a cup of herbal tea.

I explained my worries about the cult and suggested that I stay with her until my apartment was repaired. Unspoken was my hope that she'd then consent to move in with me.

I didn't mention Michael's plans for *Hecate Trivia*. She'd hear about it soon enough. I wanted no more distractions tonight.

"Let me take you out to dinner," I said. "Anywhere. Then you can take me home and have your wicked way with me."

Her smile seemed forced and artificial. "Now that's what I like to hear. I've been thinking about you constantly ever since you left the last time."

"Well think no more," I said, standing up and putting on my coat. I spoke with a confidence that I didn't feel. "I'm here to stay. You can count on that."

"Oh, thank God, Alex," she repeated. "Thank God."

She was quiet through dinner, but when we returned she fell on me with more than her usual passion, straining her bedframe and probably annoying the hell out of her neighbors. As we slipped away into exhausted sleep, she whispered softly in my ear.

"I think I'm falling for you, Alex."

* * *

Uncle Creepy was at least temporarily banished from my mind. My thoughts the next morning were of nothing and no one but Trish and what kind of life we might have once we had rid the world of Onatochee.

Maybe, I thought, Michael was right and the cult would fall apart. Maybe, I reminded myself, there was no cult at all—only our three disturbed killers. In any event, once we'd finished, Michael's work would be done and he would return to Ireland or LA or wherever he came from. More than anything else, I just wanted it to be over once and for all.

They were pleasant enough thoughts, but Terri managed to put them to a stop when she walked into my office with a copy of the *Oregonian*.

"Alex—have you seen this?"

My eyes widened as I read the headline, *I-84 Suspect Found Dead*.

"God damn." I had to read the story twice before it finally sunk in. County officials had announced that Robert Leslie, aka Pine Street Bob, chief suspect in the I-84 murder cult case, had been found dead in his cell. There were no signs of violence, and the cause of death wasn't immediately evident, but the county coroner promised a thorough investigation.

"Looks like the bastard is never going to trial, huh?" Terri lit a cigarette and fumed.

I continued to look at the paper after Terri left, shutting my door behind her. This should have been the end of it—Pine Street Bob, Maurice McMahon, and the unidentified Uncle Creepy were all dead. The I-84 case was closed for good.

But I couldn't bring myself to believe it. Images of what we'd seen at Petroco, and of the sly, echoing voice in my head persisted.

Worship me.

No. Though I desperately wished it, a lurking unease in my chest told me that it was far from over, and that it wouldn't truly be done with until after *Hecate Trivia.*

* * *

Thanksgiving came and went. I cooked a turkey for the first time in years and invited Damien, Michael, Trish, Loren, and Beowulf over to my newly-rechristened apartment. Michael was his usual charming self, Damien and Loren bonded over their favorite Linux builds, Trish flirted with everyone, and Beowulf sat patiently under the table waiting for pieces of turkey to fall. Trish stayed over again, but we just slept in a dreamless food coma.

After a good start, the holiday weekend began to drag by. I wanted nothing more than for Tuesday to come, and for Michael's ritual to be over. Trish went home, telling me that she needed a few days to prepare for the ritual, leaving me alone.

The rain returned on Sunday and time became a soft gray blur. Trish still hadn't contacted me, and I returned to work the next morning in a state of wordless shock, going through the motions like a robot. I was afraid for her, but I couldn't bring myself to call, fearful of what I might learn.

At lunch I wandered downtown, past bookstores and antique shops, eighteen-and-over strip joints, coffee houses and boutiques. I was cold, but I didn't think to bundle up. Everything seemed to hang suspended, waiting. Waiting.

It had started raining when I walked into Liberty Bell Firearms, a crowded shop squeezed between a camera store and a no-alcohol strip joint. They were advertisers with the *Ranger*, and I'd met the owner Seth a couple of times. He was decent enough for a Second Amendment freak, and he gladly provided me with the weapon I asked for—a compact Glock 19 automatic pistol, two boxes of 9mm parabellum ammunition, and two extra 15-round clips.

I was familiar with the weapon—I'd learned to shoot with my father in Wisconsin, years ago. Some wordless urge drove me to empty most of my checking account on an automatic pistol. I didn't know why, but I was still not fighting it.

Trish called me as I was returning to the office.

"Come over for dinner tonight," she said. "I need you." Then she hung up.

It was a demand, to be sure. But it was one that I needed to hear.

IX

Trish's table was set with linen and candles that provided the only illumination in the room. Incense sent up thin trails of fragrant smoke. Low music played on her stereo.

Dressed in a black satin robe, she ushered me into her apartment, bidding me to be silent as she sat me at the table. Saying nothing, I let her serve me, bringing out food and wine and sitting, gazing raptly at me as I ate it. Only after I finished did she eat, still not speaking.

"That was great," I said, putting down my wine glass as she whisked away the dishes. "What's—"

Trish pressed a finger against my lips. She stepped back and gestured, indicating that she wanted me to turn my chair to face her. I complied, curiosity and excitement growing.

She stood in front of me for a moment, our gazes locked. Then she undid the belt of her robe and let it slip silently to the floor. She was naked save for her ever-present charms and talismans.

I could only stare. Her body still enticed me, her deep violet gaze still held me spellbound. I'd seen her this way before, but now she seemed different—softer, warmer, more vulnerable, a carved goddess figurine crafted of flawless flesh.

She reached to an end table and picked something up then handed it to me. I accepted, staring, my heart suddenly pounding.

It was a pair of handcuffs.

Slowly and deliberately, Trish reached to her neck and removed her talismans, lifting them in a single mass, dangling and clicking, and placed them on the end table.

She was completely naked for the first time since I'd met her. She knelt and held her hands out, wrists together.

"Take me." Her voice was soft and supple. "Make me serve you. Please."

As I looked into her eyes, seeing them gleam in the candlelight, wide and beseeching, every one of my senses seemed to sharpen. The scent of incense was like potent perfume, the sensation of warm air from the duct above caressed my skin, the sound of Trish's excited breathing was loud in my ears.

Almost of their own accord, my hands moved, opening the cuffs, placing one on her left wrist. Then I walked behind her, softly taking her right, and placing them together behind her back, snapping the ratchet shut with a metallic sound that seemed inappropriately loud.

"Whatever you ask, I'll do." Her words hung in the air like incense smoke. "What do you want of me?"

My mind raced, thoughts flashing then disappearing in quick succession. Something whispered to me, telling me to take her, to do with her what I wished. *She wants it,* the voice said. *She's giving herself to you.*

Was it my voice, or someone else's?

I couldn't help but think of Onatochee, and what I'd felt that day at the Petroco Building. Here someone was telling me to do what I wished, be in complete control. How was it different from that strange demonic voice that nagged inside my head, "Worship me"?

Though Trish spoke in a soft, almost inaudible whisper, her words rang in my head like bells. "You tell me.."

She was mine, to do with as I pleased. She wanted it, the secret, hidden voice inside me urged.

Yet that wasn't all. There was another voice, the one that had called upon me to doubt, to think, to resist. Yes, I wanted her. Yes, she wanted me. But what else did she want? Was this how she'd been with Michael O'Regan?

Was she really giving herself to me, body and spirit?

The deeper voice, the rational voice... It told me that she was not. That there was something strange about her desire, something that didn't make sense. But that voice wasn't the loudest or most insistent. The other one was—the one that had taken her that first night, the one that had held her wrists and made her beg.

Was it what she wanted, or what I wanted?

And if it was what she wanted, how could I be the one in control?

I leaned down and placed my hand on her cuffed wrists. I felt detached, as if I was watching someone else, hovering overhead, unable to intervene.

Did I want to do this? I didn't know. All I knew was that she wanted it. And I wanted to please her more than anything.

I helped her rise. What should I say?

"Walk to the bedroom. Now."

One hand on her shoulder, the other on her wrists, I guided her through the shadows and into her bedroom. There were candles there too, glowing yellow in glass cylinders.

"Kneel."

Without a word, she complied.

"Lean forward."

Trish leaned over the edge of the bed, breasts bulging, her buttocks pale in the candlelight. I stroked them with one hand, feeling the soft warmth of her skin. Part of me wanted to take off her handcuffs, kiss her passionately, and take her there on the bed, but somehow I knew that she wanted more than that.

I drew my hand back and brought it down on her buttock, the sound loud in the stillness of the room. She gasped and writhed. I drew back and brought my hand down again. And again. A moan escaped her lips, a moan that spoke of desire deeper than I could comprehend.

I felt it. I felt her excitement, the desire to let go, to allow another to take her, to do with her what he wished. I felt the exultation of utter submission and freedom from choice and regret.

I understood what she wanted.

She wanted to surrender the need to decide, the crushing responsibility of existence. She wanted to follow, to let another lead her along the narrow path, through submission to enlightenment.

Still, there was something wrong, something that did not make sense. I'd never taken philosophy or religion classes in school—I'd shunned such things, thinking them silly and antiquated. Yet I knew there were deeper truths, and I knew them implicitly.

How did I know? Was something greater speaking to me? Did wisdom seep through the rifts as well as horror?

Silver-blue light, wings, and a single word...

Nomeus.

I didn't fear the word. I didn't fear the light. Somehow they were related, and I didn't yet understand how.

I looked down at Trish—naked, helpless, desiring only my touch and my command. But of the two of us, which one was truly submitting?

Or did we both submit to the inevitable? Were we both puppets on strings of fate, bound to each other by inexorable forces we didn't understand?

I felt a distant fear for the future, for how she truly saw me, what she truly wanted. It was there, glowing like the check engine light on a car's dashboard. And like the check engine light, I ignored it.

I stroked the red flesh of her buttocks and the back of her thighs. "You want this?"

"Whatever you want."

"Tell me you want it."

"I want it." It was more than a listless, obedient reply to my question. It was the truth. "Please. Please."

I brought my hand down again. She stiffened, and another cry of pleasure and pain issued from Trish's throat. Again and again. Her white flesh was angry red, she shuddered and bucked, and I held her down with one hand as I stroked with the other.

Trish's cries rose with each stroke. I'd heard them before— she was falling, slipping, and sliding closer to orgasm. When she finally came, she screamed loudly, drawn out and almost agonized.

I don't know how long it went on, with Trish helpless and shackled, passionately responding to my every touch, however gentle, however firm. She seemed to have a limitless capacity for it, and everything I did only seemed to excite her more. This time I didn't even bother to wonder what the neighbors thought.

It's what she wants. The script kept running in my mind, insistent and persuasive. *She wants you to do this. She wants you.*

But again the nagging thought penetrated my haze of excitement—is it what I want? I kept on. I undid my belt and folded it in half, bringing it down on reddened flesh, and she cried even louder. Never once did she ask me to stop.

I kept on doggedly. Part of my mind looked with alarm at the red weals and bruises that I was raising.

Do I want this?

A part of me did. But a part of me didn't. And I didn't know which one to trust.

Trish had come at least a half-dozen times when her cries of passion and submission finally transformed into pleas.

"Please. Please do it now." She looked back at me. Her face was wet with tears, leaving black streaks down her cheeks. "I know I can't ask you, I know it's wrong, but please, please..."

I'd been holding off for a long time so it was almost a relief to finally take her. I was painfully erect. After fumbling, all-thumbs, out of my clothes I donned a condom and slid into her without hesitation. She seemed to melt and in a few moments she was again climaxing, crying out and pressing her hips against me.

It only took a few moments for my own orgasm to finally come crashing down, sweeping over me, leaving me staggering, sliding down to my knees as Trish lay draped across the edge of the bed, gasping.

"God." I was covered in sweat, breathing hard as I lay on the floor, gazing up at Trish. "God." I reached up and touched her. "I love you."

I helped her sit up. She managed a smile. "Yes, Alex. I know. I love you too." As quickly as it had come, her attitude of submission was gone and she was her normal self. She looked back toward the living room. "The key is on the end table next to my charms."

I unlocked the cuffs and we lay on the bed for a long time.

"Is that what you wanted?" I asked at last.

"Silly question, silly man. If I didn't want it, would I have given you those handcuffs?"

It was a reasonable question.

"Did you mean it? When you said you loved me?" I realized that the answer was very important to me.

"Of course." She snuggled closer. "I never say I love you without meaning it."

It didn't ring true, but I said nothing. I was happy. Tired and spent, but happy. Tomorrow night didn't seem quite so frightening now.

"And one more thing, Alex. I'm sorry, but I need to be alone again tonight. I've got personal rituals to perform and I need to do them by myself. I need to reconsecrate all of my wards and talismans."

I frowned. "Trish, I want to—"

She fixed me with a serious gaze. "I'm sorry. I gave my protection up for you because I wanted you and I wanted you to know it. I wanted to give myself to you completely, without reservation. I don't even really want you to go, but you need to. I'll see you tomorrow. I'll even drive you home."

I was too tired to argue. So she was doing her weird mystical shit. I didn't mind too much. She'd said she loved me.

She retrieved her charms as I got dressed. She drove me home, chatting easily. Though my mind spun with questions about what we'd just done I was weary and couldn't articulate them.

We didn't talk about tomorrow night. It was as if it didn't exist.

* * *

Trish dropped me off at home with a kiss and a promise that she'd see me soon. I was utterly exhausted and when my cell phone jangled as I readied myself for bed I almost didn't hear it. The screen flashed "NUMBER BLOCKED" and when I put the phone to my ear, I heard a female voice, distant and tinny.

"Is this Alex?"

"Yes." I struggled to place the voice. "Who... Who is...?"

"It's Mia Jordan, Alex."

My gut lurched and I was suddenly awake.

"Mia? You mean Mia from..."

"From the cement plant, Alex. You and your friend saved me."

"I..." My head spun unpleasantly as I remembered what she'd said to me as they took her away. "What can I... I mean, what do you...?"

"I dreamed about you, Alex. I saw what's going to happen to you." Mia's voice took on an edge of panicky urgency. "Don't go, Alex. Don't do what they want you to do."

I frowned, icy fingers touching my spine. "What are you talking about?" I felt suddenly angry. "Who the hell is this?"

There was a muffled sound on the phone, and suddenly another voice barked at me—older and deeper, also female.

"You damned reporters leave my daughter alone! Leave her alone or I swear I'll call a lawyer!"

I heard another cry from Mia, quickly cut off, and the line went dead.

I sat staring at the phone for a long time before finally going back to bed.

X

I had another dream as I lay alone, Mia Jordan's warning still ringing in my ears. It wasn't about the winged woman—it was one of those dreams that I didn't remember, but which left me paralyzed, heart racing, convinced something horrible hid in the darkness beside me. I ended up turning on the light and watching TV for an hour before I could convince myself that all was well, and I could get back to sleep.

Tuesday. November 30. *Hecate Trivia.*

I'd done some research into the date. Hecate was a Roman goddess of magic and fertility. She also watched over roads, portals and doorways, and had dominion over ghosts and spirits. Trivia was the Roman word for a crossroads. On the festival night, some occultists claimed it was easier to contact the spirit world.

No work today; I'd told Terri I wouldn't be in. Rain lashed at the windows, driven by stiff gusts of wind. I hadn't thought that the weather could get any more depressing, but as always I was proved wrong.

As I crawled out of bed and made myself a cup of what passed for coffee, gazing at the gloomy day outside, I felt an indefinable compulsion—a need to do something. Exactly what, I couldn't say.

My head hurt as conflicting thoughts made war on each other.

Tonight. Tonight it's over. Michael performs a convincing magic show and everyone thinks he's banished the evil Indian spirit. We slap ourselves on the back and go home.

Or maybe it's real. Maybe Michael really will summon something, then send it away, proving once and for all that my entire world has been a lie. Until that day at Petroco, I'd refused to face or even acknowledge the notion, but now it was there, plain and ugly as the barrel of a gun.

Either way, it would be over and I could get back to my life.

What life, I briefly wondered? What have I really accomplished since college, save to rise sputtering to the surface of an ocean of despair and loneliness, then drag myself to shore, along with all the other driftwood? What the hell was I doing with my life?

Then, despite my night-horrors, I thought warmly of Trish, of her big violet eyes, and welcoming arms and soft, yielding body...

...And a chill passed through me as I abruptly remembered my dream.

I wore my long black coat and stood—no—floated in a vast sky filled with oily, iridescent clouds, illuminated here and there by flashes of multicolored lightning. I felt a heavy, oppressive sensation as if this was more than merely a stormy alien sky—I had the uncomfortable notion that the entire panorama breathed and pulsated with unnatural life. It was as if I was inside the head of an impossibly huge and utterly hostile creature.

I knew something terrifying lurked in that swirling, chaotic space. With growing fear I wondered whether this was truly a dream.

A voice echoed through the air around me, uttering a single word that vibrated through me, shaking mind, heart, and soul.

Alex...

Then, shining through the shimmering and shifting clouds, I thought I saw a vast sphere of burning yellow-green light, as if something unimaginably huge had opened a single titanic eye...

...And seen me.

I stumbled, my cup falling into the sink and shattering, splashing hot coffee across my chest.

It took several moments for me to regain my bearings, after which I carefully searched the apartment to make sure that none of Uncle Creepy's friends lurked there. Reassured, I got dressed.

When I opened the closet, it came again—the same compulsion I'd felt upon waking. Now it seemed more urgent and focused. Almost without thinking I reached out, my fingers touching the supple black leather of my old coat.

I'd seen it in my dreams. Cheryl's birthday present. For years it had hung in my closet, my last material reminder of her. And now I finally pulled it down from its hanger and slipped it on. It was heavy on my shoulders, substantial, and comforting.

I sighed and let my head sag. I remembered her. Remembered everything I'd wanted so desperately to forget. But even confused and troubled, her memory gave me strength, kindling warmth deep inside me, helping to overcome the fears that lurked in my shadows.

Cheryl. Cheryl, I'm so sorry.

I put on a pair of steel-toed engineer's boots, then slipped my new Glock and ammunition into the coat's voluminous pockets. It was another mindless compulsion and again I let it happen.

I rode the bus downtown. Anything was better than sitting in my apartment, watching the seconds drag by. The streets were wet and storm-tossed. A few remaining yellow leaves shivered on tree branches as the wind stirred them.

Rain continued to threaten for the rest of the day. The downpour held back, but the clouds tossed and seethed, agitated by the distant jet stream, tortured into strange shapes, looking uncomfortably like the chaos-sky in my dream. Above the ancient brick buildings along West Burnside, I imagined I could discern the image of a powerful, high-breasted woman wielding a sword, but an instant later it flew apart, blowing into wispy scraps.

I shivered, zipped the coat up to my neck, and turned my collar to the wind.

I walked the streets in a haze of contemplation. I went to the library, to the waterfront, to Powell's Books, and spent the last of my dwindling personal funds on lunch as afternoon crept unceremoniously toward evening. I knew it was time to go to Damien's place, then pick up Loren. Briefly, I considered simply heading home, pretending that Damien, Michael, Trish, and the others never existed, and try to return to something like a normal life.

The thought passed quickly, replaced by the bleak realization that my life was never going to be normal again, no matter how much I wanted it to be.

The compulsion drove me on, urgent but unknowable. Avoiding a band of street kids with torn jeans and bad attitudes, I made my way to the bus stop.

* * *

The clouds still raced and churned overhead, light pink against an indigo sky. The rain finally came, spattering down in fits and starts, driven by a harsh chill breeze from the river.

Yngwie's halogens pierced the wild swirl of water and wind only feebly, reflecting as much as they illuminated, and Damien almost ran us into a Jersey barrier while trying to park in our previous spot. The state police had gotten wise and completely blocked access, so he began to search, grim-faced for another.

I wanted to tell him about Mia Jordan's phone call, but he was distracted and didn't seem to hear anything I said. I let it go. I'd tell him later.

Loren sat in back, bundled in a winter coat, looking far more serious than usual. He had barely spoken since we'd picked him up. Maybe he felt the same shadowy portents I'd been trying to ignore all this time. Like me, he probably wished he'd brought Beowulf.

We had to drive another quarter mile down the highway before we found another place to pull over. I looked bleakly at the railroad embankment. The last time we'd walked it was during the day and in better weather; tonight it looked as if it stretched into the next county.

Damien stepped out of the driver's seat. "Ready for a hike?"

I gave him a grim look, opening my umbrella and checking, for the hundredth time that day, to make certain the Glock was safe in my pocket.

I tilted the passenger seat forward and Loren clambered out, raising his hood.

"Why can't we do this in the summer or something?" he asked.

I just shrugged. "What can I say? It's the wild, exotic life of a reporter."

We climbed up onto the tracks. As we trudged, I kept looking forward and back for the telltale white light of an oncoming train.

The place had deteriorated since our last visit. Broken fragments of wood, pieces of aluminum and plastic sheeting, old tin cans, broken bottles, twisted shopping carts and a million other bits of junk lay piled on either side of the embankment, a nightmare tangle of waste and corruption.

"My God," I muttered, feeling the reassuring slap of the pistol against my thigh as I walked. "What the hell happened?"

"It's gotten worse. Chaos draws chaos." Damien was gloomy. He had neglected to bring an umbrella, and now huddled miserably beneath mine. "There have been people here, people leaving junk and garbage, camping out beside the tracks. The doorway draws this, moves us closer to chaos and wilderness, away from organized thought and science."

The silhouette of the Petroco Building emerged from the misty gloom. I scrambled down the embankment, avoiding a jagged pile of rusty metal that might once have been a bicycle, intertwined with nail-studded timbers and a pile of foul-smelling garbage.

"God damn." Loren swore, almost tripping over the remains of a speaker cabinet. "You sure one of Uncle Creepy's friends isn't hiding out here somewhere?"

"No," I said. "I'm not. And please don't mention it again or I'll have to smack you or something."

He grinned, but still looked nervous. "Sorry, boss."

The fence was still there, surrounding the building, but there were gaps in a half-dozen places and it looked as if the junk surrounding it had been scattered and even added to. A single garish pink sodium light illuminated soaking trash and rubble, studded with rain-filled potholes, dimpled by falling droplets.

We slipped through one of the larger gaps in the fence. As we walked toward the dubious shelter of the building, I shone my light up a nearby wall. It was covered with graffiti that hadn't been there last month, and most of the plywood had been torn from the windows. A few pieces of police tape remained here and there, mute witness to Detective Maitland's visit.

As we approached, splashing through puddles and jumping over chunks of concrete and piles of brick, a piece of shadow detached itself from the darkness near the front door. It transformed into Vince, bundled in a heavy coat with the hood up, dripping water, and holding a pair of bolt cutters.

I saw a can of mace at his belt. Good. They were following Michael's advice.

"Come on! Everyone else is here already." He hustled us through the doorway, and inside.

"Oh, my holy fuck," Loren griped loudly as we stepped inside and the smell hit us.

The place still stank like an open cesspit. It was worse for the rain—cold and damp, strewn with wrecked furniture, a hundred leaks dripping water. I pictured Maitland and his team coming here. They'd probably have wanted to leave as quickly as possible.

The old marble floor was barely visible through the grime beneath our feet. Along with the sound of the wind and rain, and the drip-drip-drip of the leaks, I also thought I could hear a faint scampering sound like we'd heard before. Once more I hoped it was rats or opossums.

All in all, I preferred being outside in the rain.

We hustled quickly up the stairs and into the broad hallway on the second floor, still strewn with junk and scrawled with graffiti. There at last I saw the figures of Michael O'Regan and the others standing or crouching in the illumination provided by two electric lamps. Eric was there, but he avoided eye contact.

"Damien! Thank the Lord." O'Regan sounded uncharacteristically agitated. "We thought you'd never get here!"

I threw down my umbrella. "Parking was a bitch." I didn't feel terribly sympathetic. "All those holiday shoppers."

Trish, clad in her down coat, sweatshirt, and jeans, looked up and flashed me a smile but kept her distance and didn't say anything or step over to join me. I smiled back, hoping that the evening's foolishness would end quickly, and she and I could be together again.

"Everyone, this is Loren Hodges." Michael waved a hand at us. "Alex's friend I told you about."

The others mumbled polite greetings. They'd been busy. A couple of paint cans, one white, one red, stood nearby, with brushes tossed carelessly beside them. Nearby lay a number of empty Zap cans and an aluminum baseball bat.

Two of the familiar nested circles were painted in a cleared space on the floor. The outer ring was white, the inner red, and between them was more of the odd Hebraic writing.

Damien looked impressed. "Nice work."

"Thanks." Eric was as nervous and uncertain as the rest of us. His clothes were splashed with red and white paint. "It's from one of Michael's books."

Michael rolled up his sleeves. "A design from the Greater Kabala. Come on. Let's get this over with."

I wondered how ancient Jewish magic was supposed to summon or banish a Native American spirit, but I held my tongue as Michael unbuckled an overseas bag that lay on the floor nearby. He removed six silver candlesticks, some silver bowls, and a glass bottle filled with a clear liquid. As the rest of us watched, he carefully spaced the candlesticks and bowls around the outside of the circle, alternating one with the other, muttering briefly to himself with each action.

As I watched, I felt a light touch on my shoulder and was surprised to see Eric standing beside me.

"Alex? Alex, I..." He spoke softly, alternately looking at me and glancing down at the floor. "I... I just wanted to tell you, I'm... I'm sorry for... You know... For what happened."

I wouldn't have been more surprised if he'd starting turning cartwheels and singing show tunes, but I tried not to let it show.

"It's..." I mumbled in response, my attention torn between Michael's ritual, my own nervousness, and Trish's strange aloofness. "It's okay. Really. Everything was... was completely crazy that day."

"No, Alex. I'm sorry. There was no excuse for what I did."

"Yeah, well..." I tried to think of something to say. "I was acting crazy too. I'm sorry I hit you. I guess ancient Indian curses are like that."

He smiled. It was faint and uncertain, but a smile nonetheless.

"Thanks, Alex. It'll all be over soon."

He returned to watching Michael. I scanned the others' faces. Loren seemed torn between uncertainty and interest. Ron and Kay stood close together, watching with wide and clearly fearful eyes.

"You okay?" I asked.

Kay nodded. "So far. I just want this to be done with." Ron's expression said that he agreed but didn't want to say so.

"You bring anything?" I asked. "Weapons?"

Ron nervously cleaned his glasses with the tail of his sweatshirt then put them back on. "Taser. I just bought it yesterday."

"Good. Keep it handy."

Vince watched O'Regan with a critical frown on his face, mouthing along with his invocations. Damien ignored me, alternating between apparent unease and breathless anticipation, as if the answer to all his questions was forthcoming, but also aware that the answer might be an ugly one.

Trish was probably the weirdest of the lot. She still hadn't spoken to me but stood several feet back from the circle, observing Michael intently, but occasionally glancing into the shadows beyond our circle of lamplight. Her expression—God help me—looked not terribly different from the one she'd worn the night before, somewhere between pain and pleasure, pleading and commanding.

I remembered what she'd told me. *It said I could see and feel that power and become part of it. See the real nature of the universe, see the truth. Give myself to the truth. Surrender to it.*

Just like last night. I felt troubled for reasons I couldn't clearly identify.

"What's he doing?" Loren whispered.

I shook my head. "I have no idea. Watch and learn, I guess."

Michael began to place candles into the candlesticks—there were six this time, three white and three blue. As he lit each one in turn, then filled each bowl with water from the glass bottle, he continued to mutter words which, to my untrained ears, sounded vaguely Hebrew, but also somewhat Arabic. I thought it might be Aramaic, but this didn't seem like the time to interrupt Michael to ask.

I wasn't entirely sure what I felt as Michael finished setting up his paraphernalia. The weapon in my pocket provided less comfort with each passing moment. I caught a whiff of scent from the candles—lemon, sandalwood, cardamom—a faint counterpoint to the stench which still filled my nostrils.

Michael stood at the top of the circle. "Ready?"

XI

Outside, the rain redoubled its intensity, pelting the building like gravel as each of us nodded silently. Wind blew through the gaps in the plywood covering the tall windows, making the candles gutter.

Michael pointed. "Stand around the circle. Remember, the demon won't be tangible—just a distinct presence. You'll feel it in your mind just as you did before, possibly even more strongly this time, so be prepared. Don't move from your position, don't speak to it, and don't do anything it says. I will recite the banishment."

I obeyed, positioning myself between Damien and Loren. As he stood beside Loren, Vince's critical expression was replaced with one of intense anxiety, which I was certain mirrored my own. Nearby, Eric looked on with mounting concern. Trish stood between him and Michael, opposite me. I tried to catch her gaze, but she was staring into the circle. Her expression was intent, almost as if she was listening to something.

Michael stood calmly in his place, and began to recite another series of strange syllables.

An even stronger gust of wind thundered against the building and it seemed to shake. As Michael continued his seemingly meaningless recital, the fetor that surrounded us intensified, growing stronger, changing from moment to moment. It was the stench we'd smelled before, and the one that I'd smelled at the cement plant, but now it was the worst it had ever been. We stood our ground as Michael, holding a handkerchief over his mouth, continued his invocation.

The two electric lamps flickered and faded, then went out completely, their hot white glow fading. Plunged into darkness, I turned and started for them, but Vince's voice stopped me in my tracks.

"No! Don't break the circle!"

Chastened, I turned back toward Michael, staring toward his voice through darkness now lit only by guttering candles.

No—not just candles now. There was something else. A sick, greenish-yellow glow emanated from the center of the circle, and with growing alarm I realized that it was the same color as the great staring eye in my dream.

Through the howl of wind I could hear a faint, far-off sound that echoed in my ears, louder, then quieter. It combined a woman's sobs, a madman's wild and high-pitched giggles, the groan of tortured metal, and the shrieks of an angry infant. I'd heard it, softer and less menacing, in my dreams of the winged woman.

My heart hammered unpleasantly as the reality of the situation dawned. God—something was happening—something substantial and empirical. Something real. Something I couldn't explain. And that last thing was the most frightening thing of all.

Mounting fear and disgust kept my gaze locked on the circle, where the fetid greenish luminescence grew brighter and brighter. In one of Damien's columns he'd written about "corpse lights," the strange glow said to hover over dead bodies. This cold, unhealthy light was how I'd imagined a corpse light might look.

Michael was unmoved, still chanting in that strange Hebrew-Arabic polyglot. He reached into his pocket, drew forth a small glass vial and taking the cloth away from his face, unscrewed the lid. He flung the vial's contents into the circle, straight at the brightest portion of the foul green glow. Dark liquid splashed— was it blood?

Where the fluid landed on the floor, tiny holes seemed to open, and solid shafts of the greenish light emerged, intense as lasers. Rapidly, the holes grew in size, merged and expanded to the limit of the circle's outer ring. A solid shaft of yellow-green corpse light now rose out of what looked like a deep pit in the floor, and at its center...

At its center...

It was hard to focus on, shifting in and out of view, pixelating like the image on a snowy TV screen or a broken DVD. As it wavered and flickered, it changed shape – one moment it was a fuzzy collection of gleaming spheres, the next it was a column of swollen, veiny flesh surrounded by waving, ropy tendrils, then a roiling storm cloud flashing with yellow-green lightning and winking spheres that might have been eyes. As I watched, something stirred inside my head.

Alex...

It was the same voice that had whispered to me at the cement plant and during our last visit to Petroco. It was still a soft whisper, but it stabbed at me like sharp scissors—insistent, demanding.

Alex...

It bit and burrowed like a pig rooting in garbage, muttering at me like a lover whispering in my ear.

Alex...

They weren't true words, not really—more like a direct, unspoken connection to the deepest and most hidden parts of my psyche, where the darkness flashed with images of blood, sex, violence, and slaughter. I felt the implicit promise of Onatochee's presence.

If I surrendered to it, abandoning humanity, conscience, self, I would have absolute license to indulge every dark compulsion that roiled, black and evil, in my mind's secret corners.

The thing in the shaft of green light flickered through an array of shapes that I could barely focus on—I saw eyes and mouths, spidery wings and pincers, hooves and writhing ropy tentacles, and even stranger images. Just looking at it made my head hurt.

I tore my gaze away. The pain still throbbed and the voice still whispered, calling to me like an unclean siren, but I could resist it, at least for the moment.

This was how it had captured the Chilut and driven men like Bob Leslie to commit bloody acts of murder and rape and cannibalism—bombarding their minds with demands and promises, with threats of pain and promises of reward.

I remembered Michael's warning. *Demons—or rather, entities— like Onatochee and Abatu may not be actively malevolent or evil as we would know it—a better word might be "inimical"—they are simply incompatible with our existence in this world... No, Alex—I wouldn't necessarily call Onatochee evil but he is very, very bad. And very, very dangerous..*

Inimical? Incompatible? Yes, it was those things, but Michael had been wrong. What I felt wasn't merely inimical. It was a thing of true hate and malevolence, tangibly evil.

My hand crept to my pocket and touched the gun, a small fragment of clean human technology, a tangible counterweight to the boiling mass of otherness that held us in thrall. Pushing away the pictures that it drew from the corners of my soul, I found my voice.

"Don't!" I shouted. "Don't listen to it!"

Trying to avoid looking directly at the thing in the light and the new horrors it had transformed into, I looked toward Michael. He had dropped the cloth and stared, his face a mask of shock and fear. Something was wrong—he'd told us that the demon wouldn't be visible, yet there it was hanging in the air before us. I realized that he'd never actually seen a demon in physical form before.

"Michael!" I shouted. "The invocation! Say it, for God's sake!"

My voice seemed to snap him back for a moment. He shot me a quick glance with tired, frightened eyes, then intoned, "Onatochee!"

The green light reflected off his face, leaving its hollows in shadow, giving him a cadaverous appearance.

His words were tremulous as he spoke—in English this time— absent the deep-voiced assurance that I'd grown accustomed to. "We... We have summoned you... summoned you and called you by your true name. We invoke the powers of Yaweh and His..." He faltered. "Yahweh and the seven... The seven Archangels... Gabriel, Michael, Raphael, Uriel, Raguel, Remiel, Saraqael... to bind you and banish you."

The thing in the column of light reacted to the words by shifting again, reshaping itself into something familiar—a head, arms, legs, torso, a face... A woman, pale-skinned, red-haired, gazing at Michael with huge green eyes, bright with love, with vulnerability, with fear...

"Moira!"

Michael swayed and fell down on one knee, his hollow face now reflecting unbearable pain and guilt...

"Oh, God no! *Moira!*"

The pressure returned tenfold, like a white-hot needle injecting images directly into my brain. They flashed by like a movie on fast forward, as if I was absorbing entire memories all at once.

Biting wind and cold. The rugged, flinty countryside. The faces of my companions. The sensation of the ancient leather-bound volume in my hands. The sound of my voice as I read the words of power. The nausea and the sick touch of unclean thoughts and the horror as my resistance breaks and I surrender to them...

"Michael!" Pain clanged and echoed like the worst headache I could imagine, and I feared that if I shouted too loud my skull would burst. "Michael, don't let it..."

Oh, how good, how right it feels! Pushing Donald and sending him tumbling off the cliff, bashing Bryce's brains in with a rock, chasing down Moira, tearing her clothes from her, falling on her with perfect, unbridled, unstoppable animalistic rage, feeling not shame but joy at her screams, and mad ecstasy knowing that it is me—ME—who can cause so much pain, and holds the power of life and death, free of guilt, free of weak human hesitation... Me...

Michael O'Regan.

A tide of anger rushed up from my subconscious, made worse by the monstrous thing that boiled inside me, urging me on, pulling long-buried emotions to the surface. "You bastard! You did it! You killed..."

"I'm so sorry, Moira. I'm so very, very sorry. You must understand that it wasn't me... It was that thing, that demon that got into my head, made me do those things. Please, Moira. No one mourns for Donald and Bryce more than I do, and words can't express how I feel about what happened to you. But it wasn't me—it was that thing we summoned. We

mustn't tell anyone. The authorities… They would never believe us. This must remain a secret between you and me. Please. Please understand that, my darling. Please say you understand. Please…"

The world swam dizzily around me. It saw Michael's secrets as it saw mine and those of my companions. We were prisoners forced to stand naked and helpless before the merciless judgment of a faceless tribunal, alone in the dark knowing that there was no hope. Whatever this thing was, it was too powerful. Too powerful for any of us…

Alex…

The whisper battered me and Michael's memories were crowded out by my own. I relived a thousand forgotten sensations in an instant—the excitement I'd felt at Trish's submission to me, the possessive jealousy that had made me smash Eric in the face, my anger at Cheryl's betrayal, my rage at the dealer, my exultation at his downfall, followed almost immediately by my own self-loathing—loathing that I immediately felt for every other human on the planet, despising their weakness, hating their fear, laughing at their misery…

I saw its bubbling shape in my head, twisting and reforming itself until it took on the form of Cheryl White the way I remembered her—short blonde hair framing a delicate freckled face with an upturned nose and almost transparent white eyes. She smiled, and it was a sad, melancholy smile, at once sorrowful and cynical, from a woman who loved me but also knew that I would believe anything she told me.

I'd loved her, and she'd been taken from me. It hadn't been her fault—she'd been weak, she had a sickness, and there were others who took that weakness and used it against her.

And against me.

Her face shifted and melted, wizened into a grinning deaths-head, then reformed into the smirking face of Alan Coleman, the grinning monster who had fed her habit, taken her body, and destroyed her soul...

I still hated him. My rage wasn't gone. It was only hidden.

I felt my fist impacting his face, felt bones give, and smelled fresh blood.

You motherfucker. I'll fucking kill you.

I'd said those words, years ago. And now I couldn't escape them any longer.

Rage sustained me. The memory of what I'd done pursued me. I hid from it, worked a meaningless job, pretended to be invisible. Now that was over. Now at last I could reclaim the wrath that had given my life purpose. I could join with the power whose icy claws probed and dissected my mind and with the multitude of strange, demonic eyes that gazed unblinking into my soul...

It offered more than just vengeance. It offered power, freedom from conscience, from morality—pure, unbridled animal passion and a celebration of hunger and sex, of violence and destruction. I could take what I wanted—kill and maim, feast on hot living flesh, slake my lusts with any woman or man or child I wanted, with no thought for consequence or punishment. Onatochee's will was a ferocious wind, dragging me away from humanity, away from self, away from love and thought, toward the primal rage that swelled inside me...

Alan's face sloughed away and for an instant I saw the demon's true shape—not the many strange and horrifying forms that my fevered mind had built in a desperate effort to make sense of something that was utterly distant and incomprehensible, but its real face staring across the void at me.

Reality itself fractured, as if the sight was so strange and horrifying that I had to retreat into madness. I heard its thoughts, but they were foreign, incomprehensible, alien... No, no! *Alien* conjured images of spaceships and Klingons—*Alien* didn't begin to capture how utterly strange and repellent this entity was. Yet to gain what I wanted, to free myself of constraint and shed my own troublesome selfhood, I had to become like it, to join its essence to my own heart and mind and soul...

For a moment, that was what I truly wanted.

Then I saw light—the silver-blue purity from my dreams, the winged woman, and the word that had broken the spell when this creature and its slaves had tried to take me in my bedroom...

A voice whispered to me—not Onatochee, but something else. I had heard it before. I had been hearing it all my life and refused to listen.

Nomeus.

Shepherd.

The voice was gentle and almost mournful, but at the same time powerful and comforting. It was the voice of a bereaved mother crying at tragedy and a parent screaming in anger at those who would harm her children. Did it come from outside my mind, or from near-forgotten, impossibly ancient memory?

She loved you. She loved you, Shepherd. And she failed you because she was human. Would you fail her now? Would you surrender to the same sickness that took her, to the madness and anger and lust that is like a poison in your veins? Would you be like her?

No. Cheryl. She had loved me, and I had loved her, and no matter how we had failed each other, that love was still real. The soft voice spoke in my mind, and I felt that love again. It could save me, I realized now, because it was something that Onatochee could never understand.

The thing's crudely probing claws pulled away. Memory and sensation faded, and my heart throbbed unpleasantly in my chest, but for the moment at least I was free of the demon's presence.

In my pocket I still held the Glock, though part of me screamed that it would do no good. This aberrant thing didn't even fully exist in our reality. Nothing I did could affect it. Nothing could stop it. I was as helpless as a rabbit before a slavering wolf.

Nomeus. Her voice still echoed in my mind—a tiny cry in the night, the defiant shout of the prisoner against his captors. Do not fear the darkness.

I knew that I was the only one who could hear her. The others had to face Onatochee alone and unaided. They looked dazed, sickened and ready to bolt. Like snatches of conversation overheard in a crowded room, I felt the sensations that echoed in their minds and the vile things that Onatochee offered them.

Their thoughts were so much like mine—rage and vengeance and power and sex and thoughtless, mindless consumption. As if, stripped to our basest and most primal natures, we were indistinguishable from each other—a bloody crowd of killer apes, strangers to reason, to science, to thought and even to love.

Michael was still down on one knee, silently staring blankly up at the entity. Though it vibrated and phased in and out of focus, it retained the shape of poor, betrayed Moira.

I forced words up from my chest and out into the air.

"It's not real, Michael! It's not Moira! It's not fucking Moira! The ritual! *Say the words!*"

He didn't respond but kept staring upward, his lips moving, silently mouthing "I'm sorry" over and over again.

"Michael!" Kay cried out, and for a moment it looked as if she'd bolt. Beside her Ron held her hand tightly.

"Don't move!" barked Eric. He'd managed to overcome Onatochee's appeal to his animal lusts as well, for he looked wan and frightened. I wondered what the creature had tried to make him do. Kill me, perhaps? Take vengeance for his humiliation at Trish's hands?

I was glad he hadn't given in. Eric—surly, arrogant, jealous Eric—was stronger than I could have known. He was more like me than the horrific thing in the circle. Alone he had fought against it and held it at bay.

He is your brother. Put down your anger. Save those you can.

I knew her name.

Tsagaglalal. She Who Watches.

"Michael!" I shouted again. "Michael, God damn it! Don't listen to that fucking thing! It wasn't your fault, Michael! Listen to me! *I'm your friend!*"

My voice seemed to cut through the psychic screams that rang and hammered in my brain, and Michael's head snapped up like a man awakened from a bad dream. The image of Moira dissolved into a black, yellow-lit cloud.

Michael took up the invocation again, but his voice was thin and lifeless, nearly inaudible over the howling wind.

"By... By the seventy-two names I adjure and bind you, you all the retinues of evil spirits in the world..." He faltered as if trying to remember the words. "Be'ail Lachush and all your retinue... Kapkafuni the Queen of... Queen of Demons and all your retinue; and... Agat... Agrat bat Mal... Malkat and all your retinue, and Zm... Zmamit and all your retinue. By all these... By all these names, we bind and banish... Banish you... We call you by your true name! Onatochee!"

Nothing happened. The dark cloud remained unchanged, but a harsh metallic sound echoed rhythmically from it, a sound I had heard in my dream.

Jesus, I thought. *Is it laughing at us?*

"Oh shit!" Eric's voice rose above the tumult of demon voices and the mad shriek of the wind. "Where's Trish?"

I tore my gaze from Michael and looked toward the place where Trish had been standing a moment ago, and realized with a rush of shock that she was not there...

The circle was broken. The ritual had failed.

Michael stared at the empty spot in wide-eyed disbelief, blood draining from his face.

From the shadows behind him, Trish appeared, bearing the can of red paint.

"Take him, master!" She flung the paint into the circle, upsetting water bowls and candlesticks. The circle breached, light gushed out in a sickly green flood.

"Oh, shit!" Loren's voice echoed.

Kay screamed and turned to run.

Free from its prison, the floating horror moved, spilling forth like liquid, gliding across the floor toward Michael. A scream escaped from his lips and he stumbled backwards.

The demon loomed over him, boiling and flashing with pale lightning. Dozens of green orbs appeared among the clouds—green eyes now fixed on Michael. Thready black tendrils lashed out from the cloudy body, caressing Michael as he lay, whimpering on the floor, his hands thrown up desperately.

I pulled the Glock free, racked the slide and stood in firing stance, legs apart, pistol held steady in both hands and fired three rounds.

The report pounded my ears and recoil pounded my arm as brass went flying, but the bullets vanished into the thing's flickering, shifting bulk. I might as well have been throwing pebbles at a charging rhino.

Onatochee wasn't interested in me anyway. Its outline wavered and shifted, and then it was Moira again, but her pale arms had elongated into claws, stretching out like the limbs of a praying mantis. Michael shrieked, and the claw-hands grabbed his head, yanking him to his feet. He tried to look away, but the long, dead-pale pincers held him tight, sinking into the flesh of his head, melting into him, forcing him to stare, open-mouthed and screaming, into the face of the woman he'd violated so long ago.

"No," he babbled, tears running down his face. "No, please. Not you. Not now. Please..."

Her lips touched his, engulfing him, smothering his pleas, and her substance changed again, liquefying and flowing into Michael through his open mouth. His flesh distended, bloating like a fleshy balloon, engorged by the essence of the demonic thing that held him.

My finger tightened on the trigger and I fired again, again, again—burning rounds plunged through the melting demonic shape and slammed into Michael, leaving huge bloody craters, but neither one moved or fell. They remained together, locked in a repellent embrace as Michael absorbed the demon's unearthly substance.

The slide snapped back, but I kept straining at the trigger, my mind screaming, desperate to destroy the monstrosity before me. My hands moved on their own, ejecting the spent magazine, pulling the second from my pocket and slamming it home.

Before I could shoot again, I felt arms around my shoulders, dragging me away.

"Fuck, Alex!" Loren shouted. "We can't do shit here! We've got to get the hell out!"

His words broke the spell that had held me, and I turned to run, shooting a single glance back at Michael.

He stood alone. His entire body was shining with the demon's green corpse-light. His clothes were rent and torn where his body had swelled up and distended, but now he was returning to normal, his body shrinking back to human proportions. His hair was in disarray and his face was flushed, but when he caught sight of me our gazes locked and he smiled a thin, unfamiliar smile and a flicker of Onatochee's green flashed in his eyes.

His lips moved, and I heard a single word echo in my head.

Alex.

The comforting voice of the silver woman was gone now, and all that remained was Onatochee's voice issuing from Michael O'Regan's body and echoing in my mind and soul. With a cry I ran after Loren.

I pelted down the stairs. The others were already ahead of me and racing for the exit, but in the pink light that filtered in from outside I saw a wave of bodies appear in a rush of wind and rain, crowding through the front doors—dirty, skeletally thin, wild-eyed men and women in tattered clothes, bearing clubs, rocks, and knives.

And from the crowd echoed a mad, brutal chorus of strange syllables.

"Wo'ibunaga! Ichiloot! Onatocheeee!"

XII

The horror before me played itself out like images in a slide show. Vince fumbled for his can of mace, but he was too late—two wild-eyed men were on him, the first slashing with a rusty knife, the second shattering his skull with a crowbar. He collapsed heavily on the floor and the tide of wasted bodies swept over him.

Eric punched a screaming scarecrow of a woman in the throat and she fell then he spun away from a second attacker who swung at him with a bent piece of rebar. Beside him, Loren reached toward his ankle and yanked out a short black rod. He shook it and it extended into a flexible baton and he swung it savagely at the man with the metal bar, slashing him across the face. The man screamed and dropped his weapon, staggering away, clutching his face, blood seeping between his dirty fingers.

I heard Kay screaming, but I couldn't see her in the pink-lit shadows. Near the door, Ron lashed out with his Taser eliciting screams and angry bellows of pain. Then a thrown brick arced out of the darkness, hitting him heavily on the forehead and sending him to the ground.

Desperately I searched for Damien but was interrupted when a pair of pale, sexless creatures flung themselves at me, unarmed save for yellow teeth and jagged fingernails. Pure self-preservation drove me on, and I snapped off two shots, shattering my first attacker's face and taking the second in the leg. Screaming, he tumbled down the stairs, clutching a blasted kneecap.

Something crashed heavily down on my skull from behind, obliterating every other sensation like the striking of a vast, deafening bell. I barely saw the stairs rushing at me as I fell or felt the Glock slip from my deadened fingers. Dumbly I rolled onto my back, my brain screamed warnings as a gap-toothed man with matted hair curling out from under a tattered black stocking cap loomed above me, an old two-by-four grasped in both hands, dripping with black liquid.

My own blood? I stared at it, detached from thought. Almost calmly, I contemplated the big piece of wood as it began to swing in an arc toward my unprotected face. I willed my hands upward to protect me, but they moved with maddening slowness as if weighted down by masses of lead.

Eric appeared, wild-eyed behind the man, wrapping an arm around his thin neck, dragging him away from me.

A semblance of rational thought reasserted itself and I struggled to rise as Eric battled with the man, holding his neck in the crook of one arm while pounding him with his fist. The man didn't seem to notice, but writhed in Eric's grasp, swinging his club wildly, trying to dislodge him.

The man broke free and spun, savagely striking with his club, slashing Eric across the face. I heard the sickening thud of impact and saw blood splatter, black against the dark grime, as Eric's body slid bonelessly down the stairs.

My hand fell on something hard and it took me almost a second to realize that it was the Glock. Forcing thoughts through my still-reeling brain, I grasped the gun, clambering unsteadily up onto one knee and aiming one-handed as the man turned on me, club poised.

My finger tightened on the trigger, squeezing off a pair of shots, blasting huge bloody holes into the man's chest. His body convulsed, but he kept coming, his face a mask of rage and something that might have been pleasure.

"*Ichiloot,*" he mumbled, grinning at me through missing teeth. His face twisted like a nest of wriggling grubs. "*Onatochee...*"

I fired again, hitting him squarely in the forehead. He stood for an instant, his eyes going glassy, then flopped to the stairs, tumbling down beside Eric.

I limped toward Eric. He lay face-up, his eyes staring sightlessly, his face empty and slack. His neck was broken.

He is your brother.

The words still lingered in my head. Angry, envious, jealous, even violent, he was still a human being, and his last act had been to save me—in his eyes, the man who had stolen the woman he loved.

A wave of despair washed over me as I turned, searching for my companions.

It wasn't good. Loren was still on his feet, slashing left and right with his baton, but he was surrounded by a half-dozen assailants. Vince was down, lying still in a spreading pool of crimson. Ron was motionless and held by a couple of cultists, while nearby I saw Kay pinned to the floor by another pair, screaming as a big man with gray dreadlocks ripped her shirt open. He struck at her savagely and the screaming stopped abruptly.

Instinct took command again and, despite the pain that tore at every joint, I dropped into firing stance and pulled the Glock's trigger. The dreadlocked man's neck blossomed crimson then a second shot took him in the temple and he collapsed onto Kay, twitching.

A ragged knot of cultists raced up the stairs at me. Their eyes were mad, their faces distorted with ecstatic anger, and they carried rocks, bottles, clubs...

I squeezed off my last two shots. Then the slide locked back and they were on me. A bottle smashed into my forehead, a bat struck my shoulder. I went down under the press of bodies, expecting only a few last moments of sensation before darkness took me at last.

Stop, children. The words that were not words boomed in my head, and I felt a renewed throbbing touch upon my brain as the demon's mental tendrils brushed at me once more.

The pressure of bodies lessened and I felt myself lying prone, my face pressed against the grimy surface of the marble steps. My arm ached, my head spun and jangled, but I wasn't dead, at least not yet.

Painfully, I raised my head. The cultists had stepped back and stared reverently up the stairs at something behind me. Below, they held Kay and Ron tightly but kept their distance from Loren, who looked utterly spent but still defiant. I didn't see Damien anywhere. Maybe he'd escaped.

I was beyond fear now, but I still dreaded what I would see when I turned to look up the stairs.

Michael O'Regan strode toward me. Despite torn clothes and a bruised face covered with dried blood, he regarded me with an expression that echoed his old, self-assured, paternal self. If it hadn't been for the gleam of greenish light behind his eyes I might almost thought it was really him.

"Alex." He spoke, and the voice echoed inside my head as if speaking to me in a hundred languages simultaneously. "Alex, can you hear me?"

"Yeah," I said, though my tongue felt thick and impossibly heavy. "Yeah, I hear you, you son of a bitch."

He smiled at that. "I'm sorry that had to happen, Alex." Each word came slowly, as if he were looking them up in the dictionary as he spoke. "I find... That is... Onatochee finds it difficult to manifest in this reality without a vessel. Michael O'Regan is... I... am presently that vessel. Now he... Now I... can... communicate with less... inconvenience."

I cast a disgusted look at Eric's lifeless corpse. We could have been friends if I hadn't been such a damned arrogant know-it-all. If I hadn't slept with Trish. If he... If he hadn't...

I fixed Michael with a furious glare, tears welling up in my eyes.

"Inconvenience? How many people are dead because of you, motherfucker? How many people raped and tortured?" I rose to my knees. "I call that pretty *fucking inconvenient!*"

A look of puzzlement flashed in Michael's corpse-light eyes.

"You don't understand, do you? Onatochee is not bad, Alex. Not evil. He simply is. And he has been... That is to say... *elements* of him have been... Been... in this world for a very long..." He paused, searching for words. "A very long time."

"I saw you, Michael. I saw what you did. You killed your friend in Scotland. You raped Moira. You've been lying about that all these years."

He moved back a step, confusion once more swirling on his face. The greenish light flickered. "I... Michael... Did not... Michael..."

I got up on one knee. Behind me the cultists stirred uneasily but didn't move.

"It wasn't Abatu, was it Michael?" I persisted and felt my voice growing stronger. "You summoned Onatochee, didn't you? It possessed you and made you do those things. And you've been living in fear ever since, haven't you?"

"Onatochee does not... I do not..." His voice broke. He faltered, and for an instant he gazed at me with forsaken, hollow human eyes. "Oh God, Alex. I'm so sorry..."

"Michael?" A voice filtered down from above, saccharine-sweet and familiar. "Michael, darling, is he there?"

A pale figure emerged from the shadows behind Michael.

"Alex... Oh, my dearest, Alex... You see now, don't you? You see what a master Michael truly is?"

She was naked, her pale skin streaked with gore and grime. Her hair was a filthy matted tangle and her body a welter of cuts and scrapes. Her wards were all gone, save for a few strands and scraps in the pale valley between her breasts.

"Trish." Anger drained from me and cold, desperate despair returned as she stepped behind the Michael-thing, wrapping her arms around his shoulders. "Trish, why? What happened?"

"Sometimes sacrifice is necessary for knowledge," she whispered. Greenish light flashed behind her deep blue irises. "Sacrifice of friends, of lovers. Even of self."

Tortured almost beyond endurance, my muscles began to rebel as my adrenaline rush faded, vanishing in the face of bleak hopelessness. My knees started to shake.

"What the hell do you want?" I demanded. "You've got us. We're all either dead or at your mercy? What do you fuckers want?"

Trish shook her head slowly and smiled. It wasn't an especially sweet smile.

"It's not all that horrible, Alex. Onatochee wants us. Wants us to join with him. Be part of what he's becoming."

My knees finally collapsed and I fell back down to the stairs. "And what's that, Trish? What's he becoming? Do you even know?"

"No, I don't Alex." She laughed. "And that's the most exciting part."

Michael's eyes glowed greenish again—I'd been able to reach him for an instant, but that was long past. Seeing Trish had shattered the last of my reserves, and Tsagaglalal's soft and comforting voice had fled completely. We were alone with a monster and its fanatics.

"She understands." Michael's tone was concerned and thoughtful again, and now his words seemed to come more easily. He took a step down toward me.

"You'll understand, too." As he spoke, I thought I could see something moving inside his mouth, writhing and flickering like the worms I'd seen inside Uncle Creepy's head. "They all understand now. Don't you?"

A dissonant chorus of muttered assent echoed from the gathered cultists.

Michael reached out a hand, and it began to elongate, transforming into the claw-like appendage that had earlier seized his head.

"You will be a new vessel." Michael's voice echoed in the staircase, but also screamed in my head, reigniting the agonizing pain that coursed through me.

"You will be one with him and he with you, and your gifts will serve him." He grinned. "Shepherd."

I tried to scramble away, but one of the cultists grabbed me in an iron grip, pinioning my arm painfully behind my back. Memories of what the thing had done to Michael churned sickeningly inside me.

"Don't resist." It was a whisper, both spoke and unspoken, echoing like the sibilant hiss of a snake. "It will hurt less that way. There will be more of... more of... *you*... left that way."

His arm stretched out grotesquely and its tip grazed my face. I felt a numbing cold as if I'd just plunged my head into a freezer full of dry ice, and a hundred brittle, painful stabs, thrusting into my mouth, my eyes, my ears...

Onatochee. The voice was all now, blotting out everything else in my mind. My fears and secrets were laid bare, torn open for all to see... Every lie I'd told my parents, every secret sin I'd committed, every unspoken lust and perverse thought... I saw Cheryl staring up at me through a heroin haze, smiling stupidly as I shouted at her... I saw her with Alan. She was on her knees, paying for her sickness through her own debasement. Alan's face twisted into a sick grin as he looked at me. And I saw what I'd done... I felt the nauseous mixture of shame and pleasure as I'd pounded my fists into him, kicked him, cracked his skull, and shattered his teeth with a baseball bat...

I'd lied to Damien when I said that I'd told the other dealers. I'd lied when I'd said they had crippled him and turned him into a vegetable.

It hadn't been them. It had been me.

And now Onatochee knew it.

Somewhere in the darkness the demon exulted. Secrets and shame were like the sweetest and most treasured delicacies for a creature like that... Tearing another creature's heart and soul open to reveal that which they most wanted to keep hidden. That was Onatochee's food and drink.

Stay. The thought blasted through my mind like the discordant notes of a very bad orchestra. *Stay and join us. Tell them, Alex. Tell them how they can be one with Onatochee. Show them what he is. What I am. What we are. Be my Shepherd. Not hers.*

New images flashed through my brain. I saw cities in ruin, endless fields of corpses, the flames of war and catastrophe, the rusting detritus of a dead civilization. I saw men and women in furs, in robes, in woolen tunics and iron armor, bearing spears and swords and bows, driven to kill and pillage by the rage and madness of Onatochee and beings like him. I felt his malign presence and a renewed offer of power and blood without thought or guilt tugging once more at my heart and soul.

And through that endless icy sea of surrender, from far away, I heard someone shouting my name.

"Alex! Jesus Christ, Alex! *Look!*"

It was Damien.

Onatochee's probing essence tore free and painfully ripped itself from my mind. I screamed, but with that scream I realized that I was free again. My mind was still my own.

Michael was not looking at me anymore. He was staring, wide-eyed and fearful at something above and behind me.

Something that shone silver-blue.

I turned. Damien stood in the doorway to the outside, pointing upward, his eyes wide, his lips trembling.

I gaped, my mind trying to grasp what it saw.

It was her.

She hovered in the air near the ceiling, suspended in a sphere of pale azure light. She was even more radiant and beautiful than she had been in my dream—naked, with pale skin, high breasts over a slightly rounded belly and strong thighs. A halo of white-blonde hair trailed behind her as if weightless, and between her thighs was a light downy patch of hair the same color. Graceful white swan's wings flapped with a slow, gentle rhythm.

I knew that what I saw was not truly her, not truly the flawless naked goddess from my dreams—her real form was beyond my comprehension. The image that she presented to me and the others was merely a disguise for a being that was just as otherworldly and strange as Onatochee. But it was far better than what I'd seen so far tonight.

Deep blue pupilless eyes gazed at me from a rounded, high-boned face, then shifted to Michael, who stumbled backwards up the stairs. Beside him, Trish looked on with growing fear and wonderment, fascinated and repelled by the pale woman.

A nervous whine erupted from the cultists and they began to scramble away. Some of the cultists surrounding Loren turned and fled through the doors, ignoring Damien.

"You...?" Michael spoke with his own voice, and this time it didn't echo in my mind. The fearsome mental pressure was gone too, replaced by a gentle sensation of calm and peace. "Is... it... you?"

A spark of blue-white energy arced between them, and Michael sprang back, crying out in pain. Trish screamed as if feeling it herself.

The woman looked down on me. All across her skin, blue fireflies danced like glowing tattoos, forming arcane symbols and unreadable runes, darting and flickering, glowing hotter and brighter as I watched.

"*Nomeus*," she said in a voice like soft wind and distant thunder. She held out her hand and the spiral shape formed on it, drawn in darting blue motes. "Do not fear the darkness."

"What..." I faltered, trying to speak, but nothing more emerged from my throat. "Who are... Who are you?"

The racing blue sparks on the blue woman's skin gathered together, leaping from her, forming a slender shape in the air. I recognized it as the sword from my dream—thin and studded with thorn-like spikes near the hilt, then widening to a wicked, elongated diamond at the point, all crafted of gleaming, electric-blue energy.

Her voice echoed lyrically in my head, singing across an impossibly distant gulf, but touching me like a soft and loving hand.

Nomeus. Shepherd. You worship no God. You bow to no King. You serve no Chief. Take the weapon.

Everything that had happened served only to batter and break my rational mind until it lay smashed and irreparable. All that remained was the animal instinct that bade me run, flee, hide. And yet I stood, transfixed, staring at the vision that hovered in the air above me.

All hung there, suspended in time—Onatochee, Trish, Michael O'Regan, my friends, all horror and wonderment, the winged woman, the sword held motionless...

I reached up, grasping for the hilt...

My fingertips brushed its glassy surface.

It was as if I'd tried to grab a piece of white-hot metal. Pain shot through me, agonizing burning pain. I screamed and released my hold on the sword, then fell to the stairs, landing heavily on my shoulder.

The woman's eyes were still gentle, her expression one of patience and love...

Nomeus. When you are ready.

She glided toward Michael and Trish, who continued to retreat. Michael muttered to himself uncertainly, and Trish's eyes were wide with alarm.

The winged woman's light grew brighter, and Michael held up his hands, shielding his face.

"Ah. Ah. I'm not strong...." His voice rose to a scream. "Not yet... N... Not-not... See, Alex? She is wrong for... For this... This world... No. No. Hurts. *Hurts. Hurt-hurt-hurt...*"

Her light grew brighter and brighter, and finally exploded with solar intensity, bathing the entire hallway in blinding whiteness. All around me I heard despairing cries and the sound of running feet.

Michael's voice erupted from the white inferno, modulating higher and higher, screaming wordlessly and finally vanishing into the supersonic.

Then the light was gone and we were alone, five humans in a chamber strewn with blood and corpses and garbage.

Michael and Trish were gone. Outside I saw the last couple of cultists scurrying away through the junkyard, dragging along their wounded. We were the only ones left alive.

My limbs trembled and I felt too sick to move, but I forced myself to crawl down the stairs, then walk unsteadily toward where Kay and Ron lay unconscious. Loren knelt beside Kay, feeling for a pulse.

Damien stood frozen in the doorway. There were tears in his eyes.

"I ran," he said softly. "I ran away, Alex. But I couldn't leave you here. I had to come back. I had to..."

He fell to his knees, sobbing. The battle against his madness, and against the thing that had tested it, had almost destroyed him, but he had struggled back, unwilling to abandon us.

I knelt beside him, my arm around his shoulders, holding him close as sobs racked his body.

I realized that I loved this man, as much as I'd ever loved anyone.

"It's okay, Damien," I said softly. "It's going to be okay."

Kay moved, moaning. Loren pulled out his cell phone, punched in 911 and spoke urgently.

"Hi. Police. Loren Hodges. The Petroco Building on Highway 30. Yes. Yes. We've got people hurt and some people dead. We need help. Please."

"Why did they do it?" Damien hiccupped, still crying and trembling. "Michael and Trish. How could they have done that to us?"

"It was Onatochee," I said. "It reached out to our weakest link. It had already possessed Michael once, and when Trish broke the circle there was nothing to stop it from taking him again. Trish told me she wanted enlightenment, power, magic. She said she wanted to surrender to it, but I didn't understand. It must have gotten to her. Promised her what she wanted."

"Damn her," Damien muttered. "Damn her to hell."

"I think we're too late for that," I said.

"Who was she, Alex? The woman with the sword? Is she the one you've been dreaming about? She Who Watches?"

I nodded and glanced up the stairs to where Michael and Trish had stood.

"Do you think she killed it?" Damien asked. "Do you think it's gone now?"

Before I could reply, Ron groaned and struggled to sit.

"Kay?" he mumbled thickly. "Oh God. Kay?"

She stirred at the sound of his voice. "Ron?"

"Take it easy," Loren urged him. "Help's on the way, man. And we need to get our story straight before they get here."

He was right. We had the basic rudiments down by the time we heard the wail of sirens in the distance. Moments later I caught sight of flashing red and blue lights.

"Here they come," I said, leaning against the wall, pain throbbing in my head and every limb. "Let's hope they believe us."

* * *

Detective Maitland's attitude wasn't friendly anymore.

"That's three times you've been involved in violence with these people," he said. "If you were me, do you think that you'd start to see some kind of pattern?"

The nurse who was seeing to me shot an annoyed glance at Maitland but said nothing as she checked my pulse and blood pressure.

I lay on clean white sheets at Providence General, separated from the rest of the hospital by green surgical curtains. They'd told me I had a concussion and numerous contusions and sprains, but nothing was broken and for that at least I was grateful.

"I know what it looks like," I said. "I know I told you I'd stay away, but my friends... I'm sorry, detective. I couldn't dissuade them, so I went along."

"Along with this Michael O'Regan character in the middle of a stormy night to investigate some kind of devil cult activities." Maitland glared. "I already told you we'd been out there. We found the graffiti but nothing else."

I drew a deep breath and my chest hurt. "Well we found a lot more than that, detective. A hell of a lot more."

Maitland's eyes hardened. "And now I've got two people missing and five dead, three shot by bullets from your gun. I'm tired of playing games with you, Mister St. John. It's time you started telling me the truth."

I shook my head wearily. "I've told you the truth. We were just in the wrong place at the wrong time. We shouldn't have gone there, I know that. But we were attacked and my friends were killed by these people. I brought a gun and used it in self-defense."

"You've been doing a lot of that lately," Maitland replied. "One at the cement plant. One in your apartment. And now three at the Petroco building. You're running up quite a score, aren't you?"

I looked away, nausea surging.

"I'm sorry detective," the nurse interjected. "This man needs rest. You can interview him later. He's not going anywhere anytime soon."

Maitland favored me with a final angry glance then turned on his heel and strode out through the curtains.

The woman stepped back and turned out the light. "Now rest. You'll feel better tomorrow. I guarantee it."

Even in my injured and horrified state it didn't take long for me to sleep, but even as I did I knew that she was wrong.

Nothing would be better. Not tomorrow. Not ever.

PART THREE

SHE WHO WATCHES

D amien met me at the hospital a few days later and we drove home through the rain. The weather was getting worse.

"I tried calling Kay and Ron," he told me as he guided Yngwie along I-5, wipers slapping. "She told me never to call again; hung up on me. I think they're trying to get back to their lives and forget any of it happened."

"They won't forget," I said, feeling as bleak as the weather. "They'll never forget."

Damien grunted. "Loren's roommate says he took the dog and cleared out three days ago. He said that there was some big undefined family crisis in Kennewick."

"He won't be back, either. Nothing from Michael or Trish?"

"Not a word." Damien gripped the steering wheel tighter. "I think they're gone, Alex. They were too close to Onatochee. I think She Who Watches destroyed them both."

I didn't reply. Part of me hoped that it was true, that my friends wouldn't have to serve as a demon's living puppets. But part of me held out hope that they had survived, and would show up on my doorstep someday, hale and healthy.

I knew it was a forlorn hope, but I held onto it nonetheless.

A truck roared by, splashing the windshield with a rooster tail of rainwater.

"We're the only ones left, Damien," I said.

He drove on in silence for a while.

"Where to?" he asked. "Want to go home?"

I shook my head. "There's nothing for me there. I don't want to be alone. Not now."

"Okay." He sounded relieved. "My place it is, then."

* * *

We sat in the living room, sipping tea and coffee, as if going through the motions of our old rituals would somehow return us to the way we had been before. We both knew it wouldn't work, but we did it anyway.

There was a copy of the *Oregonian* on the coffee table. The headline read *Heavy Rains, Flooding in Western Oregon and Washington—More on the Way.*

I laughed humorlessly. "I see that we're finally off the front page."

Damien picked up the paper. "At least our story is holding up. Innocent but foolish civilians exploring an old building are ambushed by murderous transients. At this point, I don't mind admitting that I'm an idiot since I sure as hell feel like one."

The Petroco Massacre—as the media had dubbed it—had been headline news for a couple of days, and the hospital had taken pains to keep my release date discreet so that I wasn't assailed by TV crews on my way out. Damien told me he'd already changed his cell number and spent most of his time pretending not to be home. Fortunately, the worsening weather was keeping adventurous reporters at bay.

"Maitland came to see me twice in the hospital." I sighed. "He thinks we know more than we're telling, but they haven't found anything that contradicts us. He probably thinks we're a bunch of vigilantes out hunting homeless people or something."

Damien didn't smile. "No one's suggested that yet, thank goodness. They've rolled it in with the whole *Homeless Wars* narrative. It makes for better copy and lets them write editorials demanding better mental health care and more police funding. And after three whole twenty-four-hour news cycles there are sexier stories to cover."

I took a sip. My coffee was lukewarm and tasted as if it had been filtered through burlap.

There was an elephant in the room and I finally acknowledged it.

"Is it dead? The demon? Entity? Whatever the hell it was? Gone? Banished? Did She kill it or drive it off or something? Did She finish the ritual we started?"

It was another fragment of hope to cling to. Whoever, whatever *She* was—if She had vanquished Onatochee, then Vince and Eric hadn't died for nothing. And if Michael and Trish had been destroyed along with their master, maybe their deaths meant something too.

Damien shrugged. "We can only hope. Maybe we weakened it and She finished the job. And if that's the case, maybe Kay and Ron have the right idea. We need to get back to our lives and put this all behind us. We can't ever forget it, but at least we can try to learn from it."

I rolled my eyes. "You're starting to sound like an after-school special, Damien. Learn what?"

"Learn not to toy with things we don't understand, I guess." His shoulders slumped and his voice went flat and lifeless. "Learn to leave well enough alone."

I didn't reply. Glancing at the table I saw a thick book with a canvas library cover titled *Native American Mythological Cycles and Traditions* by Carl Lind.

"I see your book finally arrived," I said. "A little late for our purposes."

He picked it up. "It's interesting reading at least. Maybe it'll give us some insight into what happened." His face fell. "Though I don't think I'll be writing any more *Eye on the Unknown* columns."

The flat tone in his voice and the hopelessness of his words piled onto the guilt and pain I was already feeling. Tears stung my eyes. I'd held back too long.

"Damien, Mia Jordan called me the night before the ritual."

He dropped the book and stared at me. "Mia...? You mean the woman from the cement plant? She called you?"

"She told me not to go. Said that she'd dreamed about me and saw what had happened. I didn't listen. I guess I should have. Now I have no idea where she is and her number is blocked."

Damien's head slumped. "Oh God, Alex. She knew something was going to happen. Jesus. She might have been able to help us. If only there was some way to get in touch with her."

"We can't. It's too late." Despite my best efforts, hopelessness crept into my words.

"God, Alex."

"That's not all, Damien." The words were coming faster now, and hot tears stung my face. "I saw things when that thing got into my head at Petroco. You probably did too."

He nodded. "Yeah. I saw what a shit I'd been to my parents. I remembered all the stupid crap that I pulled and how much I really enjoyed it. The drugs, the sex, the parties. I thought about how much easier it would be to just give in to the madness and stop fighting it. It was just like before, only much worse. God, the things it showed me..."

His voice trailed off. I swallowed with difficulty and tried to keep the tremor out of my voice. "Damien, I..." I faltered. "I saw..."

He frowned, his slack expression transforming into one of concern. "What did you see, Alex? What happened?"

I shook my head. It hurt too much. "Nothing. Just the same as you. Blood, violence, death. I just can't get it out of my head."

I wanted to tell him about Alan Coleman and what I'd done to him. But I couldn't force the words out. Not yet. I just looked down and sobbed.

"I can't," I said, gulping air. "I can't tell you."

I felt Damien's hand on my shoulder.

"You don't have to tell me. Just wait. Wait 'til you're ready."

I looked up at him. "That's what She said. '*Nomeus*. When you are ready.' Jesus, Damien. I've been dreaming about Her for months and I still don't understand anything. What the hell does She want? What does She want with me?"

She had spoken to me, and only to me. She had offered me the weapon, and I'd been too weak to take it. And even now, with my friends dead and my life shattered, I had no clue.

Damien shook his head sadly. "I just don't know, Alex. I've been saying that a lot lately—'I don't know.' Now maybe I'm finally starting to realize that sometimes it's better not to know."

I brushed away tears with the back of my hand. It wasn't much of an answer but it was all we had. If it was over, it was over and there was nothing we could do about it. "Yeah. You're probably right. We need to try to get back to our lives, like Kay and Ron."

"I wish I could come up with something more, Alex, but I can't. Just trying to carry on is all I've got left." He sighed and looked as if he was ready to cry too.

I stood up. It was past noon. Time to try and put my life back together. "I should go to work. I've been out for a week, and if Loren's gone then things are probably going to hell."

Damien nodded understandingly. "Need a ride?"

I slipped on my coat and opened the door. Cold air rushed in. "I'll bus it. You stay and take it easy. Have a good rest of the day. Call me if anything happens."

I hiked four blocks through a blast of wind and ice-cold rain to the bus shelter. The sullen sky matched my mood.

My failure to come clean with Damien about Alan burned inside me. I told myself that we'd seen too many horrors over the past week; admitting that I had nearly beaten a man to death might be too much for him to take.

Or was I just afraid? Maybe I just didn't want him to know how badly I'd failed—that not telling him about Mia's phone call was enough truth for now. Maybe if I'd listened to her, none of this would have happened. Vince and Eric would still be alive, Michael O'Regan would still be spouting his mystical bullshit, and Trish would be waiting for me, eagerness and love shining in her violet eyes.

I sat down in the dubious protection of the bus shelter under a big near-naked tree. For all I could tell I was alone in the world, sitting by myself on a dead street, surrounded by deserted houses, their bright colors sad and muted.

A bus rushed by across the street, heading in the opposite direction, snorting diesel fumes. Another would be coming my way in a few minutes.

As I looked after it I fancied I could see two pale faces staring with hollow black eyes through the bus' dirty rear window. Then they seemed to shift, their mouths yawning wide and black, their outlines expanding and twisting, streamers and tendrils of wild color bursting through their skin to glimmer and writhe across the glass...

My stomach lurched. I looked away, telling myself it wasn't real, that I was upset and overwrought.

A soft footfall sounded behind me.

I spun around. Two men stepped out from behind the tree as if they'd been hiding there, watching me. They were tattered, hungry-looking men in dirty clothes with sunken red eyes—the same as I had seen when Pine Street Bob had first spoken to me, so very long ago.

"Hi, Alex," said the first. "We're looking for the Shepherd."

The second man didn't speak but opened his mouth wide, revealing an array of yellow-brown teeth. A sound emerged from his throat, the same inhuman cacophony that the demon had produced, and in my head I heard a voice speaking in warm, familiar tones.

Alex.

I stepped backwards, toward the curb, away from the pair. They moved after me, slowly and almost casually.

"He's back now." Black threads flickered in the first man's eyes and something squirmed across his face, like tiny worms crawling just beneath his skin. His torn plaid shirt moved strangely, as if something was trapped beneath it, trying to tear its way free. "But he still wants the Shepherd."

His face blurred and jumped, then for an instant it became the visage of Pine Street Bob, bearded and mad-eyed.

Alex.

The second man's mouth yawned even further open, like a snake unhinging its jaw to swallow its prey. A long tongue of shimmering greenish-yellow wriggled of its own accord, reaching out toward me...

A loud honking sound and the roar of a diesel engine made me jump. My bus was pulling up—if I'd taken another step back I'd have tumbled off the curb right in front of it.

The doors opened and the driver glared at me in silence. I looked back toward the shelter. The two men were gone.

God, I thought to myself as I stumbled on board and threw myself into a window seat. Had they ever been there at all?

I looked back as we pulled away. Through the fogged window I could see two figures standing there, silent and menacing, their faces following me as the bus moved down the street.

I shivered.

* * *

I rushed past Terri, barely acknowledging her sympathetic greeting, mumbling that I needed to sit down. A handful of other employees stared at me as I stumbled into my office and threw myself into my chair.

Terri followed me, hovering in the doorway.

"You okay, honey?" she asked, her eyes reflecting worry surrounded by thick black lines. "You didn't have to come in today. Conseuela's handling everything just fine."

I shook my head. I wasn't going to involve her or anyone else in the office. "It's okay. I'm just a little tired." I forced a grin. "I think they took most of my blood."

She returned my smile. "As long as you're okay. You want coffee or something?"

"Tea," I said. "Hot tea sounds really good right now."

"Okay, love. Just sit there and I'll get you some."

Well, if nothing else she was the nicest boss I'd ever had. More reason, I told myself, not to involve her.

Shit. I hadn't called Damien. I fumbled for my phone and hit his speed dial. The phone rang three times, then his voicemail picked up.

"Damien?" I was surprised at how frightened and weak my own voice sounded. "Damien, I saw... I think I... Jesus." I stopped, trying to slow my breathing. "Just call me, okay? Call me as soon as you get this."

I dropped the phone and leaned back, staring at the walls of my office, covered in pictures and clippings, and at my desk, a fortress of printouts and papers surrounding my workstation. It was real; it was substantial; it was my world; It was where I had lived for years.

And those men at the bus stop had been just as real.

Jesus.

I nursed my tea for another hour before I was finally calm enough to start poking at my usual pile of illiterate articles and rants. I knew I was just going through the motions, but at least it gave me some semblance of normalcy.

Idly, I checked the headlines and instantly wished I hadn't. A huge storm surge had swamped coastal properties in Bandon and Brookings. Unseasonal upwelling brought a rich haul of fish, but they were quickly followed by a plague of Humboldt squid, strangely numerous and aggressive. Winds of hurricane force struck the Olympic Peninsula.

Violence continued to ravage the homeless community as a rash of home invasions and inexplicable domestic crimes struck the Portland area. In one such crime, a store clerk in Beaverton attacked his customers with a tire iron, badly injuring one and sending another to the hospital with a fractured skull. The suspect had been taken into custody shrieking incoherently, uttering gibberish and strange-sounding words. Somehow I knew what the words were and what they meant.

Finally there was a small story about a growing scandal at the Multnomah County coroner's office. Apparently the body of Robert Leslie, aka Pine Street Bob, had been *misplaced*. He had been interred at the city morgue prior to burial, but now no one knew where he was. The coroner assured reporters that he would be doing a thorough investigation and that those responsible for the screw up would face serious consequences.

It was all too much. Nothing was right. It was all going to hell. I was reaching for my cell to call Damien again when Terri reappeared, looking at me glumly.

"I hate to further complicate your morning, Alex, but there's a very authoritarian-looking guy outside who wants to talk to you. He says his name's Maitland and he's from the Portland Police. Want me to tell him you're indisposed?"

"No." I shook my head. Detective Maitland was rapidly becoming my new best friend. "We're acquainted. Have him come in."

I waited, closing windows and saving work on my monitor. A moment later, Maitland's big shape filled the doorway.

"Hello, Alex," said a rich, Irish-accented voice. "Sorry for the deception."

A cold knife stabbed me through the gut.

It wasn't Maitland.

"We need to talk," Said Michael O'Regan.

H e was every bit the distinguished middle-aged antiquarian I remembered. He looked ready for an afternoon at the yacht club, clad in loafers, clean slacks and a dark shirt with a gray sweater tied around his shoulders. His skin was a healthy pink and his eyes were as bright and wise as I remembered. For an instant, I thought that maybe he really was Michael O'Regan, healthy and intact, returning to see his friend Alex. But something about him wasn't right, and I knew it.

He closed the door behind him. As he seated himself, I saw that he moved strangely, like a movie running a tiny fraction too fast or too slow. Greenish light flickered behind his eyes.

"It's you, isn't it?" I said. "Onatochee."

He shrugged, palms out and nodded once, still smiling.

"In a sense, yes. But as I've already told you, I don't think you truly understand."

I tried to look casual despite my fear, but probably did a bad job of it.

"Try me. Things were kind of stressful the last time we got together. Maybe now you'll find me more open-minded."

I was unarmed. The police had taken my Glock as evidence. I wondered whether it would have done me any good even if they hadn't.

"You remember how I talked to you about extradimensional entities when we met a few weeks ago?" He grinned. "You know—demons?"

I glared. "You mean how Michael talked to me? Yes, I remember. Probably better than you, since you weren't even there."

"Oh I was there, Alex. That's one of the things you don't understand."

"Have you been with him ever since Scotland, then? Riding around with him, watching what he's doing, hearing what he hears? Was it you I've talked to? Become friends with? Michael O'Regan and Onatochee, both living in the same body? Your vessel?"

Michael leaned forward. His body blurred then snapped back to normal so quickly that I might not even have noticed if I hadn't been watching him so intently.

"It's an imprecise word for what Michael... I... *We*... are now, Alex. There was a part of me... Of Onatochee... in him... in me... in Michael... all along, yes, but that doesn't fully describe what he... *we*... are. Damien and his wild theorizing are right as far as they go... Your... Our reality is multifaceted. We all coexist in the same... The same... coterminous continuum."

He frowned. "No, that's not right, not really. How can you explain life in three dimensions to a creature that has always existed as a single line? How can I make you see...?" He faltered. "What you saw that night—what shares this vessel is nothing but a suggestion of its true nature. A reflection. The merest fraction of the whole, viewed through a glass darkly, just as Damien said it was. The Chilut saw it and worshipped it as a god. The

Multnomahs saw it and called it a demon. Other people see it and it drives them mad."

"And makes them kill and maim and rape. Yes, I get it, Michael." Fear faded as anger and disgust warred inside me. "Contact with Onatochee warps his worshippers' minds and bodies. It frees them of inconveniences like conscience and morality. It makes them betray their friends like Trish did."

He looked unhappy at that and there was a suggestion of the old Michael. "Trish isn't part of this discussion, Alex."

I leaned forward abruptly and half rose, fists pounding down on my desk. "Where the hell is she then? Why did you twist her and use her?"

Michael raised a hand defensively and smiled. "All I... Or the entity that you want to call Onatochee... All we do is offer a glimpse of another reality, and freedom from the constraints of this one. How an individual reacts is up to him. Or her."

I pressed my fists into the desktop. Yes, it was rage I felt—clean and uncomplicated rage. Human rage, untainted by the demon's intrusions.

"So why are you here? What do you want with me?" I demanded. "Why does Onatochee offer freedom, knowing that it turns humans into monsters? What can an entity so complex, so intricate, possibly gain from enslaving us?"

The smile broadened, as if I was a six year old finally figuring out a math problem. "It gains more reality, Alex. It expands its influence, grows larger and more powerful. Every creature in the universe—man, god, angel, demon—must have sustenance. And Onatochee's sustenance is the darkness inside the self. The essence. The shadowy secrets of the soul, if you will. The more that join with Onatochee, the greater its power, and the more this reality comes to resemble its own."

The cool smile froze me in place. When I replied my tongue felt thick and lifeless.

"Are you saying...?" I stopped. "Are you saying that you want to expand Onatochee's reality into this one? Replace it?"

"No. Once more it's not that simple." The voice was eager now, as if the thing that wore Michael O'Regan's skin actually thought I was about to agree with it. "Realities will be joined. United. Together. Your reality will become... It will become *one*. A part of Onatochee. You must understand, Alex! There hasn't been an opportunity like this in centuries. You must see that."

I didn't reply.

"He... I... We want you to join us, Alex. You're the one with the powers, the skills, the understanding... You will be valued, honored... Your help... Your cooperation... is significant. Damien too... He can prove very useful. The others—Kay, Ron, Loren, that dog of his... They don't matter. They can join or not as they choose. My... Our... followers are not very kind to those who refuse, however. But not you, not Damien. It's you that we truly want with us."

"And if I refuse?"

He shrugged clumsily, as if he was unfamiliar with the gesture. "We'll have you either way, Alex. It's better that you join voluntarily—it's easier on us, and less painful for you. More of... More of *you* will survive and live on after the joining. Like Trish did. A portion... An *element* of a greater... A greater being, if you will."

He paused and his expression grew almost dreamy. "I am a little world, made cunningly of elements."

Onatochee, I thought, almost contemptuously. The Shakespeare-quoting demon.

Green light flashed in his eyes—brighter this time—and his face hardened. "Otherwise... Well, it won't be pleasant, but the end result will be the same for Onatochee... For me..." He paused and his tone grew almost pleading. "Why don't you understand, Alex? Can't you see what Onatochee... What *we*... offer? How glorious this new reality can be?"

"You're the one." I could barely summon the words to reply. "You're the one who doesn't understand. You think that your reality is so much more wondrous and significant than this one that I can't help but be convinced. That if you explain enough to me I'll finally understand and see that Onatochee is right. Is that what you think, Michael?"

Confusion flickered behind his eyes and more black threads squirmed. His face flushed red and a faint cloud of sparks swirled around his head.

"He sees you, Alex." The comforting, self-assured voice was gone, replaced by a low animalistic snarl. "He sees what you did. The things you keep hidden. What you did to Alan Coleman. How you and your damned moral superiority killed Cheryl White."

The words stung, but by now all they did was feed my very human, very natural rage.

"I don't know what you are," I said through gritted teeth, "but I know you don't belong here. I know you're a plague that needs to be wiped out. And if there's any way to do it, I'll find it."

A faint metallic sound emerged from Michael's throat. "You can't fight me. Any more than an insect can fight a leviathan. My storm is coming, Alex. You can't survive it alone."

I remembered the silver woman and her voice—soft, warm, comforting. She wasn't with me now, but I could at least remember.

243

"I'm not alone," I replied, still glaring, feeling rage and desire for vengeance course through me. "You fear Her, don't you? She Who Watches. The one who drove you away."

He laughed with a sound like a clanging hammer. "I saw you and Damien, Alex. All your sad, confused research and speculation. You haven't the faintest idea who or what She is, or how little power She truly has. I... we... Onatochee was at its weakest when it first took me... Took Michael... as a vessel, and even then all She could do was banish us temporarily. Now..." The anger vanished from Michael's eyes and he spoke with resolute calm. "Now, we're stronger."

With that his outlines jumped and flickered, and he was suddenly not Michael, but a mass of chaotic, shifting shapes and swirling colors, towering over me.

I jumped back in alarm, upsetting my chair. The repellent mass blurred out of focus, flickering and jumping sickeningly, then reformed, and now it was Trish who sat naked before me, her adoring violet eyes staring through a haze of static and cycling colors.

"We've been to see Damien, too," she said softly, leaning forward, holding her breasts out like offerings. She flickered and shifted, becoming something dark and foul. Then she was Trish again. "Right after you left. We made him the same offer. You see what we can do? What you can do when you step away from your own notions of reality? It would be better for you, for us, if you join us willingly, but you'll join us, one way or the other. Do it now, Alex. Do it or people will suffer."

She changed again, her eyes growing, transforming into multifaceted orbs, her face narrowing into the visage a great mantis-like thing crafted from shining orbs and streamers of greenish light. It hissed and reached for me, claws elongating...

I screamed, falling backwards over my upset chair, knocking my head against the window sill.

I'll give you a few days, Alex. The voice echoed in my head with words that were not words. *When the storm comes it will be too late. You'll be with us, willingly or unwillingly.*

I kept screaming, my hands over my head, desperate to drive out the echoing demonic voice.

I heard shouting, and the sound of the door being thrown open.

"Alex! Alex, what's wrong?"

I looked up over my desk. The chair was empty. Terri and Consuela stood in the doorway. When they saw me, their expressions of frightened anxiety deepened.

"What happened, Alex?" Terri's usual tone of slightly sarcastic camaraderie was gone, replaced by outright alarm. "Where's the cop?"

I rose unsteadily to my feet, staring at the hallway behind them and the workroom beyond.

He was gone. I pulled my coat on and rushed past them.

"I have to go," I said hurriedly. "I'm sorry, Terri. I have to go."

Terri seemed stunned. It wasn't until I was in the elevator that I heard a loud, "Alex!" echo down the hall.

* * *

I walked down the street like a man in a trance, brushing past people, stumbling toward the bus mall. In their faces I saw the same madness that I'd seen in the eyes of Pine Street Bob and Uncle Creepy and Michael O'Regan.

Numb, unfeeling, in near-total shutdown I rode the bus to Woodstock. Michael had visited Damien. I could only hope that he'd resisted, that together we might be able to find some way out of the nightmare—some way to turn back the clock and make things normal again.

I wasn't that lucky.

It was dark by the time I got to Damien's house. I scanned the front yard with its tangle of undergrowth and overhanging trees, then dashed quickly up the steps. No monsters intercepted me, but no one answered my insistent ringing, despite the fact that lights burned inside the house. There was no sign of a break-in or violence, and the door opened easily to my key. Once more wishing I had my pistol but also knowing it wouldn't have helped anything, I slipped into the living room.

There was a silence of a sort that I'd never felt before. Damien's house was almost always quiet, except for the times when we were making fun of *Paranormal Investigations,* but now there was a dull, dead quality to the place that felt wrong.

Damien wasn't anywhere downstairs. The kitchen counter was covered with dirty dishes, but Damien's ubiquitous teapot was missing.

I raced up the stairs. The lights were all on, and the door to Damien's office was open. I saw a shape sitting in the chair, facing the big flat panel monitor, motionless and slumped forward. On the desk I saw an empty pill container lying on its side, next to a half-empty bottle of whiskey and the missing tea kettle, carefully placed on a trivet.

"Damien?" Each step toward the office seemed more difficult, as if invisible hands held me back. *"Damien!"*

I grabbed the chair and spun it to face me.

Damien was gone. He slumped in the chair, his mouth half-open, his eyes lifeless and filmed over. In one hand he held a folded piece of paper, marked "ALEX." I took it and read it through a blur of tears.

Alex: Michael paid me a visit, and said he was going to see you. I hope you're still around to read this. I'm so sorry, but it's the only way out. I mailed you something. You should get it in a couple of days. You'll understand when you read it. Tell Terri that I'm sorry. Love, Damien.

I did everything you're supposed to do. I felt for a pulse, I dragged his dead weight down to the floor, tried CPR, did all the stuff from my old lifesaving classes, but I knew it wouldn't work. He'd been dead for hours and nothing I did would revive him.

Everything I'd valued had collapsed into rubble in a matter of days. Numbly I called 911 on my cell, then sat silent and staring as two paramedics went through the same rote lifesaving process, all with the same sense of futility and inevitability.

After they took him away I stepped into the bathroom, listening to the rain and wind outside. I opened the medicine cabinet and stared in disbelief at Damien's pill bottles—the ones I'd seen when I'd first visited him.

The dates on the prescriptions were over two months old, and the bottles were half full. He'd been off his medications for over six weeks.

I wanted to pick up the phone and call Loren, tell him to come get me, and ask if I could sleep on his couch again. I wanted Beowulf to jump on me and keep me awake half the night trying to get comfortable. I wanted to go home and watch TV or play video games until I fell asleep. I wanted to go to the office and edit a badly-written story about the incompetence of the city water bureau. I wanted to crawl in bed beside Trish and feel her warm and soft beside me. I wanted...

I wanted life to be normal again.

It wasn't. And it couldn't be. There was no one left. I was alone.

And there was a real, live demon out there somewhere, looking for me.

I called Terri to tell her what happened, but got her voicemail. I called a cab and paid the exorbitant cost of a ride to the airport, where I checked into a hotel.

The news scrolled by on the room TV as I ate dinner from a vending machine.

That night I dreamed of Trish's face, and her violet eyes staring at me lovingly. Slowly, she disintegrated, replaced by Onatochee's ever-changing masks, each more horrible than the last.

I spent a few days at the hotel, watching endless reruns and listening to alarming news reports about the growing storm and the violence spreading out of Old Town. The Petroco Massacre was forgotten for the moment, and the alternative was even more frightening.

I slept fitfully, troubled by dreams that I couldn't clearly remember. I saw Trish, I heard Michael, and somehow I knew that they were more than dreams. I'd frustrated them by disappearing, but they'd find me, surely enough.

Mornings dawned gray and wet, with wind-driven rain drumming on my room's sliding glass door.

I couldn't stay in Portland. I knew it. I wasn't going to end it all like Damien, but I was going to follow Loren's lead and get the hell out of town before it was too late.

On the third morning after my arrival at the hotel, I wolfed down breakfast in the coffee shop then took a cab to my apartment. If the place was secure, I'd pack just enough to get away and spend the last dregs of my savings account on a flight to California, or farther if I could. I had heard that Austin was relatively welcoming to eccentrics.

The apartment building looked normal. I checked my mail before unlocking the door. Among the bills and advertising flyers was a thick envelope doubled over and stuffed in the box, my address scrawled on it in a shaky hand.

Holding my mail clumsily, I fumbled with my keys and unlocked the door, then turned off the alarm and checked all the rooms. Nothing. For the moment I was alone. I reset the alarm, sat down at my little dining room table, and opened the envelope.

Dear Alex:

Forgive my handwriting, but I'm doing this in haste. By the time you read this, to use an old and hackneyed cliché, I will probably be dead. It's going to take all the guts I've got left to do this, so I won't delay any longer.

Michael came to see me soon after you left. I saw what he was— what he'd become. He wanted me to join with him like Trish and Pine Street Bob had, but he didn't seem terribly concerned when I refused. I think he's more interested in you, anyway. He acted as if he was up to something, that he has plans that are still unfolding. He said a storm was coming and that if I refused him now I'd beg to join him later. Very jolly fellow, that Onatochee.

You managed to hold that creature off when he got into your head. Trish didn't. She failed, but I don't think it was really her fault. For all her attitude and self-assurance she was still as weak as the rest of us. As weak as me. I almost gave in, Alex. I almost gave that monster what it wanted.

I don't think I can do it again. Onatochee knows it—my choice is to resist or serve, and I just haven't the strength to resist anymore, Alex. Life's beaten me down too much. I've failed one time too many.

What happened at Petroco destroyed a part of me that I can't live without. It's hope, Alex. That last little creature in Pandora's Box, and now it's gone. The universe is a bleak and unhappy place for me right now. When I think of the future, all I see is Onatochee staring back at me. My only hope is that there is something more lasting and sublime waiting for me on the other side.

I've spent the last few hours of my life as a free man. For a while I was the old Damien Smith again, sitting at my computer, researching, reading books, writing articles and trying to make sense of the unknowable. I've had the pieces of the puzzle for months now, but they're only now starting to fit together and make sense.

You're the one who can resist. I felt it that night, when She came. I've felt it ever since I met you. And now, I finally understand. I know who you are. I know what you are. Read the material I've attached, read the notes. I believe that there are things you must do that no one else on earth can.

Carl Lind's book on Chinook mythology includes another version of the story about the battle with Onatochee. I've attached a photocopy, along with other confirmations – Native American, Mycenaean, Persian, African, Chinese, Anglo-Saxon. It's a bit voluminous so I won't blame you if you choose to scan some of it. But read it, and read my notes—that's about as organized as I can be right now. Maybe that's where the hope lies... I just know I'm not the one to do it. I think that unlike the rest of us, your life has a real purpose, Alex.

I believe you can stop this. Don't be afraid. If it comes to a fight, think of me. Think of Cheryl and Vince and Eric. Think of Michael and Trish, and try to forgive them for their weakness. We're all human, Alex. All of us. And that's the most powerful weapon we have.

My best wishes. Carry on the work. I'm leaving you my house, the computers and good old Yngwie. Take good care of them. You have my permission to continue writing the 'Eye on the Unknown' column under my byline, so have fun with it. And find another girlfriend. Maybe that blue woman with the sword.

Love, Damien Smith.

I stared until the words bled together and ran down my face. Damien's dreams had betrayed him, and the truth he sought had proved itself so ugly that he couldn't live with it.

The top photocopy was an eleven by seventeen sheet with a page from Lind's book. I read it as best I could, wiping away tears as I went.

A story told by the Chinook as late as the early 1900s tells how the demon Onatochee was defeated by a lone warrior named Klale-Mamuk (roughly translated as "Black Hunter"), a man whose wife and child had been murdered by a rival band. In his grief he lived alone, shunning the company of other tribes. One day the goddess called She Who Watches appeared to the hunter, telling him that since he did not worship any god and didn't belong to any tribe, he would fight for them all, and he would defeat Onatochee and the Chilut.

At first Klale-Mamuk refused, saying that since men had failed him, he wanted no part in their affairs. But the goddess persisted and Klale-Mamuk saw that his heart had become black with sadness. He realized that his people needed him, and he agreed to aid the goddess.

She Who Watches then gave Klale-Mamuk a talisman that protected him from attacks by Onatochee's servants, a bow that could pierce Onatochee's hide and a stone axe that could kill him. With these weapons he led a band of warriors against the Chilut and slew Onatochee, banishing him from our world. Klale-Mamuk then went back to his camp, but having learned love and humility, returned to aid the Multnomahs when they were in peril. Many other tales were supposedly told about Klale-Mamuk, but they have long since been lost.

My hands trembled so badly that I could barely turn the page to read the second photocopy. I forced myself to concentrate. It was from a monograph on proto-Greek mythology.

The original Mycenaean legend tells of a lone herdsman who lived apart from his fellows, tending his goats and taking no part in the wars or rituals of the surrounding communities. During this time a fearsome creature, possibly a giant or minotaur, ravaged the land, devouring men and carrying off women for its pleasure.

While tending his animals, the herdsman was visited by a goddess. In later Greek versions of the myth she was Nemesis, goddess of vengeance. In earlier stories she was an earth goddess, roughly comparable with the later Gaia, but probably a more primal version, whose symbol was the sacred spiral, one of the most basic and universal of human icons.

The goddess said to the herdsman, "You do not make sacrifice to the gods, so they owe you nothing. You serve no king, so you may fight for all people. You protect your herd and do no harm. You are Nomeus, *The Great Shepherd, and I choose you to stand watch over your people, to shut the gateways through which their enemies come, to save those you can, and to avenge those you cannot."*

"Oh God." My voice was a whisper as I looked back and forth between the two legends, distantly separated in both time and space.

At first the herdsman refused to listen. He was a sad and embittered man who wished only to be left in peace to tend his herd. But the goddess spoke to the herdsman's heart and he knew that all people were his people, that he was a man of all nations and cities, that without their men and women and children he would be nothing. For the first time he looked into his own soul and saw that it was empty and barren.

The herdsman fell to his knees. "O, Goddess," he said, "I have let my grief rule me. I have been selfish and prideful. I have cursed those I should love. I have lived apart and rejected my own people. Please forgive me."

"You do not need forgiveness, mortal," the goddess replied. "You need only accept your own frailty and know that in being imperfect, you are perfectly human. In your imperfection you are greater than the gods themselves, for even they cannot accept their own transgressions or admit to their own petty failings. Rise, Nomeus, *and accept your charge. Let your imperfection and humility shake the very earth itself."*

She then gave the herdsman arms and armor—shield, spear and a dark chariot that would take him anywhere. Having accepted the goddess and admitted to his own frailty, the herdsman sought out and slew the monster.

The people proclaimed him king, but he refused. He wished only to tend his herds, he said, but in taking the goddess' charge he had learned to love his fellow man and would return if called. He lived for many years, protecting his people as he protected his herds, and when he died another took his place, so that the people would always know that Nomeus *was their champion, the guardian of the doorways, servant of the sacred spiral.*

Damien's notes were all over the paper, circling terms, drawing lines between the two tales. *Nomeus = Shepherd. Spear/ Axe/sacred weapon? Aegis/talisman? Dark chariot = ??? Nemesis = She Who Watches... She Who Watches = ?? Gods/goddesses? Sacred Spiral = ???*

I couldn't stop. My hands moved like automata, flipping through the papers, reading story after story. I read another, this one from the American southwest.

The Anaye were a group of otherworldly monsters who were defeated by the hero twins, Nayanezgani and Thobadzistshini. According to Navajo legend, the twins were given mystical weapons by the god Tshohanoai and the goddess Estanatlehi, and used them to destroy the monsters.

The legend of the Anaye is repeated with variations by many of the Uto-Aztecan nations. The Leetayo Hopi, for example, tell a slightly different story—that of a lone warrior, estranged from his community and from the gods themselves, who was visited by the spider-goddess Sotuknang and accepted a magical club and bow, using this to battle the Anaye, or Anuquoo in the local dialect. The Pima and Papago tribes tell their own version of the legend, each featuring a lone hunter named

Sheh'e Chuk who wielded a sacred spear and shield against a race of monsters sent by a wicked sorcerer...

The papers fell to the floor as I read through them, one after the other. Damien had highlighted words and scrawled more frantic notes in the corners.

...In some very old Sumerian tales, Panigara, Lord of the Frontier-Stone was a warrior given sacred duty by the goddess Belit-Ini to guard the world against incursion by evil spirits and monsters such as the red-skinned Kusariku and the demon-lord Mimma-Lemnu...

Panigara...

...When the monsters of the Alcheringa refused to dwell in the time of dreams and tried to live in the waking world as well, the ancestor-spirits grew troubled. Marawuti the Sea-Eagle visited the shaman Wurrugala, saying, "You have lost your tribe, your family and your gods. You are your own tribe, your own family, your own god. Take this bull-roarer made from the back bones of Ginga the Crocodile and use it to frighten the monsters of the Alcheringa, take this spear whose point is crafted from the rib-bones of the Rainbow Serpent to slay them..."

Wurrugala...

...The priest whom the people called only Hirdir—the Shepherd. Once a staunch skeptic who rejected all faiths, Hirdir *claimed to have had a vision of the Virgin Mary and received from her a holy sword and was bidden to fight for the lost and the innocent in her name. Hirdir fought against an army of trolls and monsters called the Fordæmdur or "Fallen Ones"...*

Hirdir...

...A ronin or masterless samurai bore a katana crafted by the goddess Ame-no-Uzume and struggled against the Kokuou Gosai (Crimson King) and the Hyakki Yako, an army of oni or Japanese demons. Though his true name is lost to history, he was known by the humble title of Kainushi, or Shepherd...

Kainushi...

...the folk hero known as Negrinho de Pastoreio *(the Black Shepherd-Boy) is still venerated in rural Brazil. According to legend, the* Negrinho *was a slave left by his owner to die in the jungle, but who was visited by an angelic being—in some versions of the story she is the Virgin Mary, in others a tribal goddess—and returned to liberate mistreated slaves and punish cruel slave-masters...*

Negrinho de Pastoreio...

...a simple Shepherd, called M'chungaji *in the Yoruba language was visited by Oya, goddess of wind and guardian of the underworld, who gave him sacred weapons and bade him defend all tribes against the minions of Gaunab, god of evil...*

M'chungaji...

...Dating as far back as the 1300s, members of a mysterious clerical order who called themselves the Filii Pastor—*Sons of the Shepherd— bore silver-tipped hawthorn staves in the form of shepherd's crooks and are said to have battled monsters and demons of many sorts. The* Filiii *claimed that every slain abomination was a scar in the flesh of Lucifer...*

Filii Pastor...

There were more. Dozens more—paragraphs, pages, whole chapters, all frantically copied or printed, highlighted, scrawled with notes. Damien had indeed spent his last few hours as the fearless researcher he'd always been, making connections that no one else could see and showing that they were more than simply the ravings of a madman.

Shepherd. *Nomeus.* Panigara. Hirdir. Kainusha, Wurrugala. Sheh'e Chuk. Negrinho de Pastoreio. M'chungaji... They all began to blur together in my mind, melting into one another until all I could think of were the words of the silver-blue winged woman as She offered me salvation.

Nomeus. When you are ready.

The last page was more of Damien's handwriting, sloppy and illegible as if written in a great and desperate hurry.

If Onatochee is a malign demonic entity who wants to open the doorways, to enter this world and prey on humans, is it possible that there are others? Others who want to keep the doors closed? If opening the doorway to our world is bad for us, is it possible that it's bad for those on the other side as well? And if there are other entities—angels? Gods and goddesses? Is that what they truly are?—who need to keep the doors closed, then they wouldn't be able to fully manifest in this world, for fear that they'd cause the very catastrophe that they are trying to avoid.

The only way to achieve their purpose is to charge humans, inhabitants of this reality, with the task of keeping the gateways closed and defeating those entities that want to enter. Nomeus. Herdsmen. Hunters. Shepherds. Warriors. Priests. Heroes. Those who have known tragedy, and have given up, but who can still learn love and compassion? Defenders of the flock that is humanity and the land that is ours. Champions who stand in the doorway with a single candle in defiance of the darkness?

And at the bottom of the page, three final words, written so heavily the paper tore...

KLALE-MAMUK=NOMEUS = SHEPHERD = ALEX???

I felt my knees buckle and I fell backwards, leaning against the wall. Damien's letter slipped to the floor along with the rest of the papers.

The pieces that I had so long wanted to pretend didn't exist were finally coming together in my mind, and for the first time the picture wasn't Onatochee's hideous ever-changing visage.

Tsagaglalal. Nemesis. Mother Mary. Gaia. Belit-Ini. Oya. Sotuknang. Marawuti. She Who Watches. Gods and goddesses...

I'd seen Her. I'd seen the spiral and touched the sword. To me She had spoken the same words She had spoken to the herdsman, countless ages ago. She had called upon me to serve, but I had failed...

...Or had I?

Nomeus. When you are ready.

I'd tasted vengeance once, and it had scarred me. But now I thought of Damien, of Trish and the others, all victims of Onatochee and his alien nature, fed upon by monsters and their own lusts. He'd tried to take me, and when I fought back he'd taken someone else. He'd twisted Trish's own spirit against her, taking what was beautiful and making it into something ugly and evil. He'd stolen Michael's mind and body, he'd killed Eric and Vince, driven Ron and Kay away to a life of constant fear and dread, even frightened off Loren—the best friend I had left. Now Damien was dead, knowing that he would not be able to resist Onatochee again.

From the beginning I'd tried to pretend that there was some easy, mundane explanation for everything. I'd scoffed at stories of demons and magic, looked down on anyone who didn't think the way I did.

The entire apartment building shook with an angry gust of wind that I felt through the weather stripping.

My choice would be the same as all the others—resist or serve.

I'd been wrong. I'd been the fool, not Damien. And now he was gone, and I had to carry on—me, with my near-fundamentalist rationalism, my blind and stupid misanthropy. I'd do penance for my ignorance, Onatochee be damned.

I wouldn't run, and I wouldn't serve—I knew that much. I would resist, even if it meant ending up like Damien. I'd felt the touch of something else, something that wasn't Onatochee.

I had done wrong. I had lied. I had failed to save people I loved. I had nearly killed a man in a quest for vengeance and couldn't even admit it to my friends. I was lost, damaged, estranged. But that was over.

In a single motion I stood, strode to the door, and opened it, letting the cold, rain-scented wind whack me in the face, blowing Damien's papers across the room. Rain slashed across the parking lot and the world beyond my portal was gray and cold.

They weren't out there. Not now. But I knew they were coming. And when they did I would be ready for them.

Gaia. Belit-Ini. Oya. Nemesis. Tsagaglalal. She Who Watches. Ame-no-Uzume. Whatever She was called, She had reached out to me, as real as Onatochee. She'd offered me the means of defeating the enemy and I had been unable to take it. I couldn't deny it even if I tried. I didn't know why She had chosen me, but the die was cast and I had to accept it.

A motion in the parking lot caught my eye. It was an old blue Ford Taurus, fenders dented, windshield cracked. As I watched, it rolled to a stop and the door opened.

"Alex?"

I stared. "Loren?"

Stepping out of the car was a blessedly familiar figure wearing a t-shirt that said *If You're Really a Goth, Where Were You When We Sacked Rome?*

Then with a happy bark Beowulf's black-furred form appeared, eyes gleaming, tongue lolling. Catching sight of me, he bounded across the parking lot and a moment later I was fending off his excited kisses.

"Sit, boy." Loren followed more slowly. His was the voice of a man who had not slept or felt any peace in days. "Terri called me. She told me about Damien, and she said she didn't know where you were. I came here hoping I'd find you. Alex, I'm sorry I ran. I just needed time. I want to help."

Tears welled up and I swallowed painfully. "Are you sure?"

He nodded. "Yeah. I wouldn't be able to live with myself if I didn't."

We stared at each other for a moment, then embraced. "Come on in," I said. "I'll make you some toast."

IV

I floated in a sea of shadows, struggling to find lucidity without startling myself to wakefulness. I stared down at my hands and moved with slow deliberation. If I was dreaming, I was determined not to wake myself up.

Nomeus. The voice was distant, but for the first time I heard it and knew what it meant. *Nomeus. Shepherd. Do not fear the darkness.*

The trash strewn wasteland near Petroco spread out below me, a labyrinth under a chaotic sky. I swooped down like a bird, tossed on the angry wind. A single figure walked unsteadily in the rain, picking his way through the maze, stopping now and then to catch his breath. He was haggard, bearded and dirty, his wild eyes darting constantly left and right. Once he looked up and for a moment I thought he might have seen me, but then he looked away and continued to limp toward the dark shape of Petroco.

His face was almost as familiar to me as my own—it had stared at me from the street outside the Pioneer Building, from the nightly news reports, and a youthful version of it had regarded me mildly from a printout in Damien's office.

Robert Leslie. Pine Street Bob. The I-84 Killer. Not dead. Not misplaced. Alive—or some unnatural semblance of it.

He blundered into a deep puddle. A sort of shiver went through his body and he seemed to go out of focus, his entire shape shifting and changing slightly, then returning to normal.

I recoiled in fear and almost woke up. It was the same kind of jumpy skip that I'd seen when Michael came to my office. Somehow, Pine Street Bob had taken on some of his master's demonic essence—merged in incomprehensible fashion with the stuff of chaos. And now a dead man was walking.

Pine Street Bob didn't look happy about it, however. His expression was confused and almost angry. He limped along, dragging one foot behind, looking all around him, searching.

"Hello, Robert." The voice echoed out of the darkness that surrounded the entrance to Petroco, easily rising above the sound of wind and rain. "We've been waiting for you."

Michael O'Regan didn't so much as step out of the shadows as materialize from them—warm, smiling, well dressed, rain dripping from a big umbrella that he held in one hand. Save for a tiny glint of demonic light in his eyes, there was nothing outwardly strange about him, but as he moved I could still see that same imperceptible out-of-synch jerkiness.

"Come on, Robert." He beckoned. "Get out of that awful rain."

Bob crouched at the foot of the concrete steps, looking at Michael suspiciously. "Who're you?" His voice was thick and gravelly.

Michael pinned Bob with a sharp, piercing stare. Green light flickered.

"You know who I am, Robert. I'm why you're here."

Bob started to speak, but then fell silent as recognition dawned.

"Onatochee," he whispered.

Michael nodded and beckoned again. "Come out of the rain, my friend."

Bob scampered up the stairs with the enthusiasm of a dog greeting his returning master.

"You've come back," he said with a crooked, gap-toothed grin. "*Ilt'sim Unachee.* You came back for me. *Gatchink. Wo'igunaba.*"

"Of course, Robert. For you and all the others." Michael waved a hand. "Come out, my friends. Robert has come back to us."

More figures appeared, stepping from the surrounding darkness, emerging from the doorway behind Michael or creeping from the trash that surrounded the building. They too moved strangely, heedless of the rain. Some flickered with the same chaotic energy as Bob, their forms changing and shifting, flashing briefly into random shapes. Some were clearly homeless, hollow-eyed and almost skeletal, but others were normal men and women in jeans, coats, jogging suits... I saw a woman who wore a pink shirt and black sweater, a frizzy-haired young man in a Portland State University t-shirt, a big man wearing a mechanic's shirt with an oval name patch embroidered with the name "Jim."

They crowded around Pine Street Bob, fixing him with intense, wordless stares. He stared back, his eyes wide and as emotionless as a dead fish, glistening faintly with the demon's greenish light. The crowd of cultists seemed to communicate in silence like ships signaling each other across a stormy sea.

"Do you feel it, my friends?" Michael asked, warmly. "Feel what will come at the great unification, the joining of realms?"

He turned and gestured at the open doors behind him. "See what's coming, my friends."

Vision and reality broke into a blurred kaleidoscope of dark colors—rich purples, dark reds, yellows and Onatochee's sickly yellow-green. They twisted and quivered, transforming from angular crystalline images to a soft, multicolored sheen that squirmed like the surface of a soap bubble. Even from my relatively safe perspective I felt nauseous and dizzy, as if gazing into a bottomless abyss with nothing to keep me from falling.

I knew that I was looking through Damien's leaky screen doors, through the unthinkable depths of the cosmos and into another reality—the face of the Gorgon. I was seeing things that I wasn't meant to see, trying to use senses that didn't exist, and my confused brain did its best to interpret the stimuli, creating instead nauseating patterns and ugly sounds. Even viewing it through the filter of my own personal dreamtime, I couldn't contemplate what lay beyond the doorway for long.

The crowd of cultists around Bob stared, silent and transfixed, bathed in the flickering light of another universe. And as they watched, they changed, bodies flickering and shifting, cycling through strange shapes and outlines that my overburdened mind could barely comprehend—I saw the vague forms of plants and animals, geometric solids, shattering fractal patterns, jarring flashes of color, negative shapes in a spinning, disordered void. My head throbbed at the sight.

Michael looked up at the sky, his shape twisting and altering along with those of his followers—an ancient tree covered in metallic leaves, an ebon-skinned giant with swooping bull's horns, a flapping mass of wings twined with sparking wires, a cloud of vibrating, multicolored particles, and other shapes beyond my comprehension. But through all the changes, his eyes remained the same—gentle human eyes, tinged with the green glow of a demon. His gaze locked with mine.

His whisper filled my skull. "See, Alex? See what we bring to your world? See the beautiful changes?"

He paused. "Where are you, Alex? Where are you hiding? It's not too late. You know where we are. You know how to find us. It'll be easy for you. But not if we find you first, Alex... Not if we find you first..."

I wrenched myself from the dream, my body convulsing, tumbling to the floor, wrapped in bedclothes, a scream rising on my lips...

And Beowulf was standing over me, his big face full of concern, his big tongue sloppily licking my face.

"Jesus, Alex." Loren appeared behind Beowulf. "It's okay, man. You just had a bad dream."

I began to perceive my surroundings. We were at the hotel. Morning light shone through a small gap in the curtains. A pile of my possessions—food, clothes, computers, notebooks—stood nearby. On a small table one of my laptops was on, connected to Damien's network via VPN. And Beowulf was here—discreetly smuggled into the room in direct defiance of the hotel's no-pet policy.

I sat on the edge of the bed, rubbing my eyes.

"Not a dream," I mumbled. "Not a dream. I saw it. I saw Michael and the cultists. They're still at Petroco."

"Petroco? Jesus. I'd have thought the cops had locked that place down by now."

"I suspect the police are too busy with the Old Town situation and the weather. That's what he wants." I shuddered. "He's got an army now. And they're..."

I faltered, remembering the wildly changing shapes of the cultists as they stood, gazing through Michael's doorway and into the realm of his master.

"They're *different*. He's changed them somehow. They look like humans, but somehow they're being drawn into Onatochee's realm, becoming part of it. And Pine Street Bob was there, too. He's not dead. He's with them now."

"You sure you didn't just have a nightmare? Michael and his buddies are bad enough without having to deal with Pine Street Bob too."

"No." I swallowed and limped painfully to the bathroom to pour myself a glass of water. "It was real. I know it. He's looking for me, but he doesn't know where I am. And I know what he's planning. I know what that bastard is up to."

"What he's up to?"

I put the glass down and looked at Loren. He was scared, and so was I.

And it was about to get worse.

"He's going to open up Damien's screen doors," I said. "He's going to invade our reality with his. And there isn't a god-damned thing we can do to stop him."

"Oh, shit." Loren was pale, as if the worst elements of his games had come to life. He paused then swallowed hard. "I think I need a cup of coffee."

V

The next few days were a blur of rain and wind and blowing leaves, grim news and grimmer thoughts. Loren and I stayed up into the small hours every night, searching without much success for details about the Shepherd legend and She Who Watches.

We moved to a succession of less reputable hotels and motels, trying to stay ahead of Onatochee's searchers. We finally ended up at the bottom of the food chain—a run-down establishment in northeast Portland that probably rented by the hour and was grandly called the "Welcome Inn" and was notable only because it boasted in-room wireless Internet. Our respective savings accounts were nearing exhaustion, but right now it didn't seem to matter.

I didn't call Detective Maitland. He'd have his hands full, and God only knew whether the cultists left any evidence at Petroco. Even in the unlikely event that he believed my story about demons and dimensional gateways, I didn't want to send the Portland cops into a place where they might get butchered. The cult and its demon-god were my problem now. Besides, I suspected that Maitland didn't like me very much anymore.

We'd have to go back to Petroco, but I knew with painful certainty that we weren't ready yet.

Above all else we waited. We waited on Onatochee, on the cultists, and on She Who Watches. We needed Her weapon desperately—I knew that. My only hope was that She'd find some way to contact me and once more offer it.

And that I'd figure out what I had to do to take it.

We made one run to Damien's place to retrieve Yngwie and as many of Damien's books and notes as we could get. I knew it was risky, especially if any cultists were watching the house, but we agreed that having two cars was worth it, and I was pretty sure we'd end up needing the books.

I went everywhere with a hat or hood pulled low over my face, avoiding eye contact, doing everything as quickly and quietly as I could. I called Terri and told her that both Loren and I would be back after New Year's. She sounded concerned and told me not to worry—she and Consuela would get the Christmas issue out. Not for the first time, I was grateful to have her as a boss.

Outside the weather grew worse still, giving the local "Stormwatch" and "Doppler Radar Bulletin" newscasters something to get excited about. We were repeatedly assured that it was the worst weather in decades, and more was on the way.

A full week after Loren's return I was sitting on the floor of our seedy room at the Welcome Inn with Beowulf—the manager didn't give a damn what kind of animals we kept in the room so long as we were paid up—filling glass beer bottles with gasoline and sealing them with fizz-keeper soda stoppers. The door rattled, Loren ambled in and dropped a heavy canvas bag on the floor with a clank.

"Order up," he said, kneeling down to pet Beowulf before opening the bag and inspecting its contents. "Clothes, blankets, crank-powered radio, entrenching tools, fireaxe. Emergency first aid kit with suture, needles, antibiotics... The whole enchilada. Two Glock 17s with ammo, two 12-gauge Mossberg 500s with seven-round mags, a hundred conventional rounds and... Wow, Alex..." He began to pull out packages of shotgun rounds. "Double slug, Rhodesian jungle rounds, dragonfire, flechette, breaching rounds... Hell, you didn't tell me you were getting all this crap."

"Yeah, well I didn't want to think about how much it was costing us." The purchase had just about melted my credit card, but at least I was keeping Liberty Bell Firearms in business. I still wasn't sure what good all this firepower would do against Onatochee, but if his followers decided to start something with us they'd get a warm reception.

"I drove past Kay and Ron's place," Loren said as I inspected one of the Mossbergs. "I saw Ron putting crap into a U-Haul. He didn't see me. I think they're trying to get out of town."

"Maybe they got a visit from Michael, too."

"Maybe," Loren said quietly. He sat cross-legged on the floor, one arm around Beowulf. "Or maybe they're having the dreams, too. It won't help, though. It didn't help me. They can run to freaking Siberia and they'll never be able to forget. Every night they'll lie awake wondering if Michael's going to come through the window." He hugged his dog closer.

"I don't blame them for trying," I said. I felt a sudden chill. "I know those bastards are looking for me. God, Loren. If they think Kay and Ron know where I am... Oh, Jesus."

"Should we go talk to them again? At least warn them? Or should we just let them get out of town and hope for the best?"

"I don't know, Loren." I didn't have a phone number or any other way to contact them. Hell, I didn't even know their last name. "When Damien tried to talk to them they told him to go to hell."

"That was right after our clusterfuck at the Petroco Building, Alex. We were all pretty crazy then. I sure as hell was. We've got to at least try. Help them. Maybe give them some weapons or something. If they turn you down again, we're not any worse off."

I swallowed. Something had kept me from approaching them—after Michael's visit I knew that the cultists were out there, searching. If I showed up, it might bring Onatochee's wrath down on both of them.

I looked at the open duffel bag and its cargo of supplies. Loren was right. Anything was better than hiding from the weather and waiting for the enemy to come to us.

"How long ago did you see the van?" I asked.

"It was on my way downtown, about four hours ago."

"Okay." I handed the shotgun to Loren. "If we're going, I'm not going unarmed. We'll each bring a shotgun and a pistol. You should take that fireaxe too."

Loren looked at the Mossberg dubiously. "I've never fired one before, Alex."

"What about all those games of *Modern Warfare?*"

He shot me a withering glance. "Uh, Alex... You know that's just a video game, right?"

I gave him a quick primer on firearm safety and how to shoot without hurting himself. A half hour later we were out in the rain-splashed darkness, the tires on Loren's Taurus humming along the grating of the Hawthorne Bridge. Below us the river was dark and high, foaming against the bridge piers, bearing great black snags and logs from upstream. The wind moaned through steel girders.

There weren't many people out—my guess was that they were staying home with warm fires and watching TV with their families, or at least with their pets. Only lunatics like me and Loren would be out in this kind of weather. And Beowulf too— he wasn't a lunatic, but he *was* very loyal.

The empty streets also made for easy parking. As we pulled up at Kay and Ron's apartment building, I saw that there was no van out front.

"I think they're gone," I said as we climbed out into the cold rush of rain.

"Let's ring anyway." Loren flipped up his hood and let Beowulf jump out before slamming the door. "Just to make sure."

Water dripped in my face from a leaky gutter as I pressed the button for the apartment. For almost a minute there was no answer. I rang again.

"Hello?" A tiny, fearful voice crackled from the speaker. "Who is it?"

"It's Alex and Loren," I said. "I'm sorry to bother you. We wanted to make sure you were okay."

There was another long pause, then the door buzzed.

"Come up," Kay said. "I'll see you in a minute."

***

Kay seemed even tinier than I remembered her, dwarfed by the yawning spaces of their nearly-empty apartment. She sat in a kitchen chair, nervously darting glances at the rain-spotted window.

"Ron's been gone for three hours now." Her voice was plaintive. "He was just going to get the last of our stuff out of storage and close the account. We're supposed to leave tonight."

271

"It wouldn't have helped," Loren said quietly. "I ran, but I couldn't get him out of my head. I know he's out there, I know he's—"

"Do you think we didn't *know* that?" she demanded, face twisting into a grimace. "You think we haven't seen the same stories on the news that you have? The storms, the killings, the violence? God, Loren... We *tried* to put it behind us. We *tried* to pretend nothing happened, but we couldn't. And I knew we never could, but at least we'd be someplace else, someplace without these memories, without this damned *rain...*"

She put her head in her hands and began to sob. I touched her shoulder and was grateful that she didn't slap it away.

"I'm sorry, Kay. Really. You've called Ron, right?"

Her eyes were red and swollen, but when she looked at me it was with an expression that suggested I was a very stupid first grader.

"Yes, Alex. I've called. It goes to voicemail."

"Sorry. I had to ask. Where's your storage unit?"

"Down under the freeway near Lloyd Center." She looked at her cell phone. "And they close in twenty minutes."

I swore. "Okay. That's as good a place to start as any. You want to come with us?"

"No, but I will anyway," she said. "Anything's better than this."

* * *

"Do you think that just maybe you could have picked a storage place that was easier to get to?"

Loren's irritation didn't do much to lighten our mood as we drove down a winding exit that led into a steep ravine and through a narrow underpass beneath the busy lanes of

I-84. Ahead, beyond a railroad crossing, was a claustrophobic complex of warehouses, its fading paint proclaiming that it was *E-Z Stor Self Storage.*

"What can I say?" Kay replied. "They were the cheapest in town."

Besides the Taurus' headlamps the only light came from the storage site. Rain sluiced down from the highway overpass, splattering the windshield as we rumbled over the railroad tracks. The whistle of wind and the roar of traffic overhead were amplified by the narrow ravine, so the lone employee who was busy locking up didn't notice us immediately.

I jumped out as we pulled to a halt, donning my coat and shoving my Glock into my waistband, out of sight behind me.

"Hey!" I shouted and he turned slightly, his features almost invisible in the shadow cast by the lot's harsh mercury lights. "Can you wait just a minute?"

"Sorry man," he replied, returning to his task and slamming the rolling gate behind him. "Lot's closed."

"Not for five more minutes. Come on—we had a friend come to drop some stuff off and he might still be in there."

"No one in there." He crouched down, his back to me as he secured the gate with a chain and padlock. "I checked. Come back in the morning."

He stood and turned around and our eyes met. I recognized him. In my vision he'd worn a work shirt with an embroidered patch that said "Jim."

With a single motion I reached behind me, pulling the Glock free, and leveling it at the man.

"Where is he?" I demanded.

The man's eyes widened in surprise.

"Hey, wait a minute, mister. I don't know anything—"

"*Ichiloot,*" I said in a low, rasping voice. "*Wo'igunaba.*"

His expression changed in an instant, from confusion and fear to delight, a sadistic smile spreading across his face.

"Shepherd," he said softly. "*Nomeus.*"

Behind me, a warning bell began to clang at the crossing, the ear-splitting shriek of a train whistle sounded and a white-hot needle seemed to stab through my brain—the same pain I'd felt in Onatochee's presence, but now it radiated from Jim. His body faded out of focus for an instant and he moved in a blur, trailing motes of light behind him, faster than I imagined possible.

I fired unsteadily with one hand, the pistol's report swallowed up by the growing roar of the train, but Jim wasn't where I'd thought he was. He moved with blinding swiftness, pivoting and slamming the side of my head with his elbow. A numbing shock passed through me and I staggered.

He had been at Petroco, and had absorbed some of Onatochee's energies along with the others. He grabbed my gun hand, twisting it, painfully trapping my finger against the trigger guard.

I tried to pull back, but he was on me, one hand still pushing the gun away, the other seizing my collar and dragging me sideways, trying to throw me off balance.

I heard a snarl and Beowulf's heavy dark body slammed into Jim's. I pulled back, wrenching the Glock free, nearly breaking my finger in the process.

We were bathed in blinding white light as the train engine appeared on the tracks, roaring like an angry metal dragon, wheels clacking on the track. Beowulf had Jim by the leg, biting and tearing, but the man swung an open hand down at the dog, making contact with a green-white spark and an electrical *crack*. Beowulf rolled away with an agonized yelp, and I smelled burnt fur on the cold wet air.

Pain still arced through my brain, jumping from synapse to synapse, slowing my reflexes. As I tried to draw a bead on Jim, he shifted and blurred again, breaking up into a kaleidoscope of geometric shapes for an instant. Then he was racing at me again.

"Hey, asshole!" Loren's voice was only barely audible over the roar of the train. "Leave my dog alone!"

Jim snapped back into a human form, whirling to face Loren, who came at him, swinging his fireaxe. A single blow and another cracking spark sent Loren flying, slamming into the side of the car.

I squeezed off two shots at Jim, catching him in the shoulder and arm. To my surprise, there was no splash of blood, but more sparks of blurred, kaleidoscopic color.

A great gust of wind drove rain into my eyes. He turned, his face contorted with anger, yet grinning madly.

"Onatochee," he mouthed as he began to stride through the mud toward me. "*Wo'igunaba.*"

Backing away, wiping water from my face, I could feel the deep vibration of the train and the rush of displaced air. It was only a few feet behind me. I didn't have any more room to retreat.

I shot clumsily, but hit him again, this time in the chest. More color sparked and he staggered slightly, as if all the damage was finally starting to overwhelm him. He began to shift and blur out of focus, and I realized that he was about to charge.

Before he could move, another explosion split the night and dozens of tiny multicolored sparks erupted all over his body— but now they were joined by spots of crimson. He slipped in the mud, falling to his knees as I shot a glance over at the car. Kay stood there, Mossberg in hand, slamming back the slide to chamber another round.

Pain and shock flashed across Jim's face, but his grin widened and his eyes flashed with greenish light. He was hurt, but not dead, and his gaze was still locked with mine.

"Shepherd," he whispered. "*Nomeus...*"

Behind him Loren staggered to his feet, hefting the fireaxe, but then Jim was in motion, blurring and shifting, trailing motes of light, racing at me with desperate, unnatural speed.

Then something cut through the pain in my brain, silencing the screams of the train and the wind, and silver-blue warmth flared. The charging man slowed, moving at almost normal speed, and I felt nerves fire, shifting me sideways almost without effort, out of the path of his headlong rush.

I released my grip on the Glock. It fell in slow motion toward the muddy ground.

I reached out as he moved past me. It felt almost casual, like swatting an annoying insect. My fingers gripped his arm and a handful of his shirt. Realization dawned and he turned to look back at me, his expression changing to one of disbelief and something that might have been fear.

Then we were moving normally again and I had him in an iron grip, using his own momentum against him, whirling him toward the rushing metal wall of the train. His body slammed into the moving barrier; it snagged flesh and fabric, snatched him out of the air, and whisked him away. His body dangled lifeless from the train like a puppet.

Loren rushed up and Beowulf trotted behind him, looking slightly singed but otherwise unhurt.

"Holy shit! What did you just do?"

I shook my head. "You tell me. Are you okay?"

"He just shook me up is all." His eyes were glazed and he stood unsteadily, but I took him at his word. "When he hit me, it was like I'd stuck a fork in a wall socket. What the fuck is going on?"

I shook my head. The pain was fading, but it still hurt. The warmth that had filled me was gone. "It's what I saw in that dream, remember? It's like what happened to Michael—he'd absorbed some of Onatochee's energy—stuff from another reality. It made him move faster and shrug off those bullets."

Loren rubbed his face. "Yeah, and shock the living crap out of me." He knelt down and hugged Beowulf. "How are you doing, boy?"

Kay hurried up, shotgun still at the ready. She handled the weapon with easy familiarity, a wild contrast to the frail, flighty woman she had been.

"Good job," she said, a deeper and more forceful tone in her voice than I'd heard before, and gestured at the clustered buildings. "They've got my husband, and I think he's in there. Are we going to go find him or not?"

I blinked, trying to focus and to comprehend the change that had come over the quiet Kay. There was a grim, slightly crazed look in her eyes that I didn't find at all comforting. Seeing the confusion on my face, she spoke impatiently. "I used to go bear hunting with my ex. Now let's *go* for God's sake."

I scanned the muddy ground. "We need to pick up all the brass first," I said. "And mess up our footprints and tire tracks."

We worked quickly, then hurried back to the fence. It was locked with a chain and heavy padlock and topped with razor wire.

"We have to get through this fence first." I looked back at the car. "Should we just ram it?"

"Nope. That only works in the movies." Loren rummaged in the trunk and held up a pair of bolt cutters. "I remembered the cement plant so I made sure to pack these."

I drew a deep breath. The rush of adrenaline and the pain in my head were fading, replaced by a trembling sense of exhaustion that I did my best to ignore. "You're a resourceful man, Loren Hodges."

"Twelve years of D&D and video games gives you a good grounding in survival techniques," he said, fitting the cutters' jaws around the lock shackle and leaning against it with a grunt. "Always scout... ahead... Never... split up... the party... Always... check... for..." He grunted again and the shackle snapped in two. "...*Traps*..."

Together we pushed the rolling gate open. The road into the facility turned sharply left into the middle of the clustered buildings, starkly lit by mercury lamps, fuzzy and angry in the swirling wet. A gust of wind almost knocked us off our feet, bearing stinging daggers of cold water.

"You ready?" I asked.

Loren flexed his arm and winced.

"As ready as I'll ever be I guess. Come on."

The wind howled mournfully between the buildings as we moved cautiously past the gate and into the storage complex.

VI

We hugged the wall of the nearest building, an ugly concrete rectangle, and slipped into the parking area, a keyhole-shaped lot in the middle of the jumbled collection of structures. Each building had a large loading bay, yawning and unlit. They were all empty save one, where the shadowy form of a U-Haul truck was visible.

"There it is!" Kay whispered, pointing. When we'd first met at her apartment, I'd thought her a little high strung. Now, noting her nervous, angry manner, I wondered whether she'd finally snapped.

We moved carefully, crouching as we stole through shadows near the buildings, but I still felt like a bug on a plate. With the floodlights on, anyone at a window could easily see us.

As if sensing the seriousness of the situation, Beowulf also moved cautiously, one foot at a time, shadowing Loren as we went.

No one spoke until we reached the loading bay where the rear of the truck vanished into gloom. I listened, trying to hear anything besides the sounds of traffic and falling rain, but there was nothing.

"Our unit is on the third floor," Kay whispered. "There's stairs and a freight elevator."

Loren looked over at the big elevator doors. "I vote for the stairs."

I took the lead, carefully edging the door open and padding up the metal treadplate steps. My footfalls echoed softly, but in my mind I made a racket every bit as loud as that passing train.

When we reached the landing at the third floor, I leaned against the door, gently depressing the handle, feeling no resistance.

"We're in 3024," Kay whispered. "Turn left and go down the corridor, then right."

I nodded and slowly opened the door.

The corridor was cold, with thin wooden walls painted light gray. Dark red metal girders crossed the ceiling overhead, and the walls were lined with padlocked doors, each with a number stenciled on it. Light came from cold, unhealthy-looking fluorescent tubes.

I fell into a crouch the moment I heard the voices. Behind me the others heard too, but none of them made a sound, not even Beowulf.

Whispers echoed down the hallway, as cold and stark as our surroundings. I looked back at the others, nodded and pointed silently.

Loren drew his Glock and I noted with satisfaction that he held it low and away from us as I'd instructed. We moved into the corridor, staying close to the walls, moving a step at a time. As we approached the corner, the whispered words grew clearer.

"...Shepherd... Onatochee... Your friend... Tell us..."

Suddenly a louder sound echoed—a drawn out scream filled the corridor.

Kay shouted Ron's name. I swore, breaking into a run, my boots pounding on the plywood floor.

As we rushed around the corner I had only an instant to take in the scene. Ron lay beside an open unit door, hog-tied, wrists to ankles, blood staining the floor and walls around him. Beside him were two of Michael's crew that I recognized from my vision—a woman with patchy gray hair and a pale, sickly kid who looked barely out of his teens. They looked up in surprise. They held knives, and their clothes were covered in a paste of blood and dirt.

My mind screamed that we could do nothing to them—like Jim, they'd traded their humanity for an existence as puppets of a demon, each wielding a tiny portion of his power in his name. The only way to fight them was to invoke the light that I'd felt inside me, the power that She Who Watches had offered...

But reaching inside, I felt nothing. It was as if I'd used up my allotment of Her powers outside, and now, when I needed it even more, there was none left.

I made a fast decision. There were four of us and only two of them. Maybe I could slow them down long enough for Kay and Loren to get to Ron and drag him to safety.

Still moving, I steadied the Glock with both hands and aimed. "Let him go!"

They pair exchanged a quick glance—light flickered in their eyes and unspoken words seemed to flash between them. The kid blurred into motion and shot toward me, holding his knife underhanded, blocking my advance while the woman knelt down beside Ron, her knife poised for a killing slash across his throat.

The sick-looking boy was only there to slow us down long enough for his friend to cut Ron's throat and finish him. He lunged at me, thrusting his knife. I ducked, knowing as I did that I was too slow.

The knife caught, but another spark of energy shot through me and it slid off the heavy leather of my coat. The kid cried out in pain and surprise, stumbling, his body shifting back to normal.

The lost fire burned inside again, brief and hot but real. I took aim past the kid and squeezed the Glock's trigger. A 9mm round struck the woman's temple—silver-blue flashed and she fell, her knife scoring Ron's neck, leaving a long crimson welt, but missing his artery. Her motionless body collapsed, surrounded by a cloud of glittering motes that quickly dispersed and vanished.

I pivoted and rolled on the shoulder I'd hurt at Petroco. The boy sprang up, his face burning with fanatical rage. I kept a grip on the Glock in my right hand and with my left grabbed his wrist, pulling him down, pressing the knife to the floor, and pinning it with all my weight.

The boy snarled and spat, trying to pull away. He moved normally—no demon-light flashed. I was fighting a normal human being.

"Fuck you... Fuck... Onatochee will..." His head thrashed back and forth, biting at me as I pressed my knee against his chest. "...Kill you... Eat your guts... Fuck you..."

Even without the other reality's energy, he was stronger than he looked, his wasted limbs infused with the strength of fanaticism and bloodlust. I'd dealt with enough of these bastards now to know that they couldn't be reasoned with. There was nothing left for them save the yawning maw of Onatochee.

I brought the Glock up to his chest and fired. He twitched once and lay still, blood blackening his shirt.

I got back on my feet, staring down and fighting back nausea, my ears clanging and jangling with the echoes of gunfire. I'd killed again, and it hadn't gotten any easier to face.

Then Kay was there, hastening to Ron's side, kneeling down to loosen his bonds. They'd tied him with bungee cords, and he was covered with a network of tiny bloody slices, but his eyes were open and he made a faint sound as she tugged at the cords. His glasses lay bent on the floor beside him.

"Kay..." Then he looked up as if seeing me for the first time. "Alex?"

"In the flesh." I grabbed one of the cultists' discarded knives and began sawing at the knotted bungee cords. Beowulf trotted up. He smelled of burnt fur. He looked at Ron with evident concern and began to lick his face.

Loren picked up the discarded shells and defaced our muddy footprints as we worked. It was several minutes before Ron was finally free.

"They wanted to know where you were, Alex," Ron said, mumbling through swollen lips, climbing painfully to his feet. "They kept calling you the Shepherd, wanting to know where they could find you. I didn't tell them anything."

"Thanks." I forced a smile, even though I didn't feel at all happy. I bent his glasses back into shape and handed them to him. One of the lenses was cracked. "Can you see?"

He put them on and nodded. "Well enough. Let's get out of here."

"How bad are you hurt?" Loren demanded as Ron limped down the corridor, away from the carnage. Beowulf trotted alongside, darting worried glances up at him. "Should we get you to the hospital?"

Ron shook his head. "Just cuts and slices. Nothing major yet. They were just getting underway when you showed up." He looked at me. "Good thing I didn't know where you were, Alex, or I might have told them."

We stumbled down the corridor and down the clanking metal steps. I kept my weapon at the ready in case any more cultists were lurking in the shadows, but we made it to the loading bay without incident.

"Let's get him back to the hotel," Loren said. "We can take a look at those cuts there."

"I'll be all right," Ron insisted. "I just need some bandages and disinfectant."

"God damn it," Kay whispered, sniffling and wiping tears from her face. "You just can't stand going to the doctor, can you?"

VII

"**S**low down, dude," Loren said as he served Ron a second McDonald's breakfast of scrambled eggs and pancakes. "You'll give yourself indigestion."

Ron ignored him, ravenously wolfing down the food and gulping coffee. He was wrapped in a motel blanket and the skin I could see was covered by a welter of scratches and cuts. Kay had stitched a couple of the worst wounds shut and injected him with antibiotics. This morning he seemed better despite the haunted expression that lingered just behind his eyes.

We'd driven through the growing storm, dodging a falling tree that took out power to most of the neighborhood, leaving the Welcome Inn dark. We'd slept in shifts, watching over Ron as he lay nearly unconscious. Morning brought restored power and continued foul weather.

The morning reports brought grim news. Out at sea, in the icy heart of the Pacific, something frightening was taking shape. The wind twisted clouds into a vast and deceptively beautiful spiral, slowly grinding eastward, carrying its wrath toward the northwestern coast.

Even the normally upbeat weatherman sounded fearful. They had never seen anything like this—it was too big, it was too far north, it was the wrong season, it was traveling in the wrong direction—yet there it was, striding across the ocean like a juggernaut. It would be coming ashore in a few days or hours. It was likely to be a distinctly un-merry Christmas.

There was other news as well. Police were investigating the discovery of several bodies at a local self-storage facility, possible victims of a drug deal gone bad, and were asking anyone with information to come forward. I reminded myself that we'd cleaned up discarded brass and gotten rid of all the forensics we could, but something else bothered me.

"You need to lay low here," I told Ron. "They'll be able to find you through that truck you rented."

He rolled his eyes. "You think I rented it under my real name?"

I leaned back in my chair. "Yeah, I guess I should have known better."

He paused, a plastic fork full of eggs half way to his mouth, and looked at me. There was a remnant of the calm assurance that I'd seen when we'd first met, but now it had to share space with shock and despair.

"I want to thank you, Alex. If you and Loren hadn't shown up last night, I'd have been..." He hesitated, as if a cold dark cloud had passed over him. "I'd have ended up like that poor bastard you found at the cement plant."

I nodded. "Thank Loren, too. It was his idea to go check on you two."

"Thanks, Loren. And thank that mutt of yours." Ron smiled, though it looked as if it hurt to do so.

Loren took the compliment with a brief smile of acknowledgement and glanced at Beowulf, dead to the world in the middle of the bed. "He's catching up on his beauty sleep, but I'll pass it on. I'm just glad you're okay."

"What happened?" I asked. "Were they waiting for you?"

Ron stared down at the fake woodgrain of the room's tiny table. In the background, the news droned on, oblivious. "That guy at the gate—the one that got snagged on the train. I'd never seen him before. Maybe he got rid of the regular guy and let the others in. I don't know how they knew I was there. I just know that when I turned that corner they were waiting for me. I tried to run, but they were on me too fast. They hog-tied me and started cutting, screaming at me, asking me where you were. 'Where's Alex?' 'Where's the fucking Shepherd?'" He rested his head in his hands, rubbing his temples. "So I guess you're this Shepherd they're looking for, huh?"

"They seem to think so," I admitted.

Kay emerged from the bathroom. I'd given her some of my clothes to wear—a baggy white t-shirt and rolled up, oversized jeans. Her skin was sallow and there were dark circles under her eyes. She looked as if she hadn't slept at all.

"So what are we going to do now?" she asked. "We can't stay here, not now, not after what they did. We have to leave."

Ron looked even wearier. "Things have changed. We need to discuss it before we do anything."

Confusion flickered across Kay's features. "What's changed, Ron? You know we can't stay here. We talked and talked and talked, and we agreed we had to get away." Her voice rose in both pitch and volume. "It's even worse now, after what they did to you. What's there to discuss?"

Ron closed his eyes for a moment, and he took a breath. "Sit down, Kay. Eat some breakfast."

She sat, tight-lipped and pale. I handed her a coffee and as she sipped it I could see her hand trembling.

"What are you planning on doing, Alex?" Ron asked. "It's pretty obvious that the whole region is going to hell pretty quickly."

"Onatochee's getting stronger," I said. "His cult's getting bigger. We have to stop him. I don't know how, but we're the only ones who can."

"At least we know where he is," Loren said. "He and his buddies are still holed up at the Petroco Building."

Kay shuddered. "You're not planning on going back *there*, are you?"

I shook my head. "Not the way things stand now. We'd have to fight our way through dozens of cultists. Even if we survive, I don't think our weapons can do anything more than just piss that thing off."

I paused and drew a deep breath. "But I can't leave. Not now. It has something to do with that woman we saw—the one who drove off Onatochee. I think She wants to help us. I think if we can find a way to talk to her She can give us something we can use to fight."

"Who is She anyway?" Kay's tone was tight and dubious. "What does She want with us?"

I stirred sugar into my tea. "I don't know. Not for certain. I think the Chinook called Her Tsagaglalal—She Who Watches. She might have aided the Multnomahs when they first fought the Chilut."

I gave a quick rundown of Damien's theories. "It looks as if She's been doing this for millennia, choosing people to act on Her behalf. To carry that sword. And it looks as if She's picked me, though I'll be damned if I can tell you why. That's why Onatochee's goons wanted to know where I am. He wants to keep me from getting the weapon that can defeat him."

Ron looked suddenly alert. "Can we contact Her? Could She help? Maybe there's something in one of Michael's books."

Kay made a disgusted sound. "Michael. Your hero, Michael. You still believe in him, don't you? You think he knew any better than the rest of us?"

"God, Kay, please don't start." Ron looked at her with an expression that was more sad than angry. "I think after what I've been through I've earned a few hours of peace, don't you?"

Kay still looked like a storm cloud ready to burst, but she said nothing as Loren set a paper tray in front of her.

"The Greeks called Her Nemesis or Gaia," I said. "We've found references to Her in other stories from a lot of different cultures. We think the Sumerians called Her Belet-Ili, goddess of fate and destiny and Her champion was called *Panigara,* Lord of the Boundary Stone. The Canaanites had some obscure legends about a goddess named Enkanasha, Ruler of the Spaces Between, and the Babylonians may have called Her Nintu. There were others, too—from every continent and dozens of cultures—all with the same basic story."

"Personally I have no idea why She'd pick a doofus like Alex to be Her hired gun," Loren said. "But She did, and I guess we're stuck with him."

"And so with that deep and moving vote of confidence," I said, "we've decided to stay and fight, and hope that we can figure out some way of contacting Her again."

Though the haunted expression still lingered in Ron's eyes, he looked at me with more resolve than I'd have thought possible. "I can't claim that I know what's really going on, Alex, but if there's a chance you can fight this thing, I'll help any way I can."

Kay's simmering resentment and anger finally boiled to the surface. "Are you saying you're going to *stay*? Are you all completely out of your *minds*?"

Ron held up a hand. "Kay..."

"*No!*" Kay stood, kicking her chair back so that it tottered and fell. "I'm done listening, Ron! I can't take it anymore. You and your precious Michael O'Regan and his damned ghosts and demons and his fucking *books* and goddamned *reality shows!* You seriously *admired* that asshole, didn't you? You never even noticed how he was screwing his way through all of his damned worshippers did you? All those adoring little occult groupies? You never even wondered *why* he spent so goddamned much time with us, did you?"

Ron stared, and what little blood he had left seemed to drain from his face.

"Kay... Did you...? You and Michael...?"

"*Yes!* Yes, I fucked him, Ron! Just like that slut Trish, just like those little sluts in every fucking town he visited! He *loved* it, Ron! He *loved* the goddamned attention, playing daddy to all his adoring little girls! Yes, I fucked him, and if it's any consolation I was fucking *sorry* the minute I did it!"

The sound woke Beowulf and he looked up, concern wrinkling his brow.

Great, I thought. Now even the dog knows.

What followed was pretty much a classic example of an uncomfortable silence, as Loren stared red-faced at the floor and I looked uncertainly from Kay to Ron and back again.

Ron looked glassy-eyed. Kay seemed torn between righteous indignation and regret at what she'd said. I'd known ever since Trish had told me of course, but now, with the secret out, as ugly and painful as an open wound, I felt sympathy for both of them, but I couldn't think of any way to help.

"Why didn't you tell me?" Ron said, softly. "I'd have forgiven you. Why didn't you say anything?"

"I didn't know what to say." Kay's anger had been like a massive wave crashing on the rocks, and now it was receding. "He knew all the right things to say to me. He kept talking about how much he admired you, and how strong and wise I was. God, Ron... I thought about telling you when he suggested that idiotic ritual, but I kept my mouth shut." She set her chair upright and slumped into it. "I'm sorry, Ron. I'm so sorry. I love you."

We all fell silent. I wanted to simply sink quietly and unnoticed into the floor, and Loren looked as if he felt the same. After a while he spoke.

"You know, I am rapidly coming to the conclusion that Michael O'Regan was a deeply flawed individual."

"In that," I said sadly, "he wasn't any different than the rest of us."

I'd certainly never warmed up to him completely. There had always been an edge of the theatrical to him. In the end he'd been a confusing amalgam of guru, father-figure, and con-man, and I wasn't sure which one he truly was.

More than anything else, he was human, and deserved better than what he'd gotten—transformed into the flesh-puppet of a demonic thing that had been stalking him for years.

The news continued to drone away. A landslide had closed I-84 eastbound, and flooding was threatening I-5 both north and south. As the big storm bore down on the coast with almost unnatural speed, port officials said that the Portland airport would be shut down later today.

Kay listened with a frightened, hopeless expression. We all knew what it meant—their escape routes were rapidly disappearing.

Ron spoke slowly and carefully, as if holding back a tide of contradictory emotions with each word.

"This isn't the time. When this is all over, we can talk about it. We can work things out, I know it."

Kay didn't look convinced. "After everything that's happened, do you really think we can?"

"Maybe not. Maybe there's no solution. But right now we have no place to go. We can either hole up and hope those bastards can't find us or try to help Alex and Loren as best we can."

Kay didn't reply.

Ron looked at me. "You're right about Michael, Alex. He wasn't any worse than the rest of us. God knows, we pretty much accepted everything he said, and I think there was a lot to admire. But he sure as hell made mistakes. It's a little late to be angry with him now."

He shifted his gaze to his wife. "I'm not perfect either, Kay. I feel like I let you down somehow. That Michael offered you something I couldn't."

She shook her head. "No, it wasn't like that. You know what a charmer he is... I mean was. If he tried, he could probably convert the Pope to Islam. I knew it was wrong, but I did it anyway. And I'm sorry."

It was obvious that Ron was still hurting, but he spoke deliberately. "We'll work it out. Or not. It doesn't matter right now. What matters is that we're here and we need to help Alex. Can we put this all aside for now and do what needs doing?"

Kay drew a deep, shuddering breath, and something seemed to click behind her eyes. It was as if she'd taken her anger and fear and resentment and locked it away. She looked at Ron, wearied resolution in her eyes.

"Okay," she said. "I'll do the best I can. Where do we start?"

* * *

After breakfast Loren set up the laptop with its VPN connection to Damien's server while I pulled out the books and research we'd taken from Damien's house. Beowulf lay curled up on the bed as we talked.

I was grateful for Kay and Ron's experience—they knew a lot more about Michael's history and magical theories than I did, and were able to provide some much-needed perspective.

Kay's demeanor had changed again, from a raw mass of emotions to cold, steady intensity. It was obvious that her feelings were still there, pent up behind a massive mental dam, held in check by willpower. But inside she was still the nervous little bird of a woman I'd first met weeks ago, and if the dam cracked, I was afraid of what might happen.

Her resolve was strong for the moment however, and she was the first to put into words what we all knew.

"You've been sitting here for days, waiting for someone else to make a move—the cultists, She Who Watches. We need to do something. We need to figure out how to contact Tsagaglalal."

There it was, the stark and simple fact that I'd known ever since Petroco. Of the many questions I couldn't answer, it was the most important one of all.

"You're right," I said. "And I have no idea how to do it. I think She's still out there, trying to contact me. I think She touched me that night that I had the vision of Onatochee and the cultists, but I haven't felt anything like that since."

"I want you to know that I have the utmost enthusiasm for this mission," Loren said, "but I'd sure as hell feel better if you had that sword."

"Me too. Unfortunately I'm the guy who couldn't manage to hold onto it."

Loren sighed. "She said 'When you are ready'. I hate to cast aspersions, Her being a goddess and all, but it seems to me that She could have given you a *little* more guidance about what She meant. It was kind of like when my ex told me 'I shouldn't have to tell you what's wrong—you should know' right before she dumped me."

"Yeah," I replied absently. His words triggered the memory of something. Something I'd read.

"O, Goddess," he said, "I have let my grief rule me. I have been selfish and prideful. I have cursed those I should love. I have lived apart and rejected my own people. Please forgive me."

The words reverberated in my mind. They meant something. She didn't have to tell me. I should know.

I glanced nervously at the TV. The sound was off but I could see a montage of images from around the region. Swollen rivers, swamped houses, bridges awash in hungry foaming water—all flashed by in quick succession.

I felt overwhelmed. It seemed apparent from the legends that our mysterious goddess chose those who had given up, who had lost their faith. Why, I wondered? Were we just empty vessels to be filled up by her will—agents of a being whose agenda was just as alien as Onatochee?

I threw up my hands. "Why didn't She choose someone with compassion and love of humanity? Why not Michael? Why not Damien? Pine Street Bob almost *killed* you, Loren, but you kept fighting. You overcame your fear and came back to help me. You're the hero, Loren, not me. Why not you? Shit... Kay, Ron—why not you?"

Ron shrugged. "I don't know. I just know that if you're the only one She chose, then you're the one we're following."

I tried to say something, but I couldn't in the face of a wave of emotion. I had always felt unworthy. I was a recluse, a misanthrope, a hypocrite. And now I had no choice but to accept the task that I was being offered.

God, Damien, I'm so sorry. I wish I'd known. I could have saved you.

All gone, all dead. All so frail, so imperfect, so human. I couldn't save them.

Save those you can. Avenge those you cannot.

I blinked away my tears, looking from Loren to Kay and back again.

I couldn't save Trish or Michael. I couldn't save Damien or Cheryl or any of the others. But I could fight for them. I could remember them. And I could at least try to help those who remained.

Kay and Ron had put aside their problems and fears and now I had to do the same. I massaged my brow for a moment, then looked up.

"Okay," I said. To my relief, my voice didn't waver. "Let's do this."

We listened to the rain and wind for another few moments, then Kay gestured at the table, where a map of Portland was laid out.

"We first summoned the entity by doing a ritual at a place of power, and so did those cultists you saw in your dream. Maybe we can do a ritual to summon She Who Watches." She pointed toward north Portland. "We already know of one thin place—the Petroco Building. There's also the cement plant. I say we go to one of those places and do the ritual."

"Even if you're right, we've got problems," I said. "Marine Drive is closed and the area around the cement plant is underwater. And call me crazy, but I think Petroco's out of the question."

"Any other places we know of?" Kay asked.

I rummaged through a pile of Damien's ubiquitous manila folders until I found one marked *Onatochee*. "I think Damien and Michael exchanged some emails about that."

The file contained more printouts and copies—tiny droplets in the deluge of paper that had made up Damien's life. After a moment I found what I was looking for—a copy of a message from Michael with the subject line *Rifts in PDX area*. I read it out loud.

Damien: Thanks for the information! I think we're onto something. Based upon your information and my own research there are at least five nearby areas that have been the scene of activity that I associate with the presence of a rift (local legends, native stories, supernatural incidents, unsolved crimes, lights in the sky, UFO sightings, etc.). For your convenience, here they are, including the ones you have already suggested:

  - The abandoned cement plant near Blue Lake
  - The northern end of Sauvie Island
  - The Portland Petroleum Company Office building (site of the Chilut village)
  - An area in Forest Park near McCaskill Road
  - Smith and Bybee Lake on Marine Drive

I have taken the liberty of creating a map with these areas noted on it. Most appear to lie in the North Portland area, which suggests to me that the area was once extremely active with extradimensional events. Once we have resolved your current issues, I might like to stay and investigate this hypothesis further.

I have made arrangements for my visit, and will be leaving in a few days. I will let you know my itinerary and I look forward to meeting you soon! Good hunting!—Michael O.

Stapled to the message was another printout, this one of the Google Map that Michael had created. There they were—all five locations, each with precise coordinates.

"Damn," Loren said. "You think Onatochee knows about all those places?"

"I don't know," I replied. "I guess there's only one way to find out. We can go scout them out in the morning, see which one is best."

"Do we know how to summon this goddess friend of yours? I don't really know any rituals." Loren looked toward Kay. "How about you guys?"

Silently Ron picked up a book titled *Extradimensional Phenomena* and opened it to a page he'd bookmarked.

"Michael described a number of summoning rituals." Ron handed me the book. "This one seems like the most appropriate."

I scanned the page—*A summoning ceremony for benevolent or indifferent entities*. It was theoretical—O'Regan himself hadn't ever used it.

No fewer than three participants; six are optimal. Damn. *Silver athame, pewter bowls, dried rose petals, mistletoe, salt water, green and blue candles, lines inscribed (if possible) with chalk or paint. If outdoors or materials are not available, the circle can be inscribed in the ground with tools, but precision is crucial.* Damn.

I wasn't sure where to get a silver athame at this point, but I was willing to give it a shot.

The invocation was a confusing mishmash of unpronounceable syllables. It wasn't in that odd Hebrew-sounding language Michael had used before—this, he claimed, was in a form of proto-Sumerian. I had my doubts but silently mouthed the words anyway.

Loren pointed to the bottom of the page, under the diagram of the elaborate summoning circle. "Check this out. We'd better get our asses in gear."

Best performed on night of solstice or equinox. At other times of year, success is questionable and less benevolent entities may be summoned.

"When was solstice again?" I pulled out my phone and looked at the calendar.

"Tomorrow," Kay said, then added wistfully, "Just a few days 'til Christmas."

I laughed. "Damn. I forgot to buy a tree."

"I'm not sure about this," Loren said, rereading the text. "Even O'Regan's not sure, and if you recall his last summoning was kind of fucked up."

"That's because someone sabotaged us." I felt a grim flash of anger remembering Trish. "I'm hoping the rest of us will be a little more resilient."

"Hey, you don't want to know what kind of pictures that motherfucking demon showed me," Loren said. "I've already turned him down, so I'm not planning on stabbing you in the back like Trish did."

I rubbed my eyes. Anger was giving way to heartache. Where was she? Was it still possible to save her?

"I know it's a long shot. If we can find a better ritual before solstice, we'll use it but I think Michael's our best bet right now. Otherwise, I think I need to locate a silver athame, whatever the fuck that is."

"It's pronounced 'a-tha-may,'" Kay said. "It's just a knife. Usually double-bladed, but I've never thought that was necessary."

Outside the rain had let up a little, but the trees still tossed and shivered in the wind. "We can hit up a gift shop for pewter bowls. Loren, you want to go shopping?"

Loren was on his feet. "I'm way ahead of you. Mind if I drive Yngwie?"

VIII

Loren returned with a load of ritual supplies he'd found at an import store minutes before it closed for the night—pewter bowls, sea salt, and bottled water to mix together, a double-bladed knife to serve as an *athame*, potpourri with rose petals. We slept in shifts again, then set out in the pre-dawn gray the next morning. After picking up provisions, we hunkered down just off Hawthorne Boulevard where there was still power and a few businesses remained open. The weather damage was less here; a few cars splashed past, lights glittering in the rain-starred windows. Sometimes a brave pedestrian trudged by, bent against the wind.

Loren chewed a piece of beef jerky. He was bundled up in a down jacket and covered in a sleeping bag. Beowulf slept curled up on the back seat between Kay and Ron.

"I feel vulnerable," Loren said. "Like those fuckers are gonna crawl out of the sewers or drop out of the sky on us. Michael knows what this car looks like. He's probably got them looking for it."

I shook my head. "I think we're okay for now." The engine was idling and Yngwie's heater did its usual bang-up job of keeping us warm. "Even if they find us, I doubt they'll attack us in the middle of the Hawthorne District." I paused and scanned the street. It was empty for the moment. "But let's stay sharp anyway."

Kay gazed through the window with a mournful expression while Ron read the O'Regan book.

"'Evening of the Solstice,'" he said. "It doesn't say what time during evening. We should start right after sundown."

I studied a copy of the map O'Regan had sent to Damien, holding it clumsily in one gloved hand, a cup of coffee in the other. We'd filled up four thermoses at the 7 Eleven and loaded up on just about anything else we could find. We had enough mini-donuts to last out the next decade.

My plan to scout out all the locations seemed impractical now and once more, every alternative seemed bad. Petroco was out, the bridge to Sauvie Island was closed, and Blue Lake was flooded, while Smith and Bybee Lakes were marshy wilderness at the best of times. That left only one place.

"Looks like Forest Park is the winner," I said.

Ron closed the book and looked at the map. "We'll need space to perform the ritual and we'll be out in the weather, but at least we can get there if the roads are clear."

"We won't be able to keep any candles lit," I noted grimly. "Will it even work without them?"

"A lot of people say the ritual trappings are there to provide a focus and the only thing that's really necessary is the circle," Kay said. "If the ritualists are skilled enough and can concentrate without them, the candles and stuff aren't necessary."

"I guess we're about to test that theory, huh?" Loren asked.

Ron looked up. "We don't know for certain that it's a real thin place, the other locations are all off the table and we're going to have to do an incomplete ritual. What do you think, Alex? Do we try anyway?"

He was asking me, and I wasn't used to being the leader of anything. Now success or failure depended on decisions that I made.

Me. The underachieving college dropout.

I shifted Yngwie into gear. "Let's go."

* * *

The Freemont Bridge was a graceful green double-tiered arch, like a suspension bridge turned upside down. With the other bridges practically awash in foaming brown water it had the advantage of being well above the flood, but it was also slick, windy and treacherous.

The growing storm battered Yngwie as I drove along the onramp, soaring up above the clustered buildings below. I knew that this weather was nothing but the curtain-raiser for the real show—the Pacific monster was still a few hours' off, but when it got here all hell was going to break loose.

"Brace yourselves," I shouted over the growing cacophony as the wind roared across the road, whistling through massive support cables and the lower deck, resounding and reverberating against protesting metal. A heartbeat later we were on the bridge, exposed to the full fury of the elements.

"Shit." The wheel seemed to want to jump out of my hands. I downshifted, gears grinding, and tried to stay on a relatively straight trajectory. High above us the arch grazed low clouds as two flags—the blue banner of Oregon flying alongside the Stars and Stripes—bravely defied the wind that threatened to tear them into rags.

Beowulf was on the front seat with Loren now—he seemed tense, sensing the danger we were in. Behind me Kay and Ron watched the road ahead anxiously.

"You guys doing all right back there?" I asked.

"We're okay," Kay said. "Just drive."

Another gust of wind broadsided Yngwie. Normally sleek and aerodynamic, the wind battered it like a toy, and we lurched sideways, tires slipping. Driving Yngwie under these circumstances was like riding a wild bull.

I grunted. "I don't think I can manage another..."

A mighty fist of wind struck us broadside and the bridge itself seemed to vibrate and lurch. The entire car slewed sideways, cargo and people sliding violently. Beowulf yelped—he hadn't been belted, but Loren managed to hold onto him.

All around us things were shaking and convulsing. The bridge's support cables stretched and groaned. We kept barreling forward even as the pavement beneath us bucked and heaved. I spun the wheel, trying desperately to keep moving, but it was too much for Yngwie. We spun, tires hydroplaning across the wet, oily pavement.

Panic urged me to jam on the brakes, to somehow stop our inexorable rush toward the railing and the sickening drop below. I forced myself to pump the pedal, fighting with the wheel as it leaped and twisted like an angry cat until at last the engine stalled and we came to a halt, facing backwards, the wind still pounding ferociously on us and the bridge. Another massive gust struck us, vibrating wires and making the entire bridge surface shake.

"Emergency warp factor, dude! We're gonna capsize!" There was an edge of terror in Loren's shout. In his arms Beowulf looked worried, but not especially scared.

I engaged the clutch and turned the key. The engine protested for a moment then roared to life. I shifted into gear and cranked the wheel, turning 180 degrees, tires spinning on the wet pavement.

The wind redoubled, blowing rain horizontally in front of us, but it seemed almost serene as I guided Yngwie off the exit and into the drab buildings of Northwest. On the wind, I heard sirens and car alarms, shrieking in a dissonant chorus. In the distance, I saw lights flashing as emergency vehicles raced around the stricken city, but there were none anywhere near us.

The radio was awash in a storm of white noise. I pressed scan and the numbers scrolled past. Static hissed across the entire radio dial, both AM and FM.

Ron looked at his cell phone. "Nothing. No bars. Everything's going down."

"You're not kidding." Loren pointed back toward Portland.

I risked a glance. A few minutes ago, lights had burned along streets and from a few homes and buildings. Now, across one sector after another, the lights were snuffed out, vanishing into gloom.

As we rolled down the now-empty Highway 30, sheltered from the worst of the storm by concrete walls on either side and big overpasses above, the hot white glow of Yngwie's head lamps in the darkness was a pointed reminder of just how alone we truly were.

Orange traffic barrels and flashing barriers toppled by the wind lay across the Vaughn Street exit and I carefully guided Yngwie through them. We turned onto Northwest 23rd Avenue and rolled along the western edge of the trendy Pearl District, past fancy restaurants and art galleries, dark and shuttered against the storm. The water was half way up Yngwie's tires, and we sloshed through as fast as I dared.

"Gonna be a lot of damage when this is all over," Loren muttered, and although he didn't finish with "*If* it's all over," I knew he was thinking it.

I steeled myself to continue. The road dipped down into the industrial district. Water rushed alongside us like a brown river. Off to our right the Columbia foamed and raged, while to the left forested slopes rose into the cold mist. "Where's the place, Loren? This is probably going to be our only chance."

He squinted at the hillside above us. "We need to drive up Clifton Way to McCaskill Road. That's assuming they aren't buried under a landslide."

"Just point the way." I didn't want to think about that right now.

I drove slowly through a half-foot of water. The wind was still determined to physically lift Yngwie and send us flying. The streets were utterly deserted and almost as dark as night. Most of these businesses had chosen not to risk the weather by staying open.

We turned off St. Helens Road and onto a winding labyrinth of dead-end streets that twisted around warehouses and undistinguished cinder block buildings that clustered on the slope. At least we were at a higher elevation and weren't driving though a river anymore.

Despite the treacherous conditions, my mind wandered. Something about me had changed—

I knew that. In just a matter of months I had found things I'd thought lost forever—friendship, love, purpose, loyalty. It was as if I had only been hiding from these things, as surely as I'd hidden from my own misdeeds, pretending they didn't exist and cringing behind a wall of affected cynicism and misanthropy.

I have let my grief rule me. I have been selfish and prideful. I have cursed those I should love. I have lived apart and rejected my own people.

Was that who She chose to be Her champion? The lost and lonely? The failures? The cynical, the sad? The ones who cared nothing for kings or crowns, for gods or priests? Those who had made of themselves empty vessels, ready for the tasks that She required?

Could only those who had seen tragedy and tasted vengeance truly understand what these things were, and how to use them in Her cause—keeping the doorways to other places shut, and holding the monsters at bay?

Only those who truly knew what it was to be human—both good and bad?

Human...

"There!" Kay exclaimed. "There's Clifton!"

It was a narrow road that ascended steeply between two nondescript buildings. I shifted into first gear and turned carefully.

The street was covered in mud and gravel. Rivulets of water poured down the steep hillside. Some trees leaned drunkenly over the road while others had been ripped completely from the soil. Yngwie's tires spun and refused to grip, propelling us along in fits and starts.

"This hillside's going to slide if there's much more rain," Ron said.

"Tell me something I don't know, dude." Loren's voice was uncharacteristically grim.

The industrial district vanished behind us and as we ascended through a landscape of dark trunks and shaggy branches. We were all on edge, our tension almost tangible. Even Beowulf sat in silence, looking ahead anxiously. I fought the urge to hurry, edging Yngwie along so slowly that the speedometer needle barely moved. Even at a snail's pace, the wheels slipped and slid, noisily seeking purchase.

"McCaskill Road is going to fork off to the right in about a quarter mile," Loren said. "The site is about a mile further past that."

Rain dripped from laden branches, splattering on the windshield in fat droplets. The trees grew thicker, crowded together like the tottering columns of a ruined cathedral, rising out of a tangled bed of green ferns. Save for the road, it looked like untouched wilderness.

Loren pointed. "It's McCaskill! Go right, Alex."

McCaskill was even narrower and less encouraging than Clifton, with a precipitous slope rising to our left and a yawning ravine on the right.

We didn't get very far before we were forced to stop. Less than a hundred yards down McCaskill, a great bite of dirt upslope had broken loose along with two big trees, blocking the road like a great earthen wall.

I stopped, mud and gravel squelching.

"Everybody out," I said. "We'll need to go on foot from here."

No one objected but filed sullenly into the cold. The air smelled of rain and dirt and wet wood. I pulled on my duster as the others bundled up in coats and gloves. I popped the trunk and we pulled out two duffel bags full of equipment and weapons.

I got back into the driver's seat. "Guide me, Loren. I'm going to turn this beast around in case we have to leave in a hurry."

Turning on the narrow road was an agonizing process, but a few minutes later as we scrambled over the landslide, Yngwie was pointed back down the road, toward Portland and civilization.

We got over the roadblock with difficulty, dragging the heavy canvas bags behind us. My coat was a hindrance, and by the time I got to the other side it was covered in mud. Loren had to help Beowulf scramble over the top and across the trunks of the fallen trees.

The wind roared through the thick boughs above us as we trudged along McCaskill. These were old trees, thick with moss and lichen. Some even sprouted ferns, growing in lush accumulations of debris at the bases of branches. In the distance I occasionally heard the alarming crack of a shattering trunk or the rattling rush of gravel and mud sliding down the hill.

I checked my watch. It was 2:30—two hours until dark. If nothing slowed us we'd make it by sundown.

If Onatochee and company decided to come after us here, we were completely on our own. But as cold minutes went by all that attacked us were the elements, ferocious and insistent— wind forcing itself between the sheltering trees, big drops cascading through their branches.

We checked the crank radio a couple of times—the stations came and went. Once we were able to listen for almost five minutes. Power and gas were out across the city. Flood waters inundated the Columbia River. Bridges were closed. Whole towns were swamped.

Communications were down too—not even shortwave radios seemed to be working in some areas and no one had any idea why. Casualties weren't known, but they were certain to be high. The storm was moving inland at high speed and didn't seem to be losing any force, inexplicably remaining the equivalent of a force five hurricane.

"Judgment Day," Kay whispered, almost to herself. "My aunt was always warning us about Armageddon and the years of tribulation. She never shut up about it."

"Yeah, we didn't invite her over very often," Ron added.

Progress was slow. We stopped for coffee, power bars, and beef jerky, then began our grim trek again. I felt as miserable as a drowned rat, and I was sure the others felt the same. My feet were soaked and numb, my hat was heavy with rain, and my coat was caked with mud and debris.

After about an hour, we approached a concrete bridge over a narrow stream that rushed along furiously twenty feet below.

Loren inspected his map. "I think this is Bell Creek. The place of power is about a hundred yards up the hill."

The span had survived the quake, but I was glad we didn't have to cross it. The slope was covered ferns and fir trees, some fallen, others leaning. I waved the others forward then began to climb, the duffel bag heavy on my shoulders.

It was even slower going up the hillside. Our feet sank into the sodden loam; thick-growing ferns seemed determined to slow us down and sabotage our progress. Sometimes the wind dropped low enough for us to hear the rushing sound of Bell Creek off to our right, but most of the time it moaned or screamed furiously through the trees, blotting out every other sound. Loren slipped once and almost went tumbling down the slope, but Ron grabbed his arm and pulled him up. Beowulf struggled but kept pace with us.

Words still echoed in my mind. *I have let my grief rule me. I have been selfish and prideful. I have cursed those I should love.*

She shouldn't have to tell me.

I should know.

I *had* to.

IX

It was almost four o'clock when we reached a place where the trees gave way to a grassy clearing with a rugged basalt outcropping in the middle. Overhead the sky was a boiling sea of racing clouds, pressing down as if to isolate us in a tiny realm of chill gray. Blown rain stung our faces as we stepped out of the trees.

"It's four o'clock! Only a half hour 'til sunset!" I shouted over the rush of wind. "We need to get started!"

I blinked the rain out of my eyes and looked again across the clearing. It looked familiar but I wasn't sure why.

We moved through the clearing toward the outcropping. Ron and I threw down our bags and began to pull out ritual gear.

"Jesus." Loren threw up his hands. "I guess we're gonna be digging the circle in the dirt, huh?"

"Clear off a space," Kay replied, crouching down and pulling up grass. "Mark it with a knife or a stick. That's going to have to do."

I looked down at the useless candles, lying in the bottom of the bag. Well, that was wasted money, I thought as I pulled out silver bowls and bottles of salt water.

A gust of wind tore across the clearing, flattening grass and almost knocking us down. In the mist beyond the clearing vague shapes of firs tossed and shook as if they were alive. Beowulf paced nervously between us as we made our preparations.

"Holy shit!" Loren's voice rose up over the wind's howl. "Look there, Alex! Look at the rock!"

I hurried over to the outcropping where Loren pointed excitedly. There, carved into the weathered basalt, so faint that I could barely make it out, was a squat, owlish figure.

I touched the wet rock with my finger. "It's her. She Who Watches."

Suddenly I remembered. "I've seen this clearing. It was in a dream, when she first offered me the sword."

Loren's eyes widened. "Damn, Alex. Maybe we should make the circle here."

By God, it was real. It was here. This *was* the place. She'd shown it to me.

In all my readings, I'd never found reference to any Tsagaglalal images outside the Columbia Gorge, but here She was on the heights above Portland, watching over us as She had Her ancient village. I'd questioned, doubted, and rejected, even in the face of overwhelming proof. And all that time She had been here, staring quietly and waiting, as She had for millennia.

Nomeus. When you are ready.

Was I ready now? Was I ready to set aside the unreasoning fear that had blinded me and the anger that kept me estranged from those I should embrace and defend?

What did I need to do? What was missing?

"Yes," I said. "We'll make the circle here. Come on. I'll help."

The dim light faded further as the sun sank invisibly toward the horizon. I set up the electric lanterns, illuminating Kay and Ron as they pulled up grass and undergrowth, creating a circle about fifteen feet across with the outcropping in the center.

Loren and I followed them, digging in the muddy ground, scribing two circles, one nested inside the other like the pattern Eric had painted at Petroco. When we were done Loren consulted the O'Regan book, shielding it against the wind and rain. Kneeling in the mud he used a hunting knife to inscribe symbols in the ring between the two circles. I sat on my haunches, watching.

Kay opened a thermos and poured coffee.

"This is kind of like camping with my folks." Ron accepted a cup and took a sip. "Remember the time we went out to Malheur County, Kay?"

She wrinkled her nose. "You mean that year it snowed in August and the tent blew down? We all had to sleep in the car that night."

Ron grinned. "And a mouse got into the car with us?"

Kay giggled at that. "Oh God, that was horrible." For the first time I saw a flicker of optimism in her bleak expression. "We all ended up staying in a hotel for the rest of the week."

"Did the mouse come along?" I asked.

"Oh yeah," Ron said. "He told us he had a great time. He still sends us the occasional postcard."

I remained quiet for a while as they reminisced and Loren completed his task.

I looked at my watch.

"It's 4:25. Just four minutes!"

Kay set out the silver bowls along the outside of the circle. They sat unevenly on the rough ground.

Salt water in the bowls. Loren and Ron located the mix that they'd made and began to pour. Check. Rose petals outside the circle. We'd pulled a bunch of petals out of a potpourri collection. Check. Sprigs of mistletoe inside the circle. Check. That had been easy to find at Christmastime.

"Let's do this," I said. "And hope we don't get anymore landslides."

As if in reply, a faint rumble rose up through the ground. From the forest came the noise of more trees cracking and crashing down.

"Alex," Loren said, "please shut up now."

Outside the circle of light from the lamps, it was almost pitch black. The trees had merged into a single, writhing mass.

"One minute!" Ron warned as I placed the last sprig of mistletoe and opened the O'Regan book to the page that Loren had marked. I'd read over the "proto-Sumerian" invocation several times and scrawled phonetic notes in the margins, but I still wasn't sure whether I'd gotten it right or not.

"Come on, man," Loren urged. "Let's get this shit over with."

I made sure that our miscellaneous weapons were close at hand. My pistol and a wrecking bar were at my feet, Loren's shotgun was near his place.

"You can shoot this, right?" I asked, handing a Glock 17 to Ron.

"I think so." He accepted the weapon gingerly. "We've been target shooting, but I've only shot an automatic a couple of times."

"I'm a better shot than he is," Kay added. "My ex was a survivalist. A real ass, but he had skills."

I checked the time. "Four twenty-nine exactly. We'll give it another couple of minutes and we'll start." I wasn't taking any chances on my watch being fast.

I was as jumpy as everyone else. Amid the slap and squelch of the thick ugly rain that still fell outside, I thought I heard the faint sound of bodies creeping through the wet grass around us. I forced it out of my head and reread my notes.

I drew a deep breath. "Get in position. Spread evenly around the circle." The others moved out, but Beowulf sat quietly as if he knew how critical this was. I looked down at the page, only barely visible in the lamplight and began, pronouncing each syllable carefully.

"*Ati me peta babka!*" I shouted, my voice filled the emptiness, rising above the wind that howled and raged. "*Kibrat erbettim. Peta babkama luruba anaku ilati! Nusku ankidu! Hebat! Gula!*"

Nothing seemed to change. We were just standing on a windswept hillside, looking like idiots. A faint tremor made the ground quiver. I swallowed hard and tried to ignore it.

I knelt down and tapped the bowl in front of me with our improvised *athame*. It rang dully, only barely audible. It was probably the best I could have expected from a bowl on sale at the import store.

I rang the bowl twice more, then set down the knife and rose again. The book said that language for the next part didn't matter, and once more I was forced to take O'Regan's word for it.

"She Who Watches," I shouted. "Gaia. Tsagaglalal. Nemesis. Belet-Ili. Whatever you're called, whatever ancient names you bear, we entreat you to join us here in our circle, here on the eve of Solstice, here where we have prepared a place for you. She Who Watches, Nemesis, Gaia, Belet-Ili, we entreat you."

Words sang in memory and I felt myself repeating them silently, my lips moving as I remembered.

O, Goddess, I have let my grief rule me. I have been selfish and prideful. I have cursed those I should love. I have lived apart and rejected my own people. Please forgive me.

What came next? What was the secret?

"You do not need forgiveness, mortal," the goddess replied. "You need only accept your own frailty and know that in being imperfect, you are perfectly human. In your imperfection you are greater than the gods themselves…"

I knew. I understood at last.

"My name is Alexander St. John," I said. My voice was weary, but I felt my strength growing as I spoke. "I wanted to be a journalist. I wanted it more than anything else."

"Alex?" Kay looked at me in confusion. "Alex, what are you doing?"

I didn't answer. A faint warmth grew in my chest and spread through my limbs, driving out the icy cold of the storm and my sodden clothes. I no longer heard the scream of the wind or felt the desperate and terrified thudding of my heart. I remembered Damien, and Trish and all the others. I remembered Cheryl. Their memories were fresh and alive. Part of them still lived in me. They would not truly die as long as I remembered.

"My girlfriend's name was Cheryl White." The words came in a rush now, thick with emotion. I felt tears but I kept on. "She was a heroin addict. She died. I couldn't save her. I let her die. I did everything to save her and I still failed."

They were all staring now, confused and uncertain. But they must have felt the growing warmth as well, for none of them moved to stop me.

"I failed. I failed her and I failed myself. So I took out my anger on the only person I could. I attacked Alan Coleman with a baseball bat. He'd been her dealer and I blamed him for everything. I couldn't accept my own weakness, my own failure."

"Alex." I could see tears in Loren's eyes. "Oh my God. Alex."

"I fractured his skull," I continued. Tears ran down my face. "I knocked out his teeth. I broke his legs. I put him in a coma and he didn't wake up for six months. Me. No one else. When I said someone else did it, I was lying. I did it, and I've had to live with it ever since."

I was frail, I was weak, I had failed. I felt many things— ashamed, lost, lonely, sorrowful...

But above all things, I felt human.

Rain mixed with my tears. "You came before. You tried to help but I was afraid. I couldn't admit to my own failings. My own frailty. But now I'll take whatever you offer. I'll stand in the doorway, I'll help keep it safe. I will be the Shepherd. I will be *Nomeus.*"

Ron, Kay and Loren stared intently into the center of the circle. There, an orb of silver-blue light appeared, rising before us. Beowulf whined uncertainly.

"She Who Watches. Gaia. Oya. Tsagaglalal. Nemesis. Belet-Ili. Whatever you're called, I'll serve you."

Here I was—the self-proclaimed rationalist, the arrogant intellectual, invoking the names of a goddess in the hope that She would share Her mystical powers with me. A few months ago, I'd have laughed at the suggestion, but now it was desperation and hope that drove me.

At last She was there—motionless, naked, sculpted from the air itself, glowing silver-blue, surrounded by dancing and darting motes of light. The wind seemed to curve around Her, leaving our improvised ritual circle calm as the eye of a hurricane. In my mind I felt Her gentle touch and soft words.

You sacrifice to no gods, you bow to no king, you obey no chief, you offer no tribute. You are of no nation, but also of all nations. Only those who are nothing can be everything. You have looked into the darkness of your own heart and no longer fear what dwells there.

I felt a deep sense of both longing and contentment, and I knew that She was speaking directly to each of us. Loren stood still, gazing intently, as if listening. To my surprise, I saw that Beowulf sat like a soldier at attention, staring fixedly at the silver woman. She was speaking to him too.

Ron and Kay seemed to hear Her at the same time, looking at each other with stricken expressions of sorrow, or forgiveness, or love, or some inexplicable combination. I wondered what She'd said to them.

The enemy comes. He seeks to draw his world into this one, to unite them in a single abominable reality. Time is short. Alexander St. John— do you bear my aegis?

At first I didn't understand, and stared without speaking

Aegis. Greek for "shield." The leather coat, filthy and covered with mud...

"Yes," I said hastily. "Yes, I bear your aegis."

Do you bear my bow?

The Glock. I guessed it was a modern version of a bow, and I'd channeled her energy to kill the woman at the storage facility, but I wasn't exactly filled with confidence. "Yeah. I mean, yes."

Do you ride the dark chariot?

Did She mean Yngwie? Jesus, this was getting obscure.

"Yeah. More or less."

Have you suffered? Have you doubted? Have you loved? Have you lost what is most dear to you, and because of it tasted bitter vengeance?

I hadn't expected such a question. I faltered, words dying on my lips.

Everything I'd ever done had been a failure. I couldn't fail now. Not again. I had to answer.

"I..."

She seemed to sense my uncertainty. *Those who have suffered know others' suffering. Those who doubt know others' doubts. Those who have failed know and forgive others' failure. Those who have loved know others' love. Those who have taken vengeance know its sadness. Those who truly know themselves have seen the darkness in their own souls. Only those can serve me, and know what it is to be* Nomeus. *Have you done these things?*

My legs shook and I fell to my knees. I couldn't conceal the avalanche of emotion that suddenly crashed over me, and my voice emerged as a sob.

"Yes. Yes, I've done all those things. I've doubted, I've loved, and I've seen how horrible vengeance is. I've failed. I've lied. I've hurt people. I've hated those I should love. I've hated myself. I've been human."

I knew why She'd chosen me.

Will you take the weapon and stand in the doorway? Will you guard this world and all who dwell in it? Will you serve the sacred spiral?

I'd been afraid. I hadn't believed, hadn't understood what She truly wanted. I'd suffered, loved and taken vengeance—yes, I'd done all those things. I'd done them selfishly, thinking that I was the only one who mattered, that the rest of humanity was worthy only of contempt. I had hidden my shame deep inside, never even admitting it to myself.

That was why it had burned, why I had recoiled and been unable to grasp it. But now I knew. I was no different than any other human being—weak, pitiable, flawless, and afraid. We shared the same sadness, the same weakness, the same fear. I had failed, I had sinned, I had lied and shamed myself. But so had everyone else in the world. We were all human, and we were all afraid, we were all weak.

I remembered Damien's last message to me.

We're all human, Alex. All of us. And that's the most powerful weapon we have.

The only real source of courage, of strength and of love was each other. I had refused to see that. I had been afraid.

I was still afraid. But only those who feel fear can be brave. And I was ready to be brave at last, after so very, very long and so many, many miles.

"Yes, I'll take it. Yes, I'll serve."

She nodded. The flying sparks that surrounded Her spun faster, weaving themselves into swirling spirals glowing with silver-blue fire. The sword drifted across the space between us, point up, grip toward me.

I name you Nomeus. *Guard this world well.*

I reached up and for the second time my fingers touched the smooth, unearthly surface.

It was as if the sun had come to earth. The camp lights were overwhelmed as the fire of mid-day burst forth in the clearing, picking out the grass and ferns and the trees beyond in a blinding white glare. I felt myself screaming, for the sword now seemed to be crafted of molten glass, searing into my fingers, melding to my flesh. I stood, clutching a burning sun in my hands, feeling a rush of new thoughts and energies pulsing through me...

And then it was over. The bubble of calm and warmth collapsed. Wind and rain returned, tearing at us with icy insistence.

Parting words rang in my head, growing fainter and more distant.

Seek the enemy in his place of power. He has opened a doorway there. Seek the enemy, Nomeus.

She was gone. The camp lights reflected off the sword as I held it, staring and blinking uncomprehendingly.

It was the first time I'd been able to truly look at the weapon. It didn't especially resemble a human weapon, save that it had a blade and a grip. It seemed more organic, as if it had been grown rather than forged. Its surface was bluish and shiny, like tempered glass. I could see the alien letters faintly, as if they were suspended in the sword's material. The edge looked sharper than a razor. Was it like those monomolecular blades I used to read about in SF stories, I wondered, able to cut through anything?

The grip was soft and seemed to mold itself to my hand. Faint warmth radiating through it, and I had the odd sense that I was both present and watching myself from a distance. Also, simmering and bubbling deep in my consciousness, I felt the foreign and almost painful throb of a demonic presence.

"Congratulations," Loren said. "I guess you got the job."

I was trying to formulate some appropriate retort when Beowulf uttered a throaty growl. An instant later, a deep roar rolled across the clearing and the ground buckled, dark cracks opening up in the earth beside us. In the forest I heard wood splintering and crashing down.

Loren grabbed for his weapons and gear. "Time to go!"

X

We could leave the ritual crap behind. I swept up whatever else I could into a bag, shoved the sword through my belt and ran.

The ground fell away beneath me as I pelted down the slope, my feet slipping and sliding on wet grass and ferns. Kay stumbled, but Ron pulled her to her feet and they rushed toward the trees. Loren plunged through after them, with me and Beowulf taking up the rear. Behind us a wall of dark earth swept down, swallowing up the clearing and burying the stone from which She Who Watches had gazed for untold centuries.

Dashing into the swaying, groaning trees, I almost tripped on the sword—maybe it was a gift from a mysterious alternate realm, but right now it was nothing but a huge pain in the ass.

The roar of displaced earth and stone went on for long moments as we scrambled down the hill. I slipped in the muddy loam and went tumbling, rolling painfully until I struck the paved surface of McCaskill road. A moment later, Beowulf bounded down and Loren landed beside me with a loud string of profanities.

"Has it stopped?" Ron asked.

The deep rumbling was gone, but the splintering and crashing of great trunks continued along with the ominous sound of sliding earth and gravel.

"For now," I said. "Come on!"

"Jesus!" Loren shouted. "The bridge is gone!"

We watched as the last remnants of the Bell Creek span crumbled and fell. The banks of the little stream slid and collapsed into muddy chaos.

"Let's get moving," I said urgently. "Now."

Loren led with a camp lantern and we followed, our eyes fixed on the bobbing white light. Torrents of mud and rocks rushed across the road, threatening to cut us off. I fell twice, tearing my jeans and ripping up my knees but I rose, groaning and pressed on.

My heart slammed into my ribs like a heavy hammer, and my lungs burned with every breath. The bag felt as if it was filled with stones, threatening to dislocate my shoulder. My soaked feet were cramped and blistered. The sword grew heavier and kept trying to trip me.

But I couldn't slow down. I had to keep going.

After what seemed like hours running through cold, wet darkness we reached the landslide that blocked the road. We climbed it blind, through mud and broken tree branches until, one by one, we half-crawled, half-fell down the other side. Loren waited until the rest of us were over, then followed, dragging a stoic Beowulf along behind.

I collapsed onto the muddy ground. Yngwie was there, tires sunk in mud, pointing back toward Portland.

From above, I heard the sound of moving earth and splintering tree trunks.

"Everyone in the car! Now!"

I forced myself to my feet, yanking the driver's side door open. I tossed in the duffel bag then threw myself against the passenger door. Ron and Kay scrambled through and dove into the back, dragging the second bag along. Loren pushed Beowulf in first, then crammed together with him in the passenger seat.

"Here we go!" I turned the key. Brilliance exploded from the headlights, illuminating the swaying, tottering trees that flanked the road ahead of us. The Holley performance carburetor sucked air, the Pertronix Flamethrower ignition fired, and the 454 cubic inch V8 roared to life. God bless Damien Smith.

I thrust the shifter into gear and let out the clutch. We lurched forward, slipping and sliding, plowing through the muck.

"Alex!" There was real panic in Ron's voice now. "The whole hillside's coming down!"

From out of the gloom, the trees advanced, a shaggy green army like Birnam Wood marching against Macbeth. Mud and water sluiced around us, heralding the greater tide of wood, earth, and stone that was to come.

"Hang onto something!" I stomped on the accelerator and the engine roared in protest. The rear wheels spun, sending up rooster tails of mud. We fishtailed, lurching from side to side. We skidded toward the steep slope below then the tires found purchase, and we shot forward, gouging deep furrows behind us.

Too fast... I leaned into the wheel, making the left turn onto the steep slope of Clifton Drive. Yngwie rose up on two wheels then slammed down with teeth-rattling force, and we plummeted down the hill, half-driving, half-sliding.

Behind us rushed a tidal wave of black earth, and uprooted trees loomed implacably on our heels. A falling bough bounced off the windshield, shattering it into a glassy spiderweb.

"*Aleeeeeeeex!*" Loren's cry seemed to almost harmonize with the cacophony of wind, the roar of displaced earth and the heated thunder of the engine. We were completely out of control now—my feet were off both pedals and the only thing I could do was try to guide our headlong flight with the wheel, which itself seemed possessed and unwilling to do anything it didn't want to do.

With another bone-shaking lurch we hit the foot of Clifton and plunged forward, across the street, toward the buildings opposite. When it reached level ground, the landslide fanned out, scattering dirt and rocks, trees and unidentifiable debris across the street.

Then we pitched suddenly down, all of us jerking forward in a single motion. Beowulf yelped in pain. The seatbelt bit savagely into my shoulder. I rebounded against the seat, and we were still at last, wind howling, rain spattering the windshield, overstrained metal pinging.

I took a deep breath. It hurt. I hoped I hadn't broken a rib.

I turned on the dome light. "Is everyone okay?"

"Define 'okay.'" Loren held Beowulf, who looked at me with an eager expression, tail wagging, as if this was all nothing more than a day at the dog park. They were tangled together with each other, but they looked relatively unhurt.

Ron held Kay close. His head was gashed and blood ran down his cheek. "I guess we're still alive," he said softly, then looked around Yngwie's interior. "They sure knew how to build 'em back then, didn't they?"

The sword was stuck between the two front seats As I picked it up, I felt a sudden flood of awareness, and a kaleidoscope of images flashed in my head, almost too fast to follow. I was still trying to make sense of them as we climbed out.

Yngwie was lodged, face-first in a ditch, rear wheels hanging three feet off the ground. It wasn't going anywhere for a while. I boosted Loren up so he could pull out the equipment bags. To my relief, the bubble-wrap had held and the gasoline-filled beer bottles were still safe in their holders.

Loren rested on his haunches, stroking Beowulf's head. Out of all of us, the dog looked calmest. "So it looks like the Dark Chariot is out of commission. What do we do now?"

"I have the sword," I said. "We need to go back. Back to the Petroco Building."

A nagging urgency flowed into my mind through the sword. I didn't know why yet, but I knew we had to go.

The wind and rain chose that moment to smack us particularly hard, forcing us to bend and bundle up. Neither Ron, Loren nor Kay seemed very enthusiastic. Beowulf just sat and looked at me, ears raised, alert despite the rain.

"Dammit." Loren threw his hands up. "Back into the shit. Exactly how far is it?"

I pointed north, into chaos and darkness. "Four miles. That way." I nudged a bag with my foot. "We can leave a lot of this stuff behind." I zipped it open and began to pull out nonessential items. "So are you coming, or what?"

Kay and Ron exchanged a glance and I saw something unspoken pass between them, along with the confusing range of emotions they'd shown when She Who Watches had spoken to them.

"Yes," Ron said. "We're going to see this through."

"And we're going to do it together," Kay added. There was decision in her voice and dedication. Was she doing this for me or for Ron? In my heart, I knew it didn't matter.

Loren reached into a duffel and pulled out a big fireaxe. "I wouldn't miss it for the world, dude."

I nodded curtly. "Let's get to work then."

XI

From a distance, we must have looked like a mad polar expedition, swaddled in muddy coats, lugging heavy packs, trudging west along the railroad tracks in the face of howling wind and needles of flying sleet. But there was no one to see us—everyone with a gram of good sense was safe indoors in the face of the oncoming storm.

Each of us also carried weapons, plus two of my improvised beer-bottle Molotov cocktails, wrapped in cloth and bundled into our backpacks. They weren't much—against Onatochee and his cultists I'd have felt unsafe with an anti-aircraft gun—but I hoped they'd make some small difference.

Beowulf trotted in the lead, occasionally looking behind to make sure we were keeping up. Since our encounter with She Who Watches, he seemed more alert, more serious and—strangely—more thoughtful. She had awakened something in all of us, and now in some incomprehensible way Beowulf was less a pet than a partner, a creature as motivated and noble as any human and—in my opinion anyway—nobler than many.

Loren loped easily after Beowulf. He had slung a shotgun and rigged the fire axe across his back with elastic belts. Under his coat he carried a holstered Glock. He'd changed too. Not into a different person, no—he was still the lanky geek who wore silly t-shirts and played video games—but I wondered whether She Who Watches simply made us more of what we were to begin with. Loren, the clownish sci-fi fan—had she awakened the hero long-dormant inside him? Had she showed him that the world he imagined was truly possible? That the things he had learned from playing D&D and watching Dr. Who were real sources of strength and inspiration?

Kay followed, also armed with Glock and shotgun. She was about as far from the mousy woman I'd first met weeks ago as I could imagine. Maybe her confession to Ron had shaken something inside. Maybe going to rescue the man she loved, and their mutual encounter with a real divine being had forged the same changes as it had in the rest of us. Regardless, she walked with confidence and I knew that she would use the weapons we'd given her.

Ron came next. He had a crowbar and a Glock, and I'd given him a quick refresher course in shooting, but he still seemed ill at ease. After the stresses and horrors of the past few days, his love for his wife seemed to shine through everything else, a beacon that kept him moving. I wished that I knew more about him—something told me he'd make a good friend.

I came last, my long coat zipped and buttoned tight, pistol holstered at my side, the sword strapped across my back. At last I had the weapon that we'd sought, and the blessing of an alien goddess whose true nature I could not comprehend. Had contact with her truly changed me, like Onatochee had changed his worshippers? Or like Loren had she simply made me recognize and understand things that I'd kept hidden deep inside me? Perhaps.

Unfortunately, I felt just as uncertain as before. Not even the sword helped. In some ways it made things worse.

In the distance the unclean throb of demonic energies grew stronger still – I could detect the alien babble of his thoughts, but like a whale trying to read the mind of a garden slug, I couldn't begin to understand any of it. There may have been some faint traces of Michael O'Regan left, but I couldn't feel them. He was nothing but a shell—a human package tied with a bow, concealing the horror that lurked inside. All I felt was a growing unease and a driving compulsion to hurry.

We'd packed goggles too—they were a godsend against the weather, as rain pummeled down, full of ice and dirt and gravel whipped up by the wind. Sometimes it struck our faces; sometimes it came at us broadside, attempting to sweep us off the embankment. Loren and I carried flashlights that barely penetrated the gloom, lighting up the tracks beneath our feet and a bit of the soggy ground below.

The area was all but lifeless. Perhaps a few people still huddled in cold, darkened offices or warehouses, and across the river I saw the occasional flash of headlights or emergency lights, but otherwise we felt utterly alone.

After a mile or two, we came alongside a parked train, its dark tanker cars providing us with welcome shelter from the wind. I called a stop to eat the last of our provisions, drink, and catch our breath. Beowulf sat down ahead of us on the tracks, looking back at us indulgently. He seemed willing to forge on even if we weren't.

I looked at my watch. The dial glowed in the darkness. "It's almost ten. We're moving at a crawl."

"Better than not moving at all I guess." Kay looked tired, but she choked down her coffee as well. She stood close to Ron, as if to gain some warmth from his proximity. "How much farther?"

"We've got at least a couple of miles to go," Loren said. "And the big storm hasn't even hit yet."

I crouched on a railroad tie and grimly threw stones down the embankment. "It's no coincidence that it's supposed to hit around midnight. Onatochee's at the Petroco Building. I can feel him, sitting there. Waiting."

"Waiting for us? Or waiting for midnight so he can do whatever it is he's going to do?"

I shook my head. "I don't know. Probably both."

Loren opened a power bar package then crouched beside me, his face as troubled as I'd ever seen.

"Alex... What you said back at the clearing... Was it true? About trying to kill the guy?"

I nodded. "Yeah. It was true. I put a man in a wheelchair, and I've been lying about it ever since. To myself and to everyone."

Loren looked down and I felt ashamed. Here was a man who had looked up to me, had been my friend, and even saved my life. And I'd just let him down.

After a while, he nodded and looked back at me. "You know, Alex, what you did was really horrible. But I can't sit here and tell you I wouldn't have done the same thing."

I swallowed and blinked away tears. "I don't think you would have, Loren. I think you'd have done the right thing."

"I guess we'll never know, huh?"

"I sure as hell hope not." I stood up. "Okay, coffee break's over. Let's get going."

We tossed away the empty thermoses, and with painful slowness continued on our way. We left the shelter of the train, where the oncoming storm assaulted us with renewed fury.

The wind was like a solid wall. The rain was mostly ice now, blasting any unexposed flesh. I felt every injury I'd taken in the past few months, from my aching head to my throbbing ankle.

Every encounter I'd had with Onatochee and his followers resonated in my mind as if it had happened only a few hours ago. I tried to think of glowing silver-blue and the comforting gaze of She Who Watches, but it was difficult. The insistent, unearthly buzzing of the demonic other reality nagged and bit at my mind.

I choose you to stand watch over your people, to shut the gateways through which their enemies come, to save those you can, and to avenge those you cannot.

Was this what it was like—being chosen? To be lost, cold, alone, unsure, and afraid? If it was, then it didn't feel much different than before. The revelations that Damien wanted so much weren't an end to uncertainty. They were just the beginning.

Off near the river, a few emergency generators were working, and a handful of lights twinkled, illuminating collapsed tanks, fallen scaffolds, and unsteady buildings. Cleanup from the disaster would take a very long time.

And the real disaster hadn't even begun.

It was nearly 11:30 when we finally approached within a half mile of the Petroco Building. Rain fell in a steady shower and the wind was down to an occasional heavy gust. I suspected that this was only a temporary respite before the real storm hit.

I called a halt, raising my goggles to scan the place with binoculars.

"Jesus," I muttered.

The Petroco Building was gone, replaced by an untidy pile of rubble—stone, wood, shingles, metal beams all tangled together. A big sphere of greenish light hung over it, shining like a baleful eye, illuminating the area with its distasteful luminescence.

The labyrinth of junk around the fallen structure had grown bigger and more imposing. Rusty cars lay on their sides; fencing and razor wire had been strung between them as crude barricades, along with pipes, cabling, fragments of crates and shipping containers. The corpses of appliances were strewn chaotically—refrigerators, TVs, microwave ovens, obsolete computers—along with every other kind of debris imaginable— tires, chairs, old doors, sofas, mattresses, bicycles, overturned dumpsters... It was as if the cult had taken detritus from every corner of the world they planned to wreck.

Shadows moved in the pale light. To a casual glance they looked normal—pale, thin, and dirty but human. But they moved with the same out-of-synch jerkiness I'd seen before, and as I watched a few of them wavered and shifted, briefly breaking up into pixelated, fractalized patterns before returning to human shape. Most were unarmed, but a few carried weapons— shotguns, clubs, bats. With growing desperation I searched for Trish, while at the same time dreading what I'd see if I found her.

My gaze focused on a tiny but familiar figure that moved with quick, nervous motions. Even at this distance I recognized him. Pine Street Bob—Onatochee's acolyte, his high priest, now no better than any of the other mortal detritus that served the demon-god.

Alex...

The voice was in my head again. Pine Street Bob hesitated, looking back and forth, as if searching for me.

I feel you out there, Alex. Coming to give yourself up? To join us? I knew you'd see sense eventually... I know you're coming. Now see what's waiting for you...

The big sphere of light vibrated and its surface shimmered. Then it seemed to open like a door, revealing something like an impossibly long tunnel that shone with strange shapes—twisting, nauseating patterns, phasing through unreal forms and colors and dimensions—a distant vista of chaos and nightmarish reality.

"Shit!" I looked away, my head swimming. The single look I'd gotten had been enough. I didn't want to look at it again. It was worse than the last time—then I'd seen it in a dream, but now it was right there in front of me. Even at this distance, it was almost painful to look at.

Ron's fingers were tight on the crowbar. "What the hell is that thing?"

"A portal," I said. "The way to Onatochee's reality. I saw it in a dream once before, but it's bigger now. I can feel it from here. He's going to rip it open even further. Let his reality spill into ours."

And if he did there was nothing we could do to stop it—sword or no sword. Even the weapon that She had given me was inadequate to stem the coming flood.

"Then what the fuck do we do?" Just a brief glimpse had rattled Loren seriously. Beowulf fixed him with a reassuring gaze and he absently patted his dog's head.

My thoughts were dark. "I don't think he knows exactly where we are, but he knows we're close. We're going to have to fight our way in. There's a maze of junk full of fanatics who know we're coming, outnumber us ten to one, and can probably shrug off most of our weapons, with the biggest fucking monster of all waiting in the middle. We either have to sneak in or go in hot. Either way we're going to get bloody. You still in?"

I received three solemn, silent nods in reply. Beowulf just looked stoic.

The wind picked up again with a thunderous roar, bearing bits of trash, leaves, branches and other debris. Rain and sleet began to pound down even harder. It looked as if the real storm was here at last.

"Buckle up as best you can." I spoke urgently over the growing cacophony. "We don't have much time."

Wordlessly, the others began to zip coats and cast off unneeded baggage. My mind was racing with schemes for attacking the site, none of which seemed remotely practical. I finally settled on one approach and tried to formulate a plan.

"This is his storm," I shouted over the growing scream of wind, loosing the sword, and feeling angry blue light flow through my hand and up my arm. "It's Onatochee's storm, but we're going to use it against him."

It was crude and improvised over just a matter of minutes, but it was the best I could come up with. I gave them as quick a rundown as I could then looked at Loren.

"There's a lot depending on you guys," I said. "Can you do it?"

He nodded. "I think so."

I threw my arms around his shoulders and hugged him close. "Good luck, both of you. For God's sake stay alive. Now get going. Kickoff's in ten minutes."

"You got it, coach." Loren grinned and led Beowulf into the tangle of debris surrounding the ruins. Moments later, they were gone from sight, leaving us crouching in the shelter of a muddy gravel slope. Kay and Ron sat close together, their parkas caked with mud, occasionally exchanging reassuring glances.

I peered at them through the haze of icy rain. Here, sheltered from the roar of the wind, we could talk for a few moments. "Can I ask you something? You don't have to tell me if you don't want to."

Ron cast me a weary but knowing glance. "You want to know what She said to us, don't you?"

"Yeah, it would be nice. If it isn't too personal." I felt a sudden need to know them both better and to understand what they felt.

"At first She didn't say anything," Kay replied, thoughtfully, a hint of wonderment in her voice. "I just felt this... warmth, I guess... Inside me, and for a few seconds I felt as if I was... Or as if Ron was..."

"I felt as if I was Kay and she was me," Ron said. "It was as if we'd switched places, and I could see myself the way she saw me."

"And I felt the same thing," Kay said. "For just an instant, I felt what Ron felt, and... Well, I guess it made me understand better than anything he could have said."

"Then I was back in my own head," Ron continued. "And I heard Her say, 'It's not too late.' That's all She said. But I knew it was true."

"If he's in my life and I'm in his, then it doesn't matter what happens." There was a loving, devoted tone in her voice that I hadn't heard from her before. "It's what we are now that matters, not what we were or what we're going to be. And right now I love Ron and I want to be with him."

Ron nodded and they exchanged another deep glance.

"I love you," he said, emphatic and without a trace of doubt.

"I love you too," she replied.

I swallowed hard and simply nodded in reply. There wasn't much I could add.

Yeah, I was pretty sick of being a cynic. Real emotions felt a hell of a lot better.

I hoped we'd all live to appreciate them better.

In nervous silence we prepped our Molotov cocktails, uncorking the beer bottles and stuffing them with the rags we'd used to wrap them. We all had windproof lighters as well, and as the seconds ticked by we carefully opened ours, ready to light and throw as soon as Loren and Beowulf got things started.

The wind had risen to an almost deafening howl, but an instant later I heard the faint but recognizable explosion from Loren's shotgun. A faint burst of orange in the distance marked where Loren had thrown one of his bombs. It was quickly followed by another, and the crack of small arms fire. Through the thickening curtain of rain I saw two cultists running past.

A diversion—something to draw the enemy away, leaving us to advance under cover of the big storm. It was probably the simplest thing we could have done, and the most obvious. But we had hoped that our opponents weren't the sharpest *athames* in the drawer. As more cultists began to run away from us, I drew some comfort in seeing that I'd been right.

"Ready?" I asked.

Kay and Ron nodded.

"Come on then," I said.

I rose, drawing my sword. The wind howled and a blanket of rain covered us as we rushed into a dark night filled with fire and blood.

XII

The full fury of the storm descended as we ran. Cold and drenching rain plummeted down in quantities that I had never thought possible. Each drop was a tiny knife of ice, stabbing down from a murderous sky. The wind picked them up and drove them into us, blowing sideways, swirling papers and sticks and other detritus, plucking at our clothes and making us feel as if great hooks on wires were trying to drag us into the churning turmoil overhead.

Though its intent was deadly, the storm also let us advance undetected into the cult's fortress of ruin. As the rain hammered down full-force, it was like a fog, kicking up mud, obscuring the green light of the great sphere, locking us into our own little world only a few yards across, concealing us from view. And the nightmare howl of the wind covered the sound of gunfire and the screams of cultists as we swept down on them.

I led the way, the sword almost dragging me along, guiding me toward disorder and aberration. The first to fall was a surprised cultist—a woman with long grayish hair who blurred into motion at the sight of me, sparking with chaotic colors. The sword moved almost of its own accord, impaling her easily

335

with a shower of silver-blue sparks. I saw—I *felt*— the demonic energies drawn from her, dissipating into a shimmering mist that vanished on the wind. Her body fell to the ground and shattered into shining fragments. A moment later they were gone, too, leaving nothing behind.

I should have fallen to my knees at the horror of what I'd done—the utter extermination of someone that had once been human. And something told me that when this was all over I would. But for now, the silver-blue flames filled me and I charged ahead.

I realized what the sword had done, and why it was so powerful. It had severed the connection between the female cultist and Onatochee's reality. She and the other cultists were infused with so much of the demonic energy that they couldn't exist in our world without it. Tsagaglalal's weapon sliced the cords that tied creatures to their realms of origin, and with it I could destroy them utterly.

We surged over a barricade of old refrigerators, twisted shopping carts, and broken dining tables, throwing ourselves upon a handful of cultists armed with clubs and rifles. Ahead of me, a cultist flashed and flickered from human form into fractured geometrics and back again. He struck at Kay but she ducked away and I swung the sword, cutting into his neck, nearly severing his head. He didn't bleed—a torrent of the flashing, multi-colored chaos-stuff poured forth and he shattered like a broken stained-glass window.

In my mind a tiny voice cried out in dismay. *He was human once. He was born, he was a child, he grew up. Who was he? Some luckless street person with a meth habit? Some misguided cultist? A sociopath who listened to Onatochee's promises?*

I told myself that it didn't matter. In embracing their demon-god, these creatures had abandoned their humanity, and with it the right to mercy—that the sword could affect them at all was proof positive that they no longer belonged in our world. The goddess had commanded that I save those I could, and these could not be saved.

Part of me didn't believe a word of it.

In the shelter of a rusted pickup truck, Ron stopped to light a Molotov cocktail, then hurled it toward the bare carcass of a tractor as a crowd of cultists swarmed over it and toward us. The wind caught it, and the fuse nearly went out, but then it struck its target and exploded spectacularly. Even with their demonic speed and strength, the cultists still burned brightly, retreating with a chorus of agonized screams.

They weren't putting up much of a fight. These weren't Onatochee's army, not really—they were nothing but cannon fodder, sent to slow us down and keep us busy until...

Until what?

A familiar shape bounded from the rubble and Beowulf sprang at another cultist, ripping with his front claws then rending with his jaws. The cultist screamed and tried to strike at Beowulf, striking sparks, but the dog didn't seem to feel it— perhaps the chaos-energy that drove them was running low, or maybe our encounter with the goddess had strengthened our resistance. I slashed with the sword, and the cultist vanished in a swirl of colored fragments.

Beowulf barked at me. He was limping and there was blood on his fur, but he seemed okay otherwise.

From behind me, I heard a shriek and saw Kay falling, overborn by two big cultists, angry motes swimming in the air as they struck and grappled with her.

I took a step toward her, but something struck me from behind. It felt as if I'd been tackled by a weightlifter as it bore me down into the mud. I twisted around in time to see a grinning face, glaring at me, his eyes flashing with inner-green light.

"Shepherd..." hissed a familiar and hateful voice, a voice I'd first heard on a Portland street what now seemed like a very long time ago. He shifted, breaking apart into spheres and spirals, and I felt an electric shock pass through my body. "He's back..."

I struggled, trying to pull the sword free.

"...And hell's come with him..."

More shocks erupted from Bob's hands as they scrabbled for purchase on my coat, but the goddess' aegis seemed to hold it off for a moment, allowing me to free one arm, bring the Glock up, jam it up under his jaw and shoot, again and again.

The bullets from the Glock–in my hands it was now Her bow—sparked silver, plowing through Bob's altered flesh. Black blood splashed and Bob howled, vibrating and shifting through shape after shape, convulsing and thrashing. I tore free from his grasping fingers and dragged myself to my feet, swinging the sword up.

Pine Street Bob shuddered and writhed in the mud, struck by 9mm rounds charged by She Who Watches' unearthly force. His ravaged face stared up at me, and for an instant the madness left his haggard eyes.

Robert Leslie's face was as serene and peaceful as the photo Damien had shown me—the image of an innocent, hopeful young man, before the pain of life and the claws of a demon had touched him.

"Alex..." he whispered softly. "Please..."

I don't know whether he was pleading for me to kill him or spare him. It didn't matter—I swung the sword. Chaos-stuff shattered into starry debris, and in a moment Pine Street Bob was reduced to a shimmering swirl of colored fragments, washed away by icy rain.

I felt an unaccountable rush of sorrow for a man lost to sickness and the worship of death.

For all he has done, Shepherd, for all his sins, he was still human.

I turned toward where Kay and the cultists struggled. Ron was there, his Glock in one hand. The cultist that had attacked his wife still crawled toward them, flickering and shifting, several bleeding holes in his side.

I finished the injured cultist off with my sword as Ron took aim at another attacker, holding his pistol clumsily in one hand, and fired the entire clip, his arm flying. He hit it a couple of times and the man staggered, sparks flashing, but then came at us again. I stepped in front of him, chopping sideways, cutting his body in half, reducing it to fading, broken pixels.

I helped Kay sit up. Her breath came in heavy gasps, she was cut and her neck was badly bruised.

"Are you okay?" I asked.

She stood painfully. "No, but I'll live."

Ron retrieved his gun and fumbled with it, trying to thumb the magazine catch and load another clip.

I motioned at him. "Give it to me."

I released the clip and slid in its replacement.

I handed it back to Ron. "Is that your last?"

He nodded, pale faced and wide-eyed. "Yeah."

I pulled a magazine from my pocket and gave it to him. That left me with one mag of my own. "Make every shot count. I think they can die, but it takes an awful lot of firepower."

I looked around. A few figures moved, darting among the junk beneath the incessant pounding of the rain. Some yellow flames still burned, flickering feebly as the wind sought to snuff them out. Onatochee's gateway was closer now, visible through the torrent like a greenish moon behind clouds. The wind howled and gusted, forcing us to hunker down or grab something for support. No more cultists came at us. We were all still alive, but we were a mess.

Beowulf loped up, one front paw held gingerly, and Loren limped behind. His left arm hung at an ugly angle, and the side of his face was beginning to swell and discolor. He held the shotgun loosely in his right hand.

He forced a tired grin and shouted over the wind. "So how's it going in your neighborhood?"

"Pine Street Bob's history," I said, putting my arm around his shoulder and talking into his ear. "What happened to your arm?"

He looked down and winced. "Big guy with a baseball bat. It took a whole clip to take him down. I pounded him with my axe too, but I still don't think he's dead. I ran."

I swore. We were low on ammo and everyone was hurt, but the center of Onatochee's power was near and we'd fought our way through most of his defenders.

I waved a hand toward the mist-shrouded sphere. "Ready?" I bellowed.

Loren nodded. Kay and Ron just looked resigned, and Beowulf remained stoic.

I stepped forward, sword in hand, pulling me toward the yawning jaws of chaos that lay ahead of us.

Almost the instant I moved, the wind died and the rain slacked off to a slow drizzle. It was as if I'd walked through a doorway into a bubble of calm amid the raging elements. Ahead of me the misty rain cleared away like a parting curtain.

When I saw what stood in the wan green light, pain struck me as ferociously as the storm.

Alex.

It... he... was there—the remains of the human shell, Michael O'Regan, his skin cracked and burnt, his grinning face more bone than flesh, his hands contorted and twisted into claws.

Hello, Alex.

The hammer-blow of Onatochee's presence struck me, its force doubled and redoubled from the last time. I stumbled and a scream dragged itself from my lungs. My head throbbed as if it had been packed with burning coals, searing my eyes, my ears, my nostrils, overwhelming every sense in a raging, irresistible inferno. The warmth of the sword was overwhelmed by pain—it and the Glock tumbled from nerveless fingers as I fell gasping to my knees.

The screams in my head roared with a thousand voices, all of them Onatochee's. Amid the incoherent babble, I heard him at last, speaking to me in his fearful amalgam of human and demon...

You came, Alex. I did not need to seek you out—you came of your own free will. You brought my vessel, you brought her weapon, but you do not know how to use it, and now you see, you see, you see...

The gate pulsed and bulged, then yawned wide—stretching out into an impossibly deep abyss where chaos and madness crawled. Raw energy flowed from it in shining greenish streamers, rising up to be caught on the angry storm that still roared on outside the little bubble of calm. Brighter and brighter it grew, and along with it the screams merged into a single drawn-out cacophony that blotted out everything save the mad echo of the demon's hateful voice.

Tonight, Alex. Tonight we become one, united. We will be the same, you and I... Your world and mine...

Loren and Ron tried to keep me on my feet as the great wave of chaos began to roll forth from the yawning portal.

The storm you have seen is nothing, Alex. This is the true storm. The storm that will carry my presence and make us all one...

A new wave of pressure burst forth from the portal, a wind as unearthly as Onatochee himself, a second storm far more terrible than the first, carrying greenish streamers of his reality, twisting tendrils curling and writhing into our world. The pressure in my head was almost unbearable...

"*Look out!*" I screamed, pulling away from Loren and Ron. "*He's going to—*"

The deafening roar cut me off as Onatochee's reality flooded out, rushing over us like an oily, shimmering tidal wave. I threw myself flat, but the others weren't quick enough. Kay stood frozen in place until Ron leaped, knocking her to the ground. The flood of nightmarish chaos-stuff smashed into him, picking him up and tumbling him through the air. Loren ducked away, but the flood caught him and he too vanished into the maelstrom.

On her knees, Kay screamed and Beowulf uttered a despairing howl. The burning pain in my head redoubled, blanketing me with hot, inexorable force, sending me falling, screaming into a bottomless void.

* * *

I lay in a shattered world, beneath a tortured sky. Ancient walls rose above me, crumbling and almost featureless. The air was stale and cold, like the musty atmosphere of a long-sealed room.

Through the gloom a light shone, bright and silver-blue, and then She was there, floating serene in Her luminous sphere, wings high and proud. Her eyes were soft and Her gaze was gentle, and behind the light I could see the faintest traces of the beautiful violet I'd once seen in Trish.

"Where am I?" I asked, painfully rising to my feet. "How did I get here?"

This is an ancient place. The voice that echoed inside my head was patient but loving, like a mother explaining something complex to a child who was too young to understand. *It was ravaged by another enemy long ago and only a fragment of it remains, floating in the place between worlds. Soon it too will be gone, devoured by the pitiless void. We cannot act in this world or yours. Only the Shepherd can carry our weapon. Only the Shepherd can face the darkness in his own world.*

"Who are you?" I asked. "Why did you choose me?"

There are many answers. You must find them for yourself. You have faced the darkness in your soul. You bear the weapon, you wear the aegis, and you bear our love, Shepherd. Those are all the gifts that we can share.

I looked down. The sword was gone.

"I have to go back," I said.

It wasn't a question, but a flat statement of reality. The sword was back there somewhere. And it was the gift She had given me that could stop Onatochee.

She nodded.

Do not fear darkness. Do not give in to despair. Investigate and chronicle. Help where you can and destroy where you must. Do this, Shepherd. Stand in the doorway with a candle and hold the darkness at bay.

They were Damien's words, scrawled on his last message to me. I would not forget.

"I will," I said. "I swear."

I swallowed. Her radiance grew, filling me and warming my heart. The pain of my injuries faded along with the ancient, ruined world around me, and I felt myself borne aloft, tumbling through the dark void between.

XIII

I opened my eyes to stare into a swirling vortex of colors that flashed and glimmered in a strange and disquieting sky—colors of a spectrum that no human was meant to see. Vast shapes flapped ponderously just beyond sight like the sails of titanic ships moving with unnatural life. The ground beneath my feet felt strange—spongy and yielding, and a faint throbbing sensation vibrated through the soles of my boots like an irregular heartbeat.

The rubble of the Petroco Building still surrounded me, but it was different too—glistening, twisting, pulsating as if alive, blurring into shapes of four, five, six dimensions.

Loren lay nearby, blood streaming from his head. He was motionless; his chest rose and fell shallowly. Ron wasn't so lucky. His body lay twisted at all angles, impaled on rusty rebar. Kay crouched beside him, weeping.

Of my companions only Beowulf remained functional, and he was in sad shape, one leg sprained or broken, a bad cut down one side of his face. Nevertheless he stood beside me, snarling at what floated in the air above us.

It was the portal, gazing at me like a vast demon's eye—just as it had gazed in my dream on the eve of Hecate Trivia. And now, also as in the dream, it focused its fearsome attention on me, and I felt Onatochee's clangor growing in my mind, stronger than ever before.

The gateway spoke with Michael O'Regan's voice. *You see now, Alex... You see what I could not explain... I am this place, and this place is me, and soon all of your reality will be me, and I will be it. Flesh and stone, blood and air, fire and sinew... All one, all part of me... All part of the thing that you called Onatochee... You saw only the tiniest fragment of what I truly am, Alex... Only the merest fraction extended into your reality, seeking purchase, seeking sustenance... Now all shall become part of me... All shall join with me...*

There was movement in the rubble and I saw that it was the surviving cultists. Some still looked human, but their eyes were pale and lifeless, their faces confused, bewildered or utterly expressionless. Others were unstable—flickering through different shapes—broken geometric solids, flapping sheets of multicolored radiance like those in the sky, swirls of bright motes pulsating yellow-green, folding and unfolding origami sculptures in rough human shape.

The first inhabitants of a new reality, I thought. The products of Michael's great unification.

I waved a hand at the remains of his cultists. "Join you like they did? You promised them freedom. You promised them power. Just like you promised me, just like you promised Damien. But we saw through you, didn't we? We knew what a liar you really are, Onatochee."

I remembered the goddess' charge. There were many I'd failed to save, but there were also many I could avenge if I had the chance.

You do not understand power, Alex. You don't understand that true power comes from union with power, with surrender, with acquiescence. We create power from what we consume... They did not just gain power, they have become *power...*

The words were hard to make out, and again I realized that my brain was simply trying to make sense of incomprehensible concepts being spewed by a creature as different from me as I was from a cold virus. Bandying semantics with a giant demon-eye was wasting time. If there was any chance of stopping Onatochee, I would have to take it now.

I'd seen his vision, perceived what he intended. Amid the pain and burning torment in my head, the sword and my connection to She Who Watches had allowed me to see the demon's psyche and his plans.

He was telling me the truth—he and his reality were one. His evil was that of an entire single-minded, demonic universe. The thing in the air above me wasn't merely a gate—it was Onatochee himself, manifesting in our world, transforming it into a semblance of his own. He had his foothold now, and if we didn't stop him, it would expand outward, devouring our world and our entire reality, incorporating it into his very essence. Our reality would not simply become another realm, it would become *Onatochee*.

As I watched, a nearby cultist seemed to melt away into the confused, altered landscape, broken up into random shapes, fading from sight and joining with the substance of the other reality. Others began to change, too—their once-human outlines blurring and softening into shining shapes and glittering fog.

This was what Onatochee's promises meant—to fade away and be absorbed into their master. We weren't his children. We weren't his servants. We weren't even his slaves.

We were his food.

I struggled to my feet. My ankle almost gave way and I staggered, scanning the ground, looking for the lost weapon. All I could see was an iridescent shimmer against a shifting, fragmenting surface.

"We're not going to just roll over and give up," I shouted. "We defeated you once, and we can do it again!"

Impudence. The word didn't even begin to encapsulate the creature's cosmic disdain and indifference, but it was all I could perceive. *You defeated nothing. The Multnomahs drove off a small speck of my substance. They were beaten and did not know it. Beaten by the very things that give Onatochee nourishment. They were weak, and they paid the price for their presumption. You are weak, Alex. You are afraid. You feel sorrow, not anger. I see that when I touch your mind. You are weak like Michael O'Regan, like Damien Smith. Like all the others. Like your woman. You are weak.*

The words stung, but in a way they gave me strength, reminding me of the very qualities that made me who I was. I swallowed fear and shame and focused on anger. "I'm the Shepherd now, Onatochee. *Nomeus.* You killed my friends. You took Michael and Trish from me, made them into your puppets. Now you need to pay for what you've done."

You are wrong. They are not puppets. They are the flesh of Onatochee.

I shook my head, trying to clear away the sorrow that welled up, threatening to drown the fires of rage. I reminded myself that I was running out of time—that with each passing heartbeat the demon-thing's influence expanded and grew stronger. I searched the chaotic ground with growing alarm, my heart racing. How long now? How long did I have left?

From a few feet away I heard a faint yip, so soft that only I could hear it. I looked toward Beowulf, who stood beside what might once have been a pile of trash, staring at me urgently.

Projecting from the iridescent ground was the hilt of the sword, dark and inert.

The demon felt the weapon's presence the moment I fixed my gaze on it. A deafening mental scream erupted from the great staring thing in the sky, blotting out every other thought. It screamed incoherently, but its message was unmistakable.

Onatochee was a being so unnatural and distant that I couldn't even fully perceive him, and he only barely understood me. But there were things that we could both grasp easily— anger, rage, bloodlust, and the drive to survive. The compulsion for self-preservation flooded out from the demon-eye, spurring what remained of his followers to action.

The altered landscape around us was suddenly alive with motion as the remaining cultists emerged from hiding. There was at least a score of them—some still human-looking, others like amalgams of crackling geometric shapes, still others swirling clouds of multicolored motes, almost entirely transformed into the stuff of Onatochee's realm.

A knot of them rushed to block my path, cutting me off from the sword. I had no weapons, I was near-dead from weapons and exhaustion, but I kept moving, charging into their midst. Hands and shimmering appendages reached out, grabbing at me but slipping from my coat. I pressed on, still intent on the weapon. Then a pair of human cultists slammed into me and I felt myself falling.

Gunshots exploded, pounding my eardrums and bullets struck the pair, showering sparks and making them blur and fragment. It didn't hurt them, but it distracted them. I dodged past as Kay strode forward, firing and firing until the Glock's slide locked back. Then she smoothly ejected the clip, slipped in another, chambered a round, and kept firing.

"You fucking sons of bitches! You killed my husband, you fucks!" Her voice was a scream of pure, unadulterated anger and hatred. *"Die, you fuckers! DIE!"*

What remained of the cultists was no more than a collection of instinct and impulse. They turned on Kay, reaching out and overwhelming her. Sparks flashed and she went down under a tide of altered bodies.

She'd bought me a moment, but the sword was still long paces distant. Realizing what they'd done, the crowd of semi-human cultists rose as one and came after me again. I moved without thought, desperately dashing toward the weapon.

Then Beowulf was in motion, a sleek canine shadow, ripping and rending, leaping into the midst of the crowd of my attackers, biting and snarling. More sparks flashed—I didn't even know if he was hurting them, but like Kay he had given me precious moments. A few continued to pursue, their faces twisted, eyes flashing.

But I'd reached the sword. I seized the grip and yanked it free.

The power that flowed through the weapon was like what I'd felt when I first touched it—a white-hot explosion of pain and energy, but channeled inward by the bizarre reality surrounding me, stoking a growing fire in my chest. If Onatochee was inimical to my reality and my existence, then I was now inimical to *him*.

I spun, the sword whirling, slashing effortlessly through the first rank of attackers. They didn't even scream but only vanished into clouds of particles, sucked back into the vortex of the demon-gate. Almost nothing of our world remained in them, and the sword's power tore them free, sending their otherworldly energies back to where they had originated.

The swarm of chaos-motes cleared, revealing Beowulf, hurt but alive, panting and limping toward where Kay's motionless form lay.

I turned, the sword over my head. The great shimmering eye-sphere hovered there and its dissonant metallic voice shouted again in my head. The words were only barely comprehensible, as if in its rage and fear it had lost the ability to express itself coherently.

No. Go back. Come no closer. We kill you if you do.

It didn't matter anymore. I wasn't going to communicate, taunt or reason. The thing in the swirling unfamiliar sky was an interloper, an invader, a disease. Its very presence was an affront to my reality, and to the mind that reality had spawned.

I ran toward it, the sword blazing, clutched in both hands. Onatochee was a cosmos-spanning consciousness and I knew somehow that I couldn't ever truly destroy it, but I could sever its ties to the chaos-place that had spawned it. I could close the doorway and cut it off forever.

There was a piece of shimmering stone between me and the hovering sphere. My foot touched the stone, transforming it back into familiar earthly matter, and I pushed off. I felt myself carried higher and faster than I could ever have jumped on my own.

The sphere retreated through the writhing air. It was afraid. It knew what it could do and now it fled.

Then it hesitated, stopping like a single frame of stuck film, vibrating and groaning.

Michael O'Regan's voice echoed in my head, clear and undistorted by the demon that had possessed him.

Now, Alex! I can't hold it... very... long...

Onatochee screamed in rage and frustration. Then the sword sliced into it and it shattered, green light flooding out and vanishing like mist on the wind. A final agonized shriek pounded through my brain like a rusted nail.

I tumbled to the muddy ground and rolled to my feet, sword at the ready. All around me the other reality retreated, sucking back the last remnants of the cultists, draining back into the collapsing gateway. The pulsating, shimmering ground vanished, replaced by the familiar dirt and rock and rubble of the fallen Petroco Building. Onatochee's final wail faded away into the clean sound of falling rain and the muted roar of wind.

A feebly-flickering mass lay nearby, blinking in and out of focus, transforming from one vile shape to another. All of the shapes were broken and weak, reaching out toward me with feeble tendrils and broken claws, their forms random and unfinished.

I raised the sword. Did it feel anything, I wondered? Terror? Regret? Impotent anger? Could it even conceive of human emotion or intellect?

No, I thought. This was nothing but the last fragment of an invader, the flapping severed tail of a vast serpent, a mindless and soulless thing that needed to be finally vanquished.

As I stepped closer the thing shifted, changing again, transforming into a human shape.

"Alex..." Michael O'Regan said through ruined lips. "Alex, I'm sorry."

I faltered, sword still drawn back for a final blow, my mind whirling with a thousand conflicting thoughts.

"Michael...?"

He seemed to deflate, slowly collapsing, his weary eyes closing, his substance draining away.

I spoke quietly. "Thank you, Michael."

A look of peace settled over the lined, mutilated face, all that was left of the man I had known. "Thank you, Alex."

I swung the sword. A moment later the last remnants of Michael O'Regan were gone as if they had never existed.

The wind died away. Rain still fell in torrents, but now it fell straight down. I felt no triumph, only grim satisfaction and regret at the fearsome cost of victory.

From nearby I heard a weak groan and saw Loren roll onto his back. Beowulf stood astride him, deliberately licking at his face and whining, urging him to wake up. His eyes flickered open.

"Hi, boy." It was a thick, incoherent mumble. "Alex? Whass... Hap'nin?"

A new roar of sound, deeper than the wind, erupted from the oil tanks and scaffolds by the river. The Willamette rushed over its banks in a dark, foaming flood, sweeping through the tank farm toward us.

"Shit," I muttered. Loren groaned in pain as I lifted him by one arm. "Come on, unless you want to drown."

Beowulf bounded toward Kay's still form. He sniffed her briefly, then looked up, barking urgently.

"Shit!" I let Loren go and hastened to her, grabbing her wrist and feeling for a pulse.

"Oh God." Her chest rose shallowly, and I felt a faint pulse—she was badly hurt but still clinging to life.

I looked back at Loren, still struggling to rise. I couldn't carry both of them, and the black wall of water was rushing closer, rupturing oil tanks, collapsing cranes, engulfing buildings.

At last Beowulf had had enough and bit Loren on the leg, eliciting an angry yelp.

"Fucker!" Loren's voice was thick with pain and weariness, but he was awake. "What the fuck'd you do that for?"

"Go!" I shouted. "Go, God damn it!"

Some of my desperation finally penetrated and Loren moved clumsily, limping away from the water, toward the railroad embankment.

My muscles ached and screamed in protest as I lifted Kay and stumbled after. The sword was clumsily jammed into my belt and again more hindrance than help. We struggled toward the railroad embankment, a wall of black water racing along behind. When Loren flagged, Beowulf barked and bit him again.

We made it up the embankment just ahead of the water. It crashed upon the gravel slope ferociously, then receded back toward the Willamette, leaving the land behind sodden with mud, water and oil.

I let Kay fall to the tracks and collapsed beside her.

Resting on hand and knees, Loren groaned.

"Jesus, Alex." He was sobbing, breathing in short, painful gasps. "Jesus. Why are we still alive?"

"Good question." I truly had no idea. "But I'm grateful anyway."

Loren let Beowulf lick his face, then hugged his dog close and looked at Kay, unconscious on the tracks. "Where's Ron? Did he make it?"

I shook my head. I was weary and could barely form the words. "No. We're the only ones left."

Loren buried his head in his hands. His shoulders shook. "Oh, God, Alex. Is it finished? Is it really over?"

I stared out across the ruins of the old building and the wrecked tank farm beyond. Pools of water shone in the moonlight. The wind was gone and the roar of the flood was fading.

"I don't know, Loren," I admitted. "I really don't know."

Epilogue

The Bedford-Stuyvesant neighborhood of Brooklyn had always been a war zone—run-down brownstones, abandoned apartment complexes, blasted vacant lots, drug deals in alleys, prostitutes on the corners. Yet to those who lived there it was home, and a strong community stood against chaos, fighting rot and corruption, holding its own in the asphalt heart of New York City. For the first time in my life I understood how they felt.

The place had once been called Brooklyn Gardens, a housing development intended for low-income families. Now it was a shell, overgrown with weeds, surrounded by razor wire, abandoned by a city that couldn't afford to tear it down. And here, on a street lined with burned and rusted-out hulks of cars, full of blowing papers, broken bottles and old toys, I stopped Yngwie, climbed out, locked the doors, and strode along a trash-strewn sidewalk.

Without hesitation I cut through the fence. I wasn't the first to do so—it had been patched numerous times and there were bottles, needles, crack pipes, and cigarette butts everywhere. The building's windows were boarded up, but most of the boards had been torn off, and what remained was covered in graffiti proclaiming ownership by several competing gangs.

I pushed a door open against a barricade of junk, forcing my way inside. It reeked as badly as the cement plant had, and it triggered unpleasant memories.

She was in one of the apartments, crouched in the corner amid a nest of tattered blankets, newspapers, dirty clothing, food containers, and garbage. She was naked, her once-white skin now dirty black, a welter of scars.

She looked up at me with wide, haunted eyes. Though their whites were rheumy and yellowish, the pupils remained the same intense violet-blue that I remembered.

"Alex?" she said, in a cracked voice that still retained some trace of her old enthusiasm. "How did you find me?"

I reached under my coat and withdrew the sword.

"It told me, Trish. Just a couple of weeks ago."

Trish began to cry.

"I'm so sorry, Alex." There was a trace of her old voice in the sad words. "Please don't hate me. I didn't mean for it all to happen the way it did. When Onatochee spoke to me that day at the Petroco Building... I knew I had to do what he told me. I'm sorry I told them where you lived, Alex. I'm sorry that I left your window unlocked so they could get in. But I didn't have any choice, Alex. He promised me that if I did what he asked, I'd see his world, share his power... Please, Alex. Please forgive me."

In my heart I'd known it. She was the only one who could have left the window unlocked to let Uncle Creepy into my apartment. I'd figured it out a long time ago, but I still felt a knot of sickness in my gut when she admitted it.

"A few cultists escaped when I closed the gateway to Onatochee's reality." I tried to keep the quaver out of my voice, to overcome the emotion that I felt at the sight of her. "His last resort. They all carried a remnant of that damned demon inside them. If any survive with even the smallest fragment of his reality they could call him back." I paused. "But you're the last one, Trish. I found all the others but you."

My shoulders slumped as I remembered discovering the final awful truth. "The Multnomahs closed the gateway just like I did. But Onatochee lived on in his surviving worshippers, and through them he took his revenge on the Multnomahs. He possessed or killed them one by one, until they were wiped out. Parts of him lived on, still connected to his reality, seducing and controlling the weak, making them do his will over the centuries, carrying on the cult."

Trish sobbed, her face hidden by matted hair.

I went on mechanically, reciting what I'd learned, and the fearful truths that I didn't want to speak out loud.

"Eventually we came along—you and me and Damien and Michael O'Regan. After we contacted Onatochee at the Petroco Building, he got into our heads. He was subtle, but he got us to do what he wanted. Michael performed the ritual, you left the window unlocked, Damien agreed to go along with the whole scheme. It was Onatochee's plan all along. When we performed the second ritual, we didn't just summon his spirit—we opened the doorway just enough for his scattered remnants to reform and connect to his reality. He was drawn back into this world, leaving him free to open his gateway and absorb our reality into himself. It was our fault."

She kept crying, fists pressed into her eyes.

I couldn't hurt her. I had to help. There was still a chance. Back home we were healing and repairing the damage that Onatochee had done. I'd moved into Damien's house and was continuing his work. Kay, Loren, Beowulf, the car, the city... they were all healing.

We could help her too. I'd killed others without hesitation, but her... Maybe there was a way...

"Trish. Please. Come with me. I'll take care of you." I felt tears on my face. "Trish, I love you."

When she looked at me, I saw a glimmer of greenish light in her weary eyes.

"Trish?" My voice broke with despair. "Oh God, Trish..."

She sprang at me, a knife in one hand.

"*Ichiloot,*" she snarled.

I swung the sword up instinctively, thrusting it through her throat and her entire body went rigid, sparking with a whirl of unearthly colors. Her screams rebounded off the walls—there was nothing human in the sound—no love, no passion, none of the things I remembered.

I staggered away, old feelings struggling against revulsion. This was not Trish, I told myself. The Trish I'd known briefly but passionately had died at the Feast of the Crossroads.

She was gone, the last remnants of Onatochee's reality flickering into nothingness, vanishing into the still air.

My legs went weak. I leaned against the graffiti-covered wall and let the sword fall to the floor. Tears poured down my face and I couldn't stop them.

Onatochee's last vessel. And his last victim.

I drove away as quickly as I could, toward the Williamsburg Bridge and beyond it, Manhattan.

Michael O'Regan believed that he had a mission to track down demons and destroy them. Perhaps She Who Watches passed his mission to me. But I accept it freely, fully aware of what it entails.

Damien was right. The world has changed in some fundamental way and what lies ahead is dark with the terror of the unknown. He was the sane one, and I was the fool. Mine was the blindness of the intellect, the madness of the rational.

But I will not give in to despair. I will investigate and chronicle. I will help where I can and destroy where I must, or be destroyed myself. Though it seems the height of arrogance to assume that I can save the world, I know at last in my heart and soul that, imperfect as it is, the world is worth saving.

I stand in the doorway with a candle, holding the darkness at bay.

I am *Nomeus.*

I am the Shepherd.

About the Author

During the day Anthony Pryor helps keep computers running at a large school district, but by night and on lunch breaks he's been editing, developing and writing for more years than he cares to admit, producing fiction and support material for popular games like Battletech, Dungeons and Dragons, Pathfinder and A Song of Ice and Fire, and working for publishers like Wizards of the Coast, White Wolf, Paizo Press, Green Ronin and others.

He lives in Milwaukie, Oregon with an overweight cat, plays more games than is strictly healthy and tries with minimal success to master the bass guitar in his copious spare time. With a mom who used to hang out with Diego Rivera and Frida Kahlo and a daughter who attends graduate school while fighting injustice and poverty in her spare time, Anthony's actually the boring one in his family. His greatest ambition is to be a world-famous rockstar, but being a writer is okay, too.